LILAH STURGES ·

LUMBERJANES™

THE INFERNAL COMPASS

BOOM!
BOX™

ROSS RICHIE...CEO & Founder
JOY HUFFMAN...CFO
MATT GAGNON...Editor-in-Chief
FILIP SABLIK.............................President, Publishing & Marketing
STEPHEN CHRISTY.................................President, Development
LANCE KREITER.................Vice President, Licensing & Merchandising
PHIL BARBARO..............Vice President, Finance & Human Resources
ARUNE SINGH...Vice President, Marketing
BRYCE CARLSON............Vice President, Editorial & Creative Strategy
SCOTT NEWMAN.................................Manager, Production Design
KATE HENNING..Manager, Operations
SPENCER SIMPSON...Manager, Sales
SIERRA HAHN...Executive Editor
JEANINE SCHAEFER...Executive Editor
DAFNA PLEBAN...Senior Editor
SHANNON WATTERS...Senior Editor
ERIC HARBURN...Senior Editor
WHITNEY LEOPARD...Editor
CAMERON CHITTOCK..Editor
CHRIS ROSA..Editor
MATTHEW LEVINE..Editor
SOPHIE PHILIPS-ROBERTS.........................Assistant Editor
GAVIN GRONENTHAL.................................Assistant Editor
MICHAEL MOCCIO.....................................Assistant Editor
AMANDA LaFRANCO............................Executive Assistant
JILLIAN CRAB....................................Design Coordinator
MICHELLE ANKLEY.............................Design Coordinator
KARA LEOPARD...................................Production Designer
MARIE KRUPINA...................................Production Designer
GRACE PARK........................Production Design Assistant
CHELSEA ROBERTS.................Production Design Assistant
SAMANTHA KNAPP.................Production Design Assistant
ELIZABETH LOUGHRIDGE................Accounting Coordinator
STEPHANIE HOCUTT................Social Media Coordinator
JOSÉ MEZA...Event Coordinator
HOLLY AITCHISON...........................Operations Coordinator
MEGAN CHRISTOPHER..........................Operations Assistant
RODRIGO HERNANDEZ.............................Mailroom Assistant
MORGAN PERRY...................Direct Market Representative
CAT O'GRADY.................................Marketing Assistant
BREANNA SARPY.........................Executive Assistant

BOOm! Box™

LUMBERJANES: THE INFERNAL COMPASS, October 2018.
Published by BOOM! Box, a division of Boom Entertainment, Inc.
Lumberjanes is ™ & © 2018 Shannon Watters, Grace Ellis, Noelle
Stevenson & Brooklyn Allen. All rights reserved. BOOM! Box™ and
the BOOM! Box logo are trademarks of Boom Entertainment, Inc.,
registered in various countries and categories. All characters, events,
and institutions depicted herein are fictional. Any similarity between
any of the names, characters, persons, events, and/or institutions in
this publication to actual names, characters, and persons, whether
living or dead, events, and/or institutions is unintended and purely
coincidental. BOOM! Box does not read or accept unsolicited
submissions of ideas, stories, or artwork.

For information regarding the CPSIA on this printed material, call:
(203) 595-3636 and provide reference #RICH – 812278.

BOOM! Studios, 5670 Wilshire Boulevard, Suite 400, Los Angeles,
CA 90036-5679. Printed in USA. First Printing.

Softcover Edition
ISBN: 978-1-68415-252-0, eISBN: 978-1-64144-114-8

CBLDF Hardcover Edition
ISBN: 978-1-68415-406-7

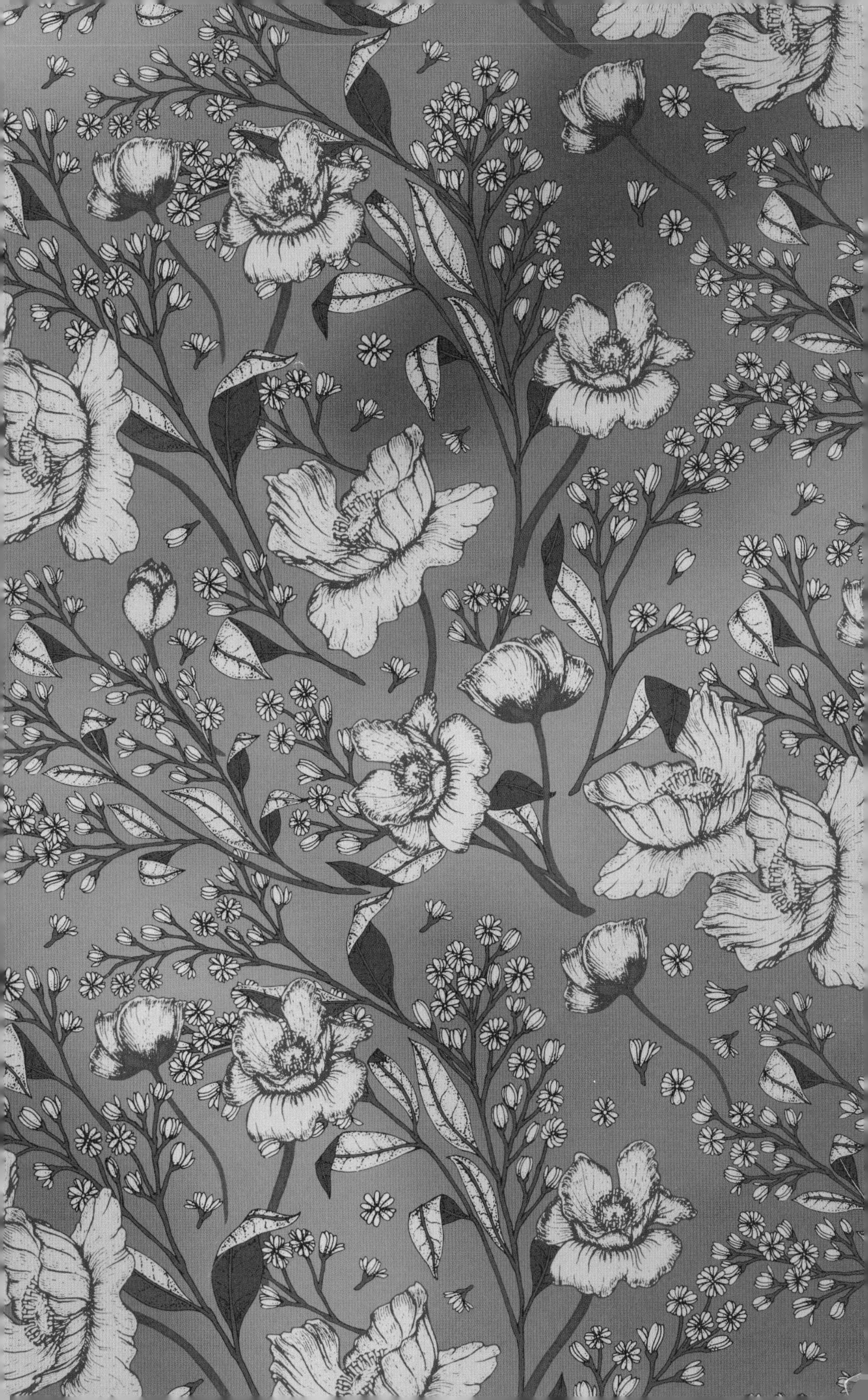

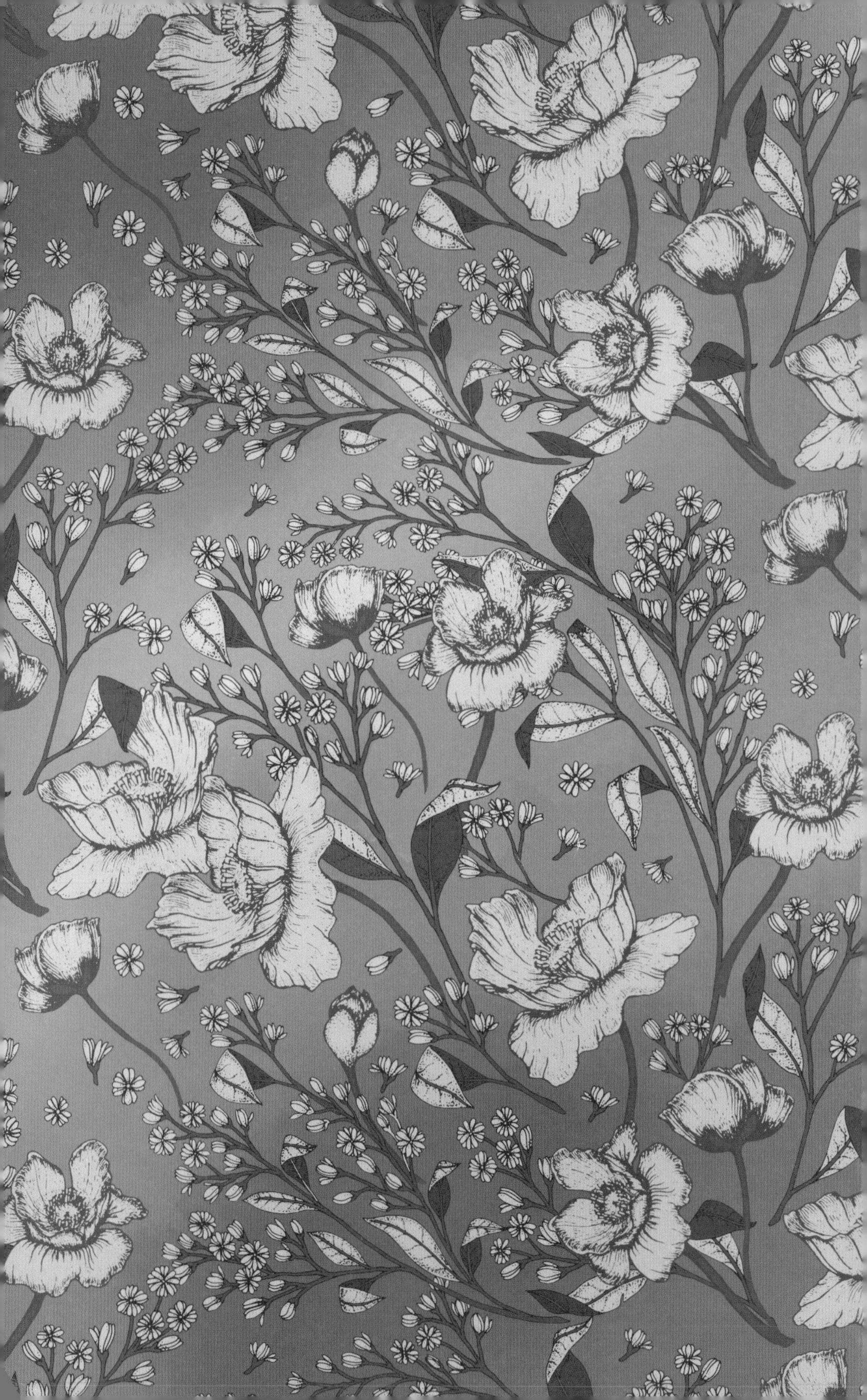

LUMBERJANES™
THE INFERNAL COMPASS

Written by
LILAH STURGES

Illustrated by
POLTERINK

Lettered by
JIM CAMPBELL

Cover by
ALEXA SHARPE

CBLDF Exclusive Cover Design by
JILLIAN CRAB
with illustration by **POLTERINK**

Designer
JILLIAN CRAB

Assistant Editor
SOPHIE PHILIPS-ROBERTS

Editors
JEANINE SCHAEFER
DAFNA PLEBAN

*Special thanks to **Kelsey Pate** for giving the Lumberjanes their name.*

Created by
SHANNON WATTERS, GRACE ELLIS,
NOELLE STEVENSON & BROOKLYN ALLEN

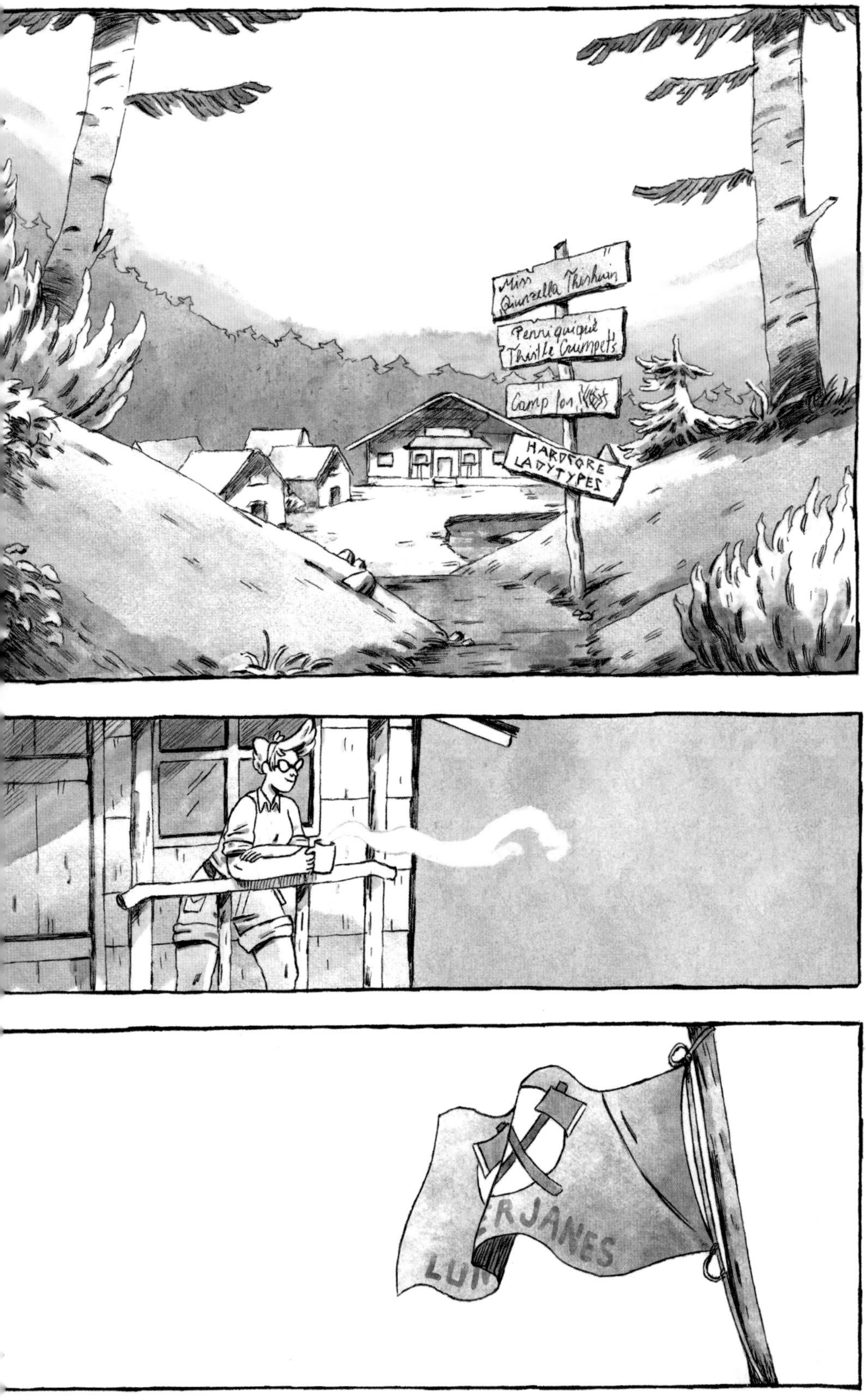
Miss Qiunzella Thiskwin
Penniquiqui Thistle Crumpets
Camp for
HARDCORE LADYTYPES
LUN
ERJANES

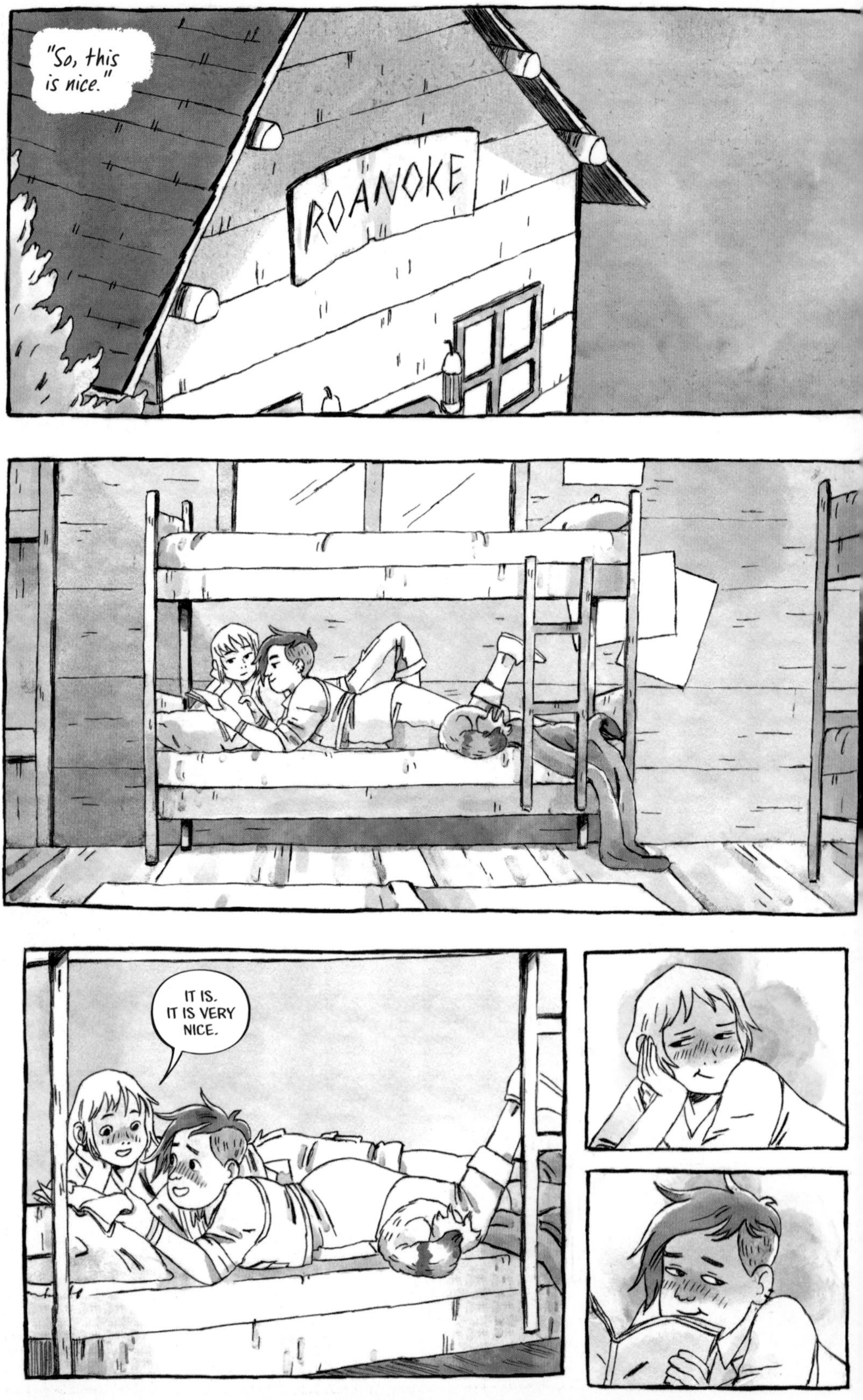
"So, this is nice."
ROANOKE
IT IS. IT IS VERY NICE.

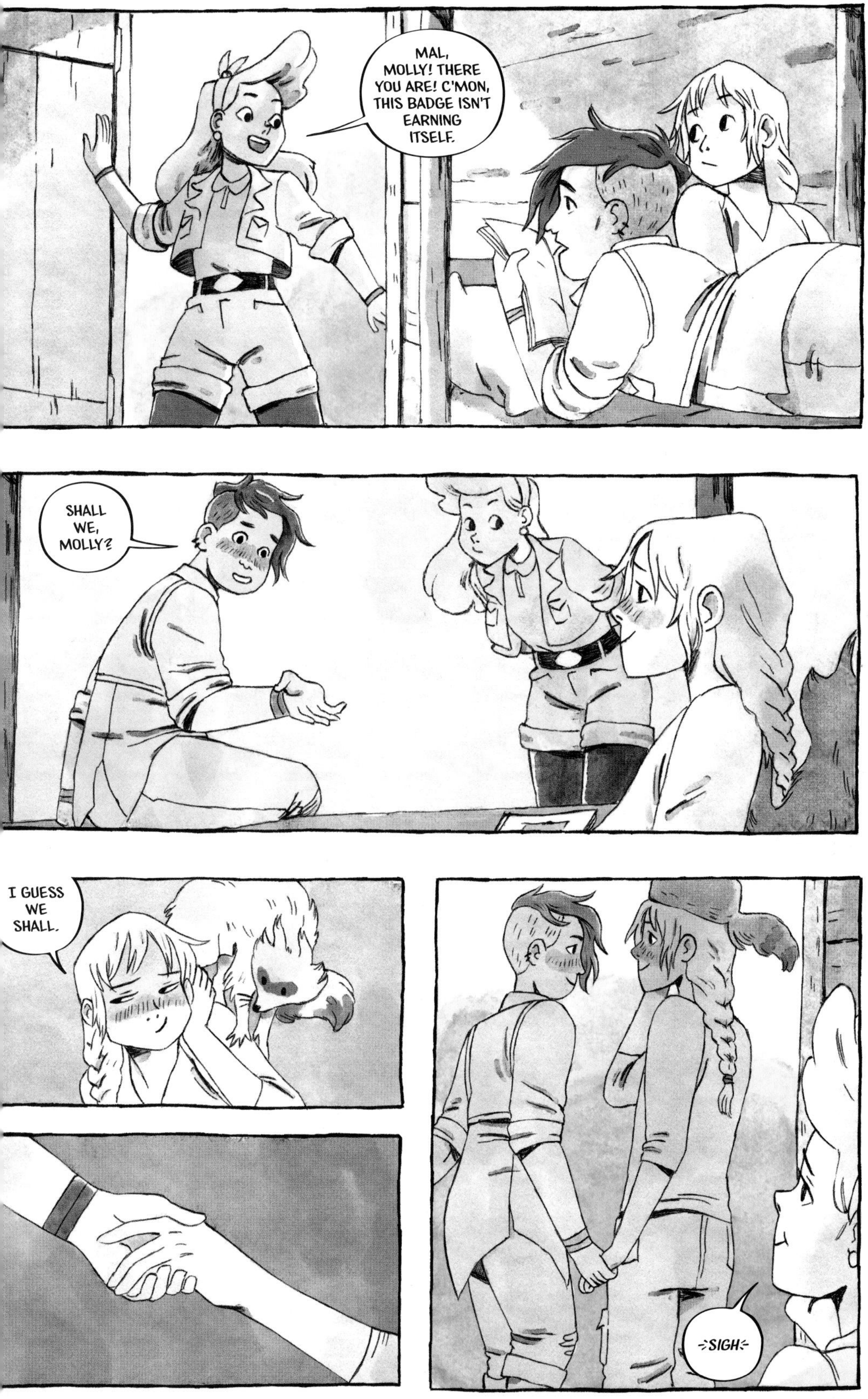
MAL, MOLLY! THERE YOU ARE! C'MON, THIS BADGE ISN'T EARNING ITSELF.
SHALL WE, MOLLY?
I GUESS WE SHALL.
SIGH

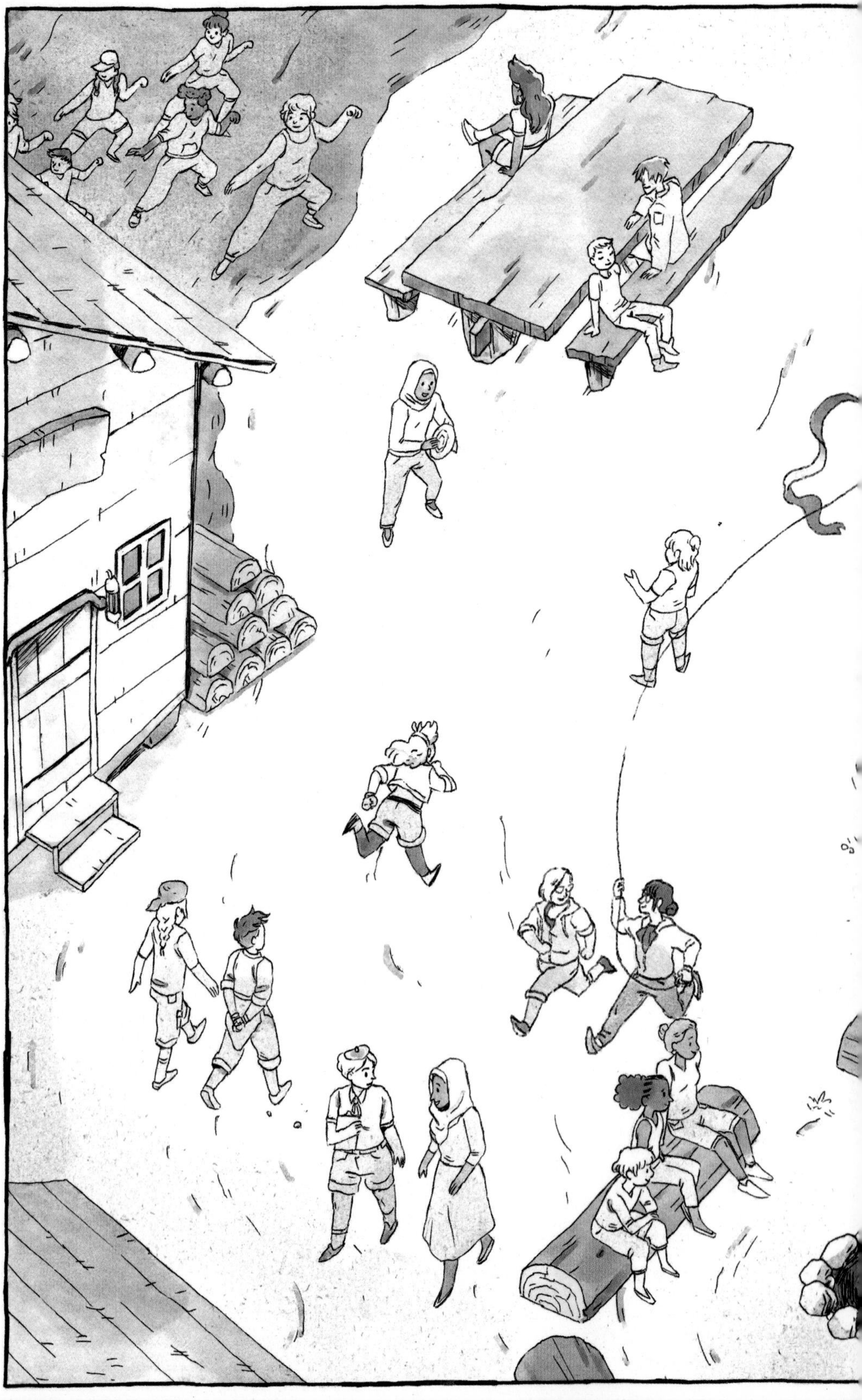

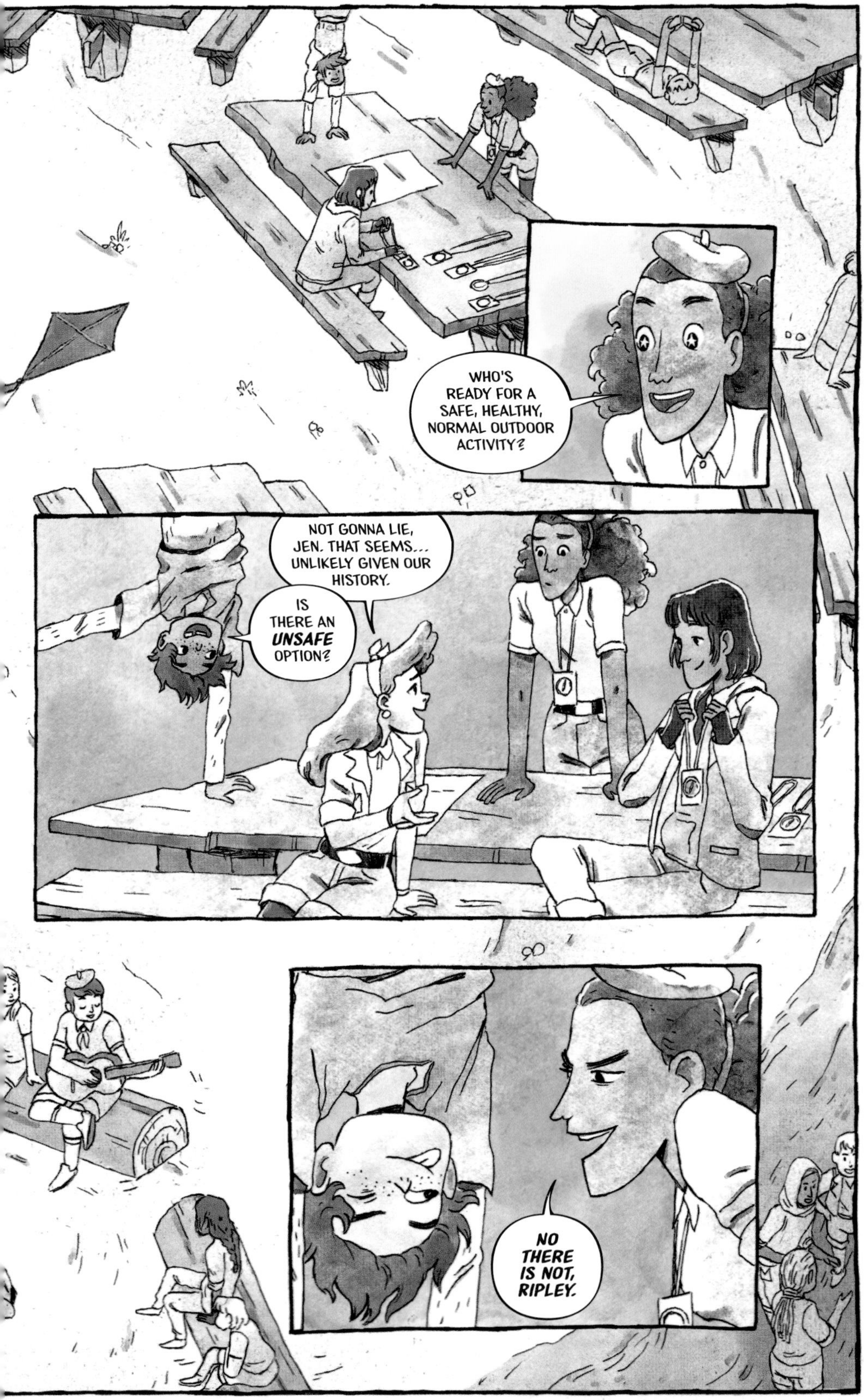
WHO'S READY FOR A SAFE, HEALTHY, NORMAL OUTDOOR ACTIVITY?
NOT GONNA LIE, JEN. THAT SEEMS... UNLIKELY GIVEN OUR HISTORY.
IS THERE AN *UNSAFE* OPTION?
NO THERE IS NOT, RIPLEY.

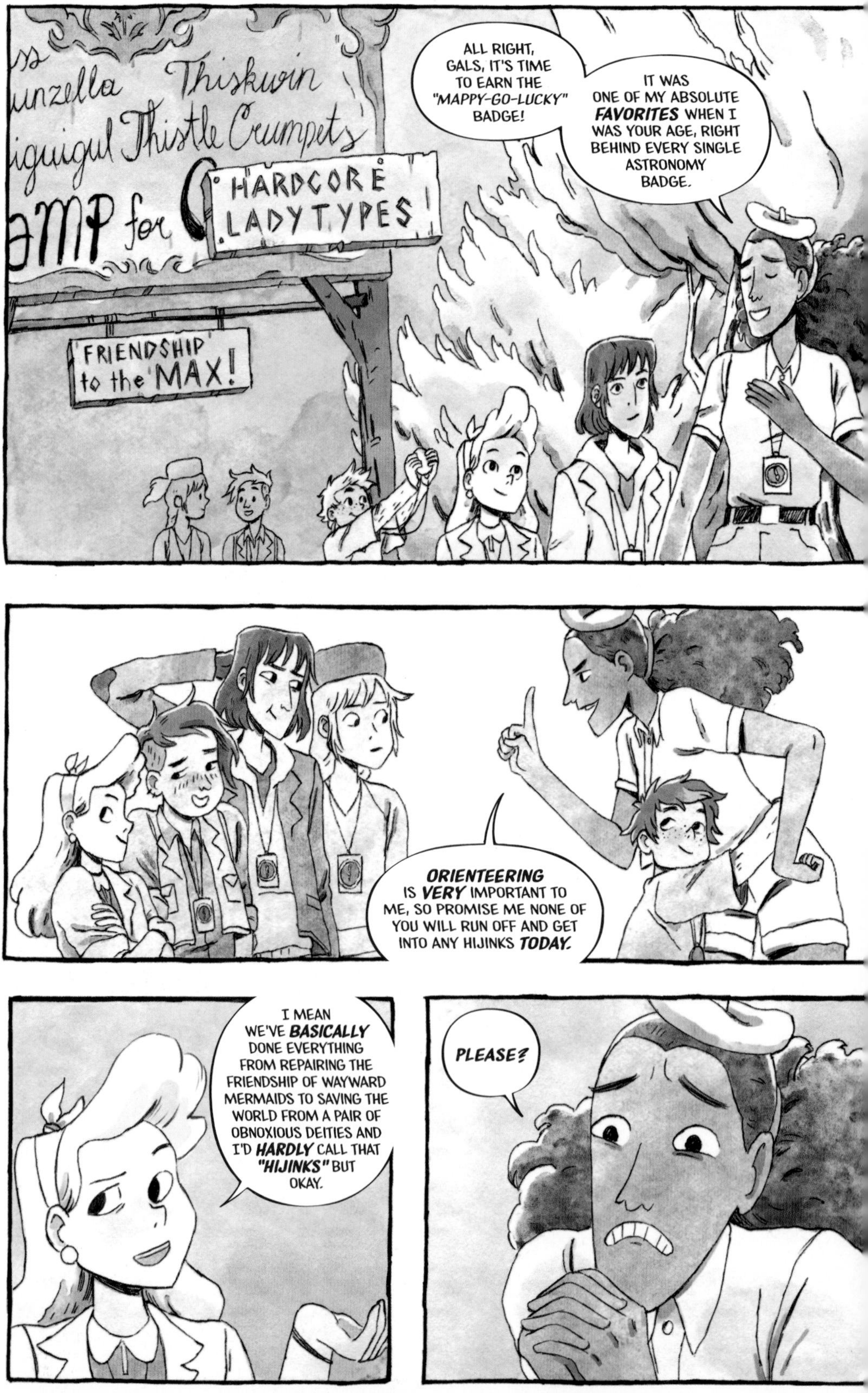
Thiskwin
Thistle Crumpets
HARDCORE LADYTYPES
FRIENDSHIP to the MAX!
ALL RIGHT, GALS, IT'S TIME TO EARN THE "MAPPY-GO-LUCKY" BADGE!
IT WAS ONE OF MY ABSOLUTE FAVORITES WHEN I WAS YOUR AGE, RIGHT BEHIND EVERY SINGLE ASTRONOMY BADGE.
ORIENTEERING IS VERY IMPORTANT TO ME, SO PROMISE ME NONE OF YOU WILL RUN OFF AND GET INTO ANY HIJINKS TODAY.
I MEAN WE'VE BASICALLY DONE EVERYTHING FROM REPAIRING THE FRIENDSHIP OF WAYWARD MERMAIDS TO SAVING THE WORLD FROM A PAIR OF OBNOXIOUS DEITIES AND I'D HARDLY CALL THAT "HIJINKS" BUT OKAY.
PLEASE?

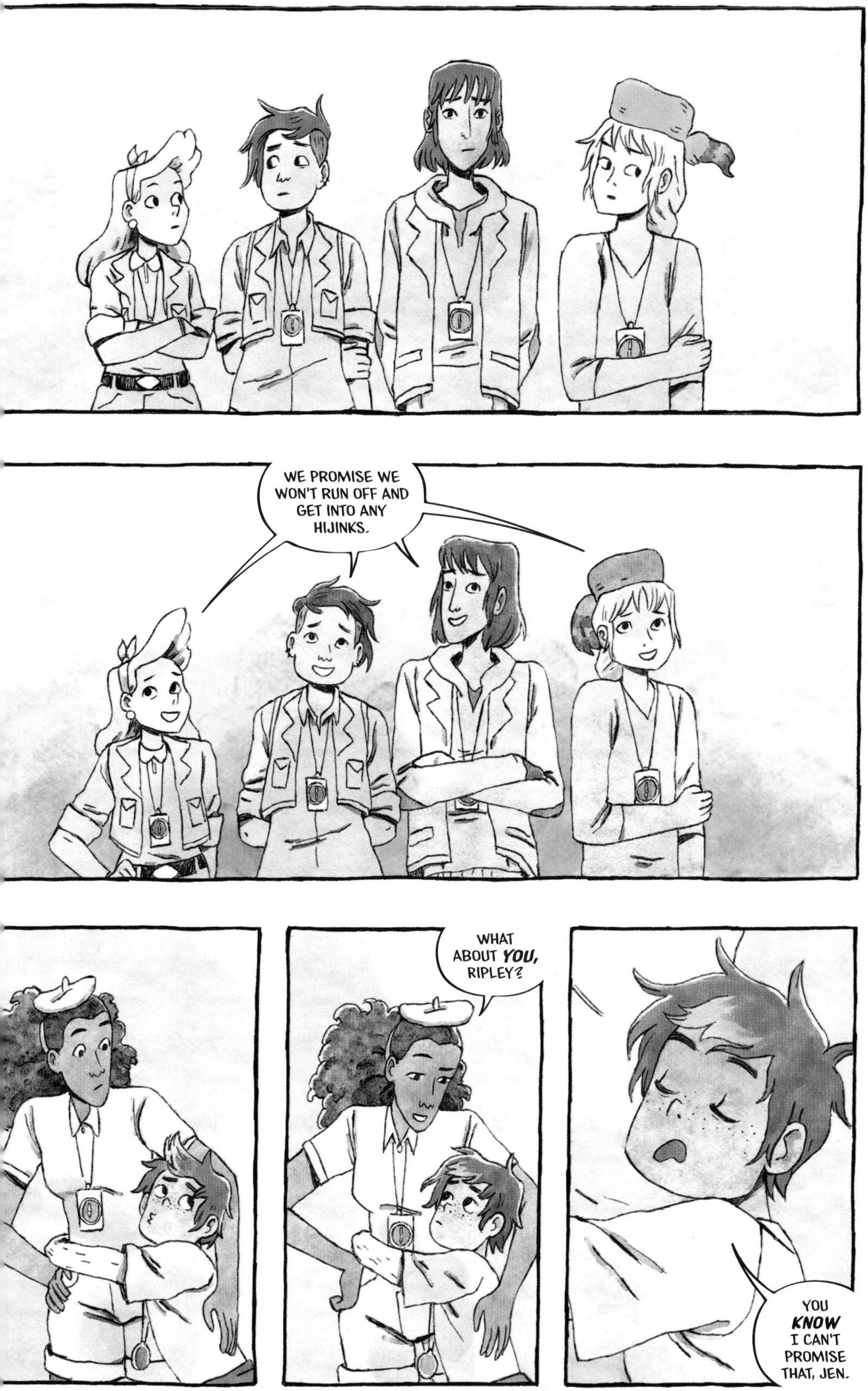
WE PROMISE WE WON'T RUN OFF AND GET INTO ANY HIJINKS.
WHAT ABOUT **YOU,** RIPLEY?
YOU **KNOW** I CAN'T PROMISE THAT, JEN.

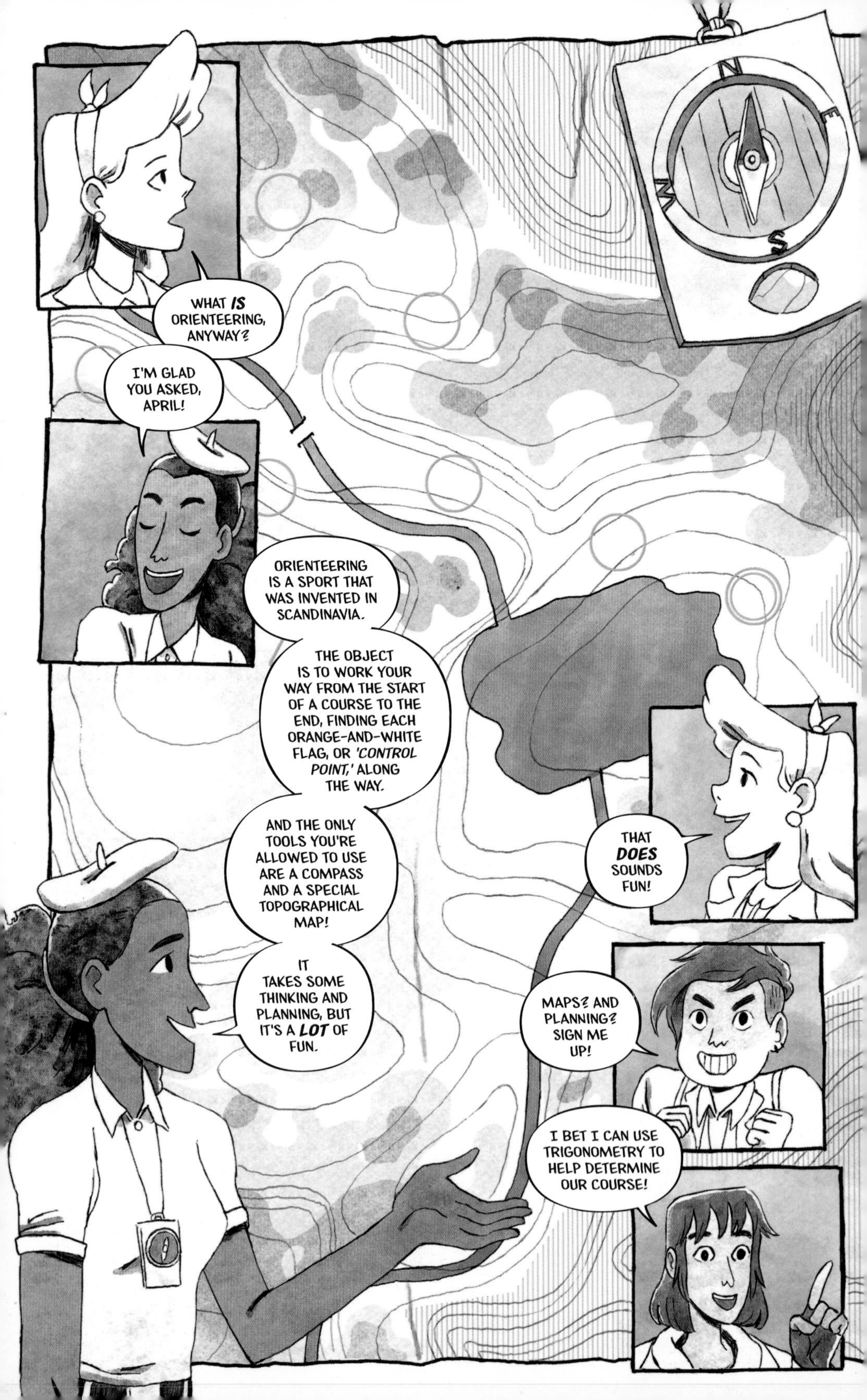
WHAT *IS* ORIENTEERING, ANYWAY?
I'M GLAD YOU ASKED, APRIL!
ORIENTEERING IS A SPORT THAT WAS INVENTED IN SCANDINAVIA.
THE OBJECT IS TO WORK YOUR WAY FROM THE START OF A COURSE TO THE END, FINDING EACH ORANGE-AND-WHITE FLAG, OR *'CONTROL POINT,'* ALONG THE WAY.
AND THE ONLY TOOLS YOU'RE ALLOWED TO USE ARE A COMPASS AND A SPECIAL TOPOGRAPHICAL MAP!
IT TAKES SOME THINKING AND PLANNING, BUT IT'S A *LOT* OF FUN.
THAT *DOES* SOUNDS FUN!
MAPS? AND PLANNING? SIGN ME UP!
I BET I CAN USE TRIGONOMETRY TO HELP DETERMINE OUR COURSE!

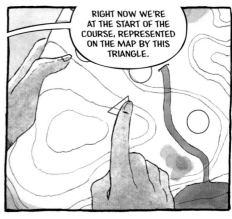

THIS FLAG IS CALLED A *'CONTROL POINT.'* WE'LL BE LOOKING FOR MORE LIKE IT, SO STUDY IT CAREFULLY. LEARN ITS DISTINCTIVE MARKINGS.

RIGHT NOW WE'RE AT THE START OF THE COURSE, REPRESENTED ON THE MAP BY THIS TRIANGLE.

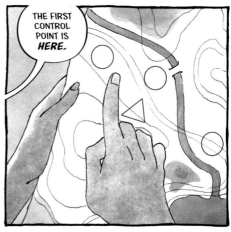

THE FIRST CONTROL POINT IS *HERE.*

OH, I GET IT. SO WE USE THE COMPASS TO DETERMINE HOW TO GET TO THE FIRST POINT ON THE MAP.

THAT'S IT, JO. EXACTLY!

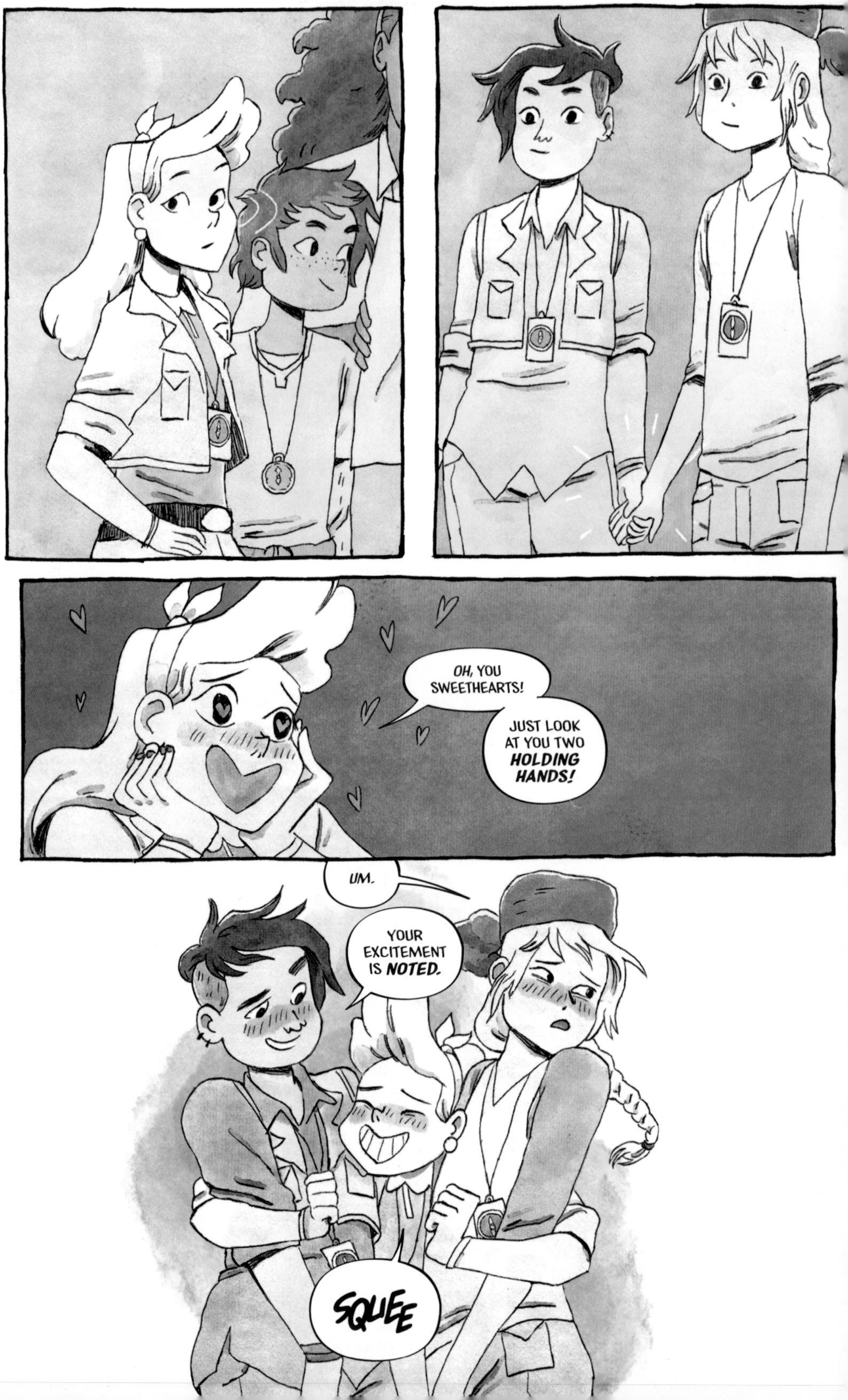
OH, YOU SWEETHEARTS!
JUST LOOK AT YOU TWO HOLDING HANDS!
UM.
YOUR EXCITEMENT IS NOTED.
SQUEE

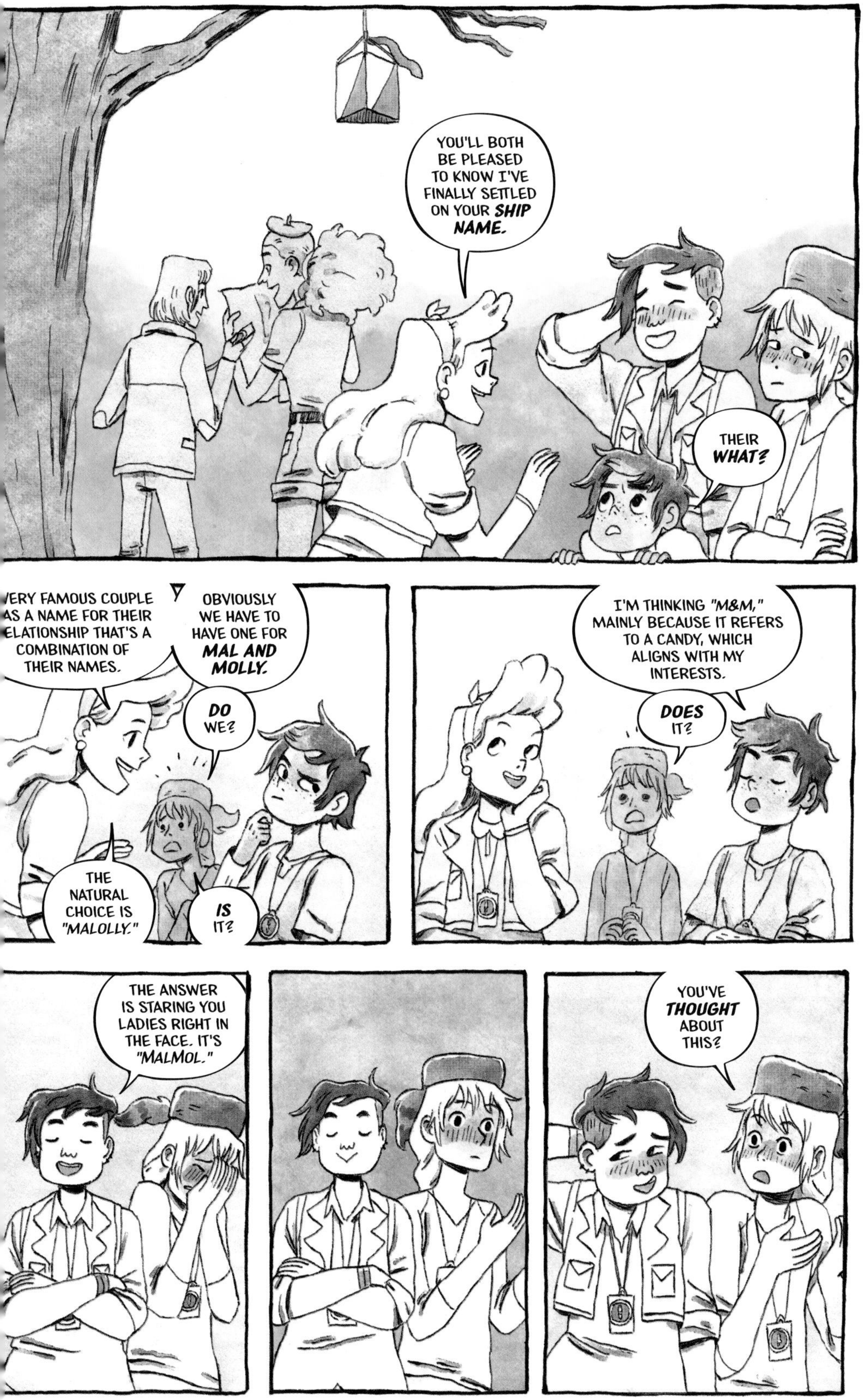
YOU'LL BOTH BE PLEASED TO KNOW I'VE FINALLY SETTLED ON YOUR SHIP NAME.
THEIR WHAT?
VERY FAMOUS COUPLE AS A NAME FOR THEIR RELATIONSHIP THAT'S A COMBINATION OF THEIR NAMES.
OBVIOUSLY WE HAVE TO HAVE ONE FOR MAL AND MOLLY.
DO WE?
THE NATURAL CHOICE IS "MALOLLY."
IS IT?
I'M THINKING "M&M," MAINLY BECAUSE IT REFERS TO A CANDY, WHICH ALIGNS WITH MY INTERESTS.
DOES IT?
THE ANSWER IS STARING YOU LADIES RIGHT IN THE FACE. IT'S "MALMOL."
YOU'VE THOUGHT ABOUT THIS?

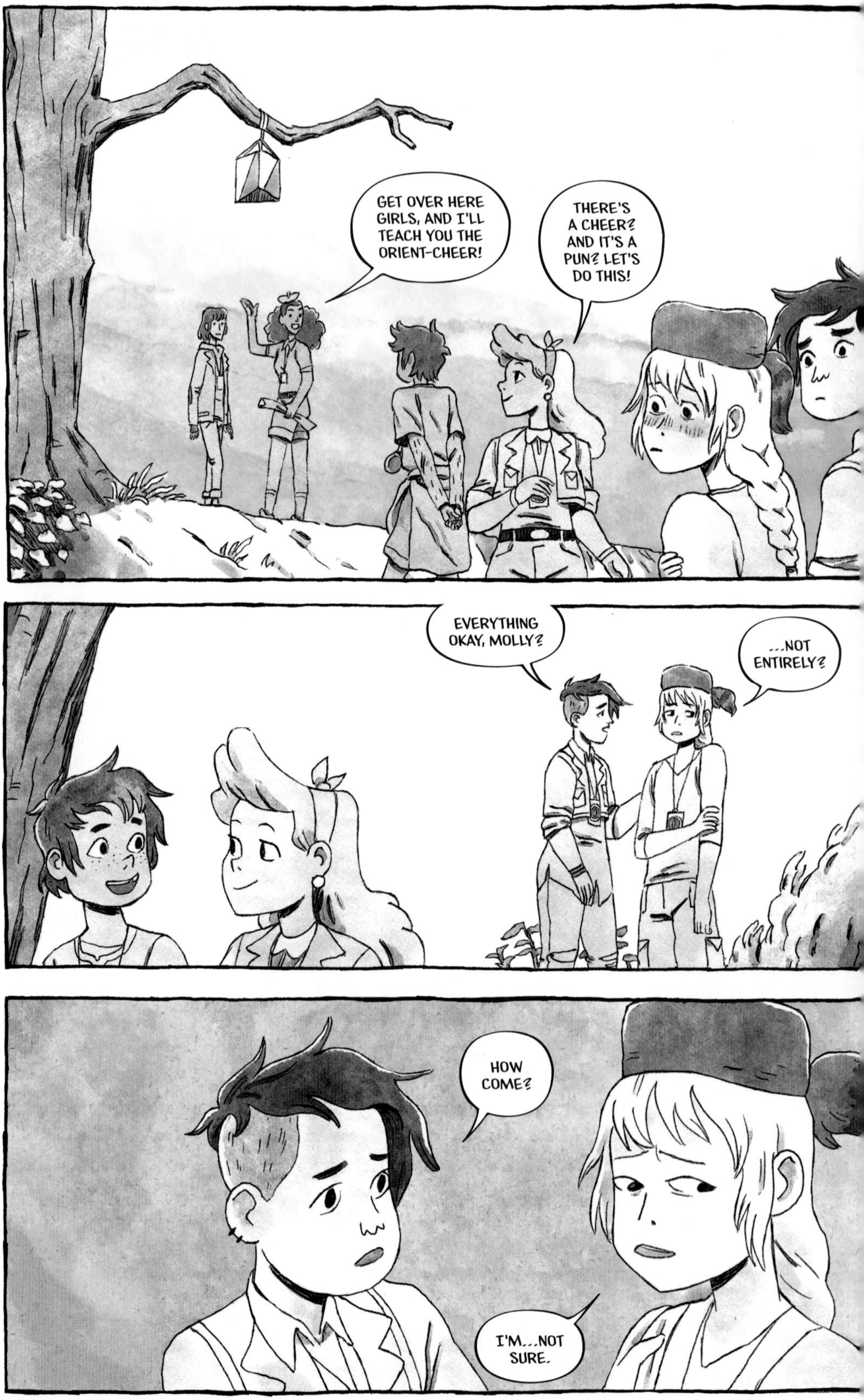
GET OVER HERE GIRLS, AND I'LL TEACH YOU THE ORIENT-CHEER!
THERE'S A CHEER? AND IT'S A PUN? LET'S DO THIS!
EVERYTHING OKAY, MOLLY?
...NOT ENTIRELY?
HOW COME?
I'M...NOT SURE.

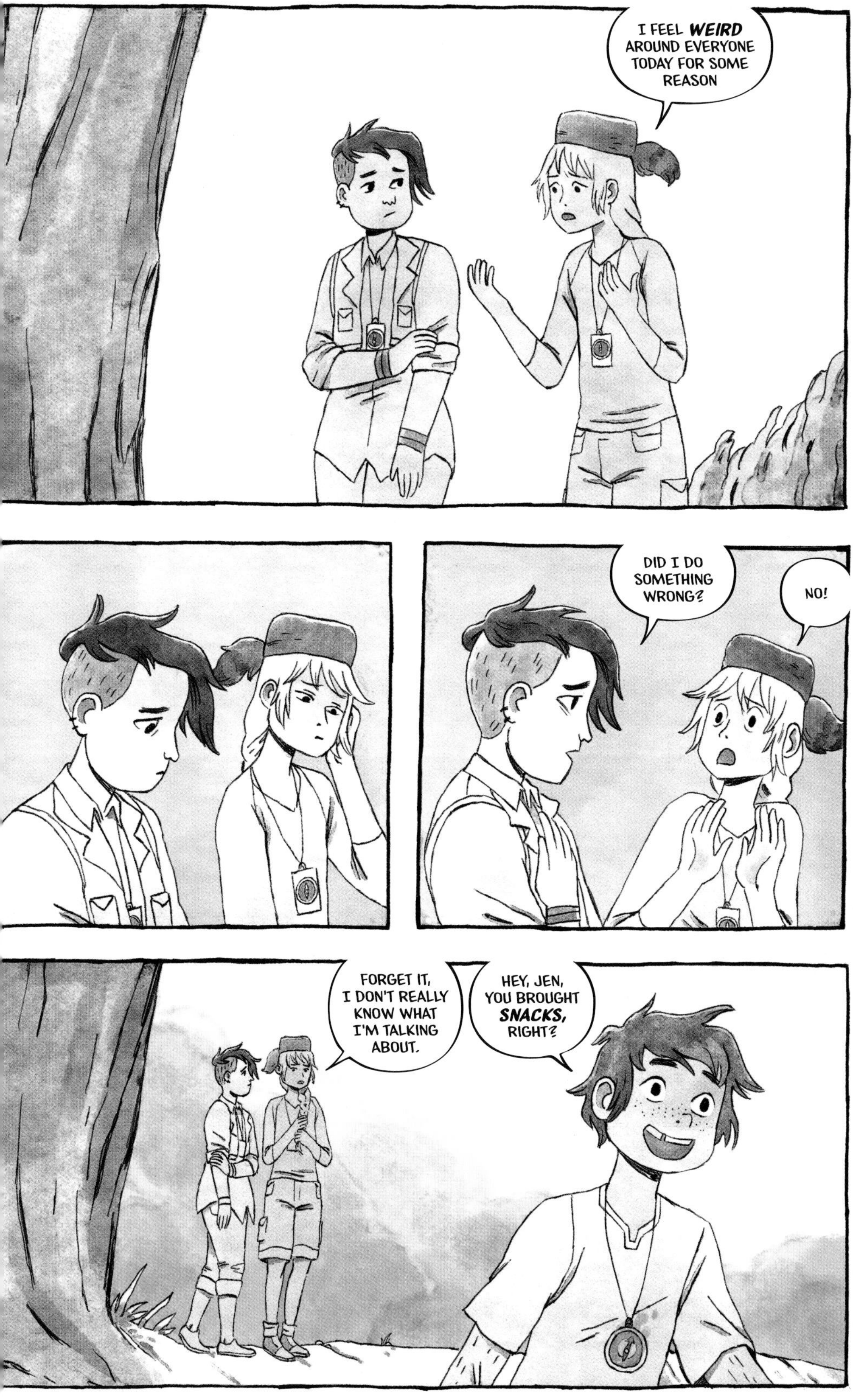
I FEEL WEIRD AROUND EVERYONE TODAY FOR SOME REASON
DID I DO SOMETHING WRONG?
NO!
FORGET IT, I DON'T REALLY KNOW WHAT I'M TALKING ABOUT.
HEY, JEN, YOU BROUGHT SNACKS, RIGHT?

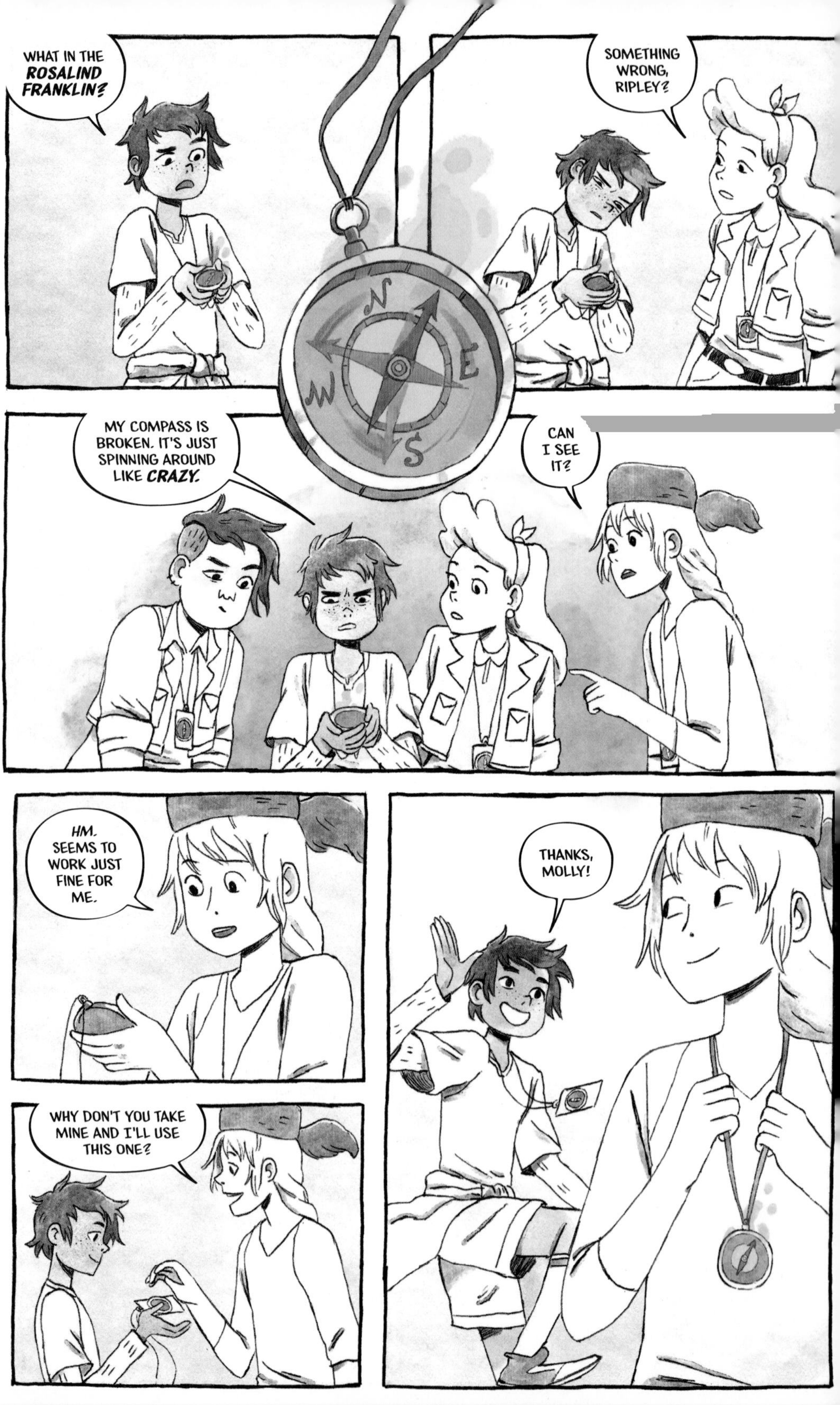
WHAT IN THE *ROSALIND FRANKLIN*?
SOMETHING WRONG, RIPLEY?
MY COMPASS IS BROKEN. IT'S JUST SPINNING AROUND LIKE *CRAZY*.
CAN I SEE IT?
HM. SEEMS TO WORK JUST FINE FOR ME.
WHY DON'T YOU TAKE MINE AND I'LL USE THIS ONE?
THANKS, MOLLY!

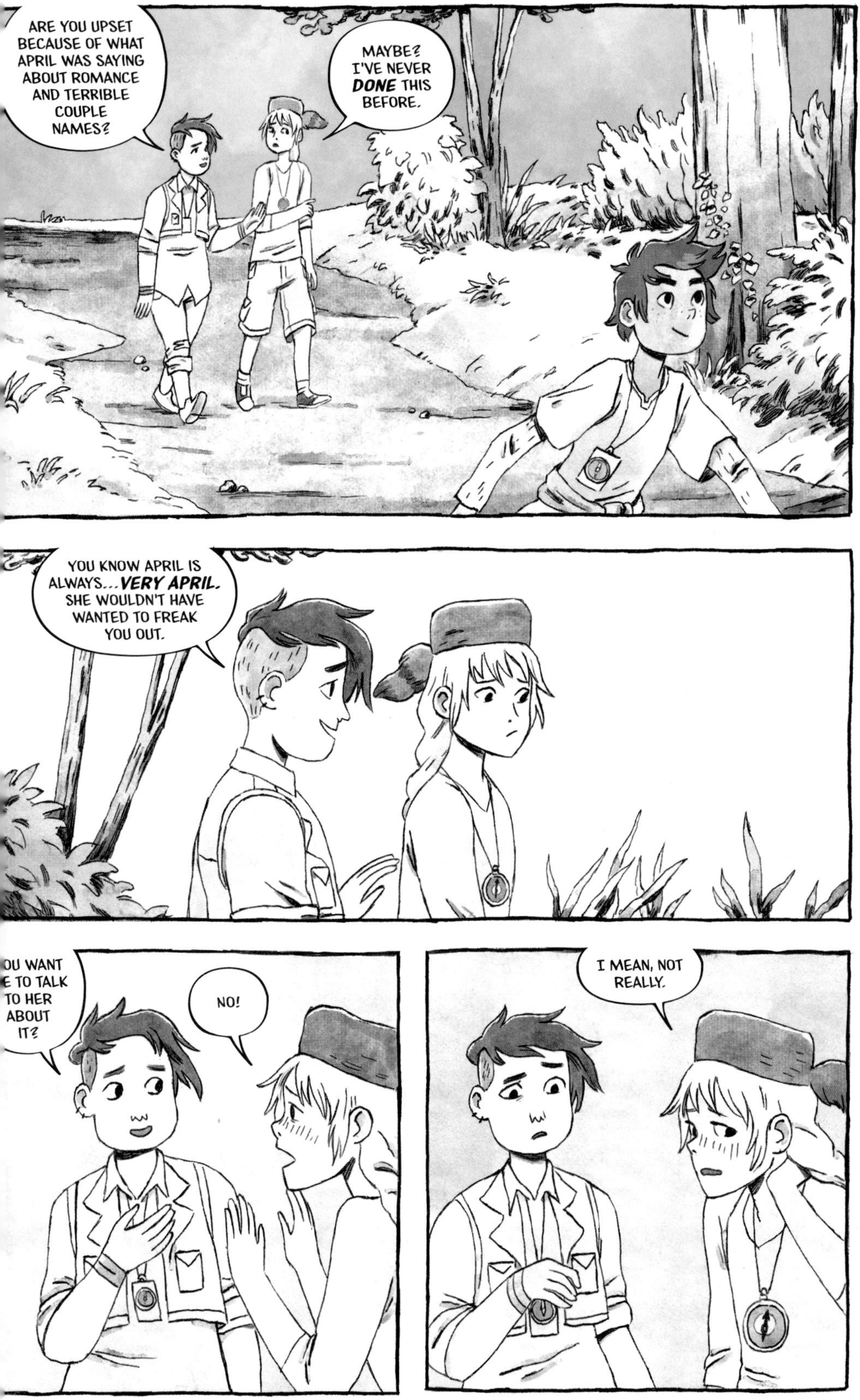

ARE YOU UPSET BECAUSE OF WHAT APRIL WAS SAYING ABOUT ROMANCE AND TERRIBLE COUPLE NAMES?
MAYBE? I'VE NEVER **DONE** THIS BEFORE.
YOU KNOW APRIL IS ALWAYS... ***VERY APRIL.*** SHE WOULDN'T HAVE WANTED TO FREAK YOU OUT.
OU WANT E TO TALK TO HER ABOUT IT?
NO!
I MEAN, NOT REALLY.

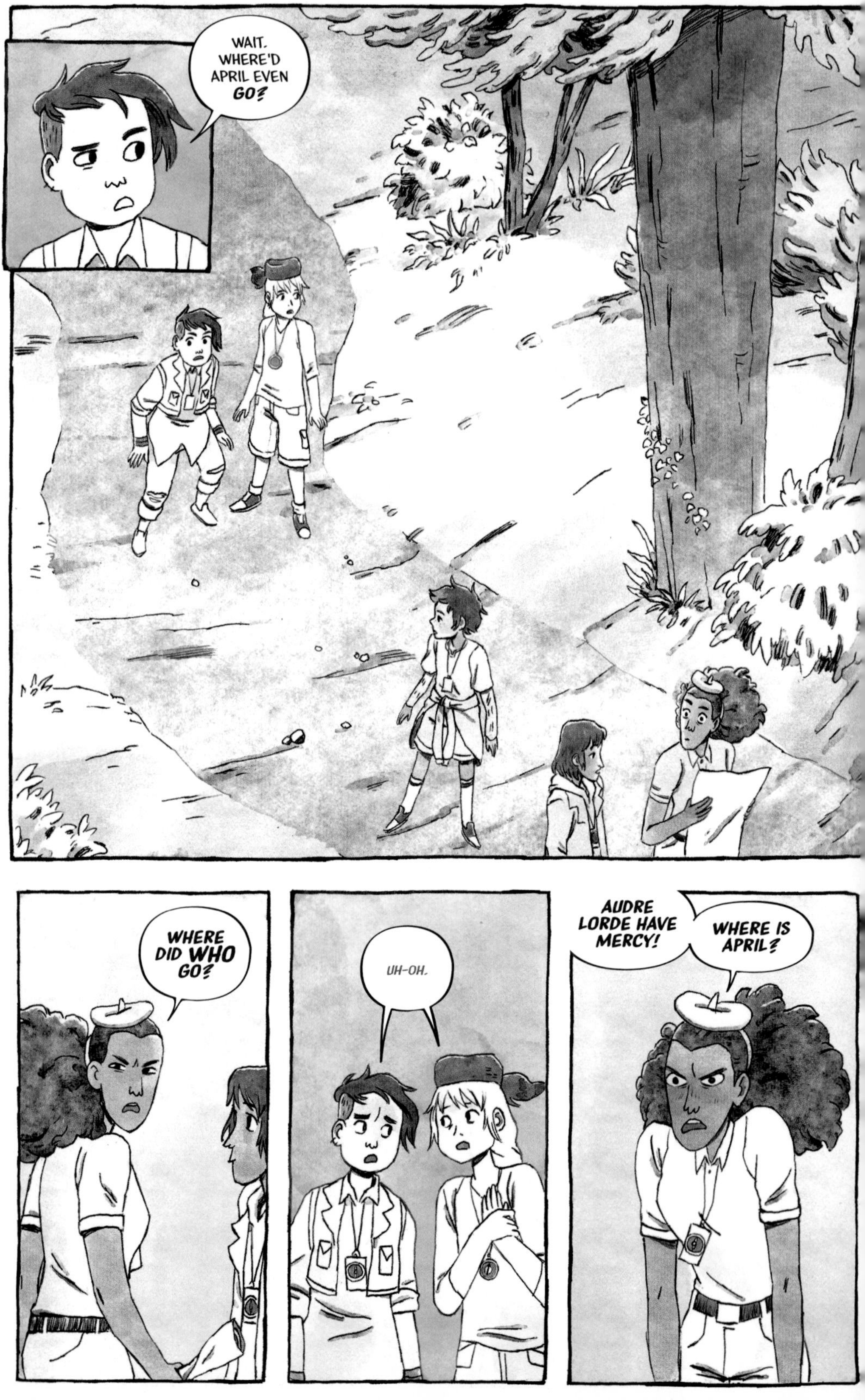
WAIT. WHERE'D APRIL EVEN GO?
WHERE DID WHO GO?
UH-OH.
AUDRE LORDE HAVE MERCY!
WHERE IS APRIL?

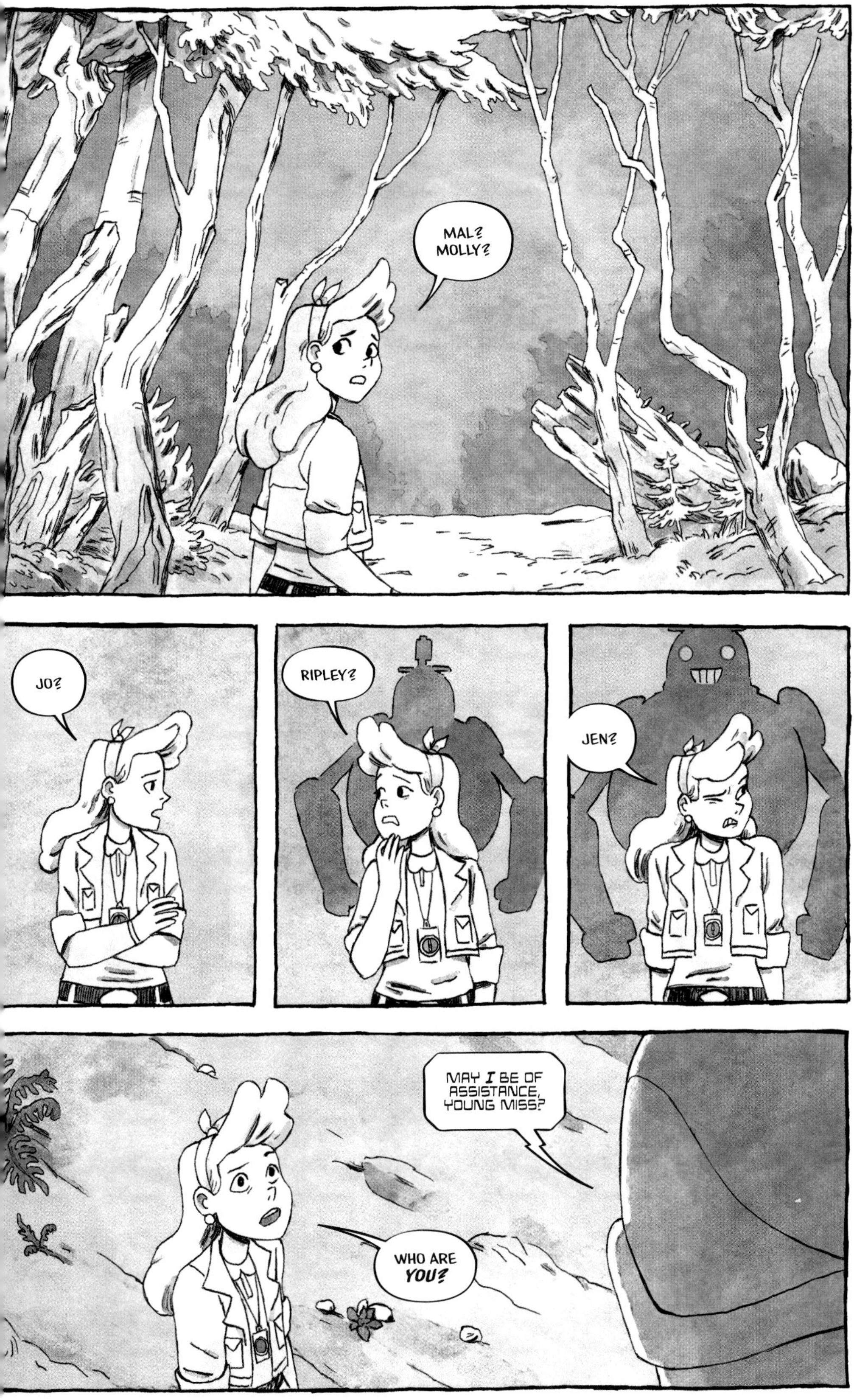
MAL?
MOLLY?
JO?
RIPLEY?
JEN?
MAY I BE OF ASSISTANCE, YOUNG MISS?
WHO ARE YOU?

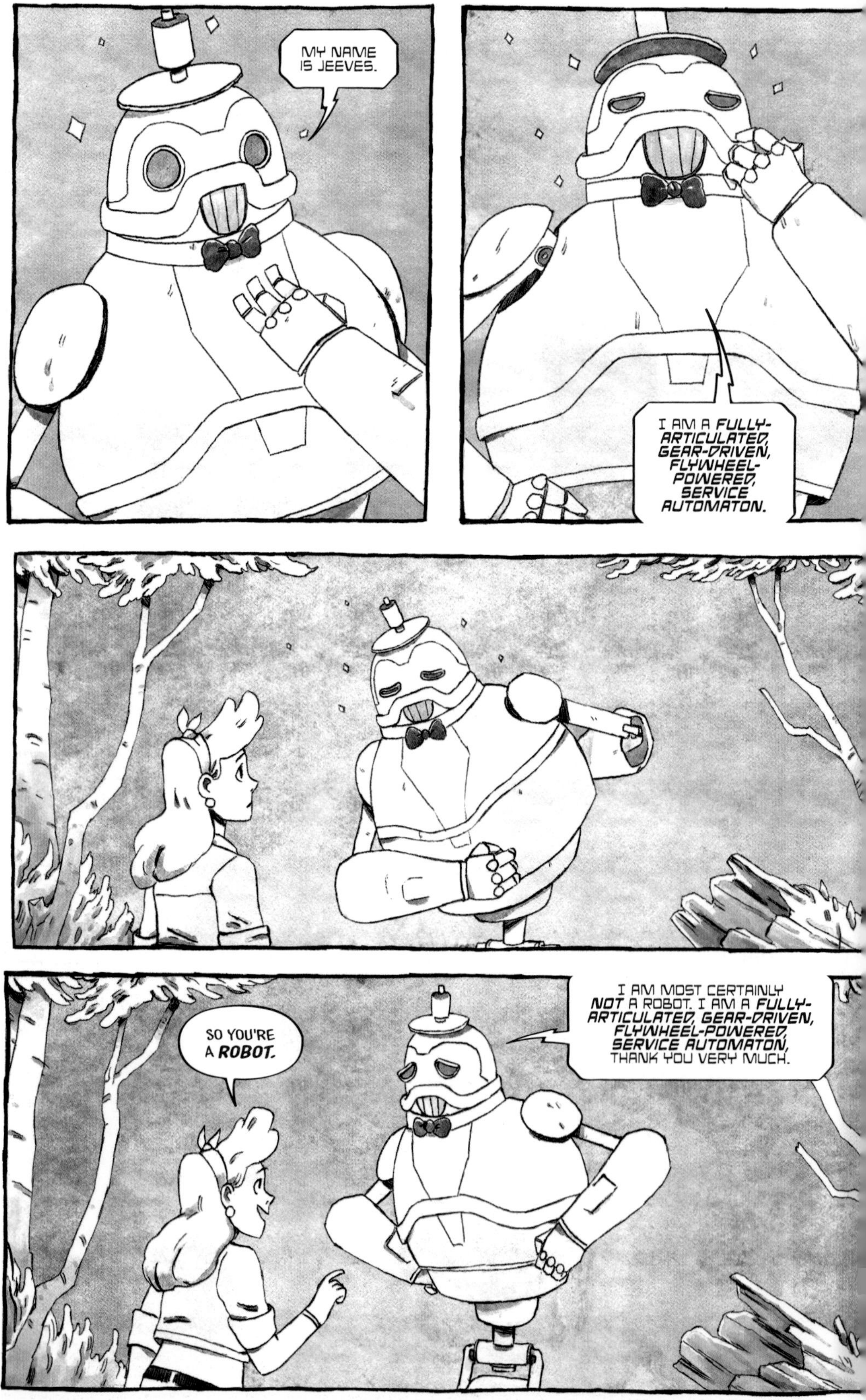

MY NAME IS JEEVES.
I AM A *FULLY-ARTICULATED, GEAR-DRIVEN, FLYWHEEL-POWERED, SERVICE AUTOMATON.*
SO YOU'RE A ***ROBOT.***
I AM MOST CERTAINLY ***NOT*** A ROBOT. I AM A *FULLY-ARTICULATED, GEAR-DRIVEN, FLYWHEEL-POWERED, SERVICE AUTOMATON,* THANK YOU VERY MUCH.

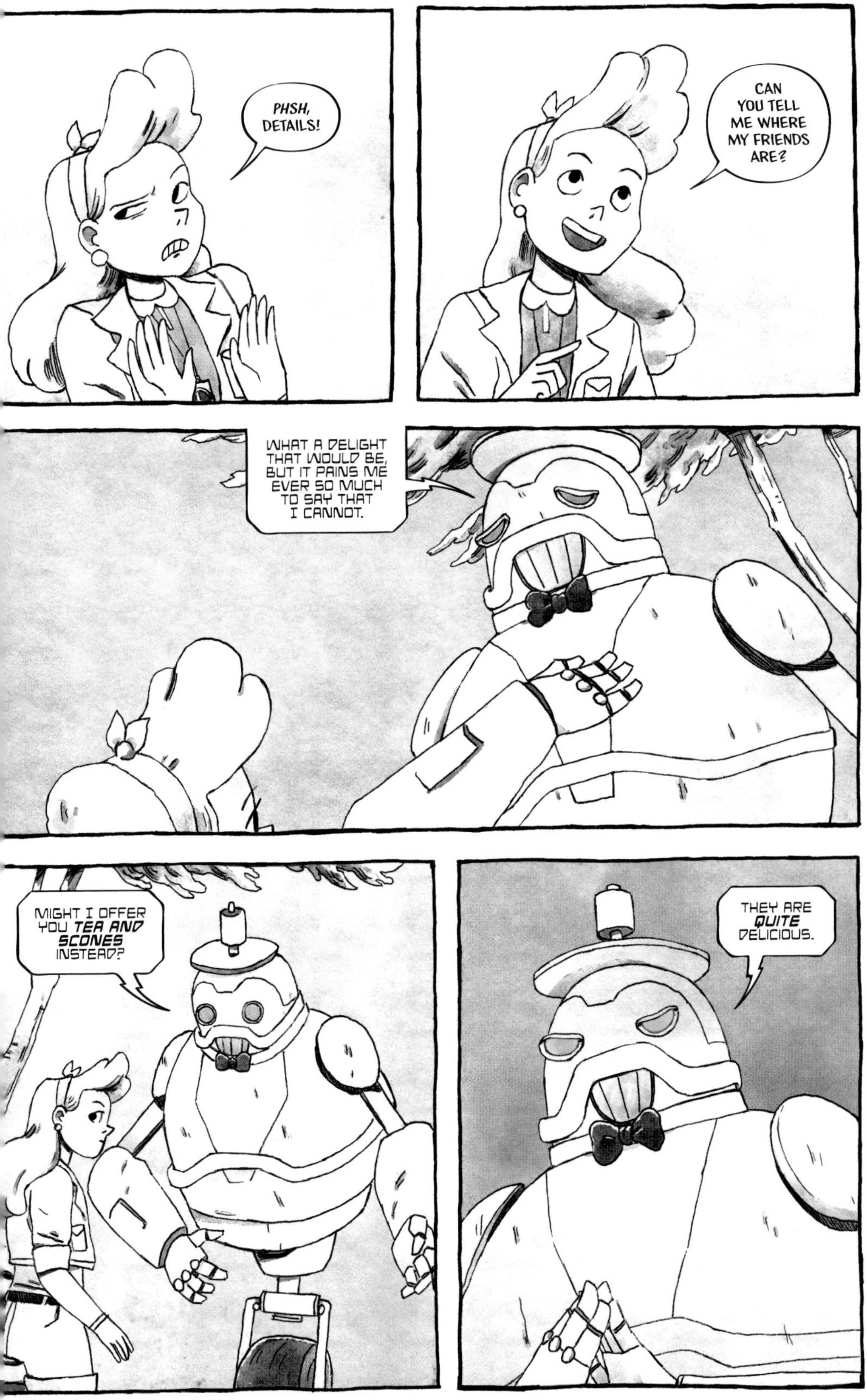
PHSH, DETAILS!
CAN YOU TELL ME WHERE MY FRIENDS ARE?
WHAT A DELIGHT THAT WOULD BE, BUT IT PAINS ME EVER SO MUCH TO SAY THAT I CANNOT.
MIGHT I OFFER YOU TEA AND SCONES INSTEAD?
THEY ARE QUITE DELICIOUS.

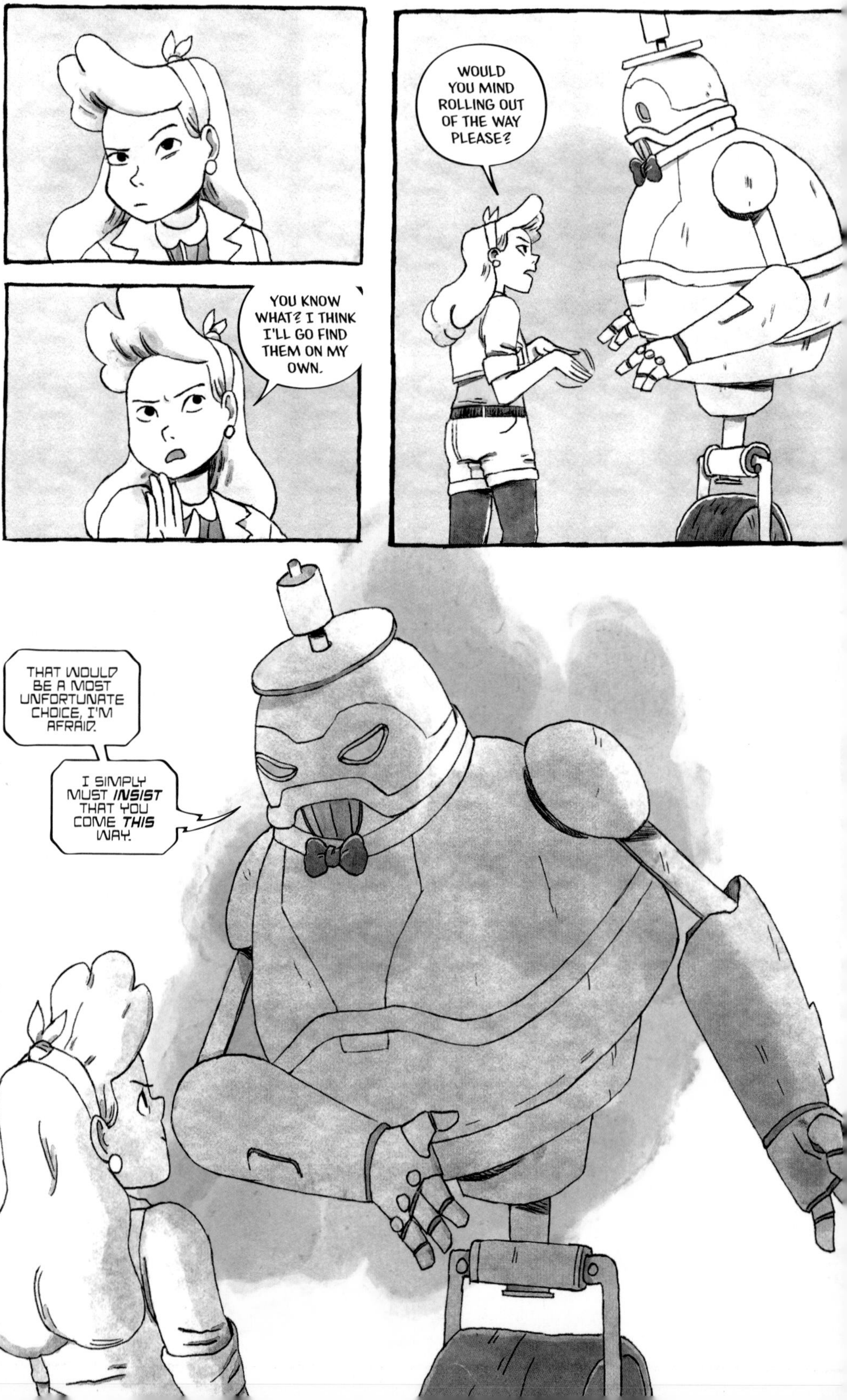
YOU KNOW WHAT? I THINK I'LL GO FIND THEM ON MY OWN.
WOULD YOU MIND ROLLING OUT OF THE WAY PLEASE?
THAT WOULD BE A MOST UNFORTUNATE CHOICE, I'M AFRAID.
I SIMPLY MUST INSIST THAT YOU COME THIS WAY.

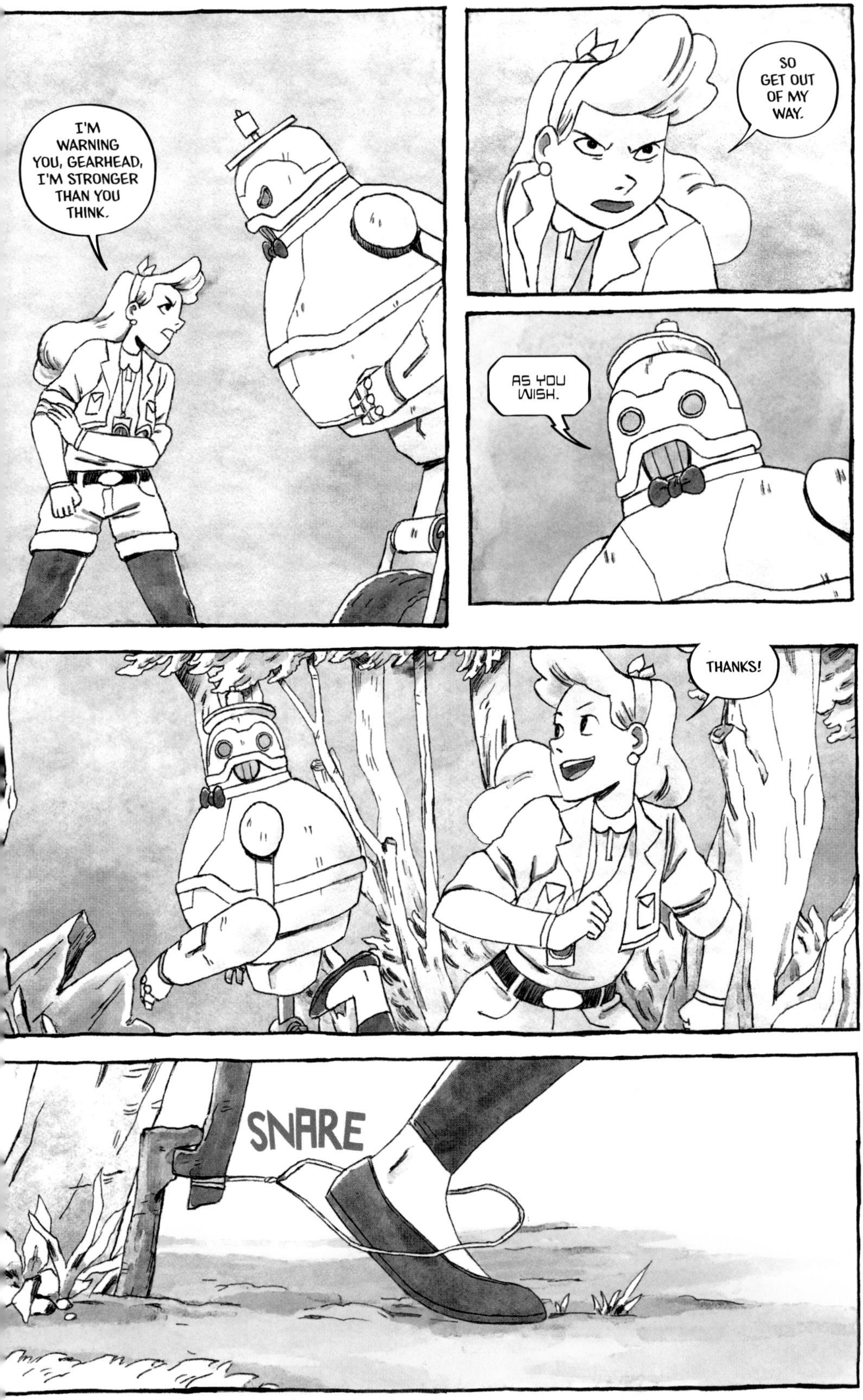
I'M WARNING YOU, GEARHEAD, I'M STRONGER THAN YOU THINK.
SO GET OUT OF MY WAY.
AS YOU WISH.
THANKS!
SNARE

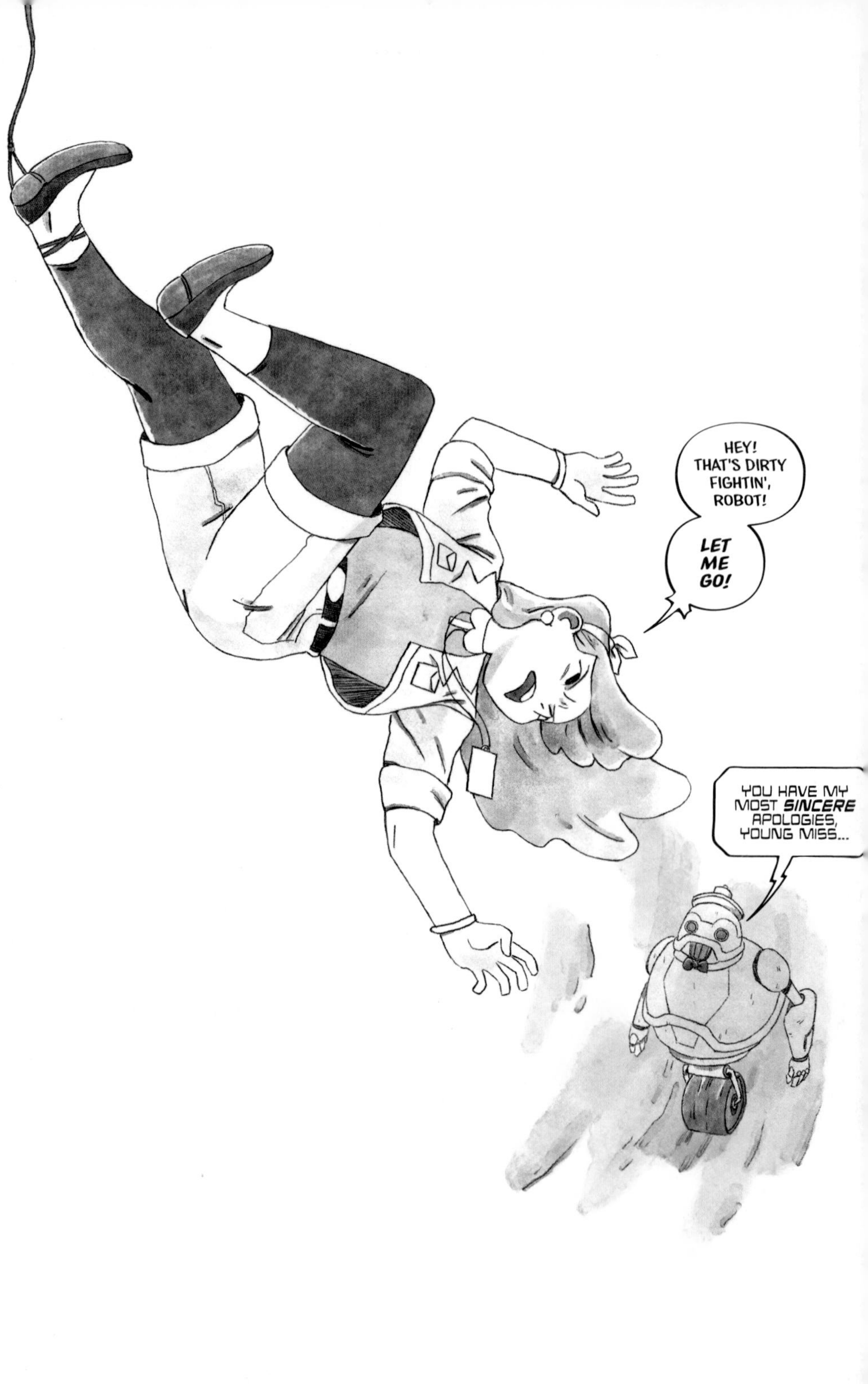
HEY! THAT'S DIRTY FIGHTIN', ROBOT!
LET ME GO!
YOU HAVE MY MOST SINCERE APOLOGIES, YOUNG MISS...

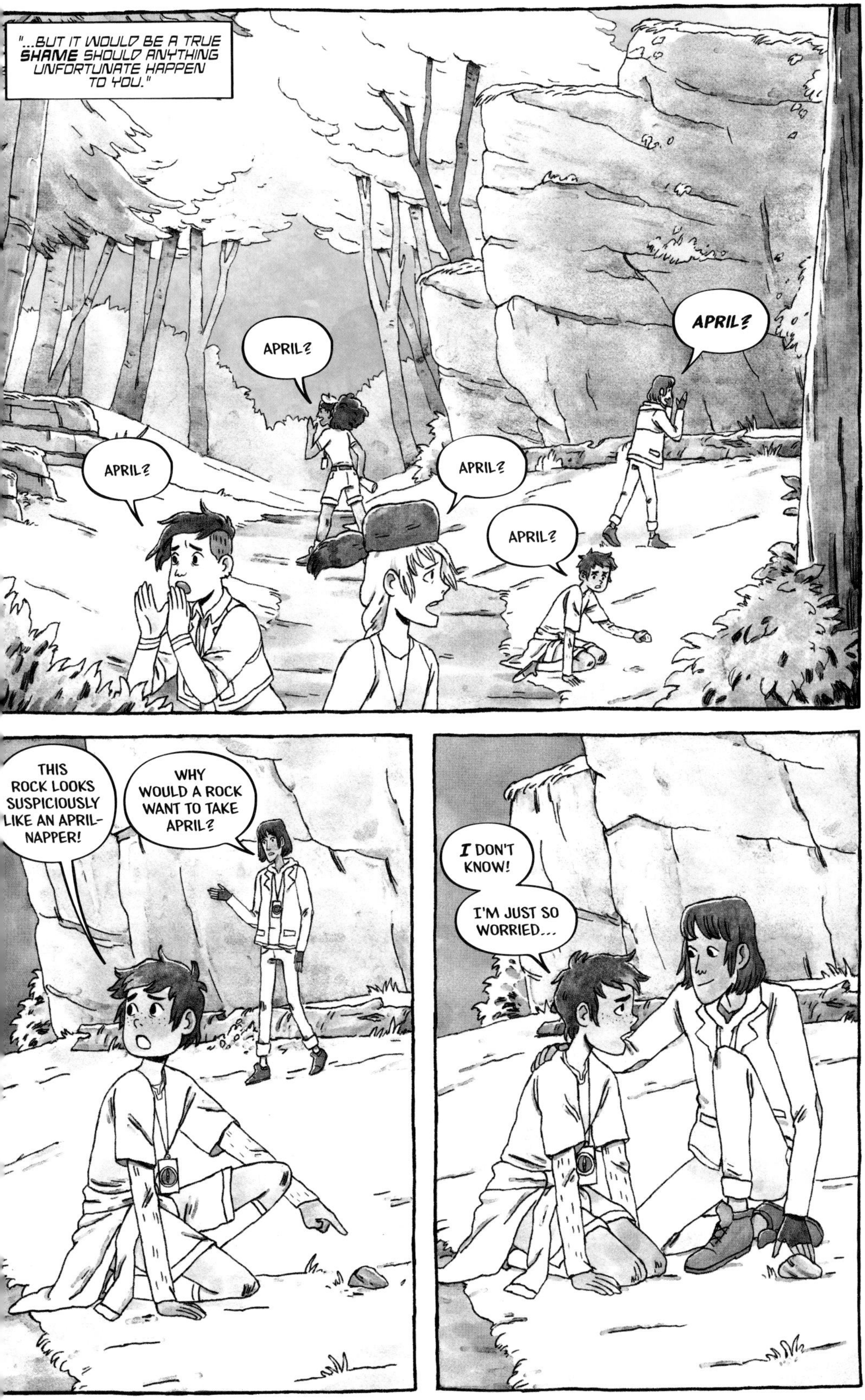
"...BUT IT WOULD BE A TRUE SHAME SHOULD ANYTHING UNFORTUNATE HAPPEN TO YOU."
APRIL?
APRIL?
APRIL?
APRIL?
APRIL?
THIS ROCK LOOKS SUSPICIOUSLY LIKE AN APRIL-NAPPER!
WHY WOULD A ROCK WANT TO TAKE APRIL?
I DON'T KNOW!
I'M JUST SO WORRIED...

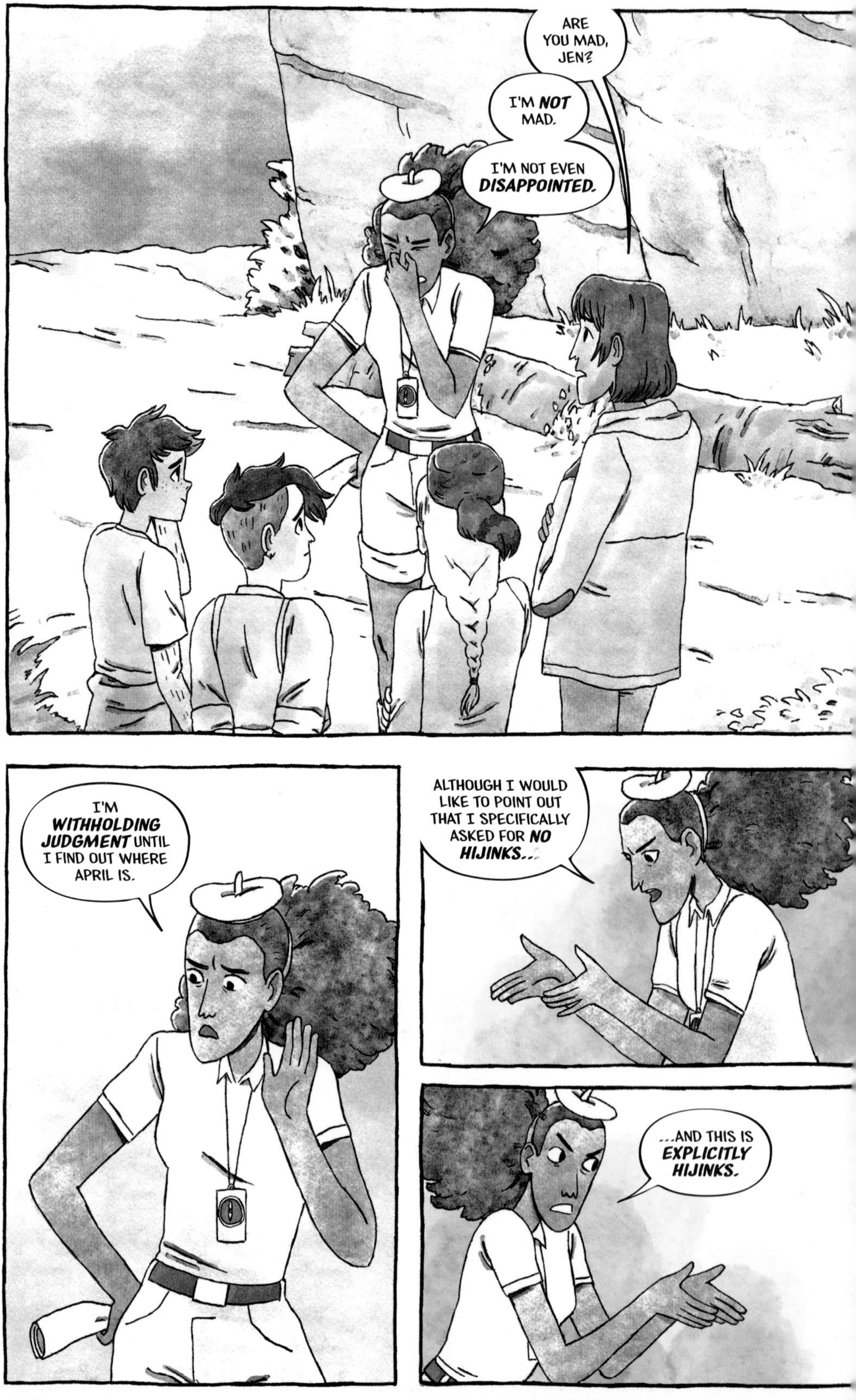
ARE YOU MAD, JEN?
I'M NOT MAD.
I'M NOT EVEN DISAPPOINTED.
I'M WITHHOLDING JUDGMENT UNTIL I FIND OUT WHERE APRIL IS.
ALTHOUGH I WOULD LIKE TO POINT OUT THAT I SPECIFICALLY ASKED FOR NO HIJINKS...
...AND THIS IS EXPLICITLY HIJINKS.

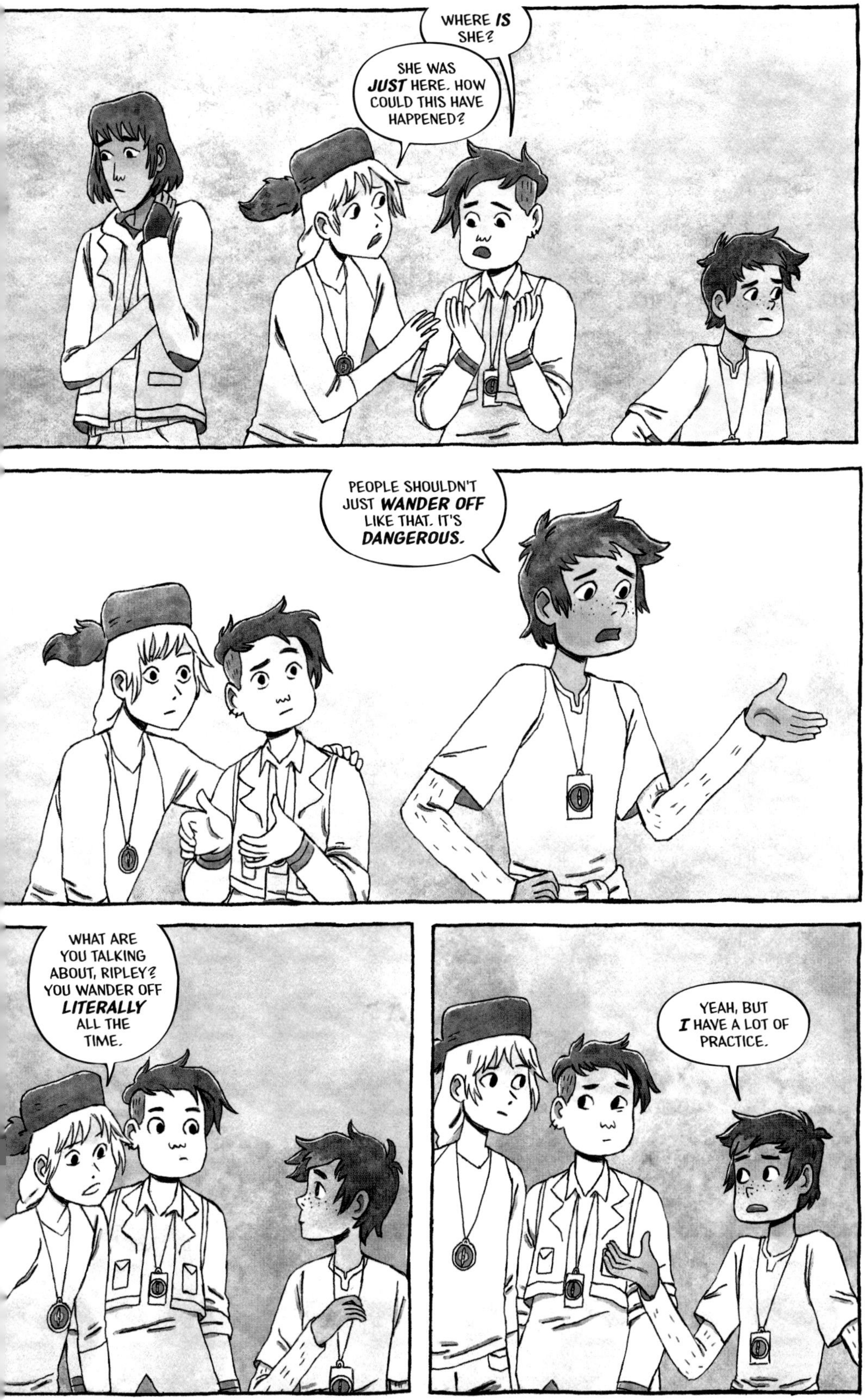
WHERE IS SHE?
SHE WAS JUST HERE. HOW COULD THIS HAVE HAPPENED?
PEOPLE SHOULDN'T JUST WANDER OFF LIKE THAT. IT'S DANGEROUS.
WHAT ARE YOU TALKING ABOUT, RIPLEY? YOU WANDER OFF LITERALLY ALL THE TIME.
YEAH, BUT I HAVE A LOT OF PRACTICE.

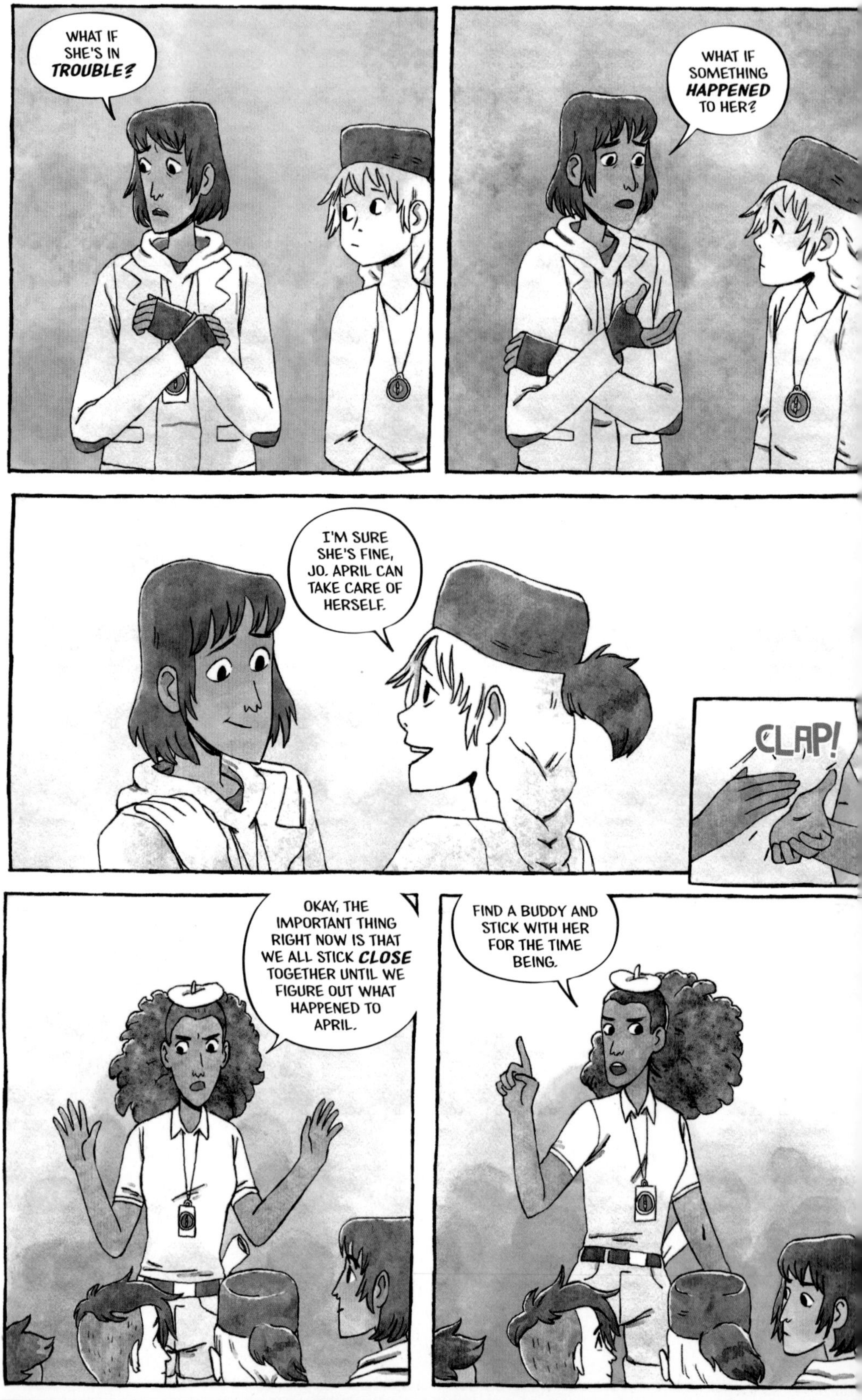
WHAT IF SHE'S IN TROUBLE?
WHAT IF SOMETHING HAPPENED TO HER?
I'M SURE SHE'S FINE, JO. APRIL CAN TAKE CARE OF HERSELF.
CLAP!
OKAY, THE IMPORTANT THING RIGHT NOW IS THAT WE ALL STICK CLOSE TOGETHER UNTIL WE FIGURE OUT WHAT HAPPENED TO APRIL.
FIND A BUDDY AND STICK WITH HER FOR THE TIME BEING.

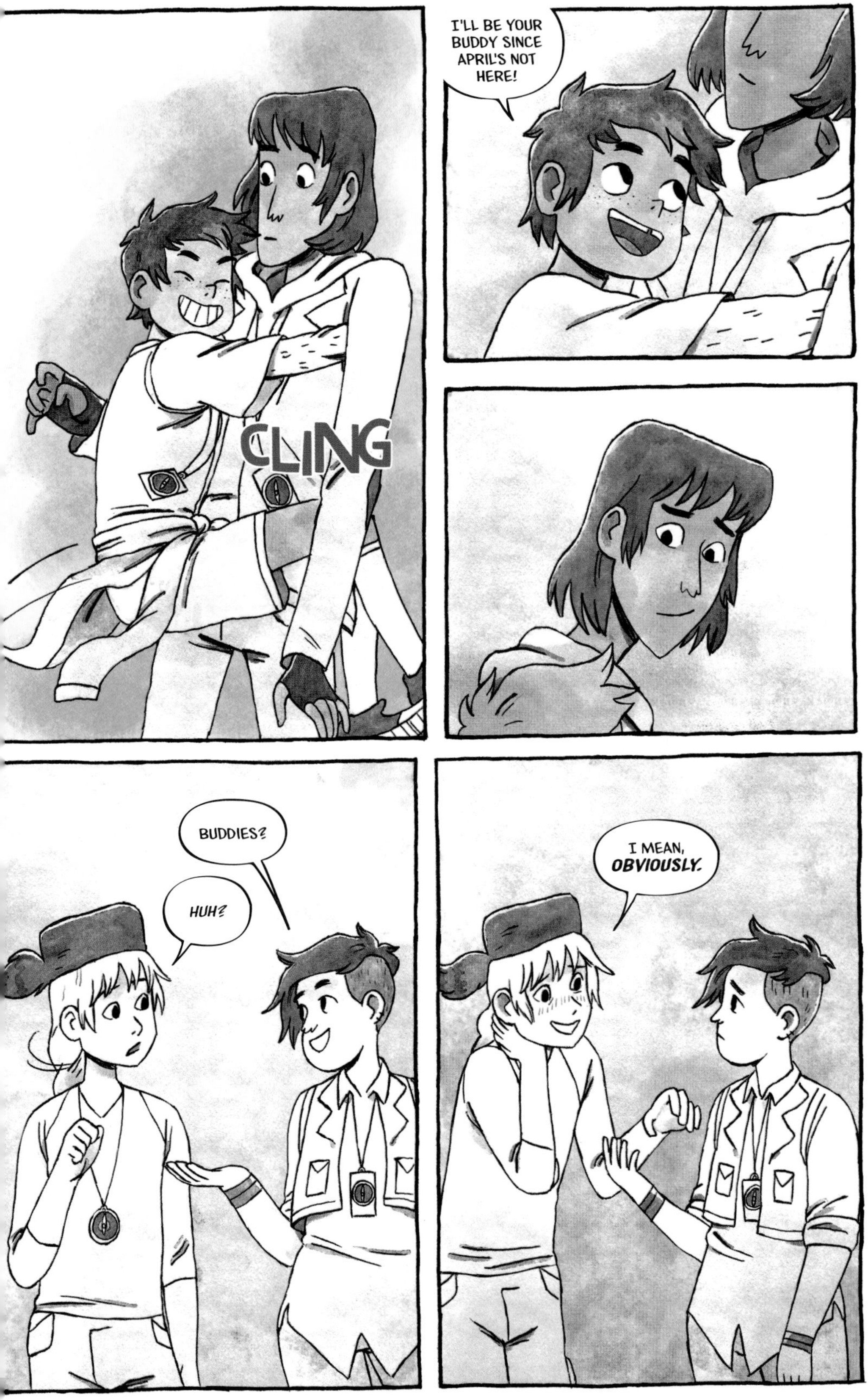
CLING
I'LL BE YOUR BUDDY SINCE APRIL'S NOT HERE!
HUH?
BUDDIES?
I MEAN, **OBVIOUSLY.**

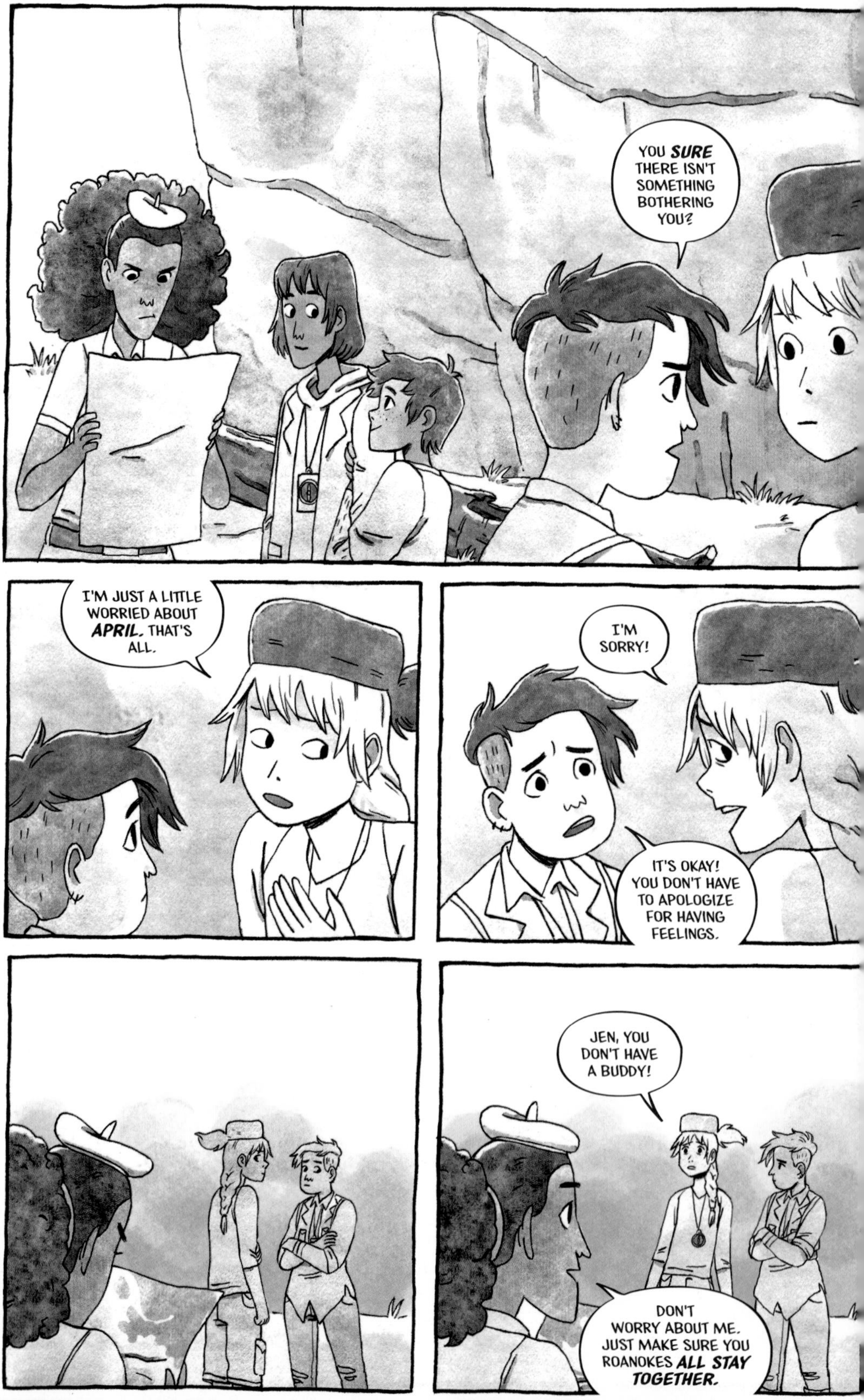
YOU SURE THERE ISN'T SOMETHING BOTHERING YOU?
I'M JUST A LITTLE WORRIED ABOUT APRIL. THAT'S ALL.
I'M SORRY!
IT'S OKAY! YOU DON'T HAVE TO APOLOGIZE FOR HAVING FEELINGS.
JEN, YOU DON'T HAVE A BUDDY!
DON'T WORRY ABOUT ME. JUST MAKE SURE YOU ROANOKES ALL STAY TOGETHER.

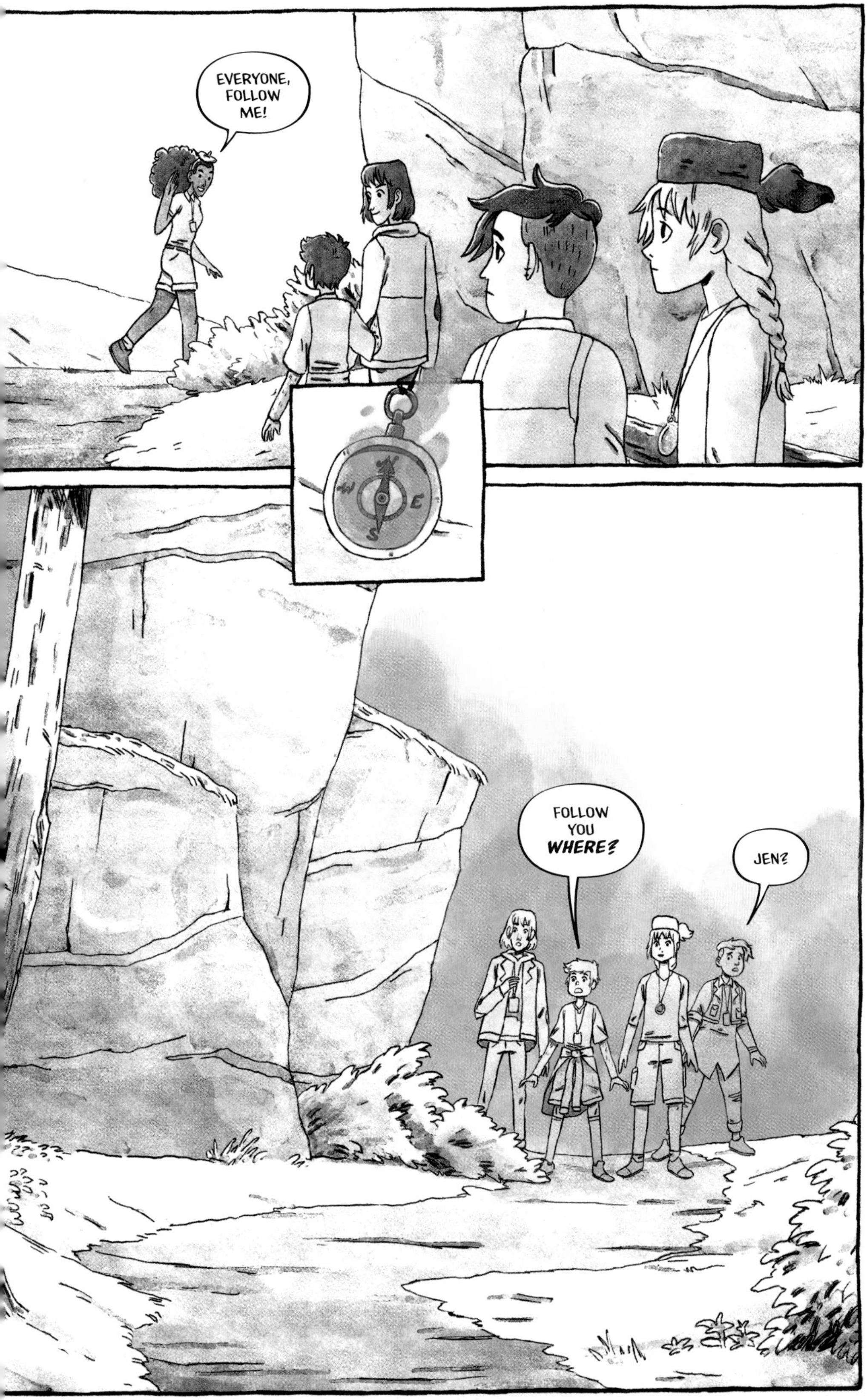
EVERYONE, FOLLOW ME!
FOLLOW YOU WHERE?
JEN?

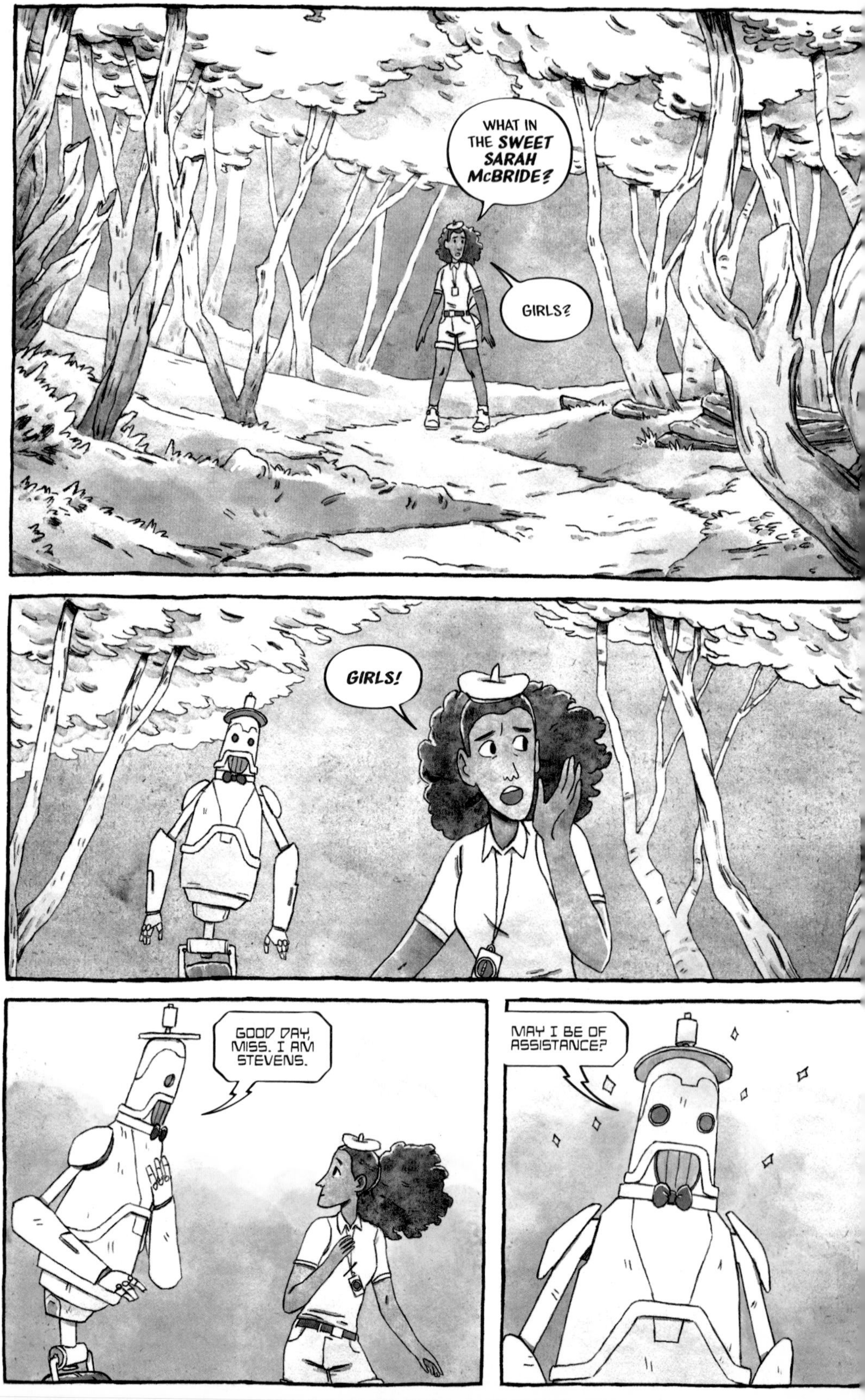
WHAT IN THE SWEET SARAH McBRIDE?
GIRLS?
GIRLS!
GOOD DAY, MISS. I AM STEVENS.
MAY I BE OF ASSISTANCE?

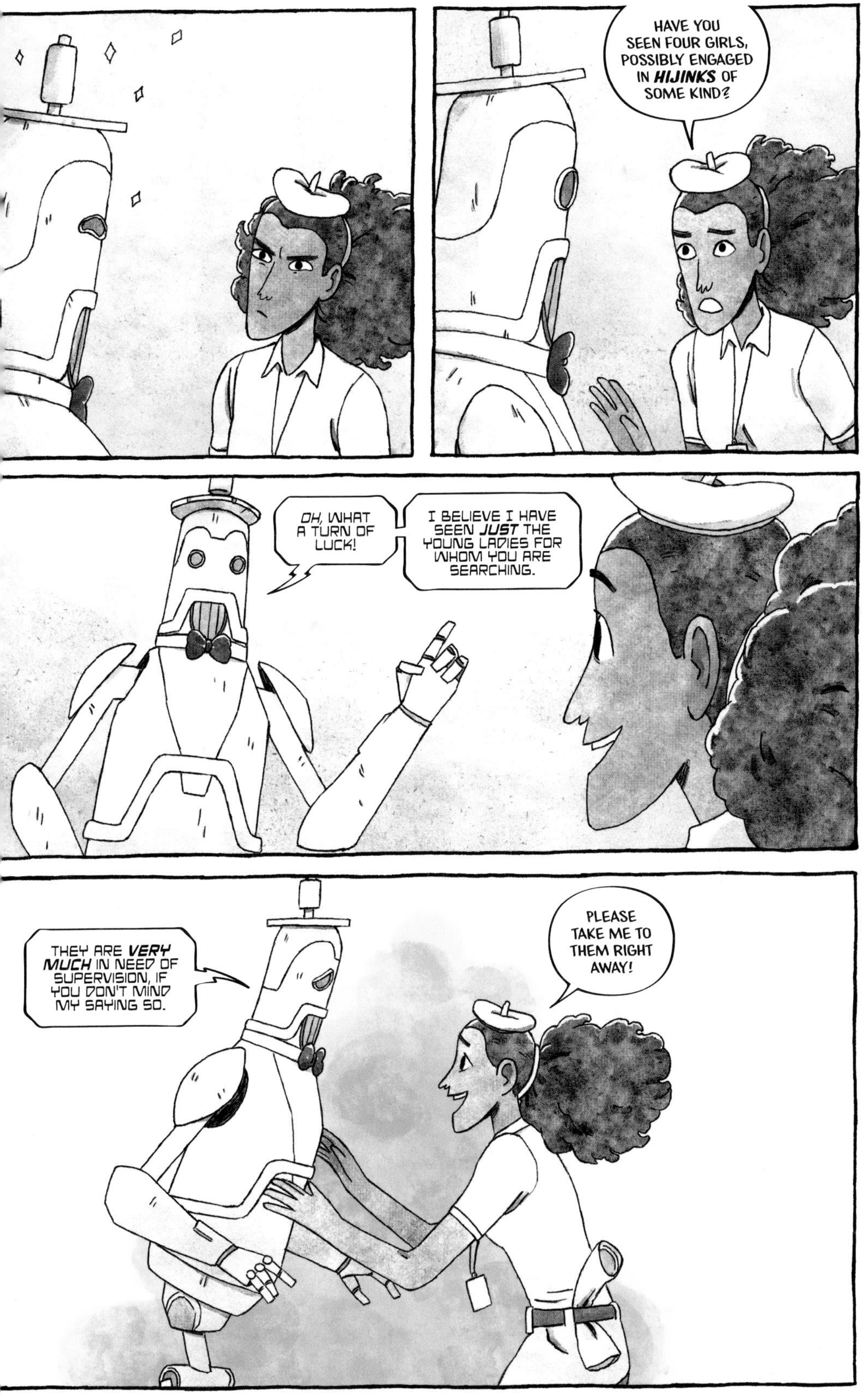
HAVE YOU SEEN FOUR GIRLS, POSSIBLY ENGAGED IN HIJINKS OF SOME KIND?
OH, WHAT A TURN OF LUCK!
I BELIEVE I HAVE SEEN JUST THE YOUNG LADIES FOR WHOM YOU ARE SEARCHING.
THEY ARE VERY MUCH IN NEED OF SUPERVISION, IF YOU DON'T MIND MY SAYING SO.
PLEASE TAKE ME TO THEM RIGHT AWAY!

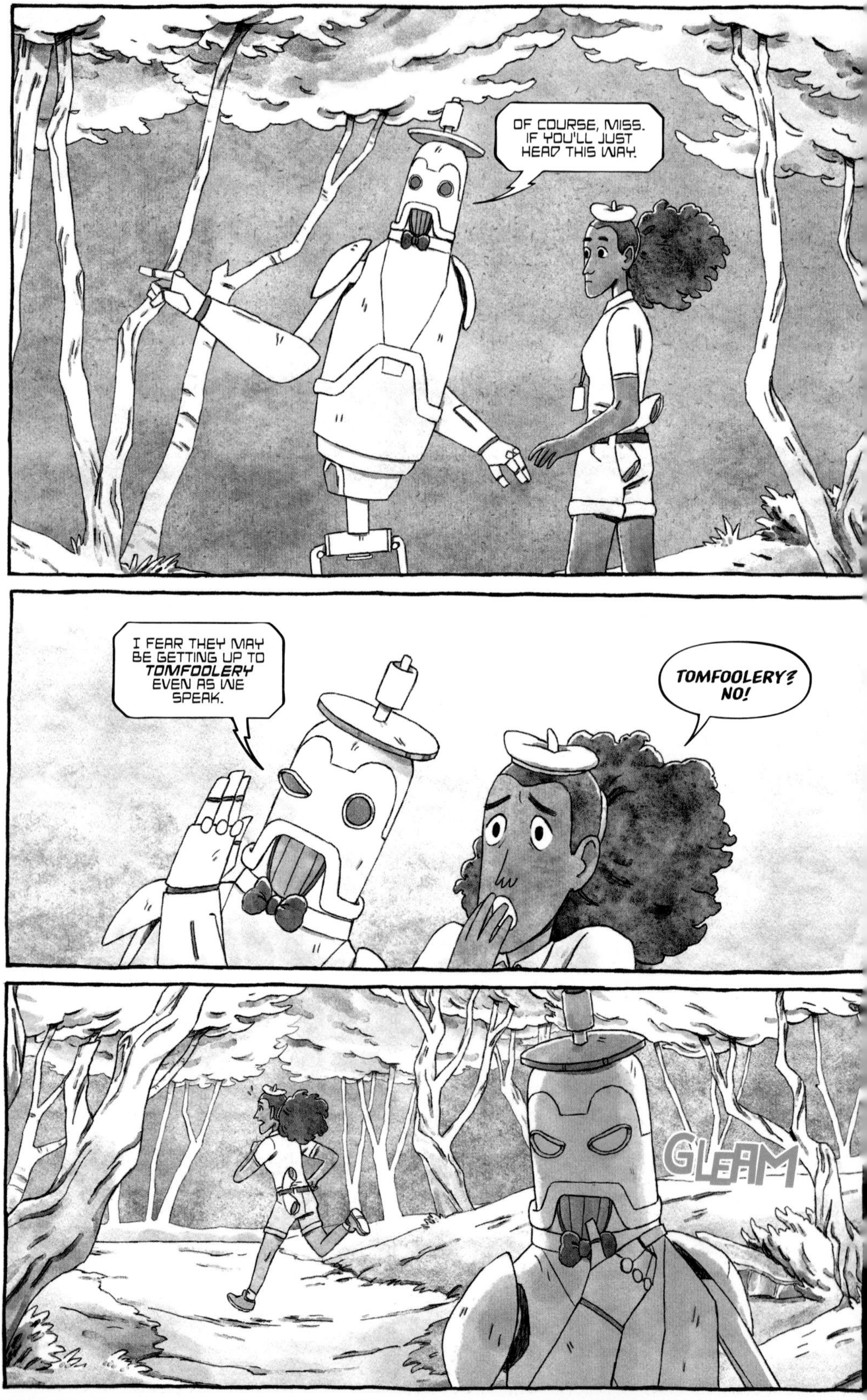
OF COURSE, MISS. IF YOU'LL JUST HEAD THIS WAY.
I FEAR THEY MAY BE GETTING UP TO *TOMFOOLERY* EVEN AS WE SPEAK.
TOMFOOLERY?! NO!
GLEAM

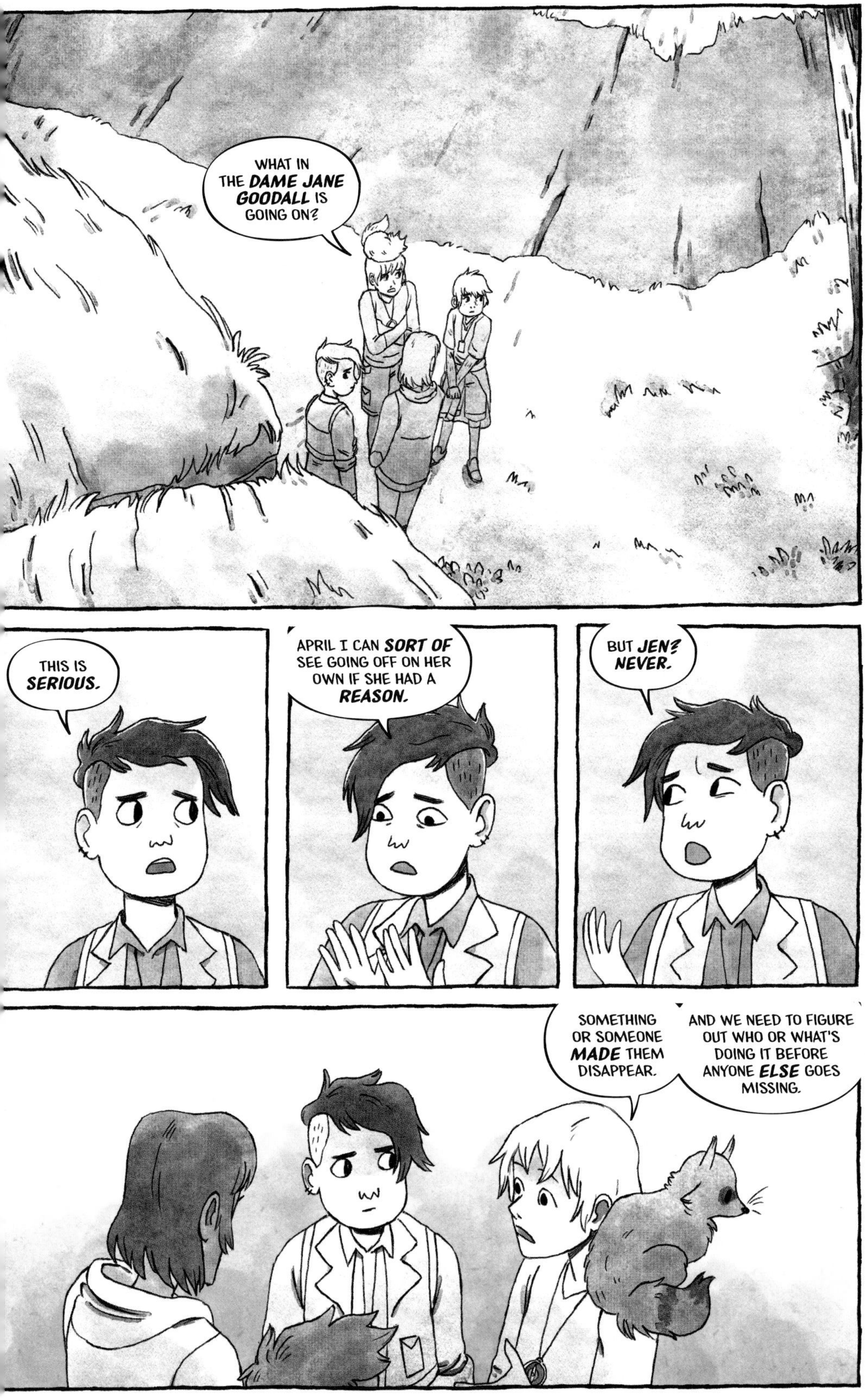
WHAT IN THE DAME JANE GOODALL IS GOING ON?
THIS IS SERIOUS.
APRIL I CAN SORT OF SEE GOING OFF ON HER OWN IF SHE HAD A REASON.
BUT JEN? NEVER.
SOMETHING OR SOMEONE MADE THEM DISAPPEAR.
AND WE NEED TO FIGURE OUT WHO OR WHAT'S DOING IT BEFORE ANYONE ELSE GOES MISSING.

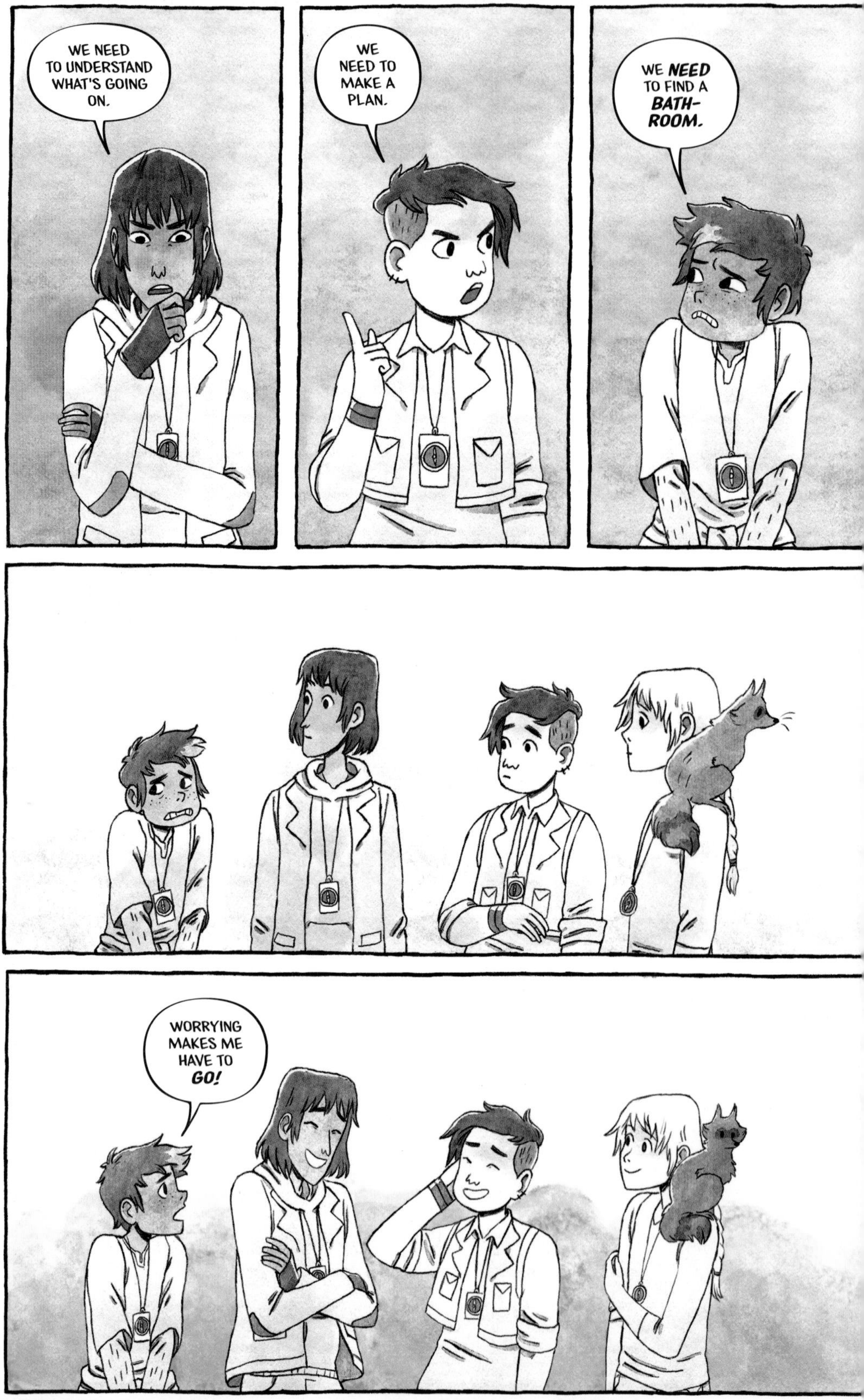
WE NEED TO UNDERSTAND WHAT'S GOING ON.
WE NEED TO MAKE A PLAN.
WE NEED TO FIND A BATH-ROOM.
WORRYING MAKES ME HAVE TO GO!

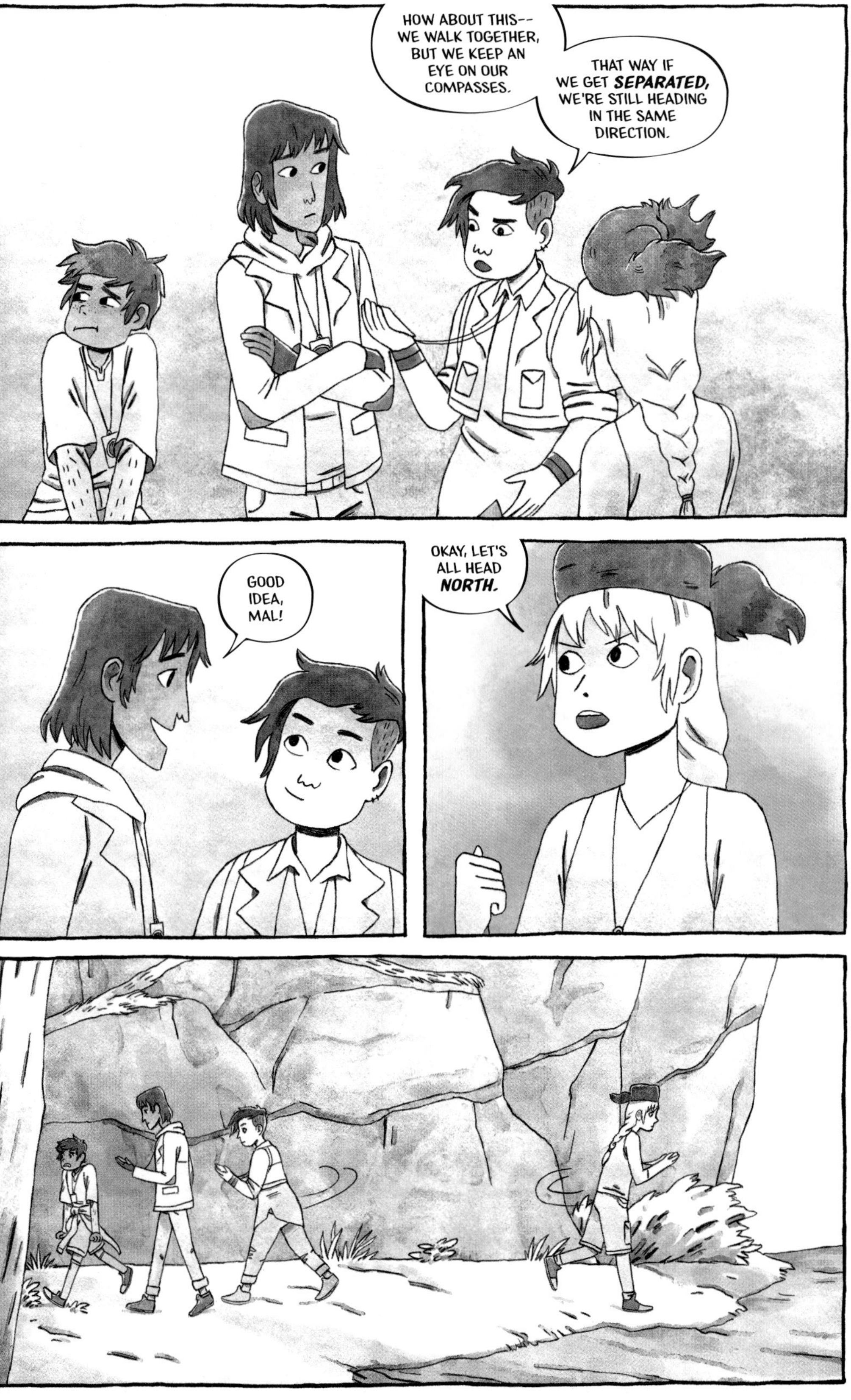
HOW ABOUT THIS-- WE WALK TOGETHER, BUT WE KEEP AN EYE ON OUR COMPASSES.
THAT WAY IF WE GET SEPARATED, WE'RE STILL HEADING IN THE SAME DIRECTION.
GOOD IDEA, MAL!
OKAY, LET'S ALL HEAD NORTH.

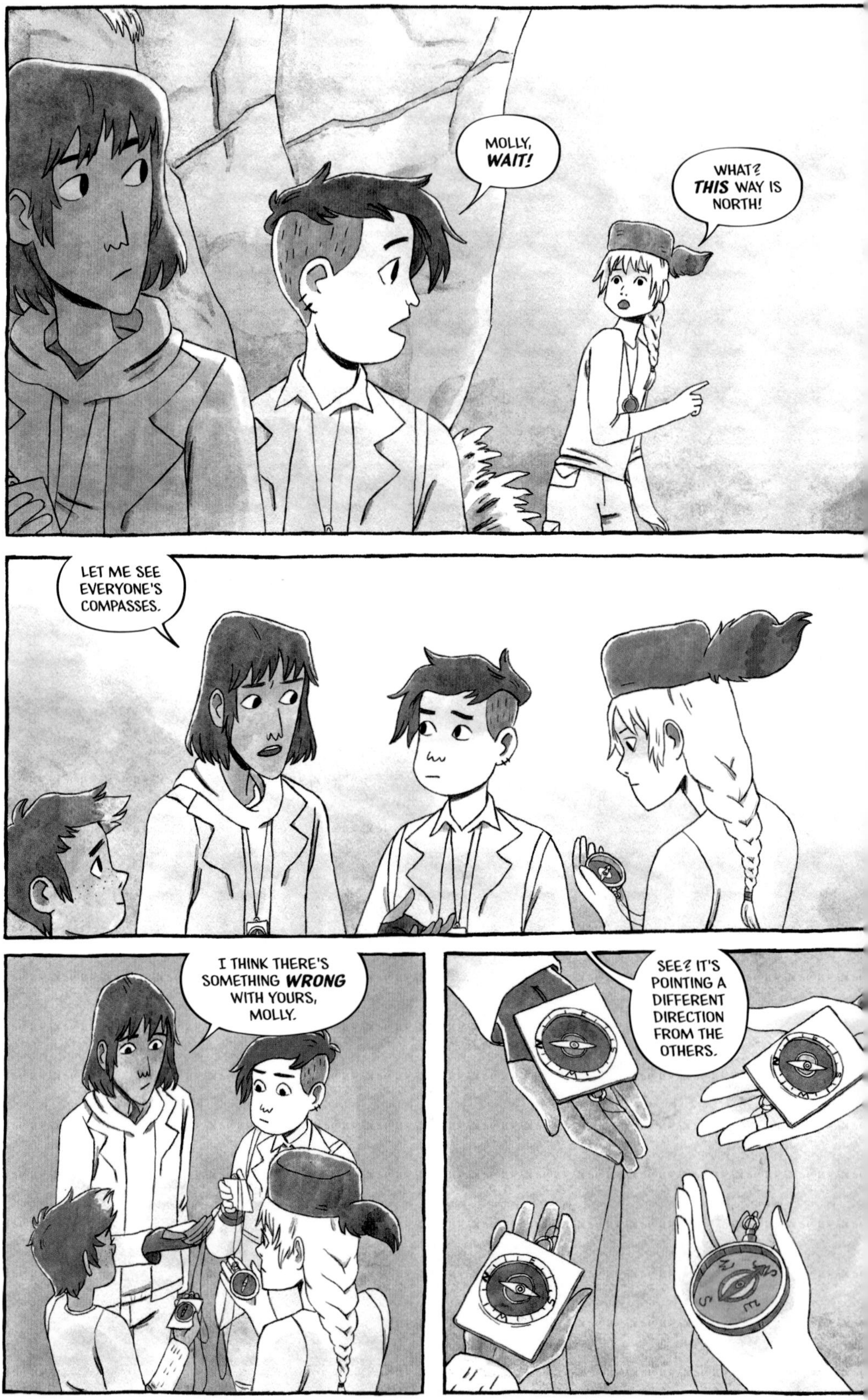
MOLLY, **WAIT!**
WHAT? **THIS** WAY IS NORTH!
LET ME SEE EVERYONE'S COMPASSES.
I THINK THERE'S SOMETHING **WRONG** WITH YOURS, MOLLY.
SEE? IT'S POINTING A DIFFERENT DIRECTION FROM THE OTHERS.

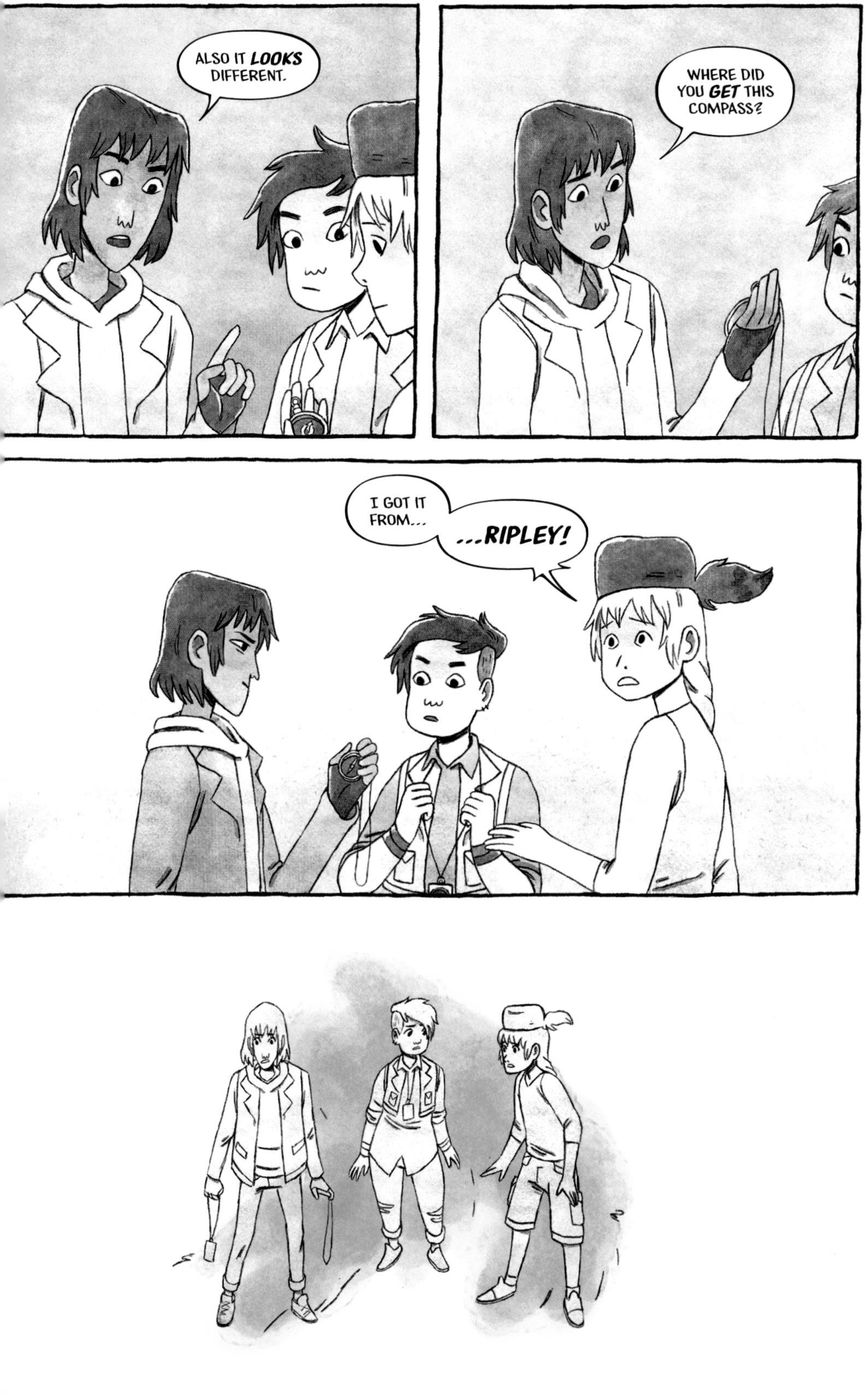
ALSO IT LOOKS DIFFERENT.
WHERE DID YOU GET THIS COMPASS?
I GOT IT FROM...
...RIPLEY!

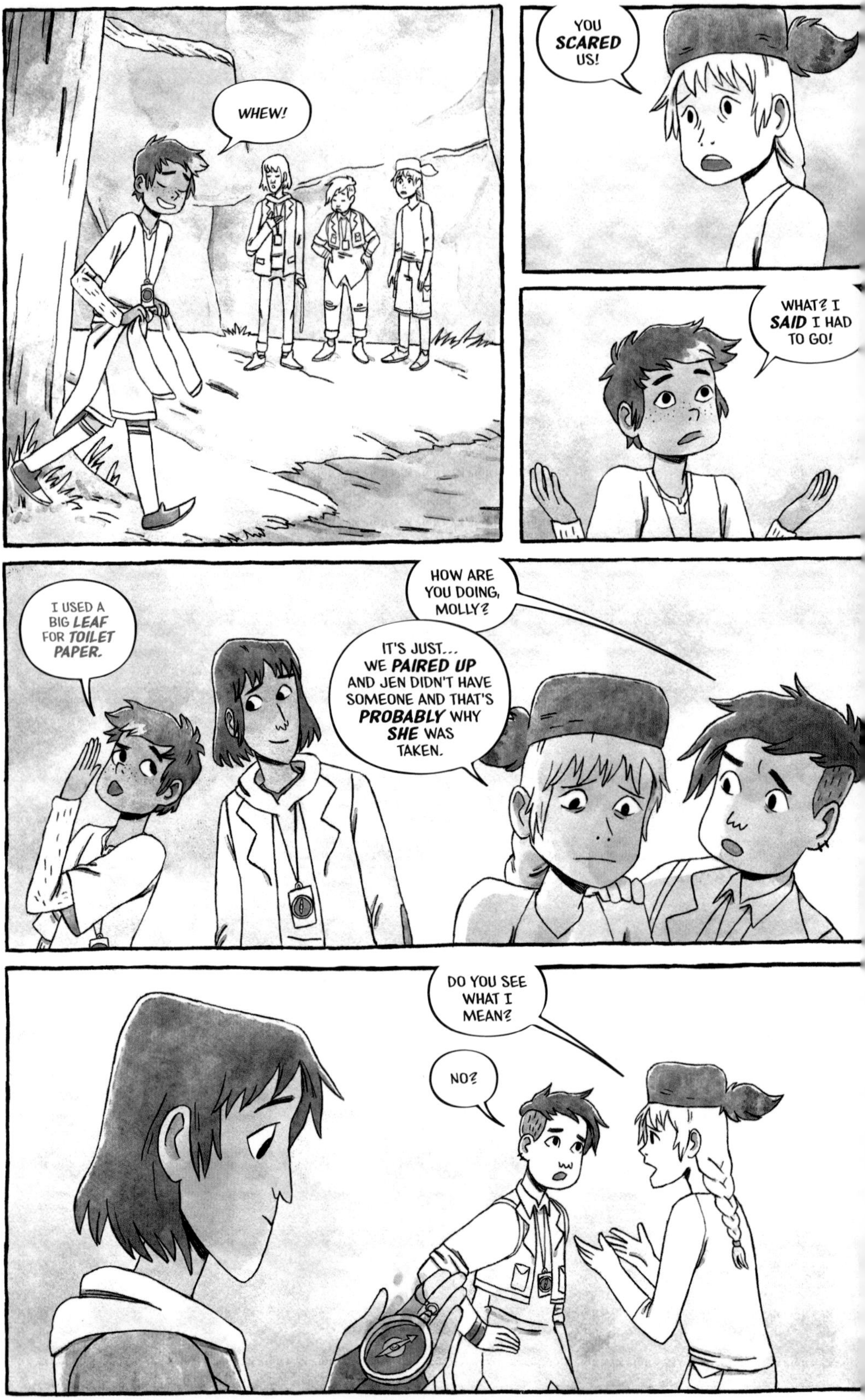
WHEW!
YOU SCARED US!
WHAT? I SAID I HAD TO GO!
I USED A BIG LEAF FOR TOILET PAPER.
HOW ARE YOU DOING, MOLLY?
IT'S JUST... WE PAIRED UP AND JEN DIDN'T HAVE SOMEONE AND THAT'S PROBABLY WHY SHE WAS TAKEN.
DO YOU SEE WHAT I MEAN?
NO?

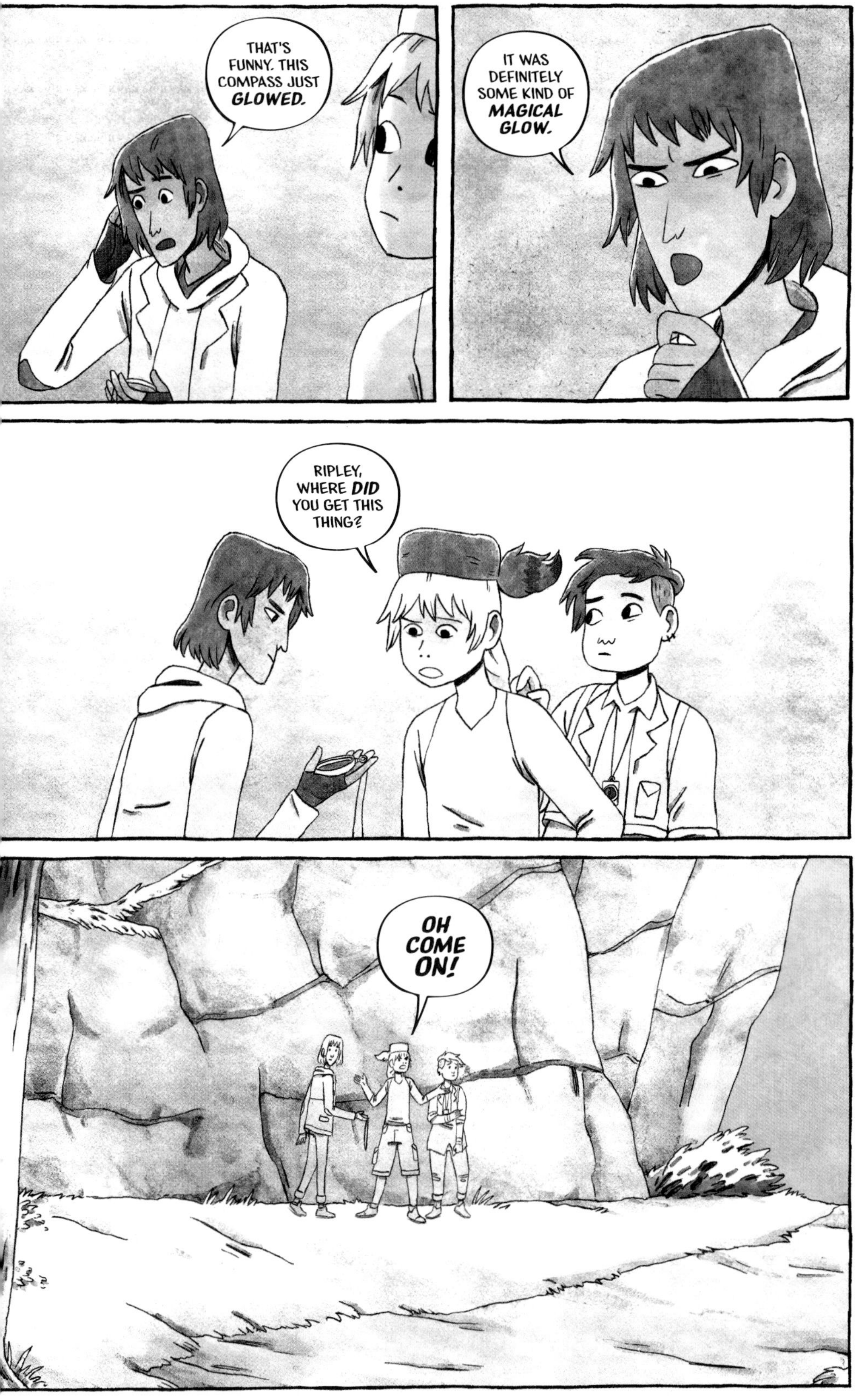
THAT'S FUNNY. THIS COMPASS JUST **GLOWED.**
IT WAS DEFINITELY SOME KIND OF **MAGICAL GLOW.**
RIPLEY, WHERE **DID** YOU GET THIS THING?
OH COME ON!

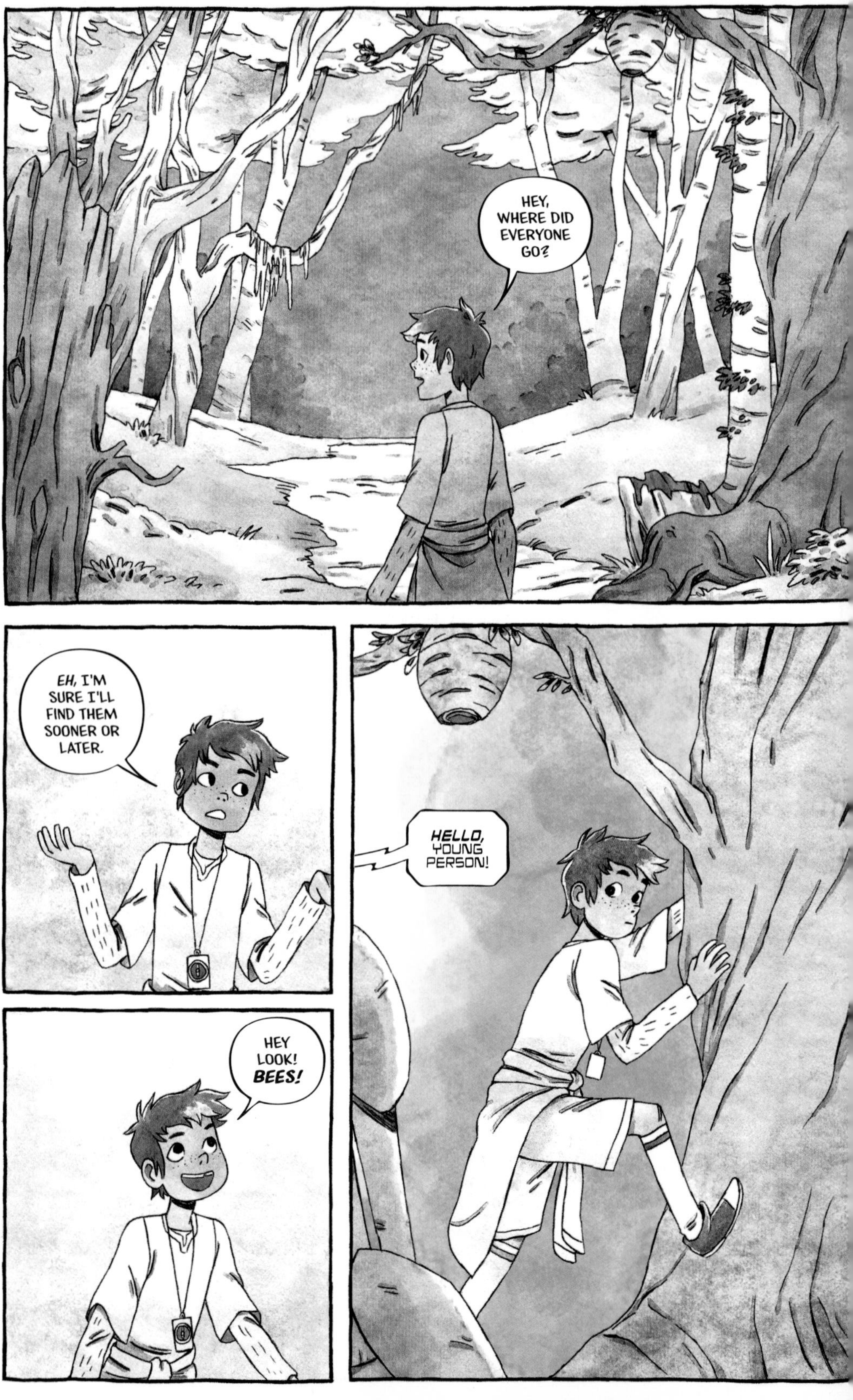
HEY, WHERE DID EVERYONE GO?
EH, I'M SURE I'LL FIND THEM SOONER OR LATER.
HEY LOOK! BEES!
HELLO, YOUNG PERSON!

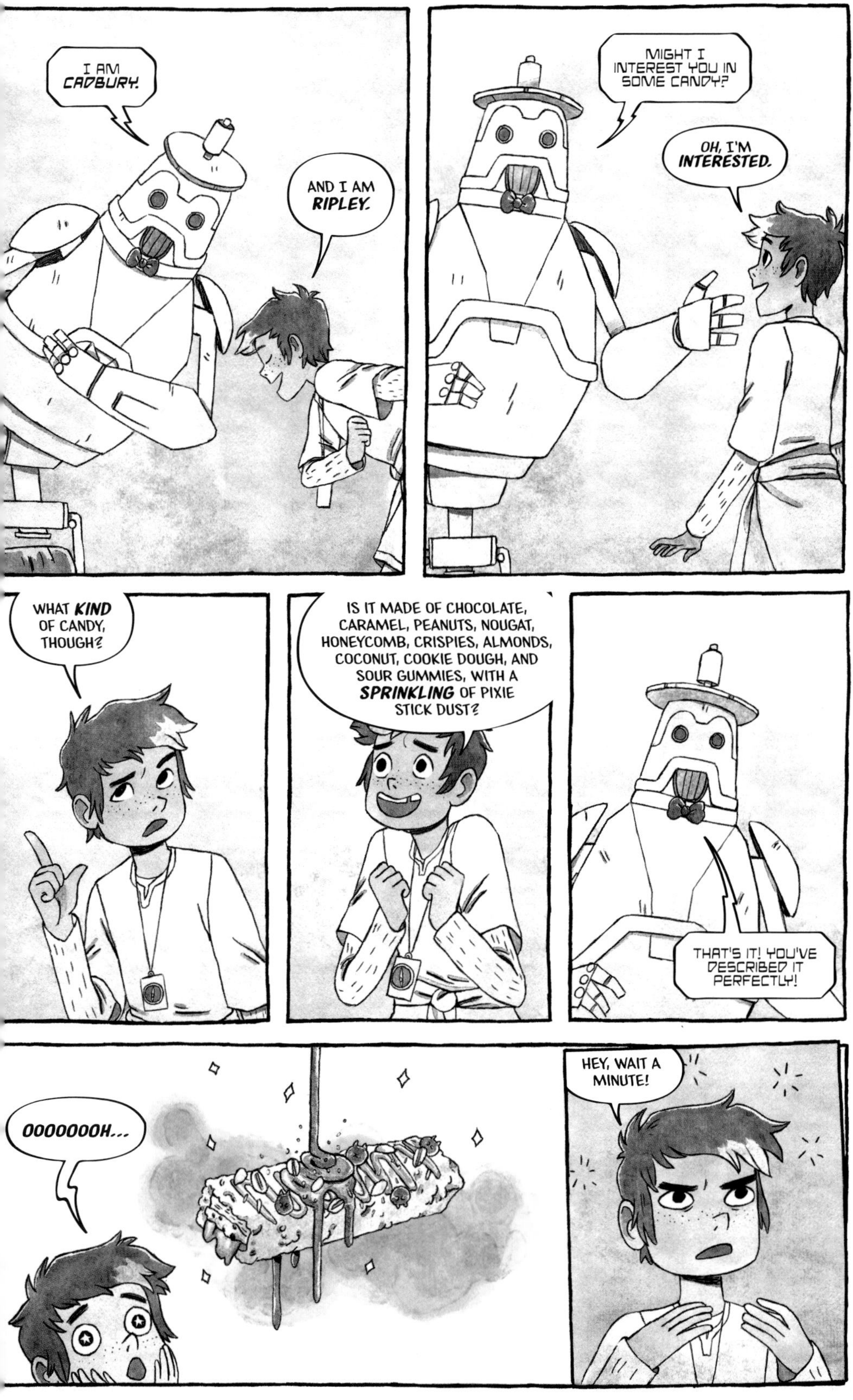
I AM CADBURY.
AND I AM RIPLEY.
MIGHT I INTEREST YOU IN SOME CANDY?
OH, I'M INTERESTED.
WHAT KIND OF CANDY, THOUGH?
IS IT MADE OF CHOCOLATE, CARAMEL, PEANUTS, NOUGAT, HONEYCOMB, CRISPIES, ALMONDS, COCONUT, COOKIE DOUGH, AND SOUR GUMMIES, WITH A SPRINKLING OF PIXIE STICK DUST?
THAT'S IT! YOU'VE DESCRIBED IT PERFECTLY!
OOOOOOOH...
HEY, WAIT A MINUTE!

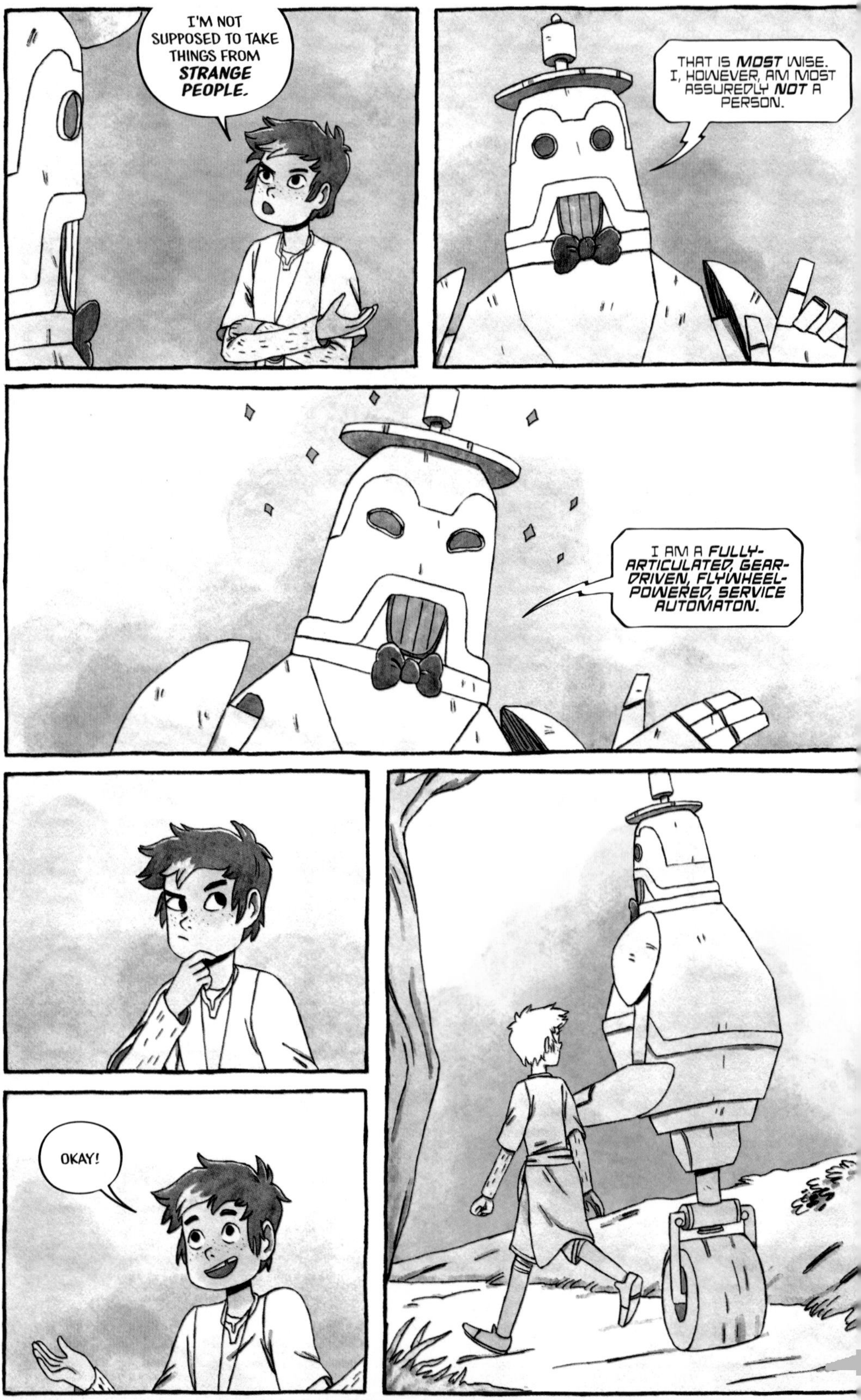
I'M NOT SUPPOSED TO TAKE THINGS FROM STRANGE PEOPLE.
THAT IS MOST WISE. I, HOWEVER, AM MOST ASSUREDLY NOT A PERSON.
I AM A FULLY-ARTICULATED, GEAR-DRIVEN, FLYWHEEL-POWERED, SERVICE AUTOMATON.
OKAY!

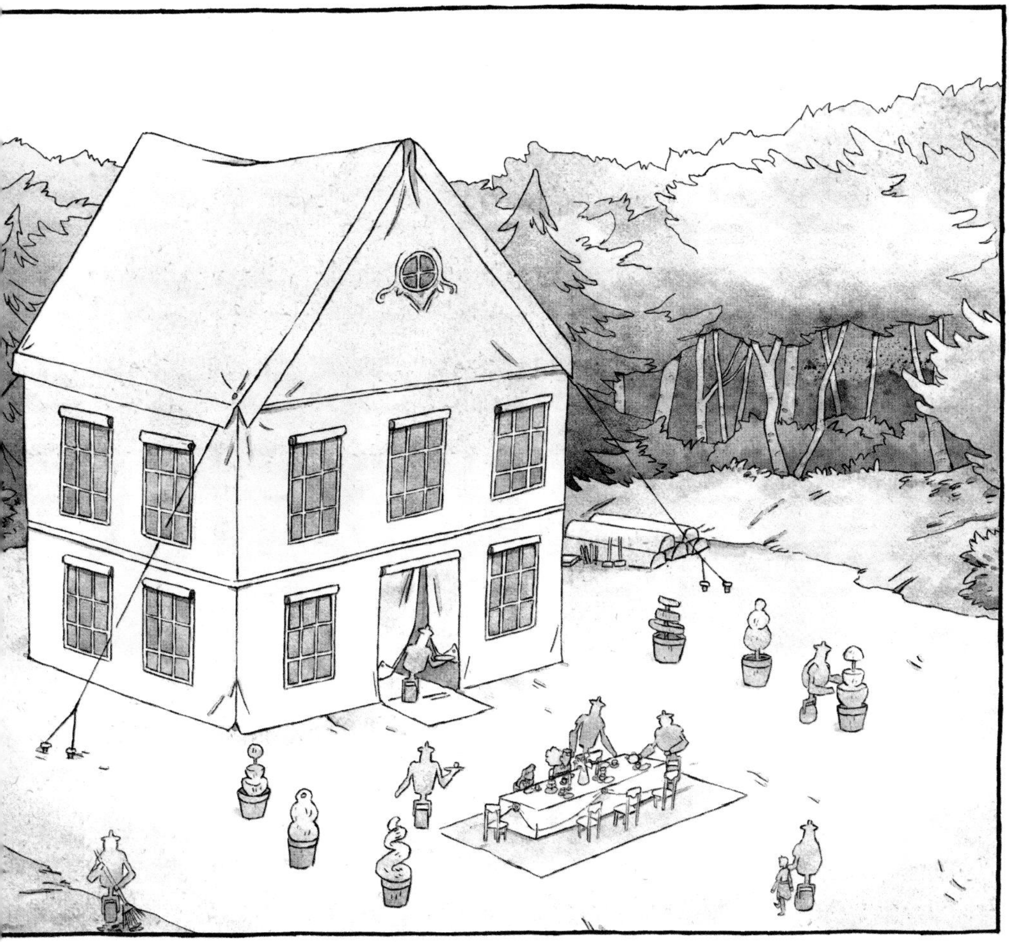

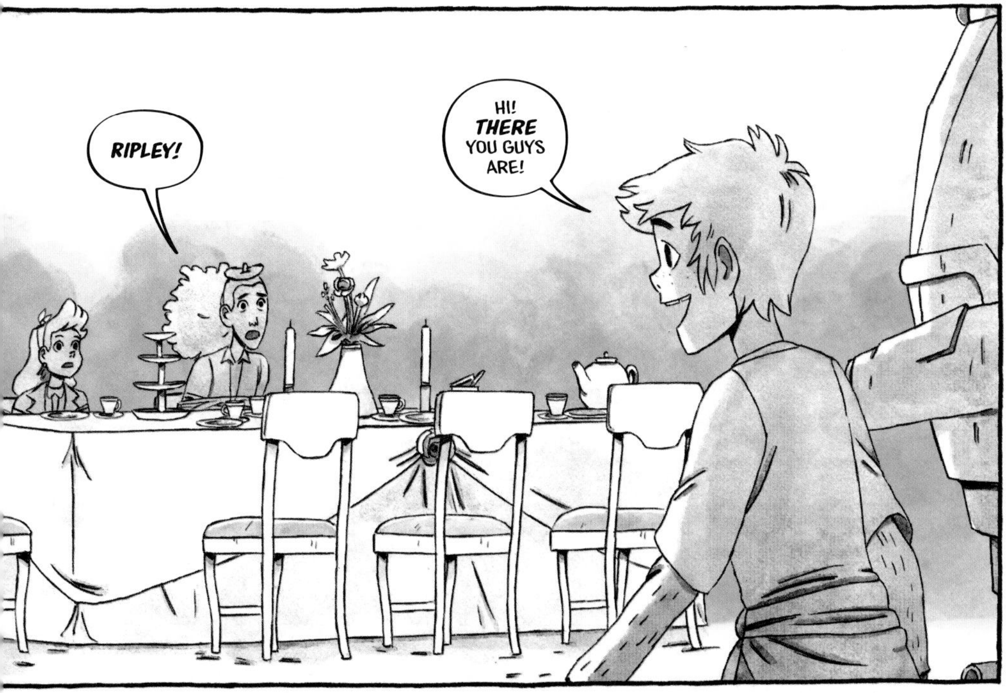
RIPLEY!
HI! THERE YOU GUYS ARE!

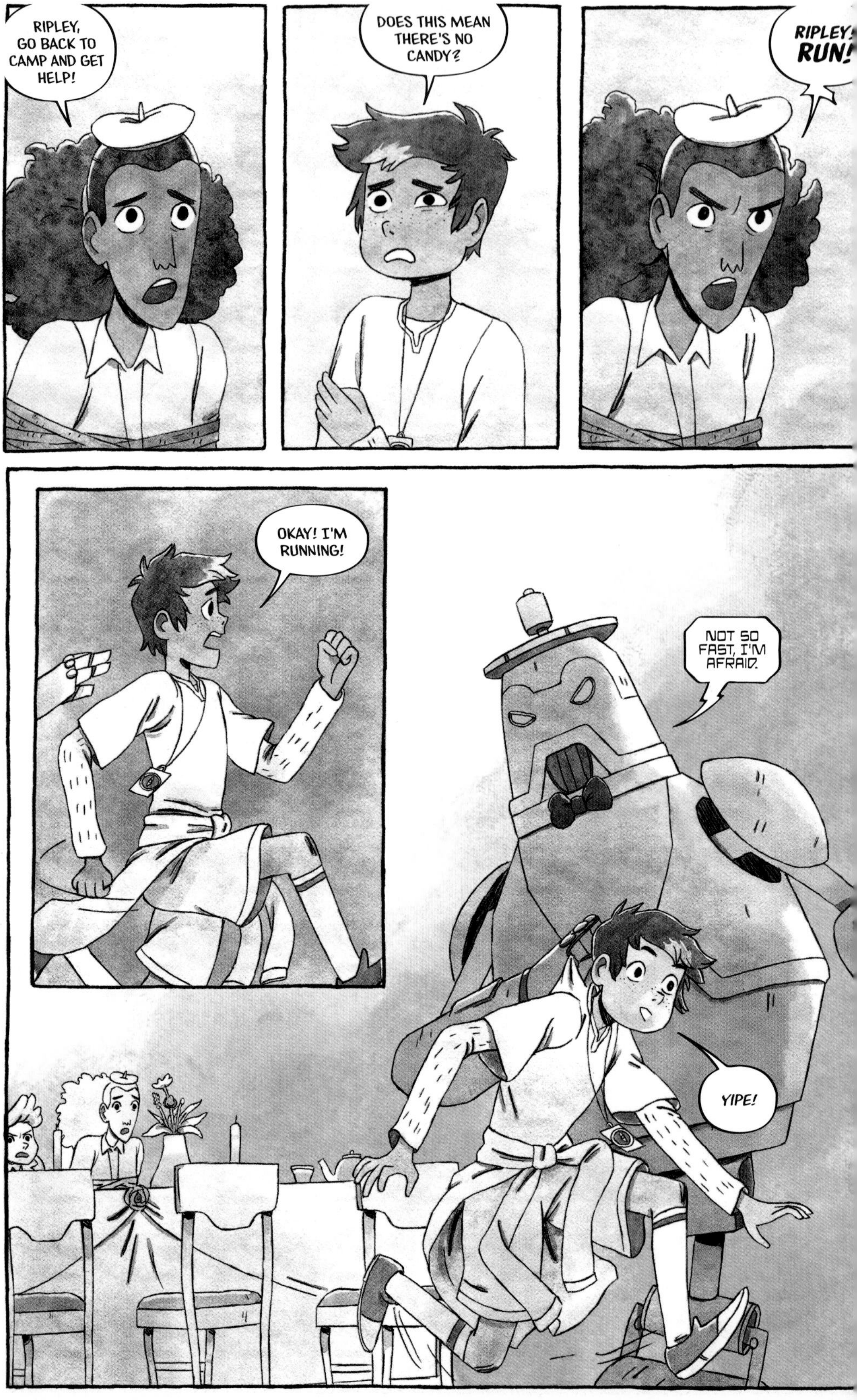
RIPLEY, GO BACK TO CAMP AND GET HELP!
DOES THIS MEAN THERE'S NO CANDY?
RIPLEY! RUN!
OKAY! I'M RUNNING!
NOT SO FAST, I'M AFRAID.
YIPE!

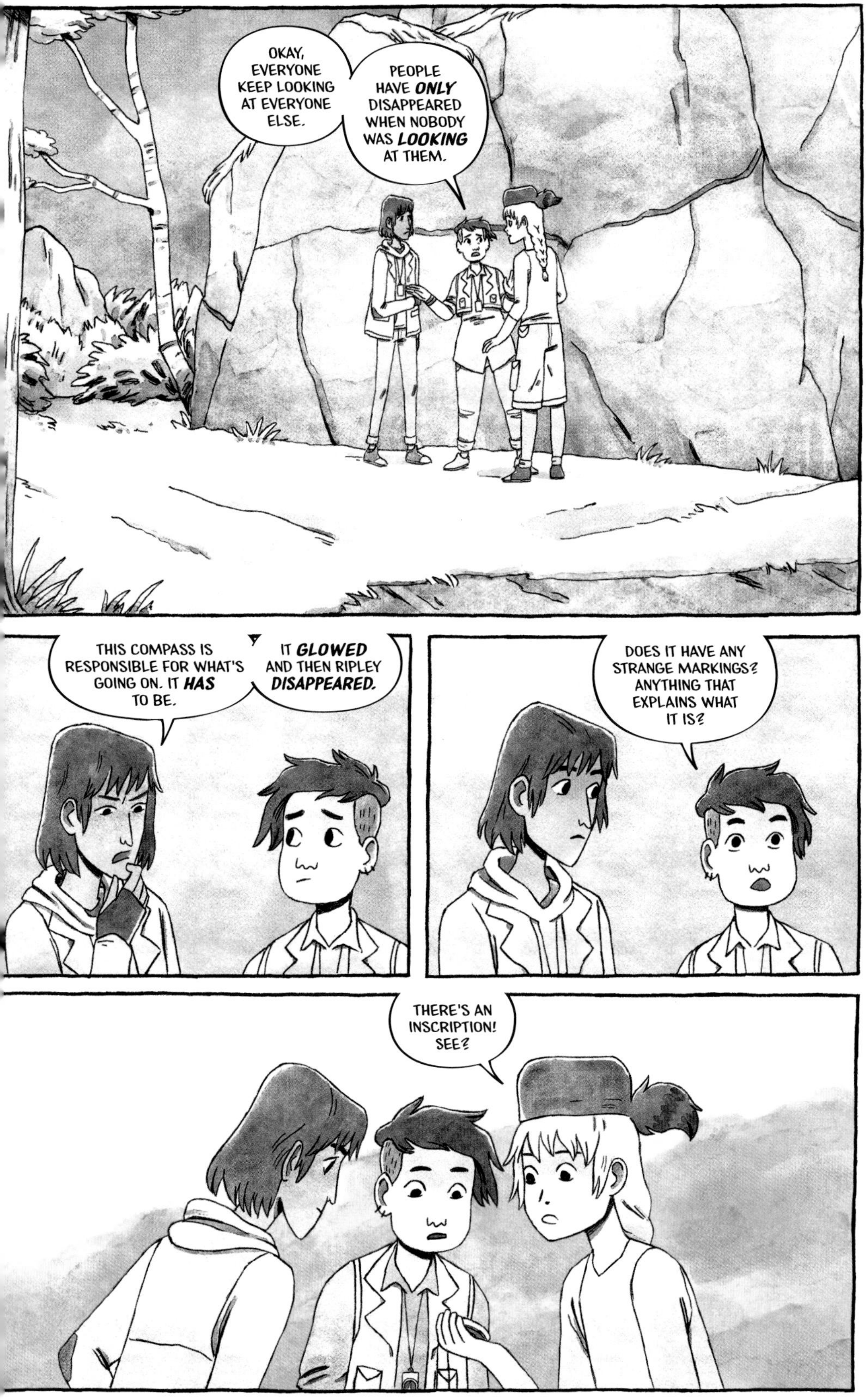
OKAY, EVERYONE KEEP LOOKING AT EVERYONE ELSE.
PEOPLE HAVE ONLY DISAPPEARED WHEN NOBODY WAS LOOKING AT THEM.
THIS COMPASS IS RESPONSIBLE FOR WHAT'S GOING ON. IT HAS TO BE.
IT GLOWED AND THEN RIPLEY DISAPPEARED.
DOES IT HAVE ANY STRANGE MARKINGS? ANYTHING THAT EXPLAINS WHAT IT IS?
THERE'S AN INSCRIPTION! SEE?

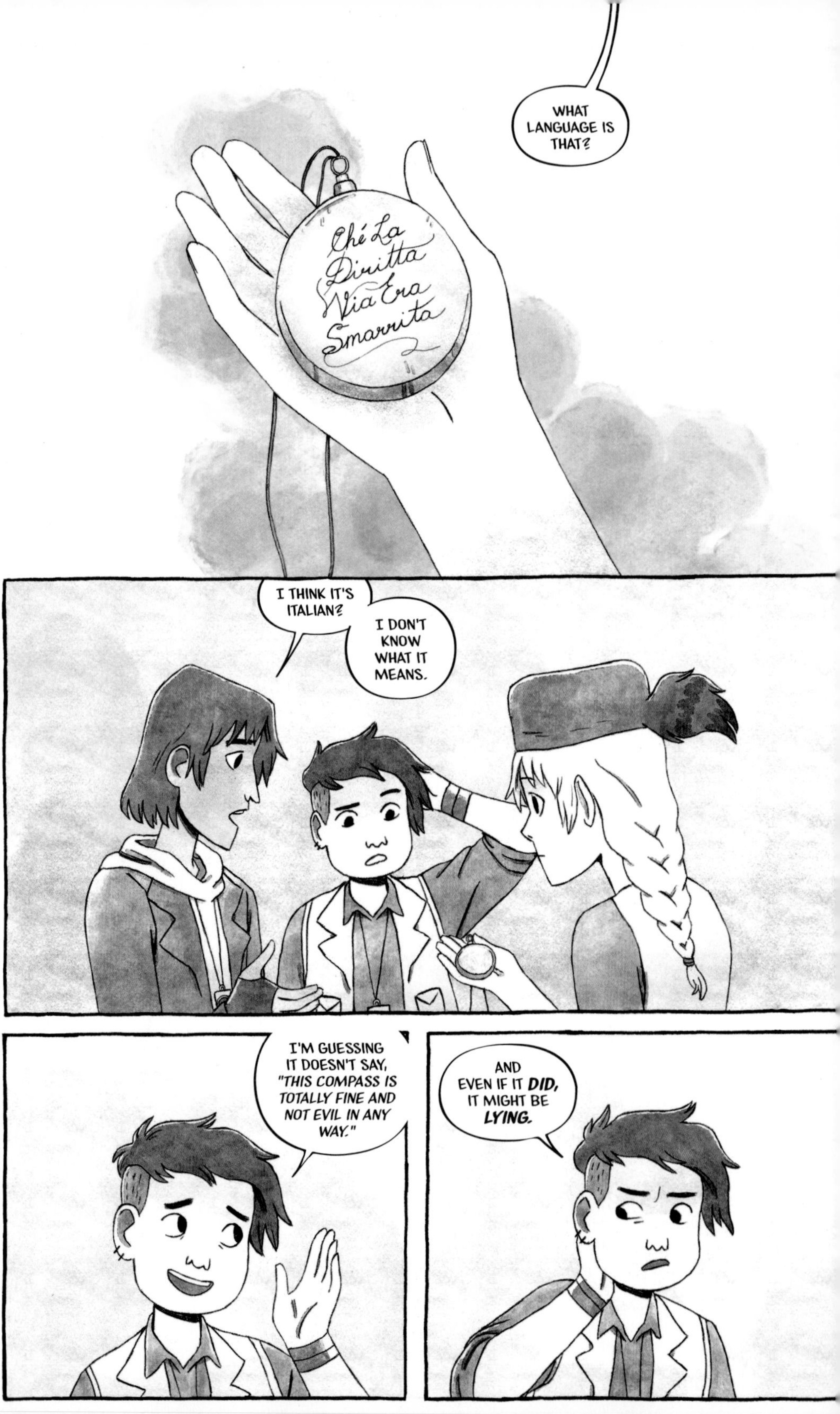
WHAT LANGUAGE IS THAT?
Ché La Diritta Via Era Smarrita
I THINK IT'S ITALIAN?
I DON'T KNOW WHAT IT MEANS.
I'M GUESSING IT DOESN'T SAY, "THIS COMPASS IS TOTALLY FINE AND NOT EVIL IN ANY WAY."
AND EVEN IF IT DID, IT MIGHT BE LYING.

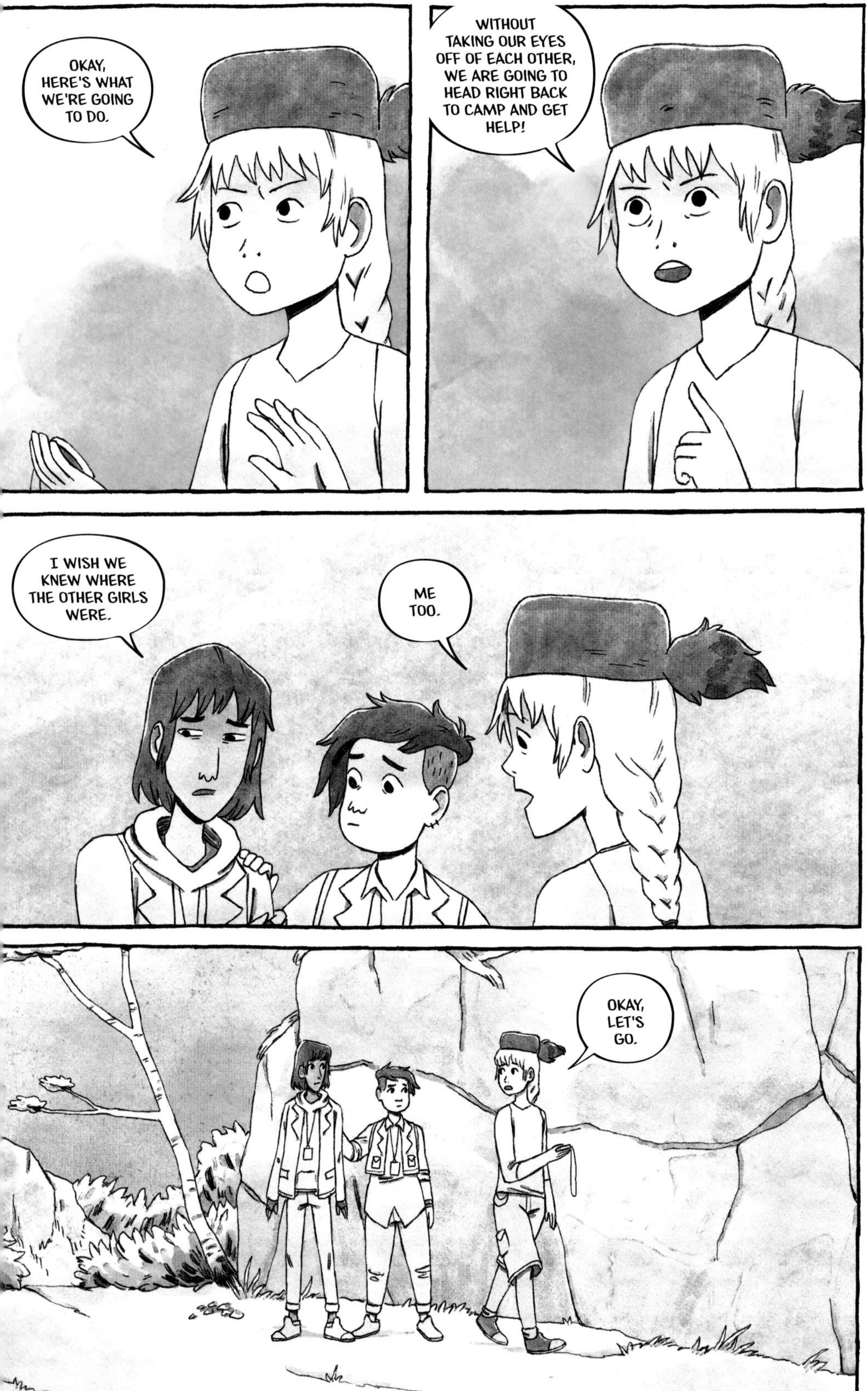
OKAY, HERE'S WHAT WE'RE GOING TO DO.
WITHOUT TAKING OUR EYES OFF OF EACH OTHER, WE ARE GOING TO HEAD RIGHT BACK TO CAMP AND GET HELP!
I WISH WE KNEW WHERE THE OTHER GIRLS WERE.
ME TOO.
OKAY, LET'S GO.

HEY, LOOK! THE COMPASS IS *GLOWING!*

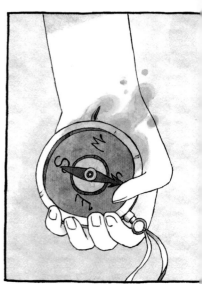

SEE?

WOW! JO, YOU WERE *RIGHT!* THAT I? *DEFINITELY* A MAGIC GLOW!

WAIT! EVERYONE KEEP LOOKING--

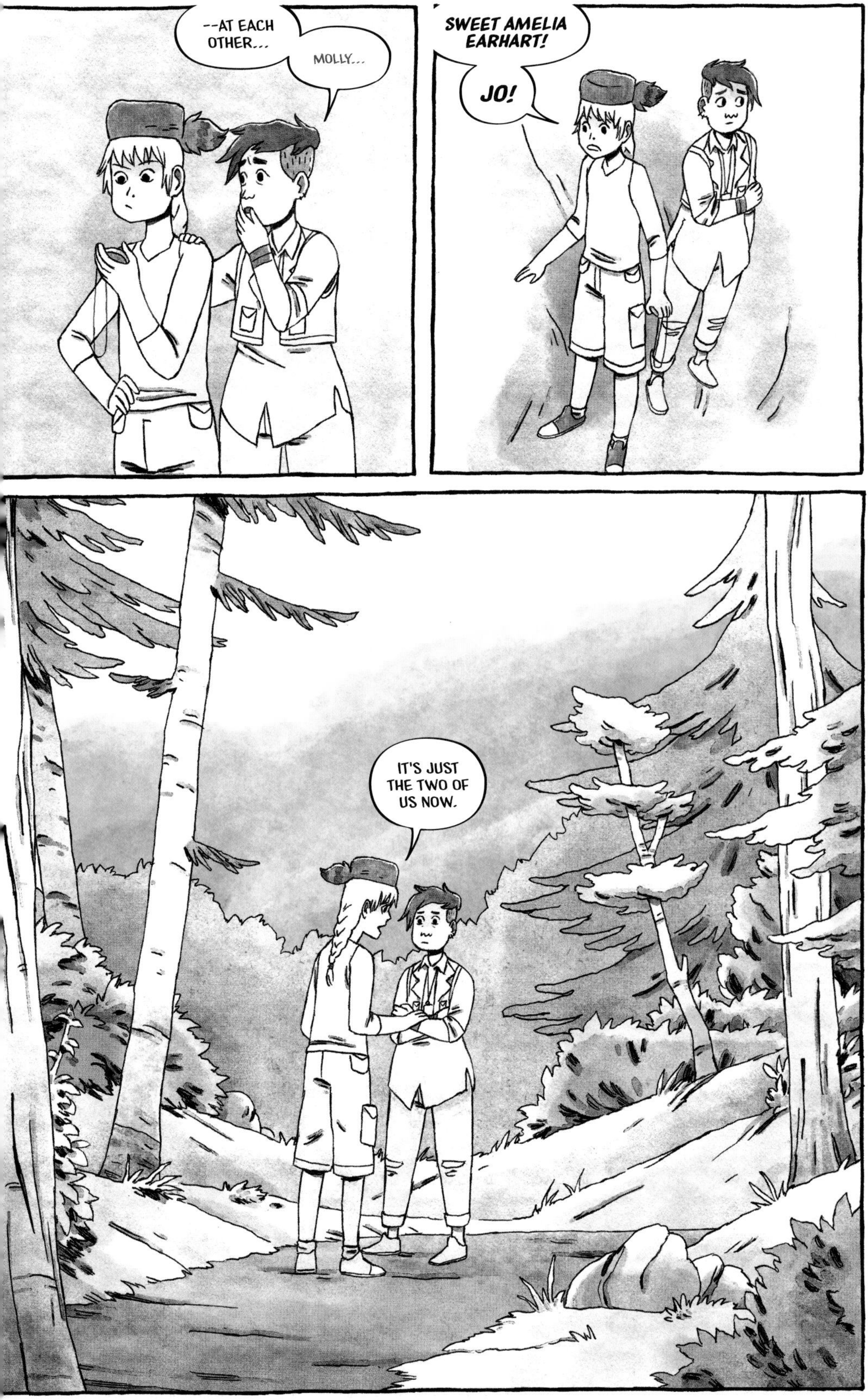

--AT EACH OTHER...
MOLLY...
SWEET AMELIA EARHART!
JO!
IT'S JUST THE TWO OF US NOW.

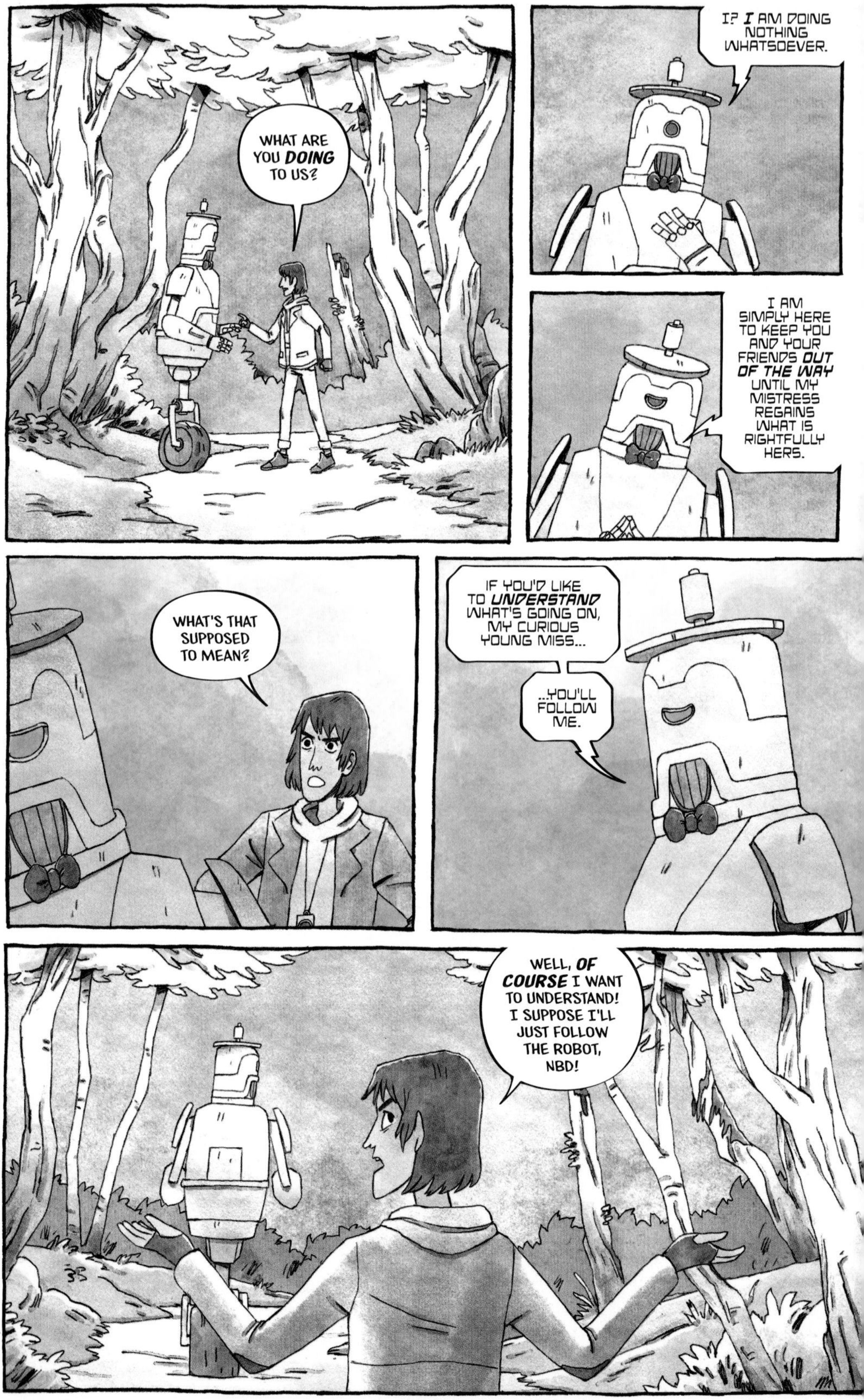
WHAT ARE YOU DOING TO US?
I? I AM DOING NOTHING WHATSOEVER.
I AM SIMPLY HERE TO KEEP YOU AND YOUR FRIENDS OUT OF THE WAY UNTIL MY MISTRESS REGAINS WHAT IS RIGHTFULLY HERS.
WHAT'S THAT SUPPOSED TO MEAN?
IF YOU'D LIKE TO UNDERSTAND WHAT'S GOING ON, MY CURIOUS YOUNG MISS...
...YOU'LL FOLLOW ME.
WELL, OF COURSE I WANT TO UNDERSTAND! I SUPPOSE I'LL JUST FOLLOW THE ROBOT, NBD!

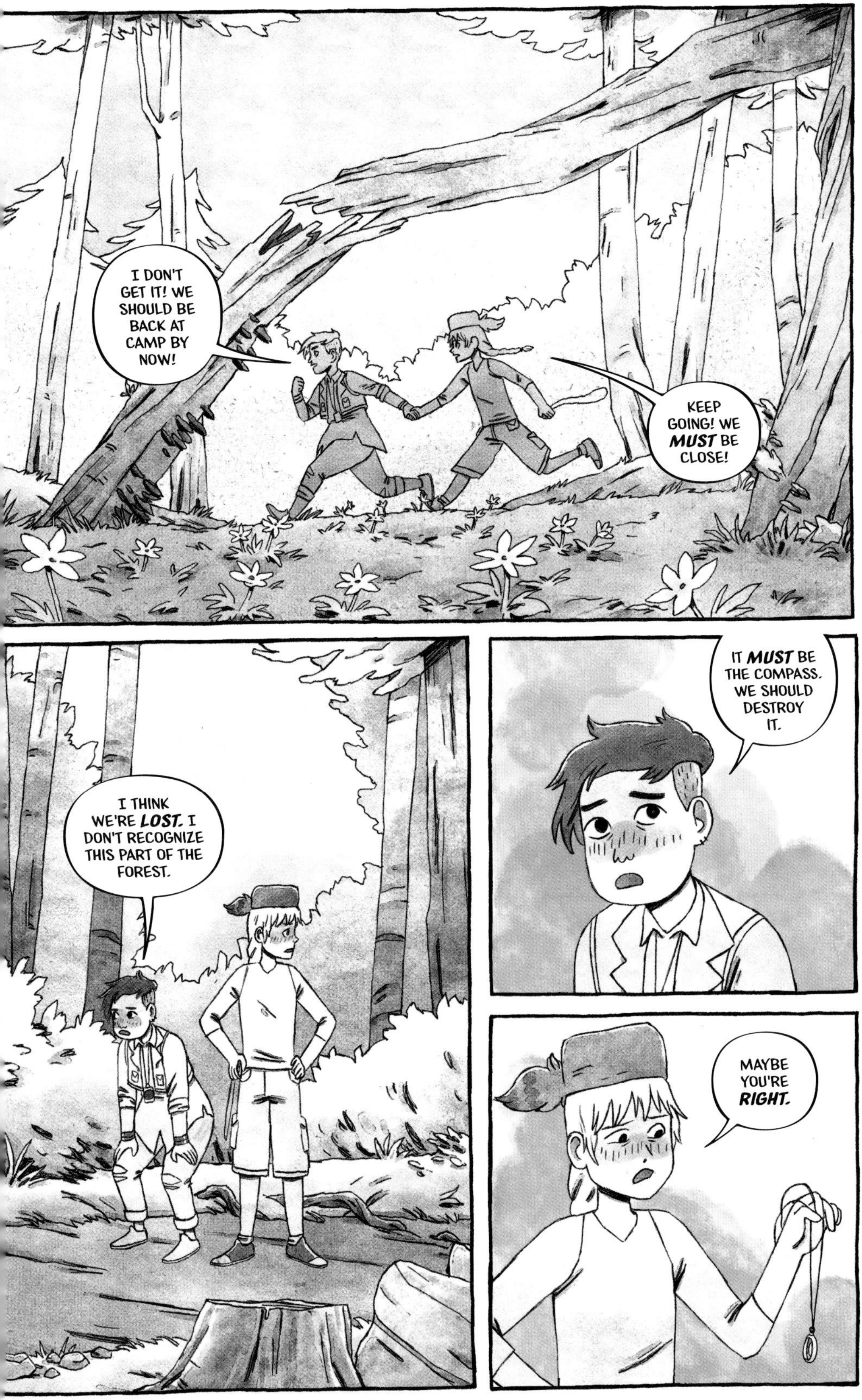
I DON'T GET IT! WE SHOULD BE BACK AT CAMP BY NOW!
KEEP GOING! WE MUST BE CLOSE!
I THINK WE'RE LOST. I DON'T RECOGNIZE THIS PART OF THE FOREST.
IT MUST BE THE COMPASS. WE SHOULD DESTROY IT.
MAYBE YOU'RE RIGHT.

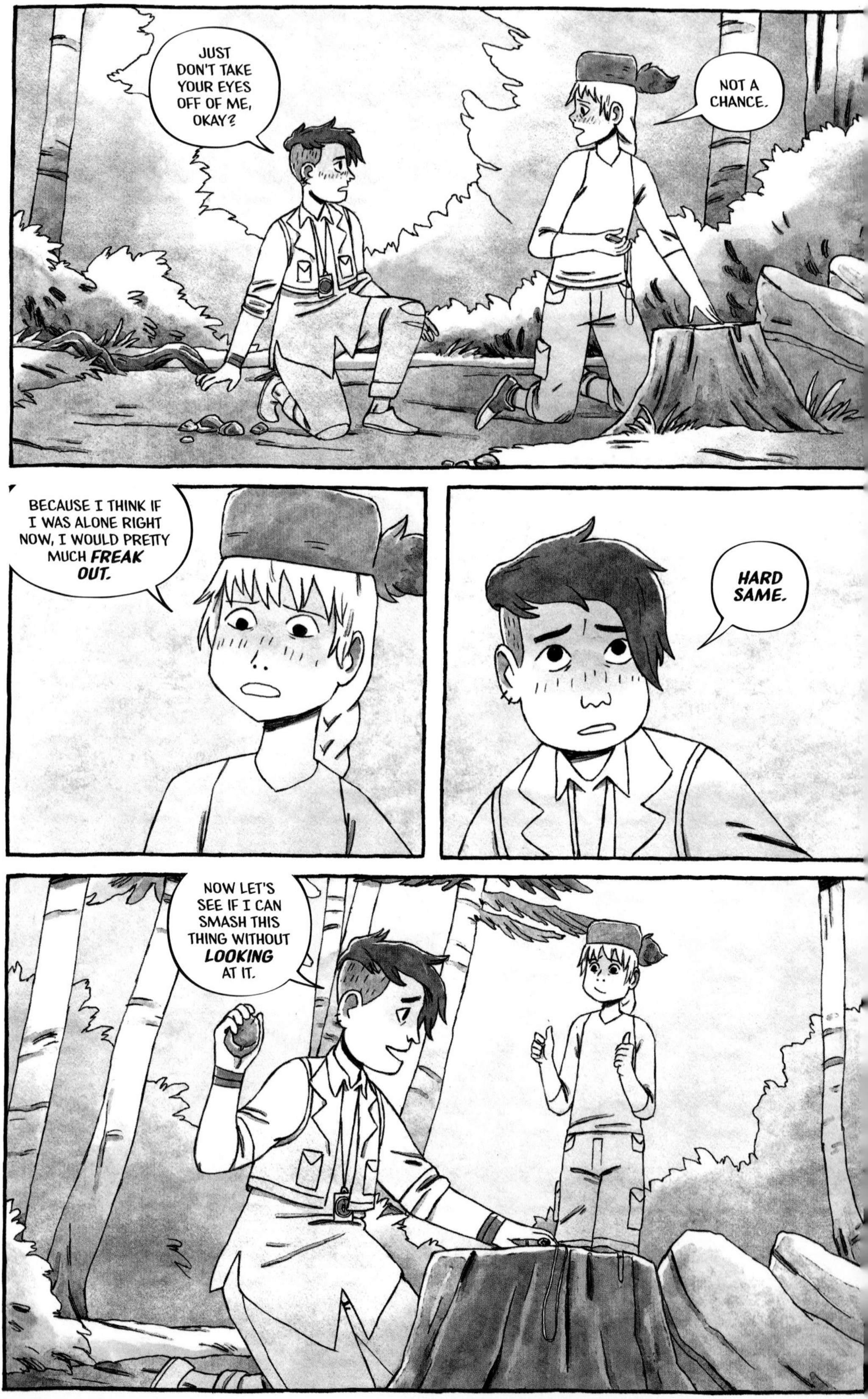
JUST DON'T TAKE YOUR EYES OFF OF ME, OKAY?
NOT A CHANCE.
BECAUSE I THINK IF I WAS ALONE RIGHT NOW, I WOULD PRETTY MUCH FREAK OUT.
HARD SAME.
NOW LET'S SEE IF I CAN SMASH THIS THING WITHOUT LOOKING AT IT.

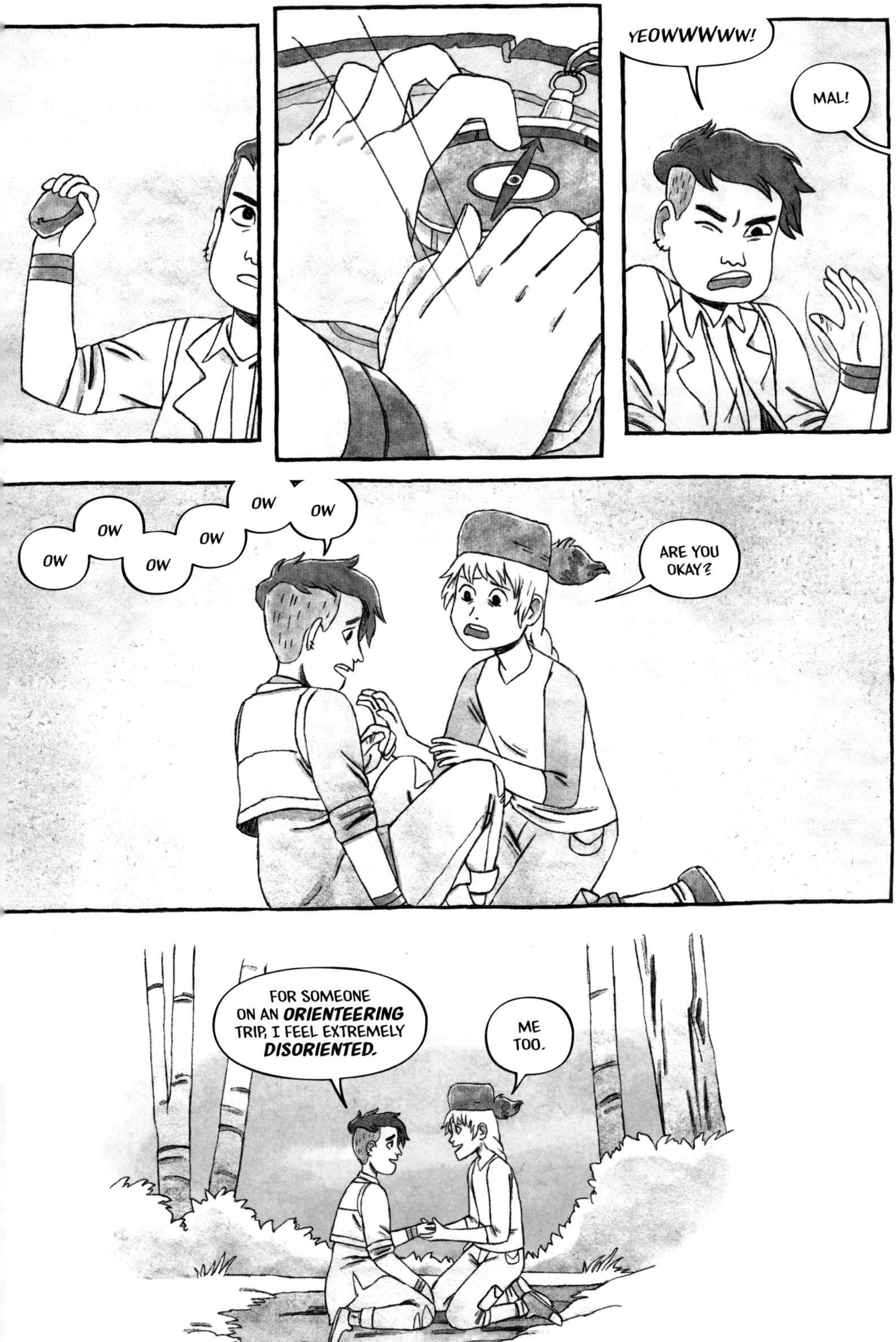
YEOWWWWW!
MAL!
OW OW OW OW OW OW
ARE YOU OKAY?
FOR SOMEONE ON AN ORIENTEERING TRIP, I FEEL EXTREMELY DISORIENTED.
ME TOO.

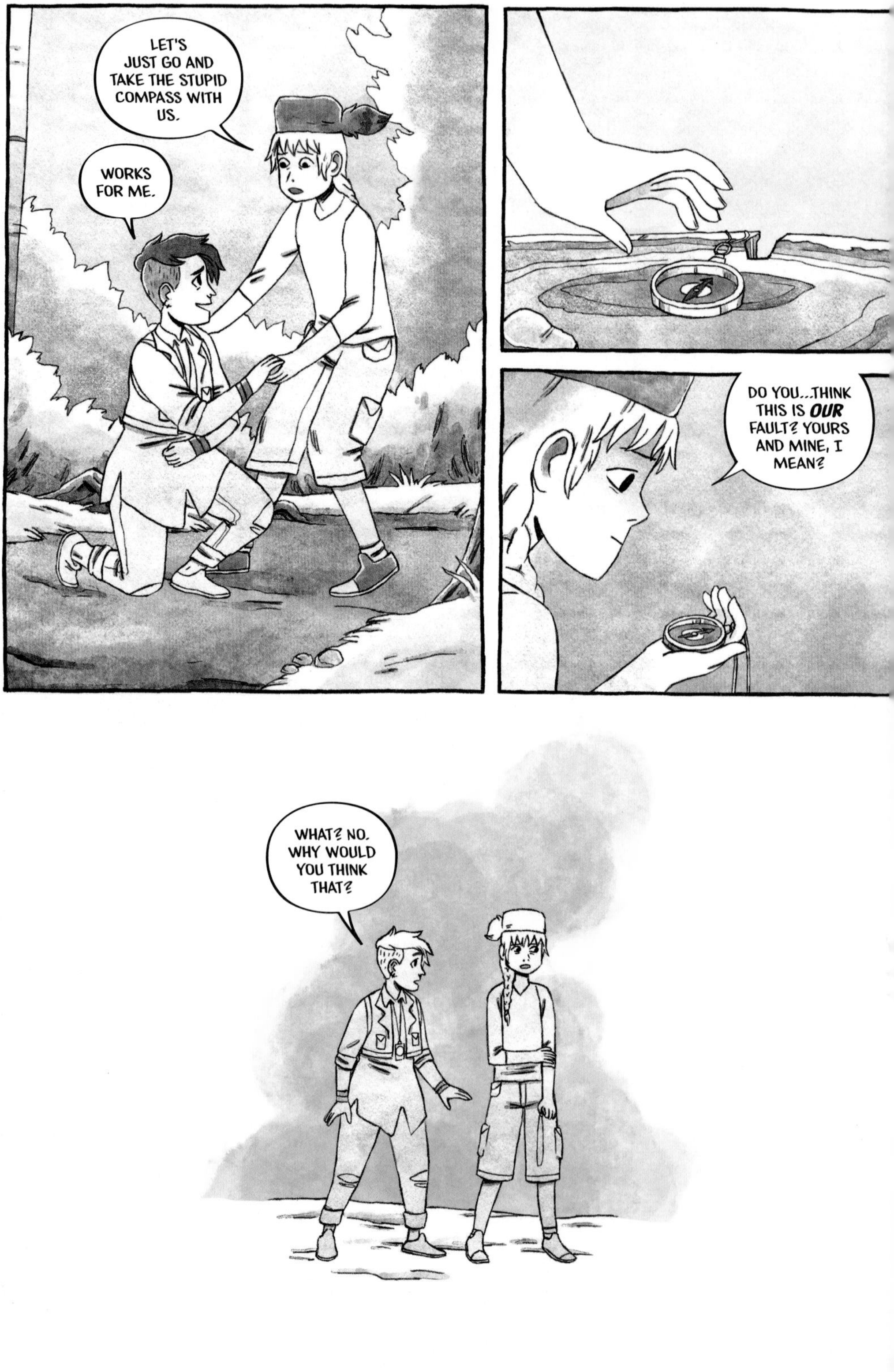
LET'S JUST GO AND TAKE THE STUPID COMPASS WITH US.
WORKS FOR ME.
DO YOU...THINK THIS IS OUR FAULT? YOURS AND MINE, I MEAN?
WHAT? NO. WHY WOULD YOU THINK THAT?

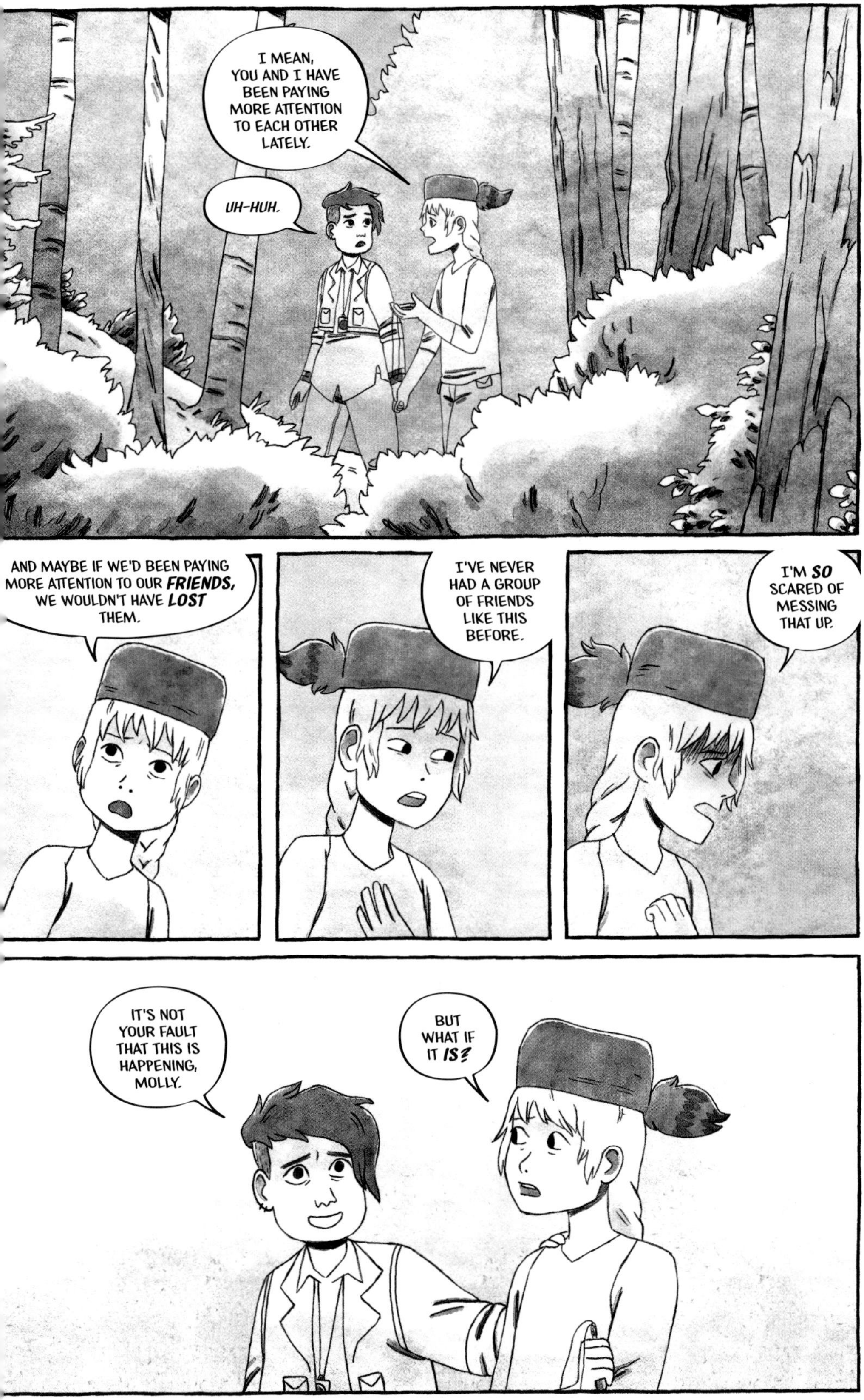
I MEAN, YOU AND I HAVE BEEN PAYING MORE ATTENTION TO EACH OTHER LATELY.
UH-HUH.
AND MAYBE IF WE'D BEEN PAYING MORE ATTENTION TO OUR FRIENDS, WE WOULDN'T HAVE LOST THEM.
I'VE NEVER HAD A GROUP OF FRIENDS LIKE THIS BEFORE.
I'M SO SCARED OF MESSING THAT UP.
IT'S NOT YOUR FAULT THAT THIS IS HAPPENING, MOLLY.
BUT WHAT IF IT IS?

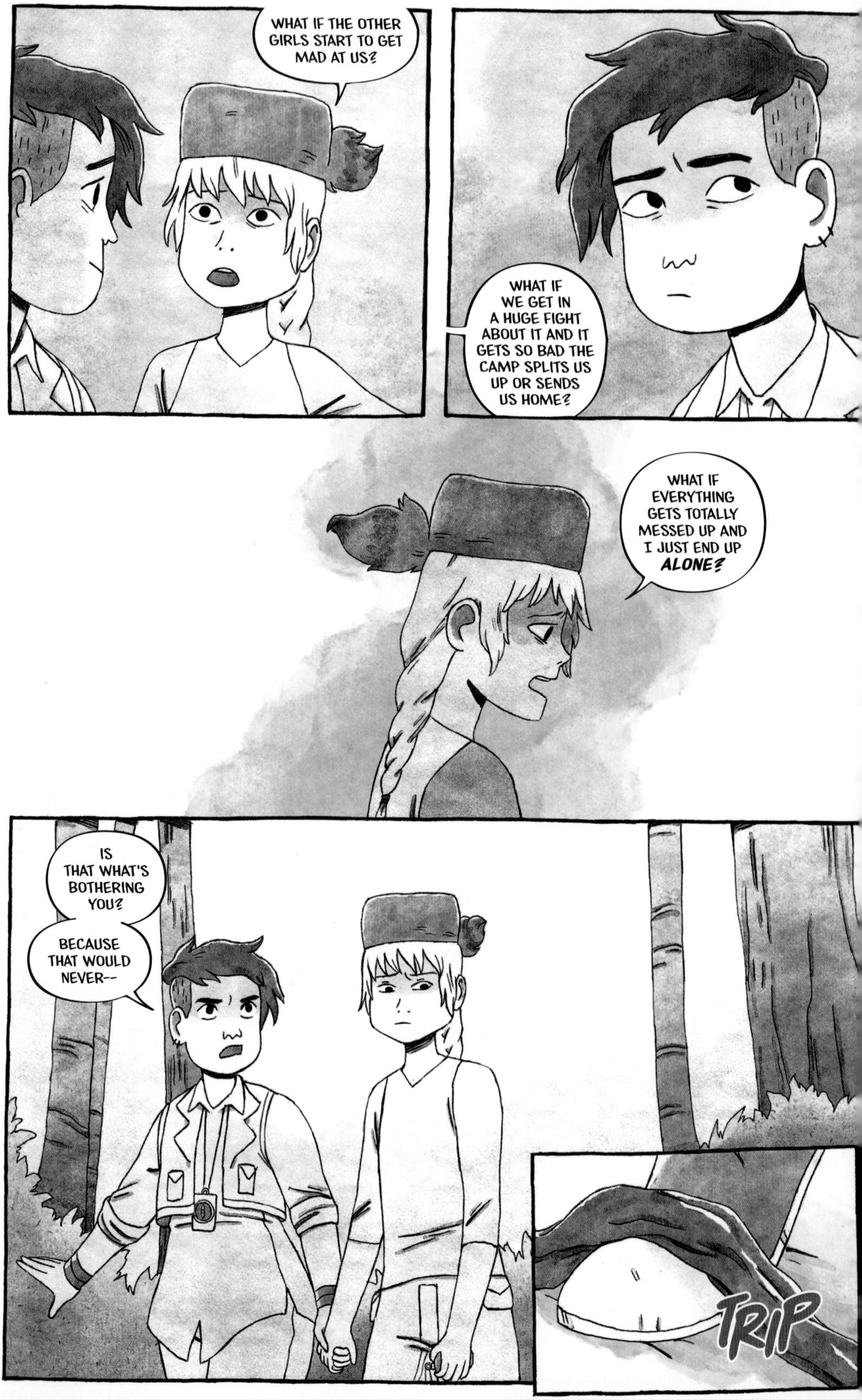
WHAT IF THE OTHER GIRLS START TO GET MAD AT US?
WHAT IF WE GET IN A HUGE FIGHT ABOUT IT AND IT GETS SO BAD THE CAMP SPLITS US UP OR SENDS US HOME?
WHAT IF EVERYTHING GETS TOTALLY MESSED UP AND I JUST END UP ***ALONE?***
IS THAT WHAT'S BOTHERING YOU?
BECAUSE THAT WOULD NEVER--
TRIP

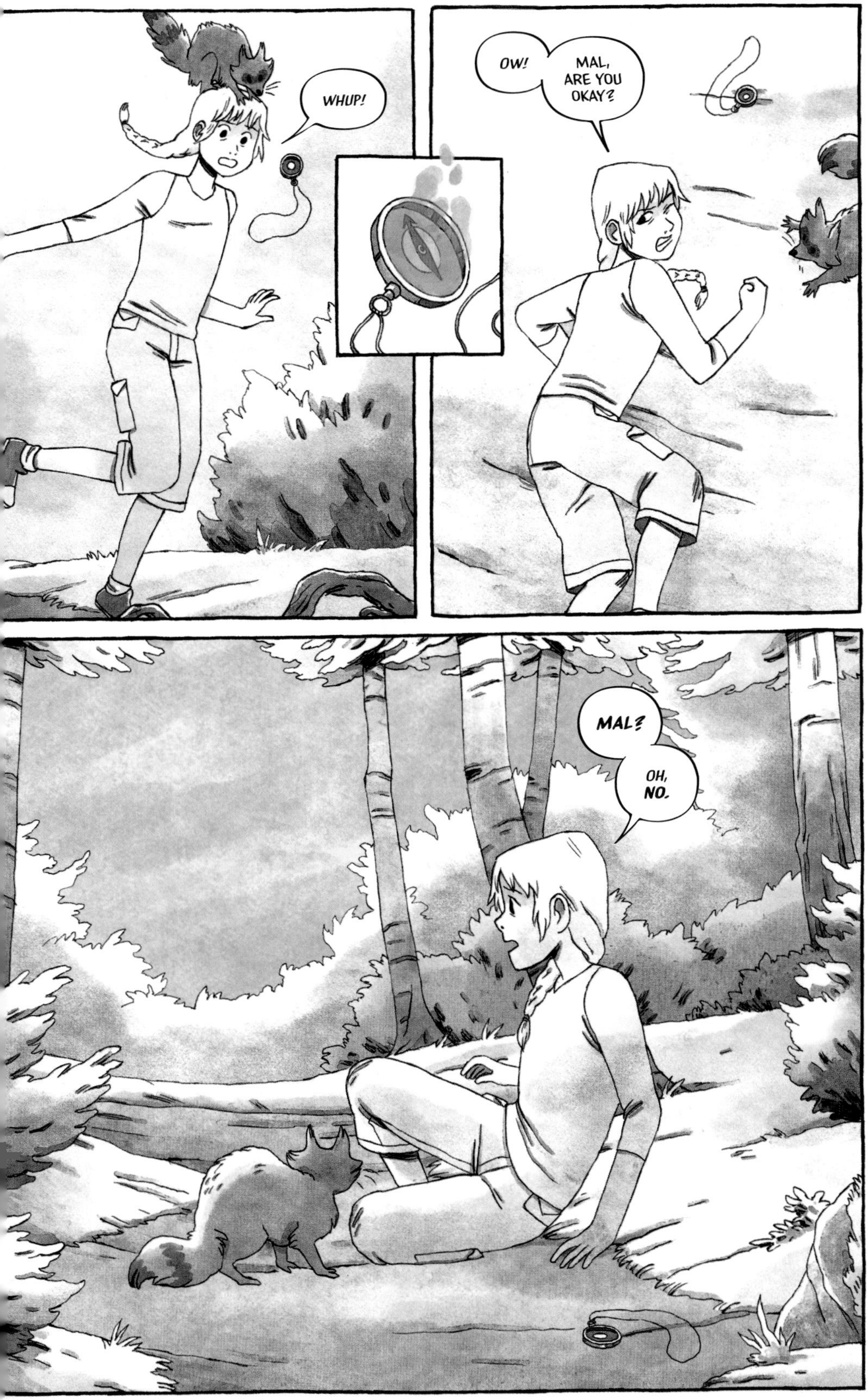
WHUP!
OW!
MAL, ARE YOU OKAY?
MAL?
OH, NO.

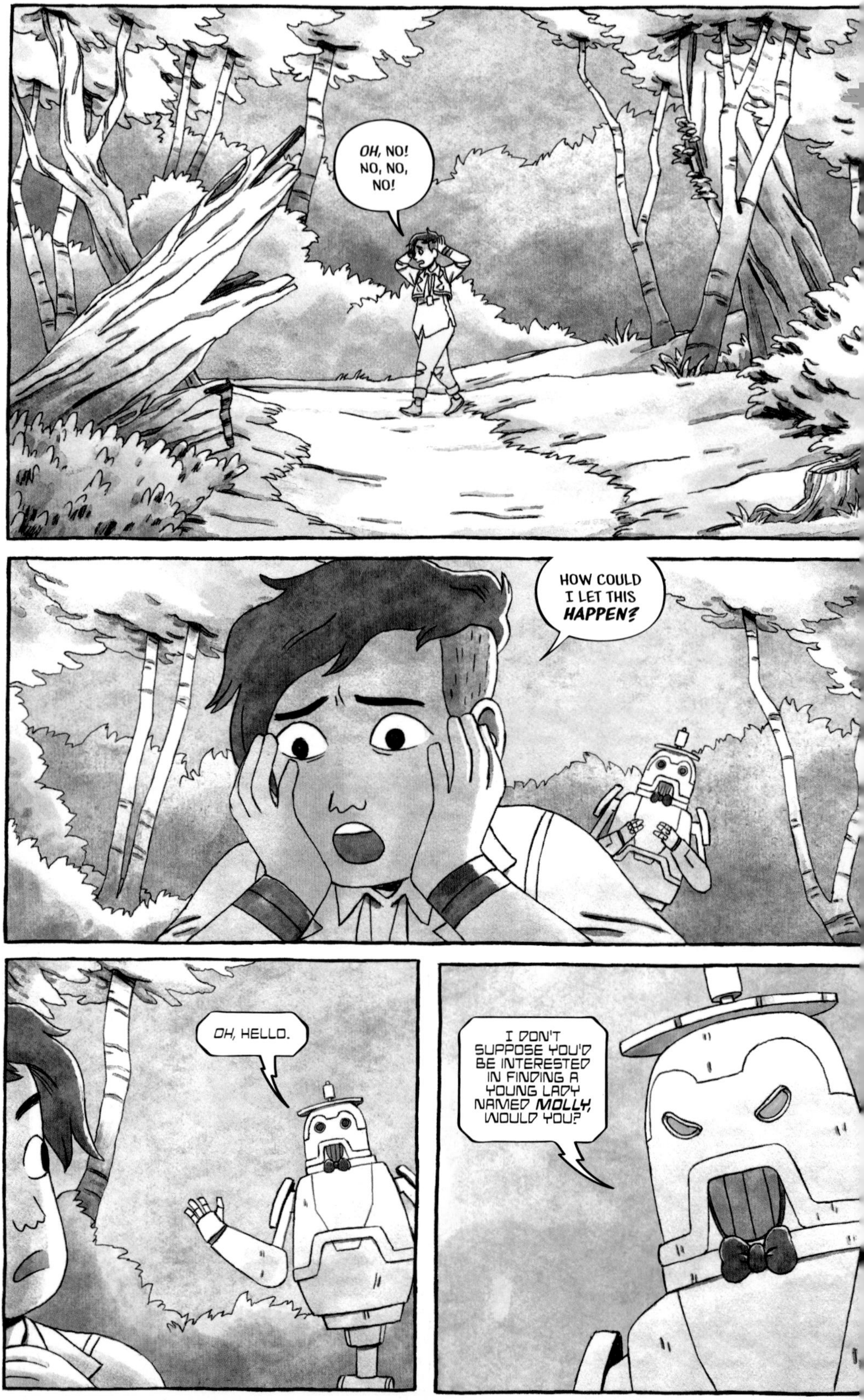
OH, NO! NO, NO, NO!
HOW COULD I LET THIS HAPPEN?
OH, HELLO.
I DON'T SUPPOSE YOU'D BE INTERESTED IN FINDING A YOUNG LADY NAMED MOLLY, WOULD YOU?

I SHOULD JUST *LEAVE* THIS THING AND *GO.*

NO! WHAT IF SOMEONE *ELSE* FOUND IT? THEN *THEY'D* BE IN THE SAME TROUBLE *I'M* IN!

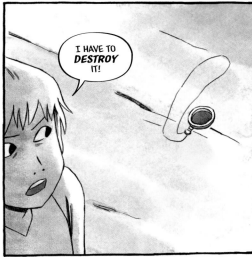

I HAVE TO *DESTROY* IT!

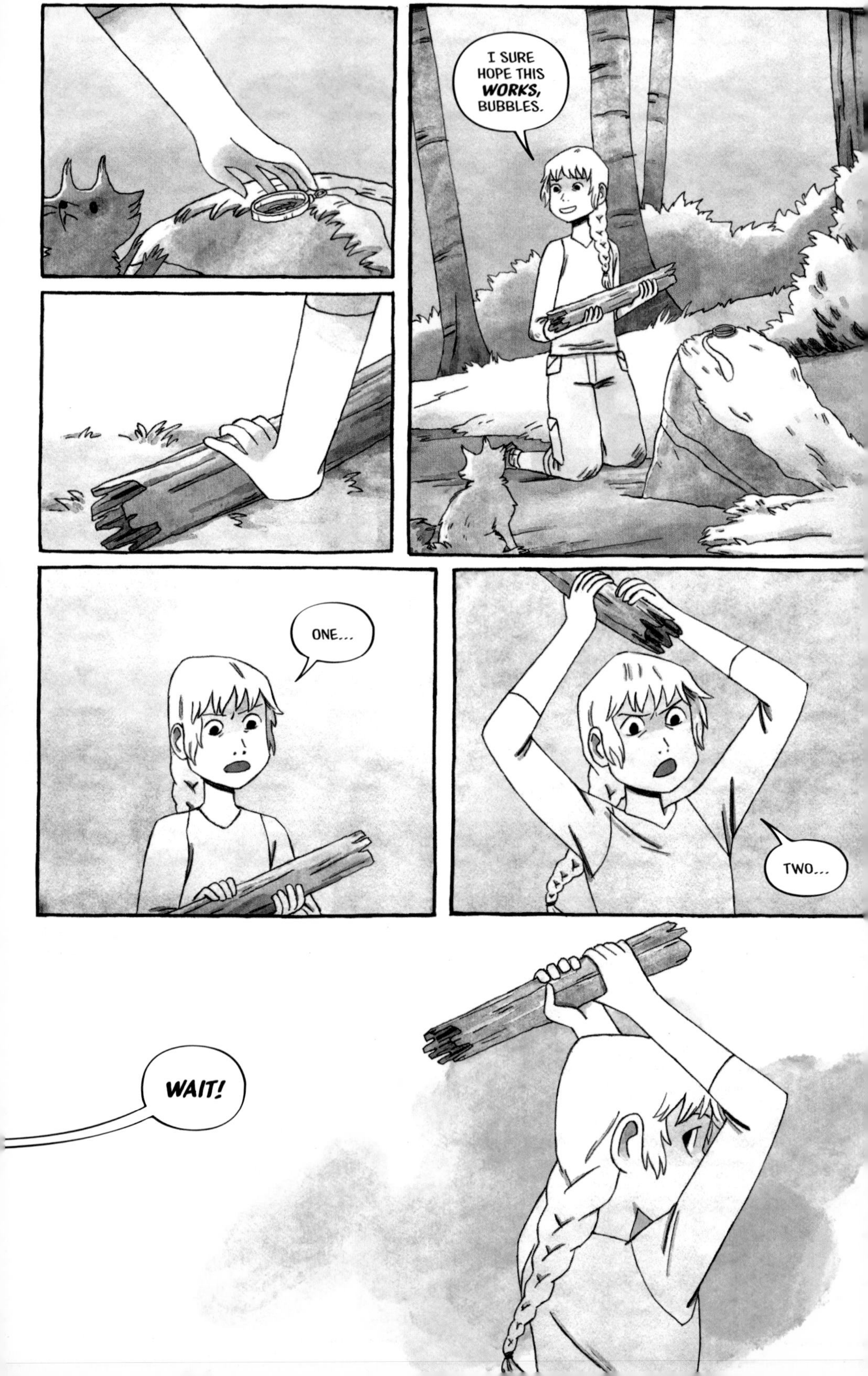
I SURE HOPE THIS ***WORKS,*** BUBBLES.
ONE...
TWO...
WAIT!

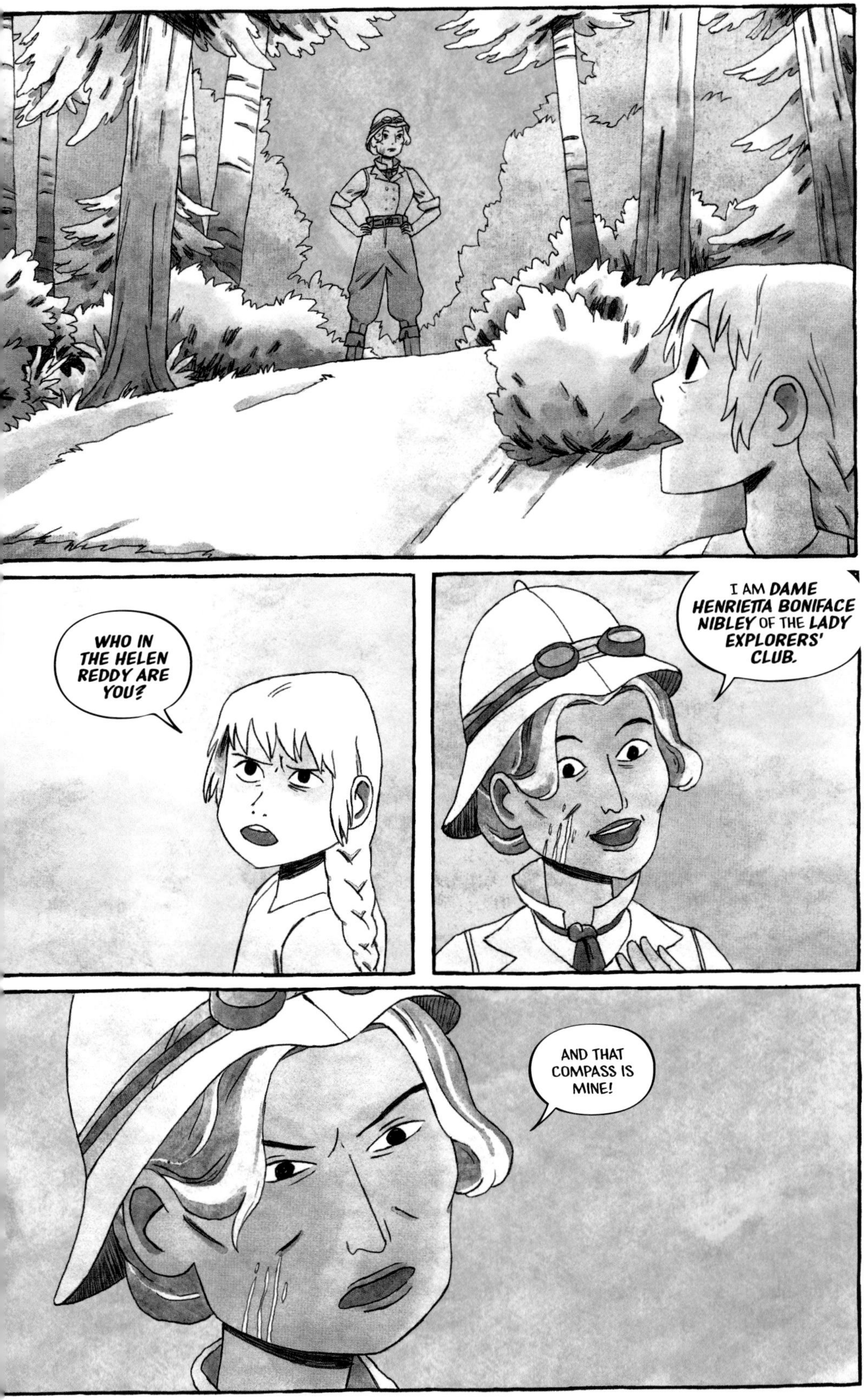
WHO IN THE HELEN REDDY ARE YOU?
I AM DAME HENRIETTA BONIFACE NIBLEY OF THE LADY EXPLORERS' CLUB.
AND THAT COMPASS IS MINE!

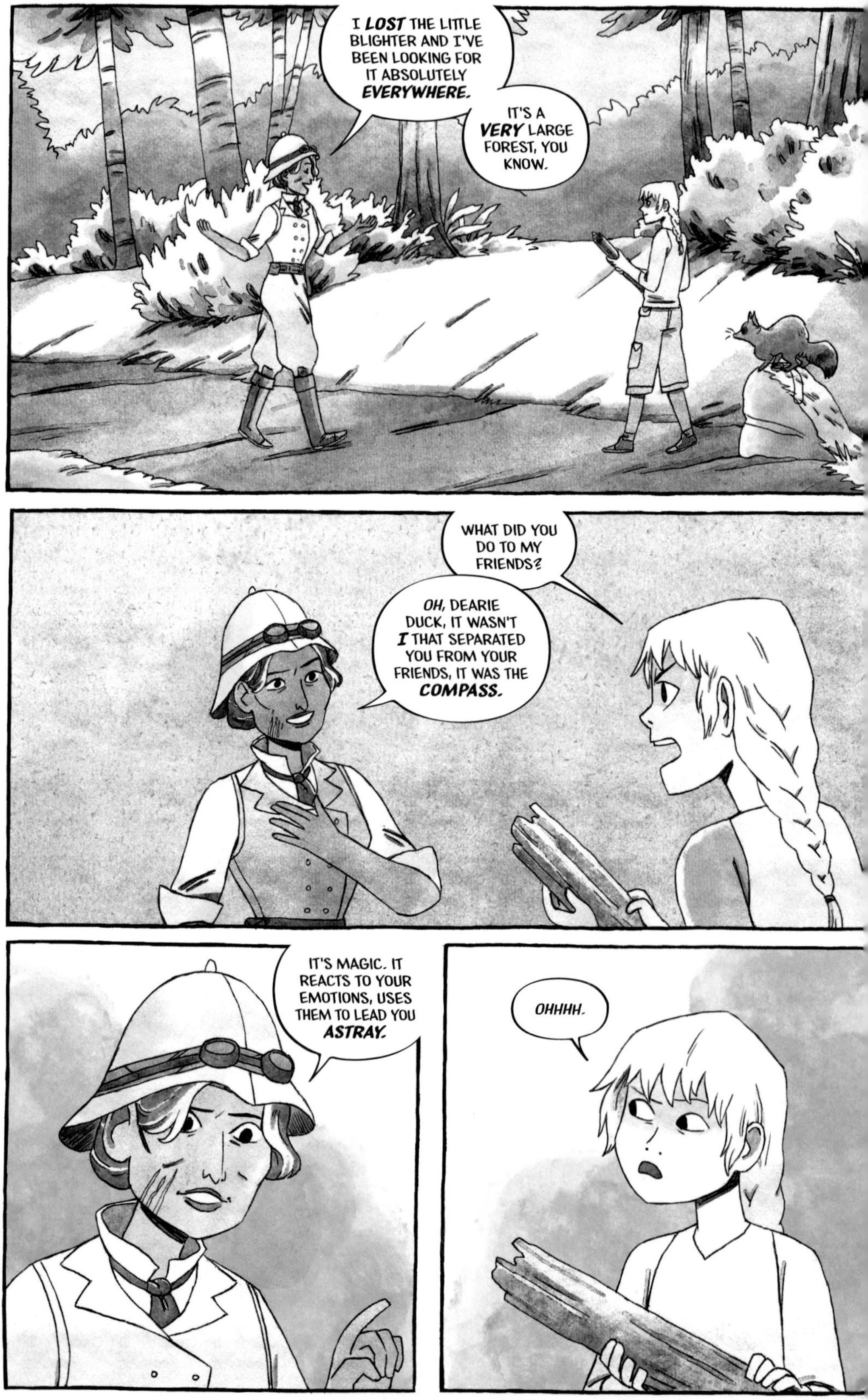
I LOST THE LITTLE BLIGHTER AND I'VE BEEN LOOKING FOR IT ABSOLUTELY EVERYWHERE.
IT'S A VERY LARGE FOREST, YOU KNOW.
WHAT DID YOU DO TO MY FRIENDS?
OH, DEARIE DUCK, IT WASN'T I THAT SEPARATED YOU FROM YOUR FRIENDS, IT WAS THE COMPASS.
IT'S MAGIC. IT REACTS TO YOUR EMOTIONS, USES THEM TO LEAD YOU ASTRAY.
OHHHH.

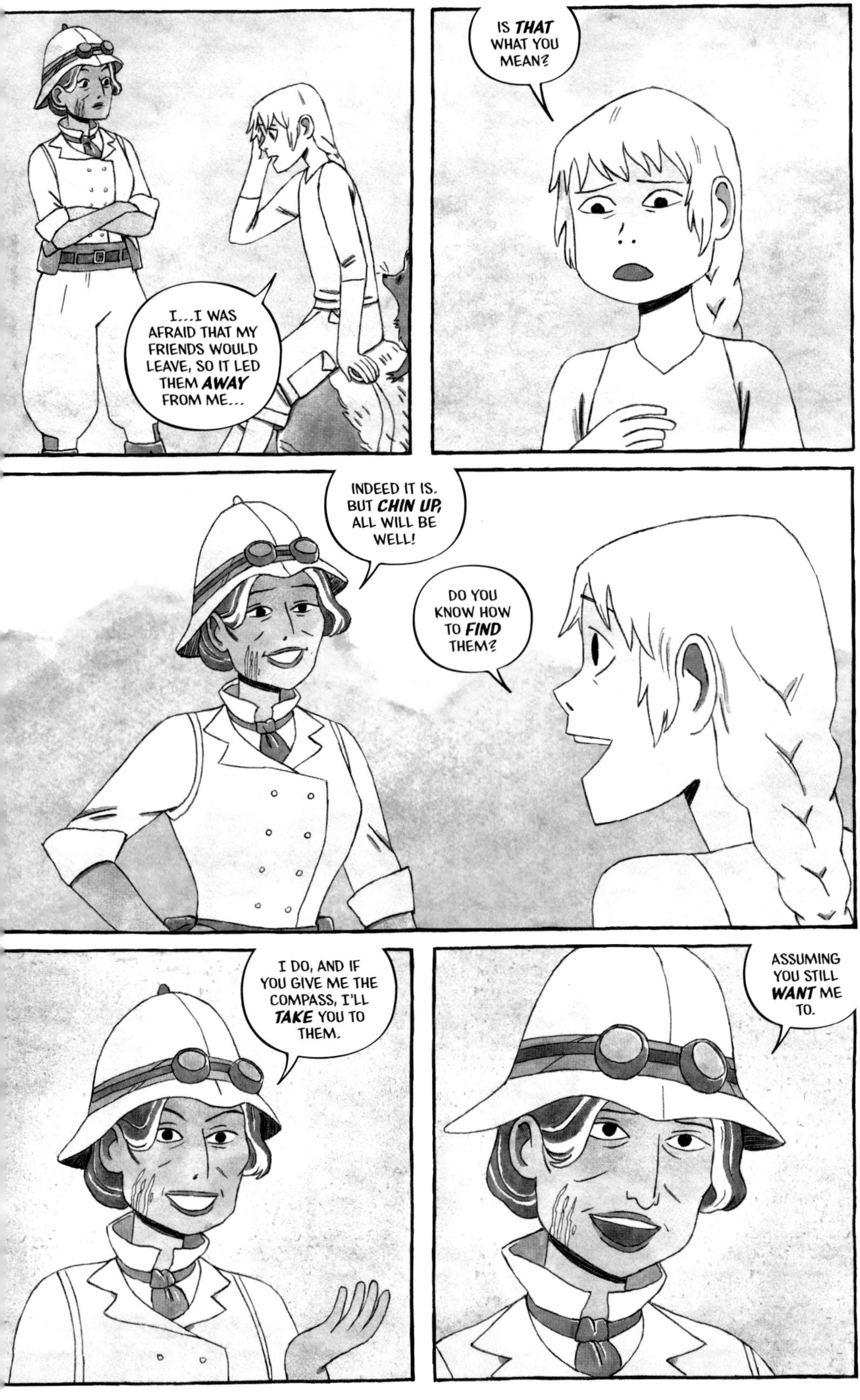
I...I WAS AFRAID THAT MY FRIENDS WOULD LEAVE, SO IT LED THEM AWAY FROM ME...
IS THAT WHAT YOU MEAN?
INDEED IT IS. BUT CHIN UP, ALL WILL BE WELL!
DO YOU KNOW HOW TO FIND THEM?
I DO, AND IF YOU GIVE ME THE COMPASS, I'LL TAKE YOU TO THEM.
ASSUMING YOU STILL WANT ME TO.

YOU HAVE MY **WORD** AS A LADY EXPLORER.

I DON'T KNOW...

OH, PLEASE LET'S NOT QUIBBLE OVER THIS!

I DO SO **HATE** A QUIBBLE!

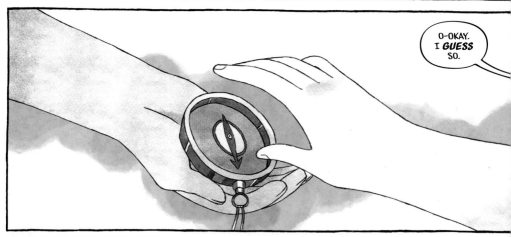

O-OKAY, I **GUESS** SO.

BRILLIANT! **RIGHT** THIS WAY!

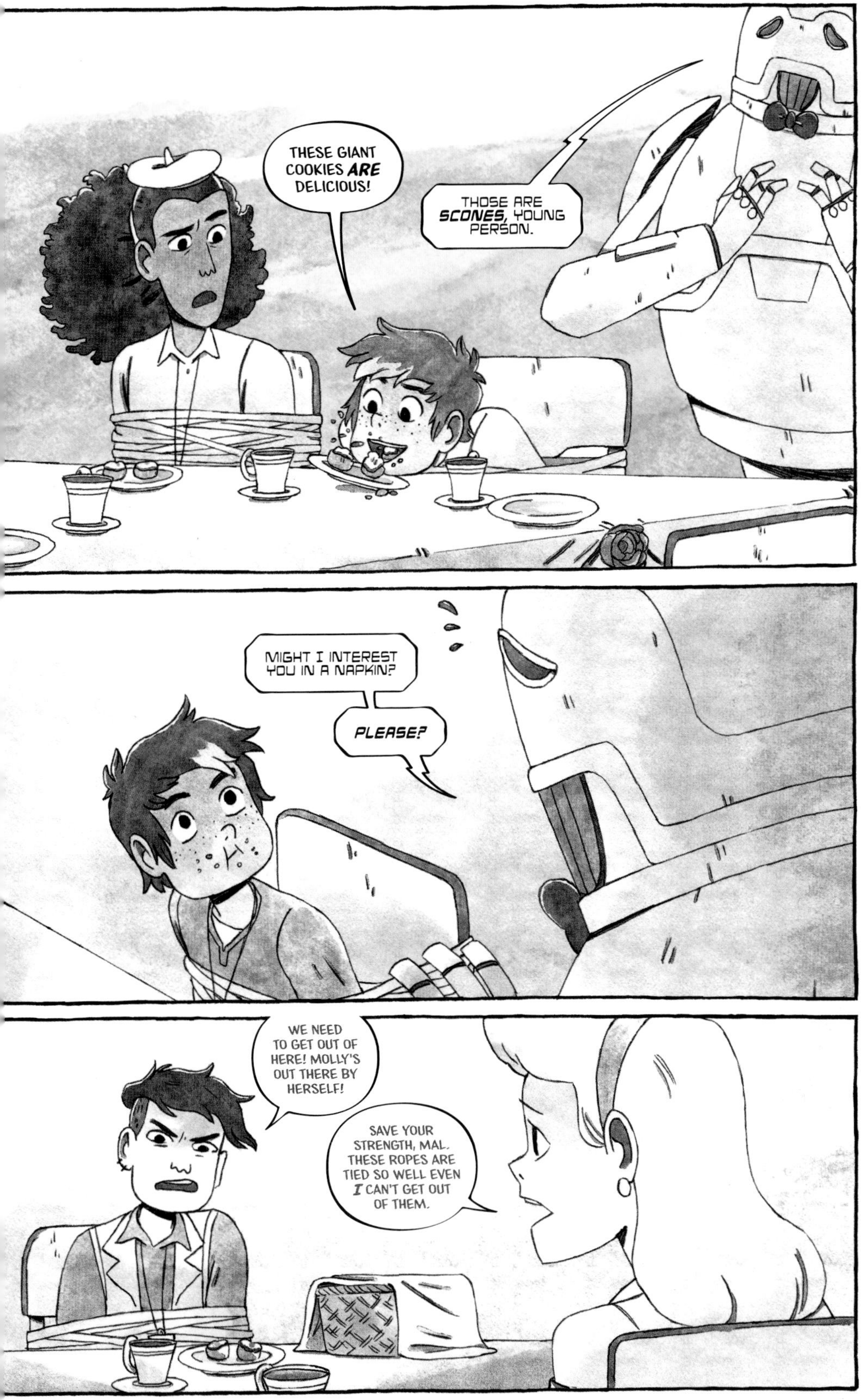
THESE GIANT COOKIES ARE DELICIOUS!
THOSE ARE SCONES, YOUNG PERSON.
MIGHT I INTEREST YOU IN A NAPKIN?
PLEASE?
WE NEED TO GET OUT OF HERE! MOLLY'S OUT THERE BY HERSELF!
SAVE YOUR STRENGTH, MAL. THESE ROPES ARE TIED SO WELL EVEN I CAN'T GET OUT OF THEM.

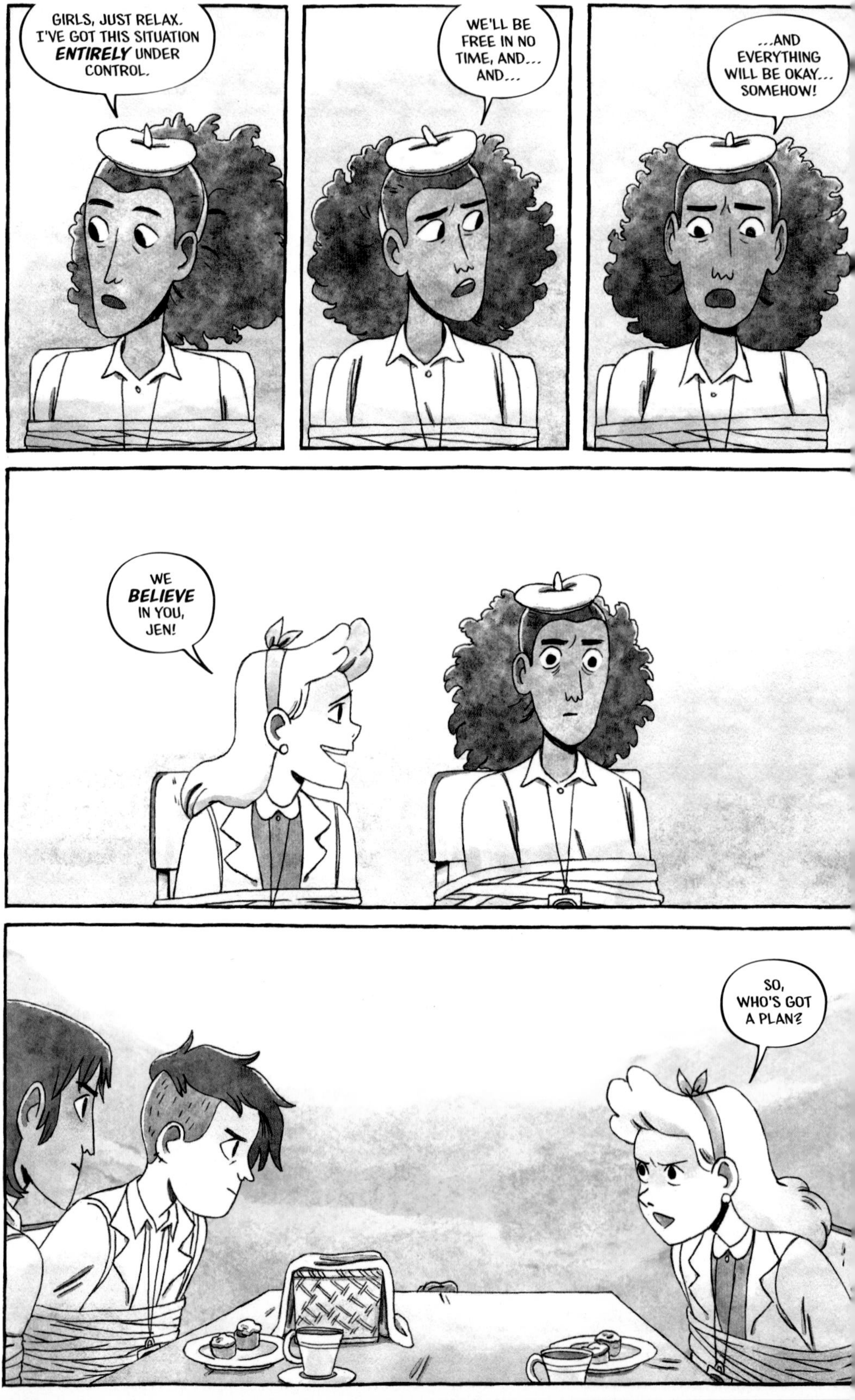
GIRLS, JUST RELAX. I'VE GOT THIS SITUATION ENTIRELY UNDER CONTROL.
WE'LL BE FREE IN NO TIME, AND... AND...
...AND EVERYTHING WILL BE OKAY... SOMEHOW!
WE BELIEVE IN YOU, JEN!
SO, WHO'S GOT A PLAN?

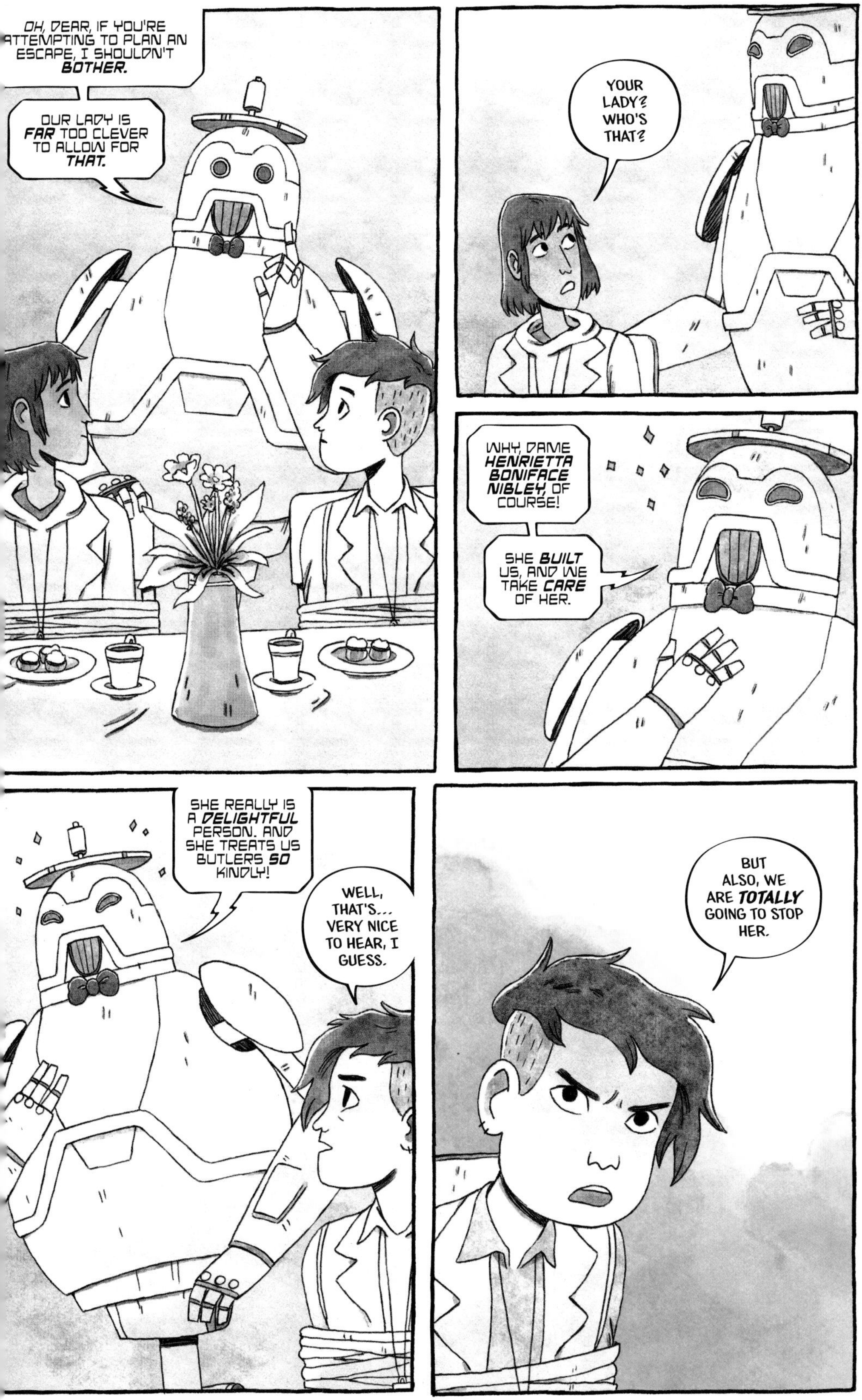
OH, DEAR, IF YOU'RE ATTEMPTING TO PLAN AN ESCAPE, I SHOULDN'T BOTHER.
OUR LADY IS FAR TOO CLEVER TO ALLOW FOR THAT.
YOUR LADY? WHO'S THAT?
WHY, DAME HENRIETTA BONIFACE NIBLEY, OF COURSE!
SHE BUILT US, AND WE TAKE CARE OF HER.
SHE REALLY IS A DELIGHTFUL PERSON. AND SHE TREATS US BUTLERS SO KINDLY!
WELL, THAT'S... VERY NICE TO HEAR, I GUESS.
BUT ALSO, WE ARE TOTALLY GOING TO STOP HER.

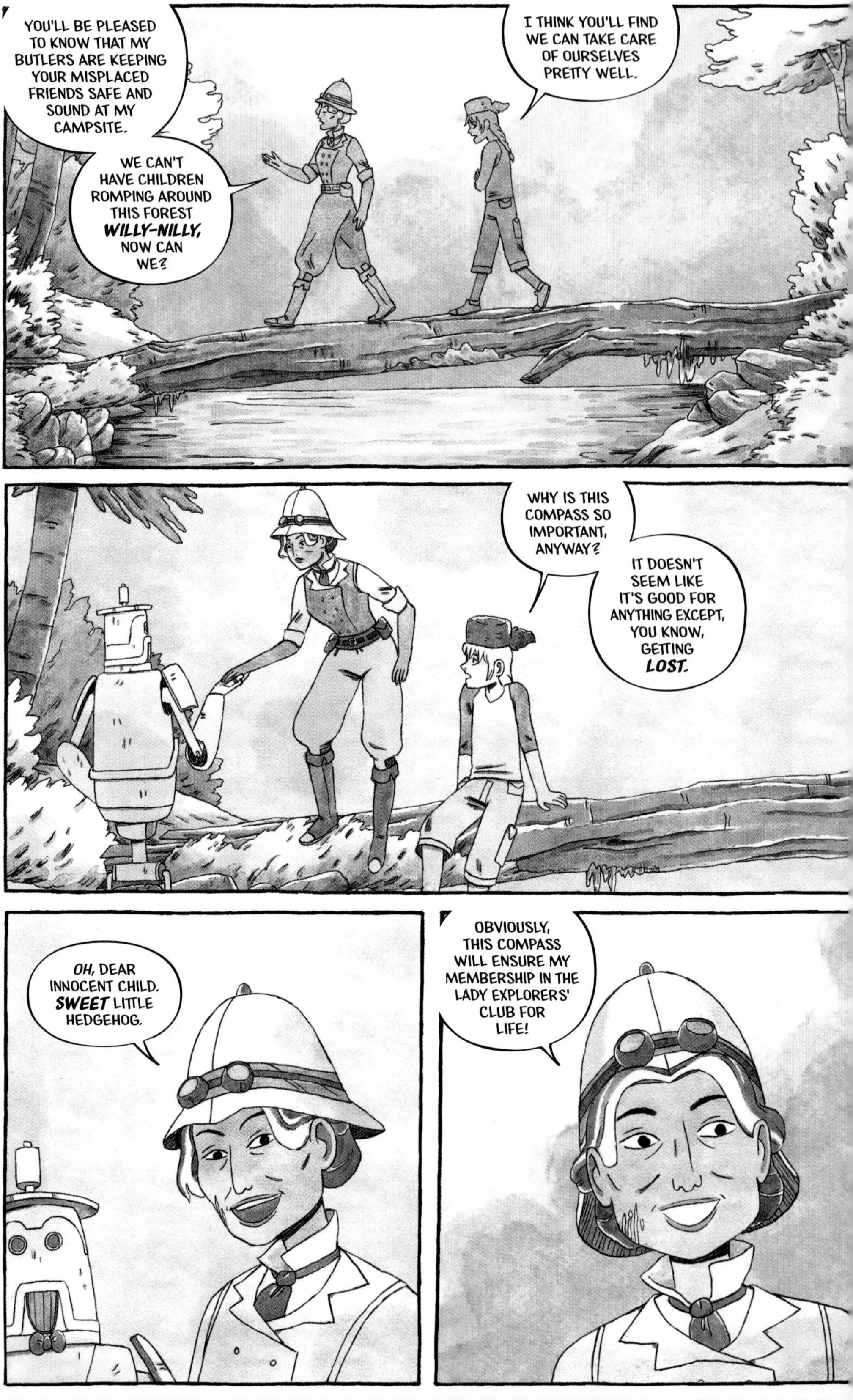

YOU'LL BE PLEASED TO KNOW THAT MY BUTLERS ARE KEEPING YOUR MISPLACED FRIENDS SAFE AND SOUND AT MY CAMPSITE.
WE CAN'T HAVE CHILDREN ROMPING AROUND THIS FOREST WILLY-NILLY, NOW CAN WE?
I THINK YOU'LL FIND WE CAN TAKE CARE OF OURSELVES PRETTY WELL.
WHY IS THIS COMPASS SO IMPORTANT, ANYWAY?
IT DOESN'T SEEM LIKE IT'S GOOD FOR ANYTHING EXCEPT, YOU KNOW, GETTING LOST.
OH, DEAR INNOCENT CHILD. SWEET LITTLE HEDGEHOG.
OBVIOUSLY, THIS COMPASS WILL ENSURE MY MEMBERSHIP IN THE LADY EXPLORERS' CLUB FOR LIFE!

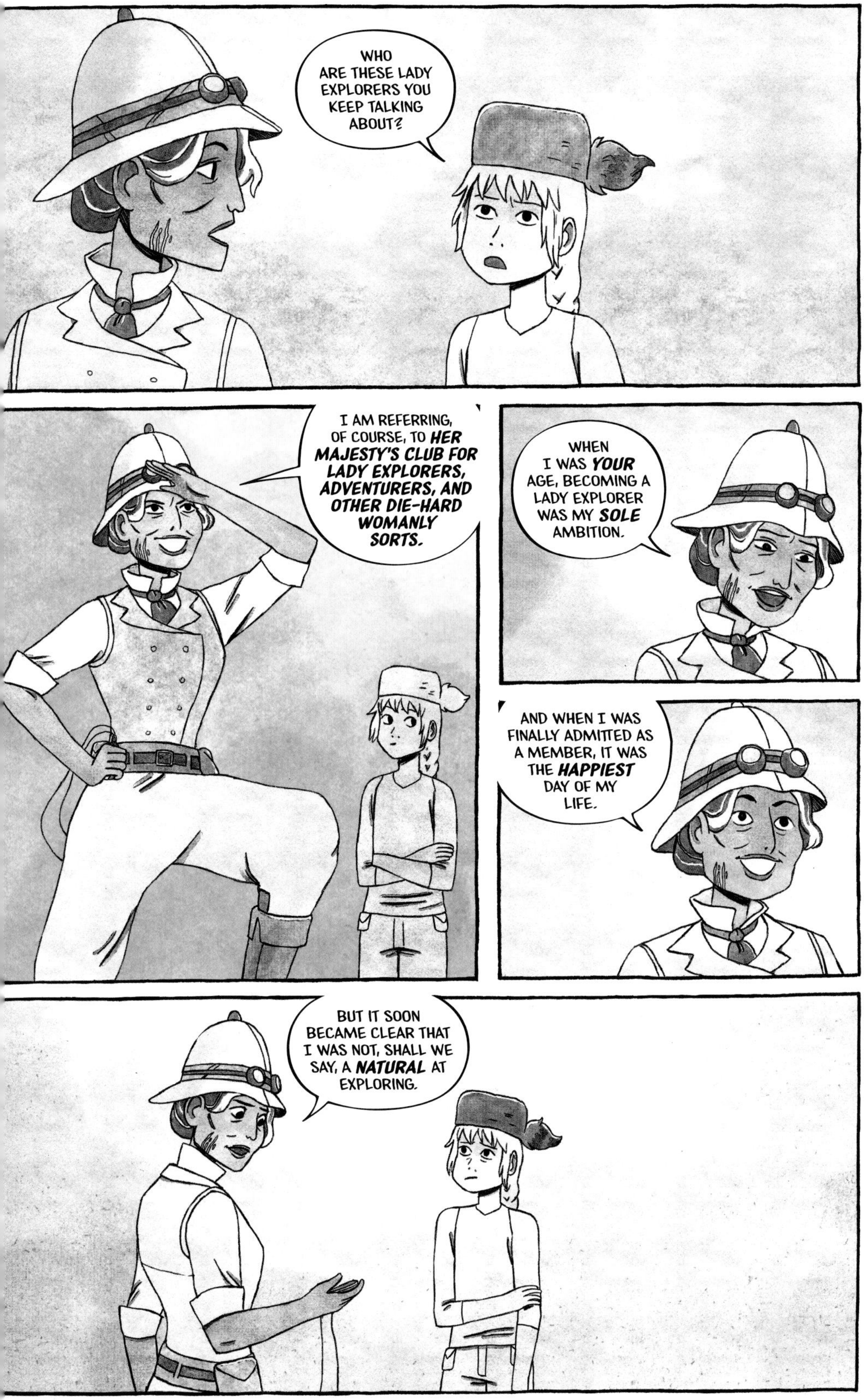
WHO ARE THESE LADY EXPLORERS YOU KEEP TALKING ABOUT?
I AM REFERRING, OF COURSE, TO HER MAJESTY'S CLUB FOR LADY EXPLORERS, ADVENTURERS, AND OTHER DIE-HARD WOMANLY SORTS.
WHEN I WAS YOUR AGE, BECOMING A LADY EXPLORER WAS MY SOLE AMBITION.
AND WHEN I WAS FINALLY ADMITTED AS A MEMBER, IT WAS THE HAPPIEST DAY OF MY LIFE.
BUT IT SOON BECAME CLEAR THAT I WAS NOT, SHALL WE SAY, A NATURAL AT EXPLORING.

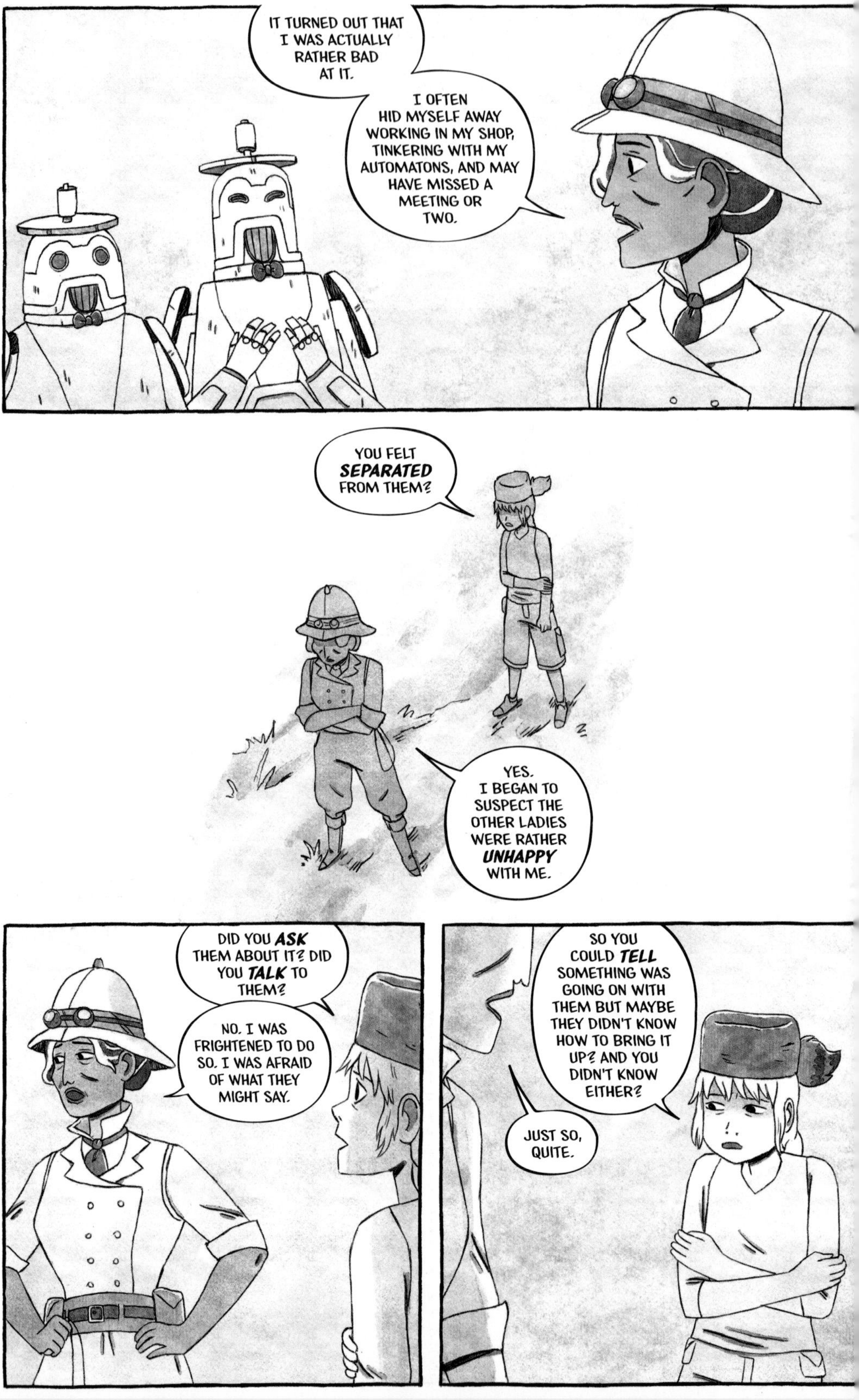
IT TURNED OUT THAT I WAS ACTUALLY RATHER BAD AT IT.
I OFTEN HID MYSELF AWAY WORKING IN MY SHOP, TINKERING WITH MY AUTOMATONS, AND MAY HAVE MISSED A MEETING OR TWO.
YOU FELT ***SEPARATED*** FROM THEM?
YES. I BEGAN TO SUSPECT THE OTHER LADIES WERE RATHER ***UNHAPPY*** WITH ME.
DID YOU ***ASK*** THEM ABOUT IT? DID YOU ***TALK*** TO THEM?
NO. I WAS FRIGHTENED TO DO SO. I WAS AFRAID OF WHAT THEY MIGHT SAY.
SO YOU COULD ***TELL*** SOMETHING WAS GOING ON WITH THEM BUT MAYBE THEY DIDN'T KNOW HOW TO BRING IT UP? AND YOU DIDN'T KNOW EITHER?
JUST SO, QUITE.

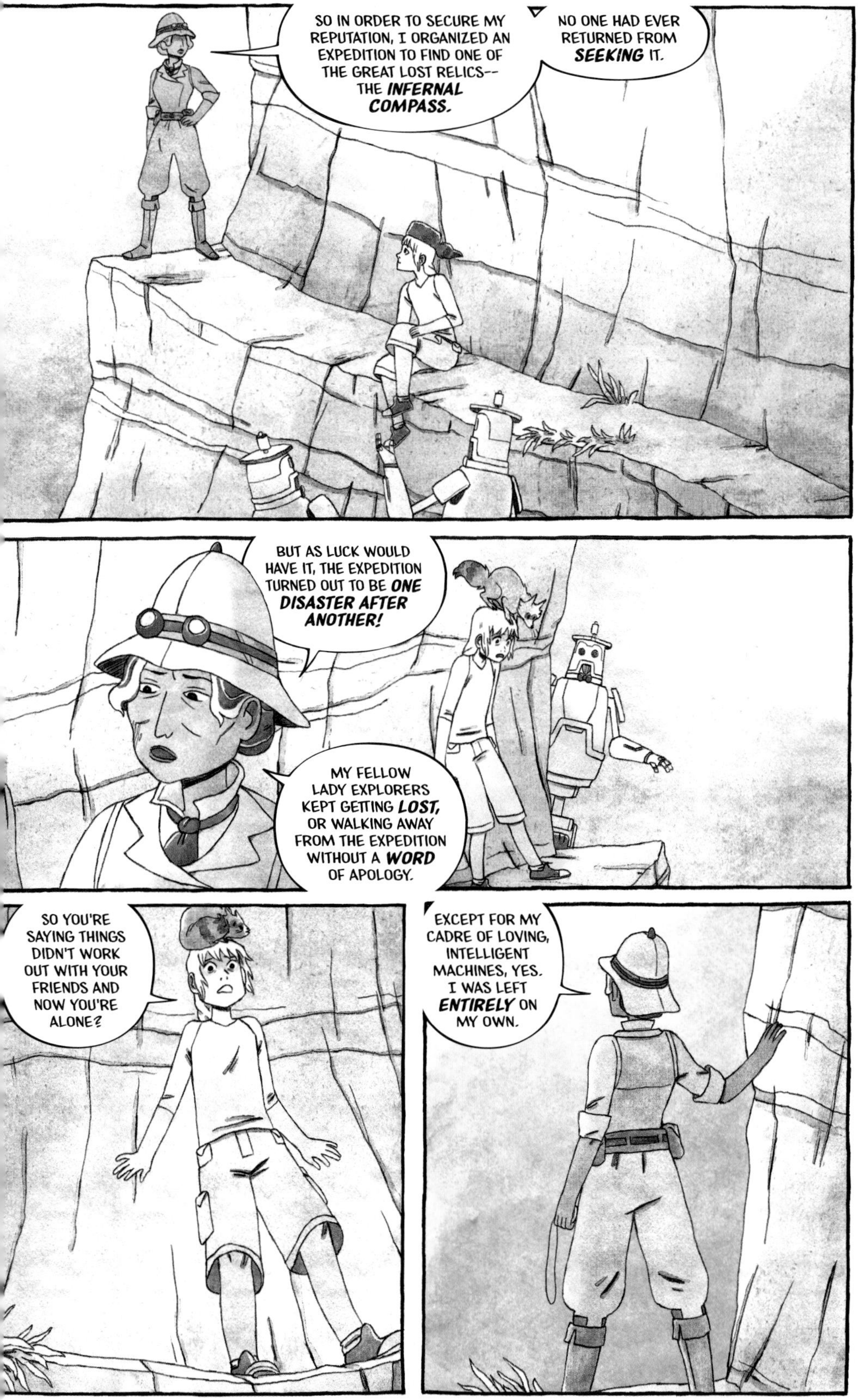
SO IN ORDER TO SECURE MY REPUTATION, I ORGANIZED AN EXPEDITION TO FIND ONE OF THE GREAT LOST RELICS-- THE *INFERNAL COMPASS.*
NO ONE HAD EVER RETURNED FROM *SEEKING* IT.
BUT AS LUCK WOULD HAVE IT, THE EXPEDITION TURNED OUT TO BE *ONE DISASTER AFTER ANOTHER!*
MY FELLOW LADY EXPLORERS KEPT GETTING *LOST,* OR WALKING AWAY FROM THE EXPEDITION WITHOUT A *WORD* OF APOLOGY.
SO YOU'RE SAYING THINGS DIDN'T WORK OUT WITH YOUR FRIENDS AND NOW YOU'RE ALONE?
EXCEPT FOR MY CADRE OF LOVING, INTELLIGENT MACHINES, YES. I WAS LEFT *ENTIRELY* ON MY OWN.

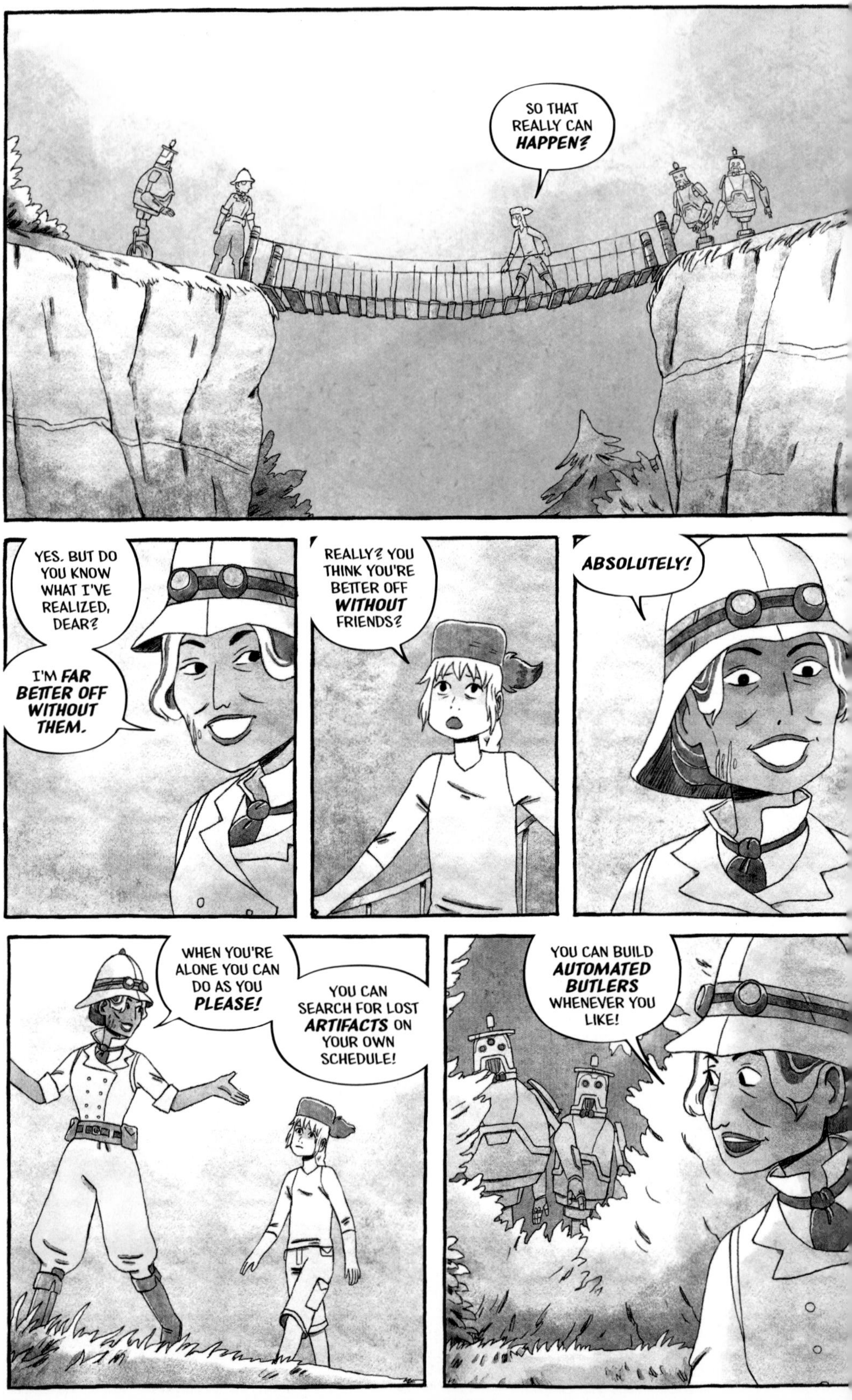
SO THAT REALLY CAN HAPPEN?
YES. BUT DO YOU KNOW WHAT I'VE REALIZED, DEAR?
I'M FAR BETTER OFF WITHOUT THEM.
REALLY? YOU THINK YOU'RE BETTER OFF WITHOUT FRIENDS?
ABSOLUTELY!
WHEN YOU'RE ALONE YOU CAN DO AS YOU PLEASE!
YOU CAN SEARCH FOR LOST ARTIFACTS ON YOUR OWN SCHEDULE!
YOU CAN BUILD AUTOMATED BUTLERS WHENEVER YOU LIKE!

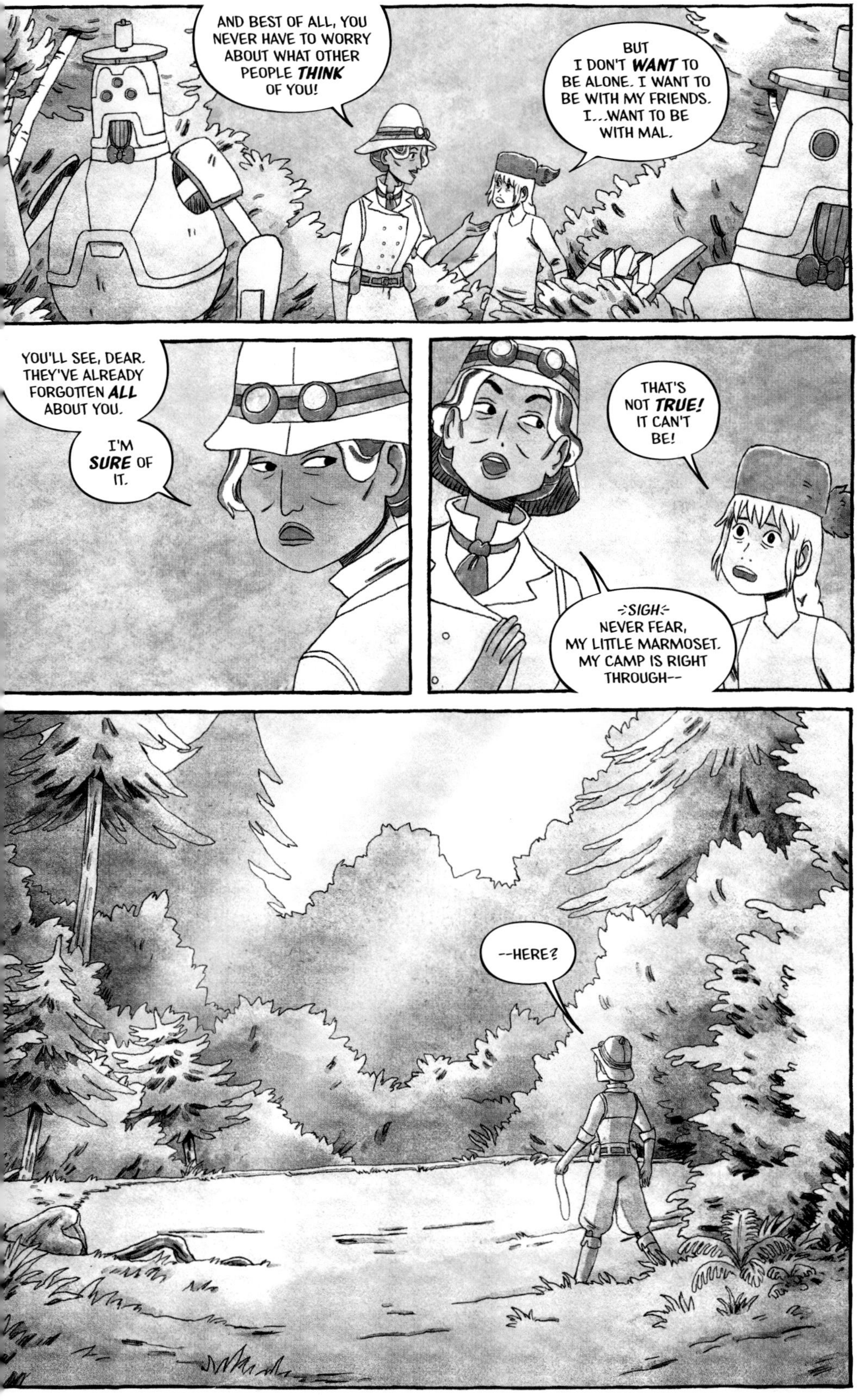
AND BEST OF ALL, YOU NEVER HAVE TO WORRY ABOUT WHAT OTHER PEOPLE THINK OF YOU!
BUT I DON'T WANT TO BE ALONE. I WANT TO BE WITH MY FRIENDS. I...WANT TO BE WITH MAL.
YOU'LL SEE, DEAR. THEY'VE ALREADY FORGOTTEN ALL ABOUT YOU.
I'M SURE OF IT.
THAT'S NOT TRUE! IT CAN'T BE!
SIGH
NEVER FEAR, MY LITTLE MARMOSET. MY CAMP IS RIGHT THROUGH--
--HERE?

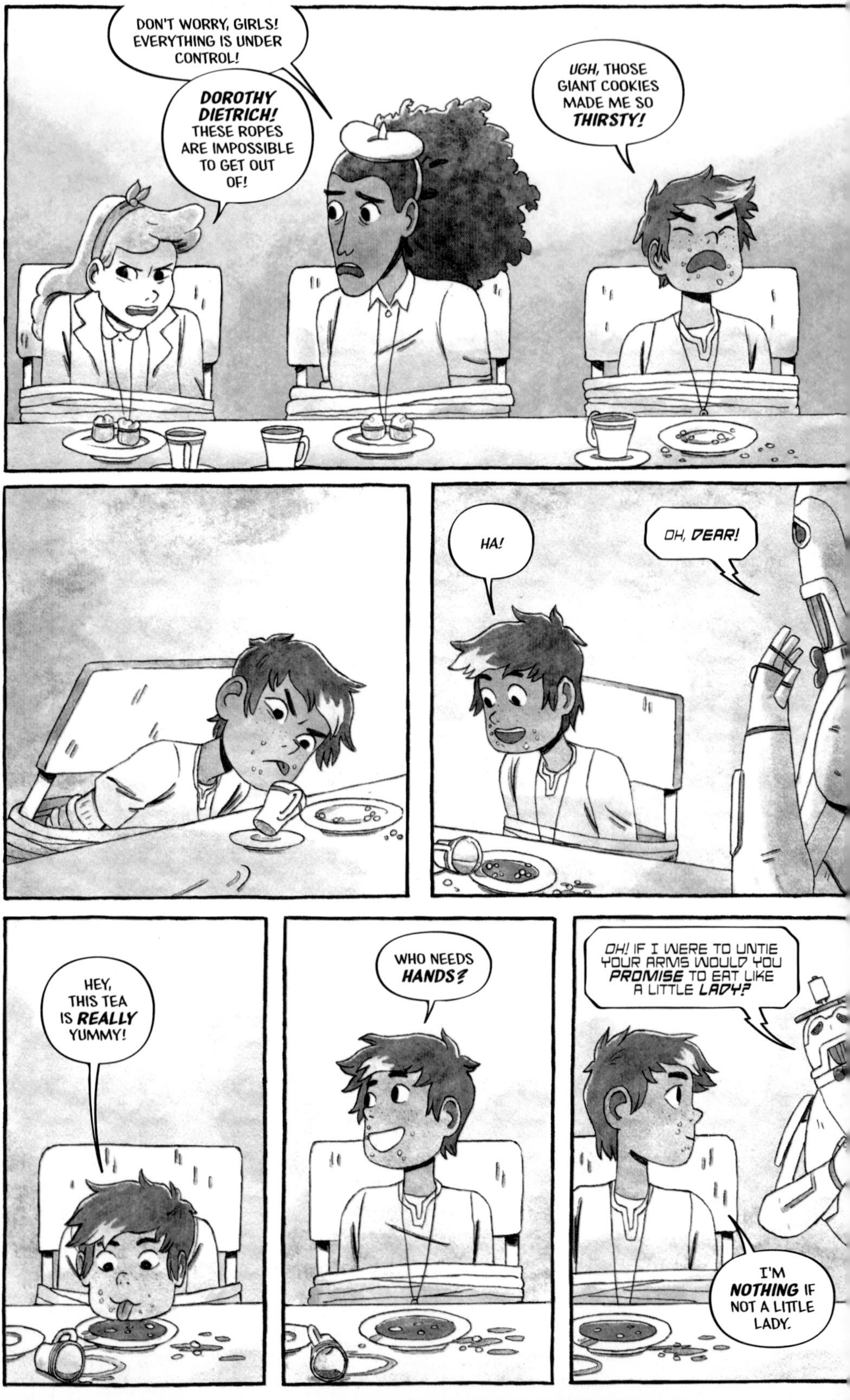
DON'T WORRY, GIRLS! EVERYTHING IS UNDER CONTROL!
DOROTHY DIETRICH! THESE ROPES ARE IMPOSSIBLE TO GET OUT OF!
UGH, THOSE GIANT COOKIES MADE ME SO THIRSTY!
HA!
OH, DEAR!
HEY, THIS TEA IS REALLY YUMMY!
WHO NEEDS HANDS?
OH! IF I WERE TO UNTIE YOUR ARMS WOULD YOU PROMISE TO EAT LIKE A LITTLE LADY?
I'M NOTHING IF NOT A LITTLE LADY.

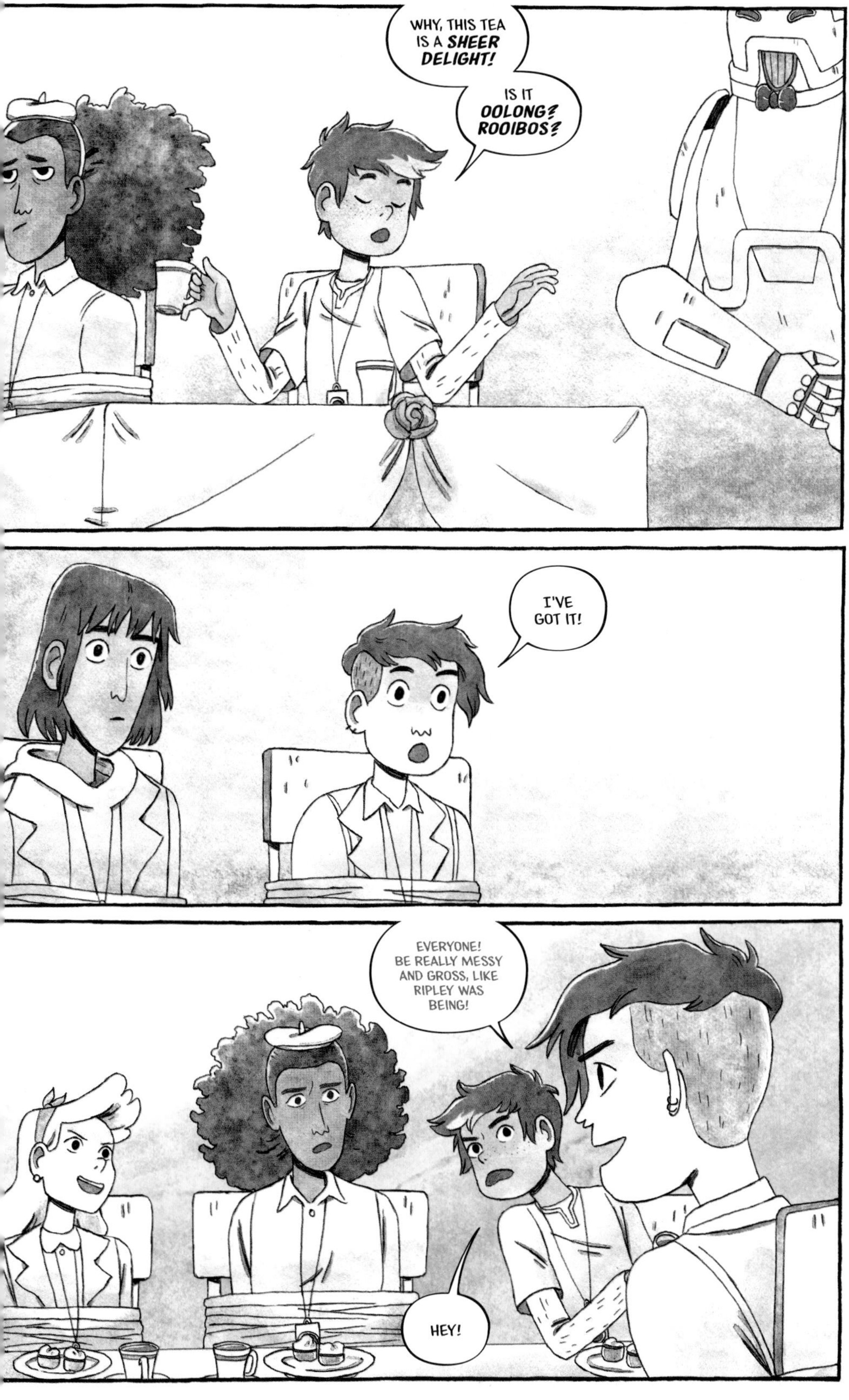
WHY, THIS TEA IS A SHEER DELIGHT!
IS IT OOLONG? ROOIBOS?
I'VE GOT IT!
EVERYONE! BE REALLY MESSY AND GROSS, LIKE RIPLEY WAS BEING!
HEY!

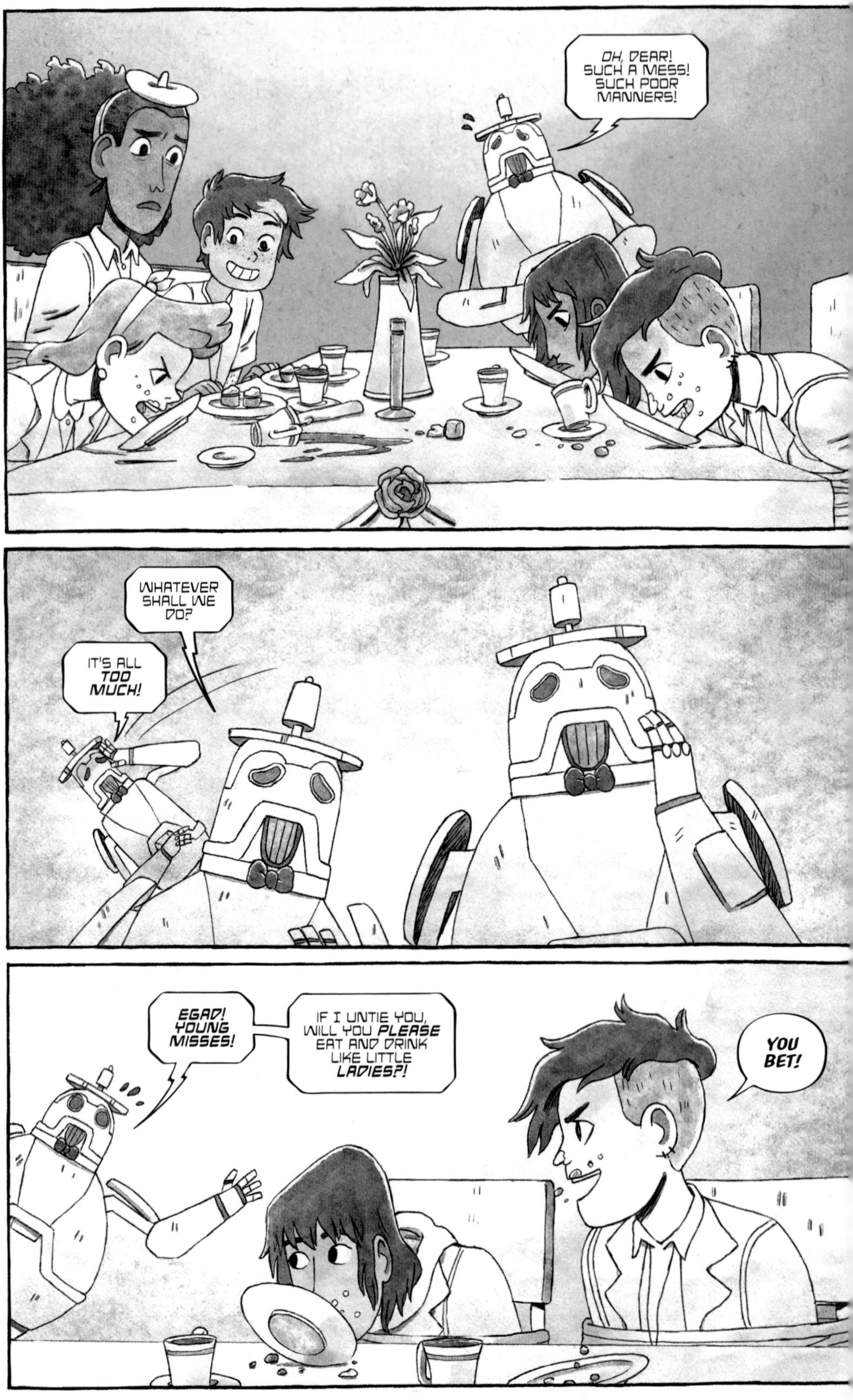
OH, DEAR! SUCH A MESS! SUCH POOR MANNERS!
WHATEVER SHALL WE DO?
IT'S ALL TOO MUCH!
EGAD! YOUNG MISSES!
IF I UNTIE YOU, WILL YOU PLEASE EAT AND DRINK LIKE LITTLE LADIES?!
YOU BET!

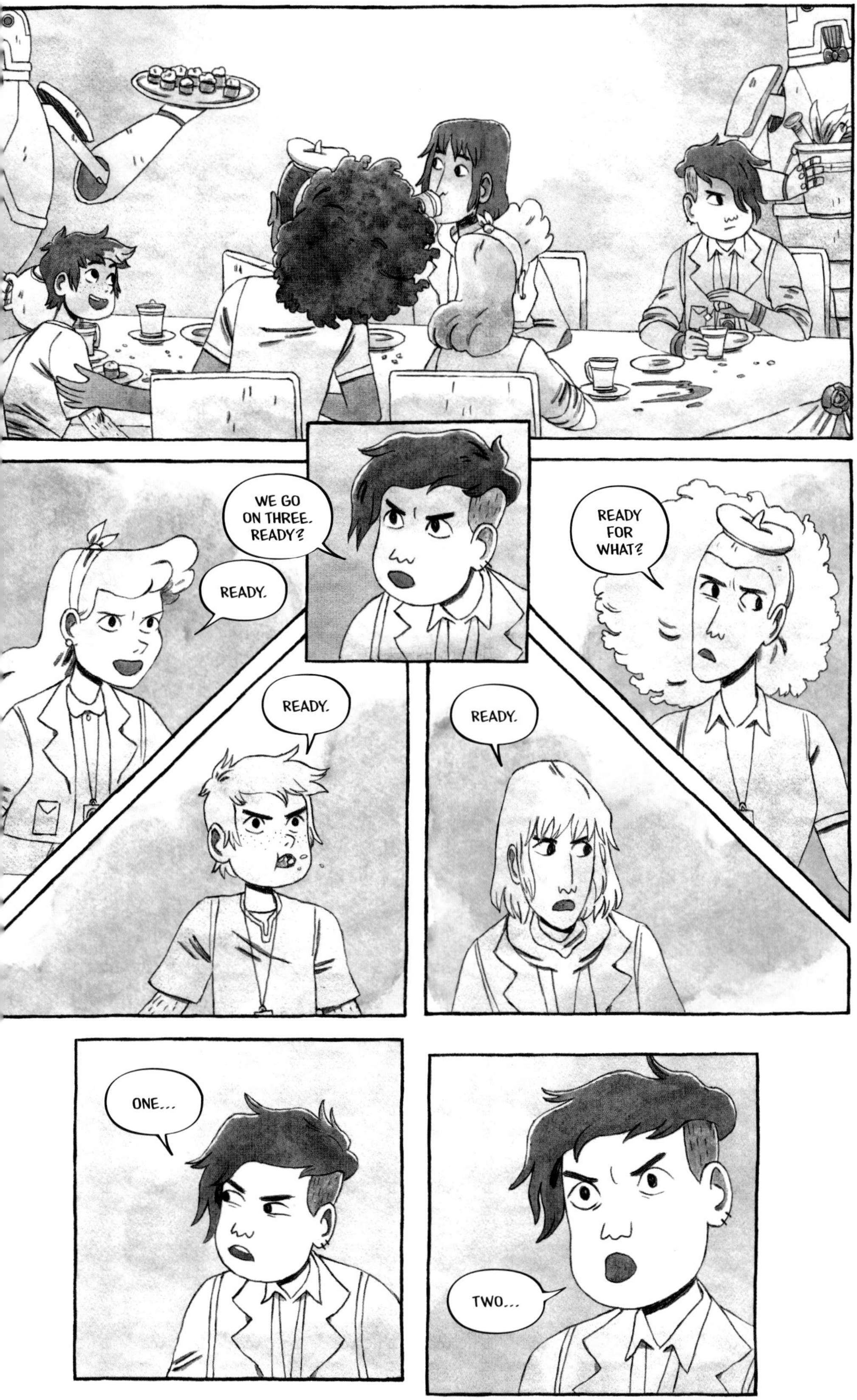
WE GO ON THREE. READY?
READY.
READY FOR WHAT?
READY.
READY.
ONE...
TWO...

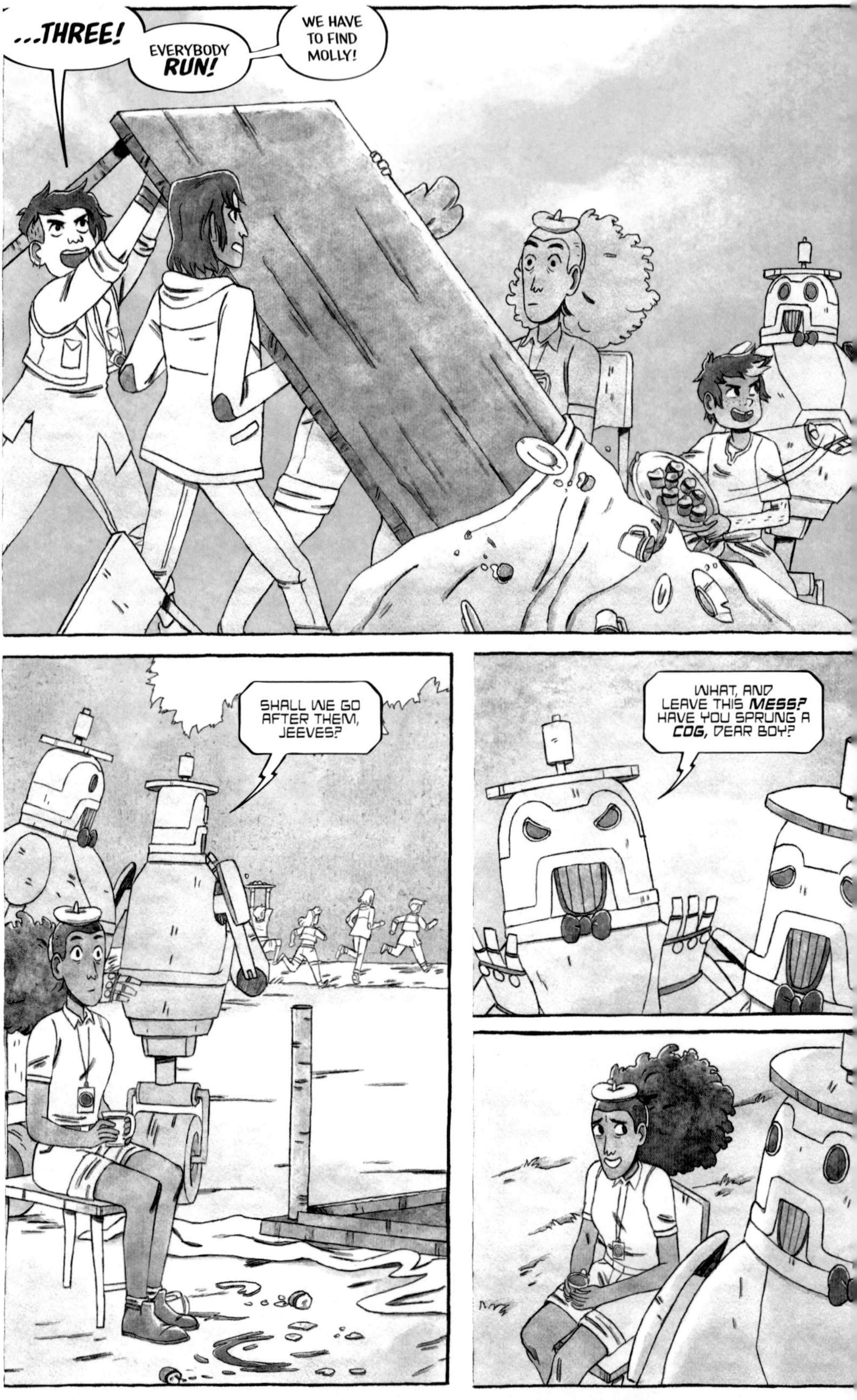
...THREE!
EVERYBODY RUN!
WE HAVE TO FIND MOLLY!
SHALL WE GO AFTER THEM, JEEVES?
WHAT, AND LEAVE THIS MESS? HAVE YOU SPRUNG A COG, DEAR BOY?

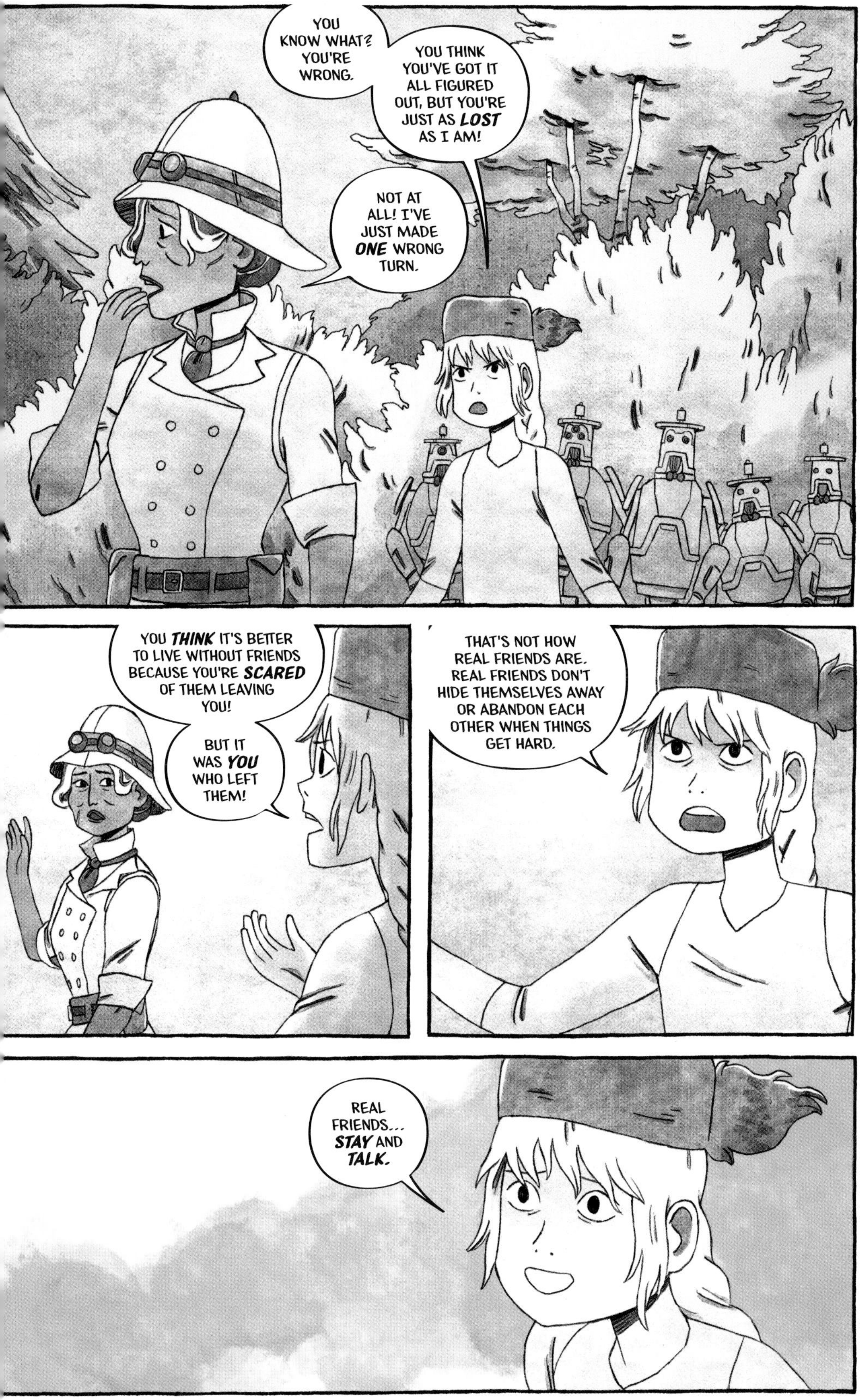
YOU KNOW WHAT? YOU'RE WRONG.
YOU THINK YOU'VE GOT IT ALL FIGURED OUT, BUT YOU'RE JUST AS LOST AS I AM!
NOT AT ALL! I'VE JUST MADE ONE WRONG TURN.
YOU THINK IT'S BETTER TO LIVE WITHOUT FRIENDS BECAUSE YOU'RE SCARED OF THEM LEAVING YOU!
BUT IT WAS YOU WHO LEFT THEM!
THAT'S NOT HOW REAL FRIENDS ARE. REAL FRIENDS DON'T HIDE THEMSELVES AWAY OR ABANDON EACH OTHER WHEN THINGS GET HARD.
REAL FRIENDS... STAY AND TALK.

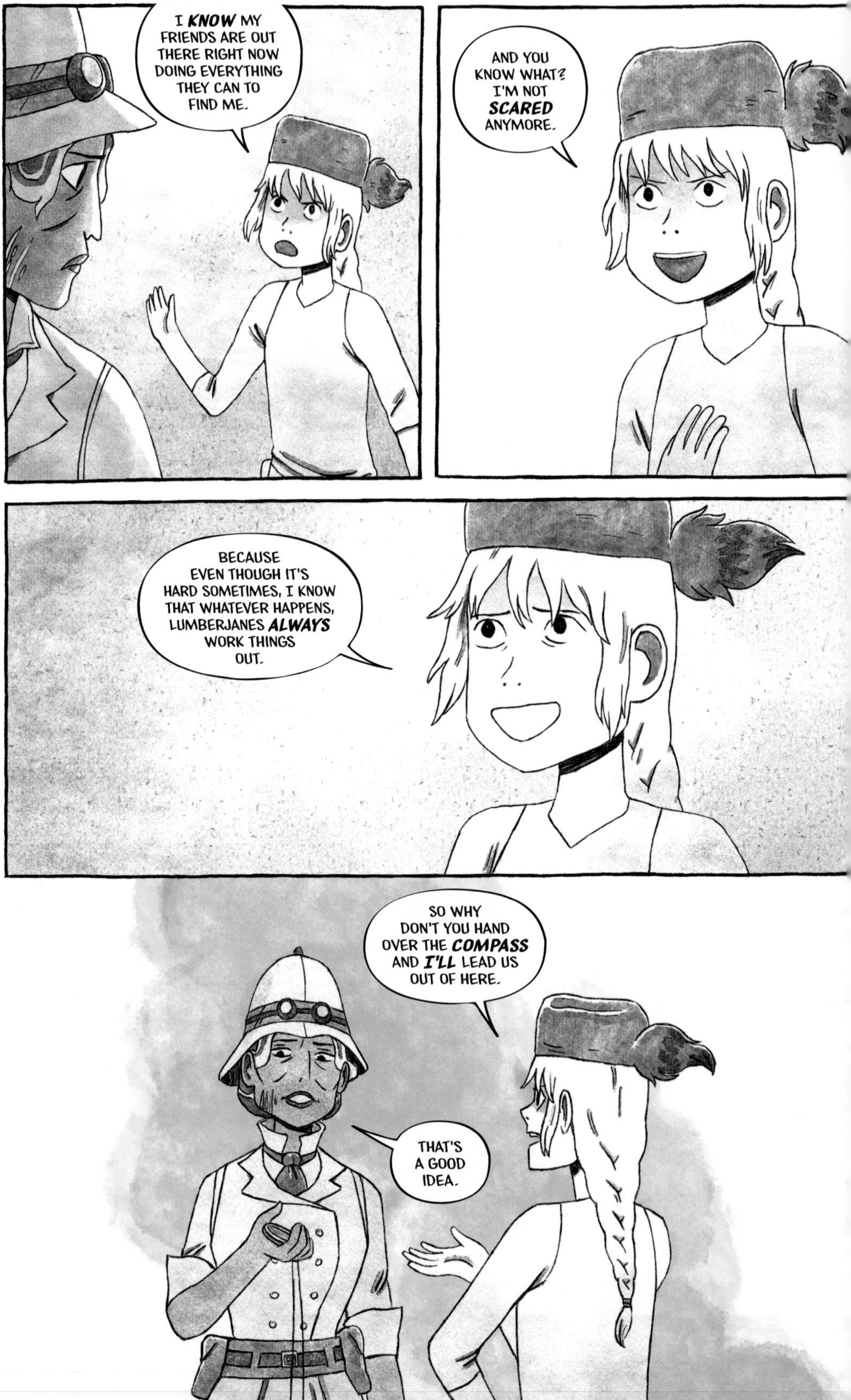
I KNOW MY FRIENDS ARE OUT THERE RIGHT NOW DOING EVERYTHING THEY CAN TO FIND ME.
AND YOU KNOW WHAT? I'M NOT SCARED ANYMORE.
BECAUSE EVEN THOUGH IT'S HARD SOMETIMES, I KNOW THAT WHATEVER HAPPENS, LUMBERJANES ALWAYS WORK THINGS OUT.
SO WHY DON'T YOU HAND OVER THE COMPASS AND I'LL LEAD US OUT OF HERE.
THAT'S A GOOD IDEA.

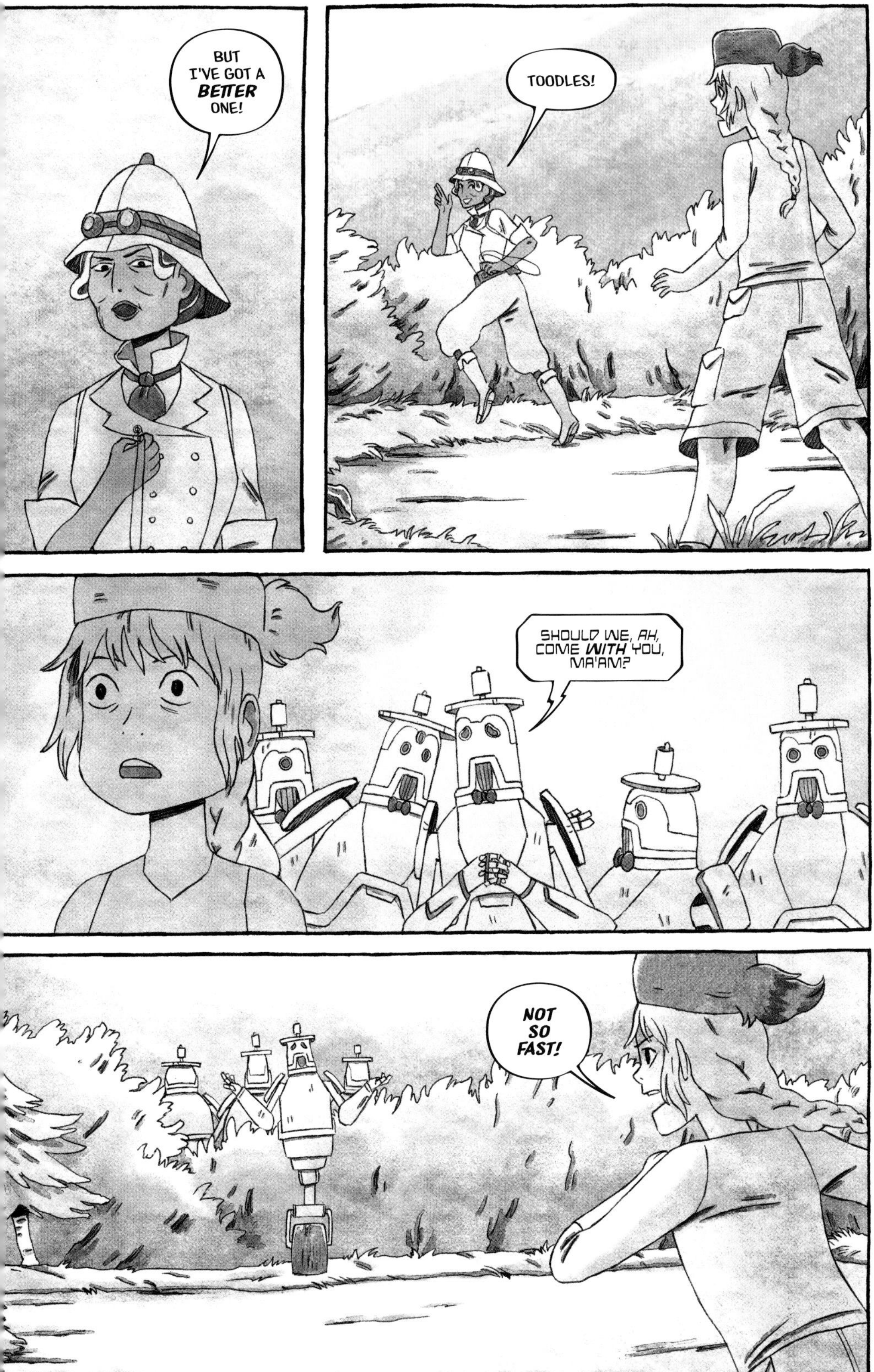
BUT I'VE GOT A BETTER ONE!
TOODLES!
SHOULD WE, AH, COME WITH YOU, MA'AM?
NOT SO FAST!

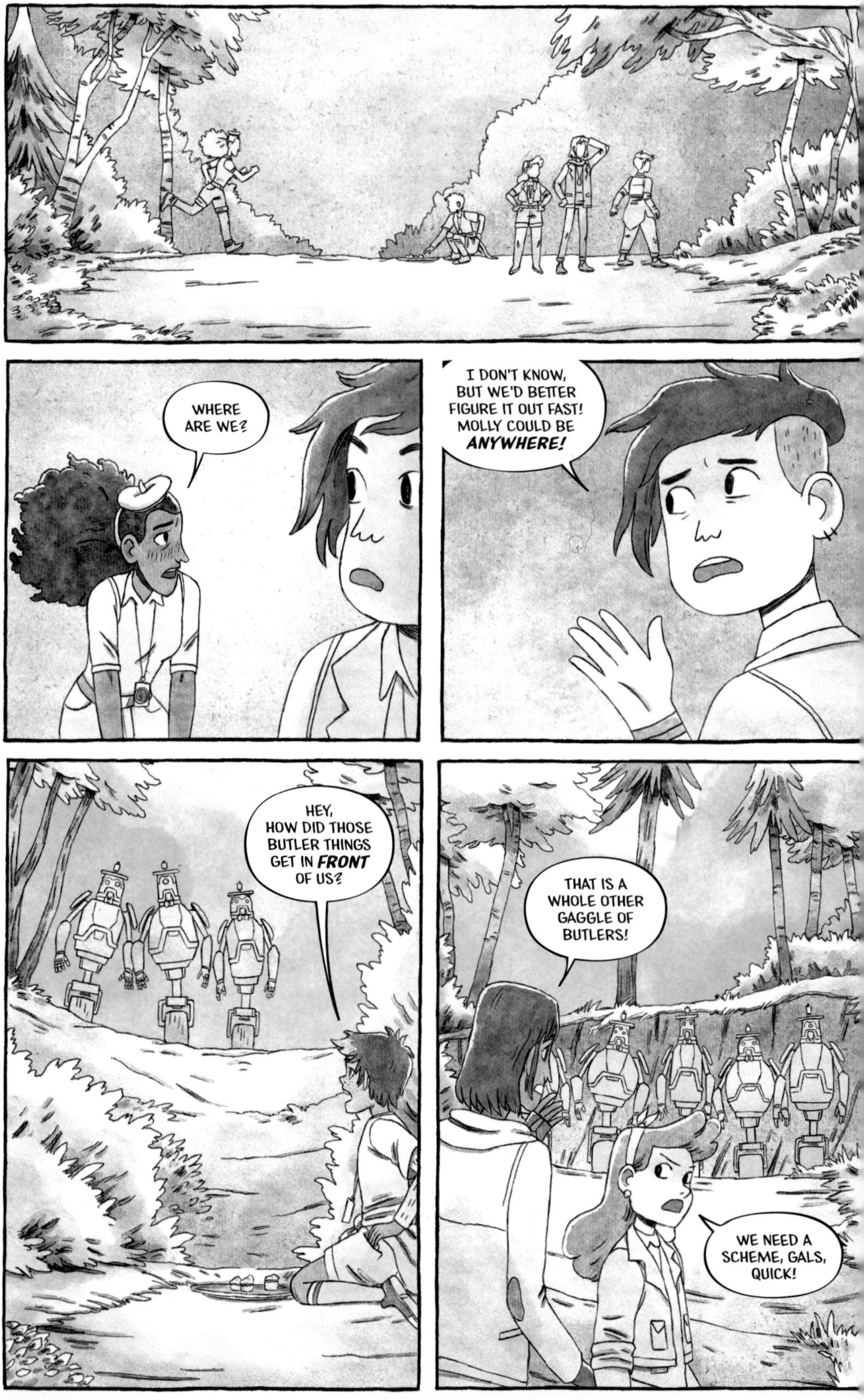
WHERE ARE WE?
I DON'T KNOW, BUT WE'D BETTER FIGURE IT OUT FAST! MOLLY COULD BE ANYWHERE!
HEY, HOW DID THOSE BUTLER THINGS GET IN FRONT OF US?
THAT IS A WHOLE OTHER GAGGLE OF BUTLERS!
WE NEED A SCHEME, GALS, QUICK!

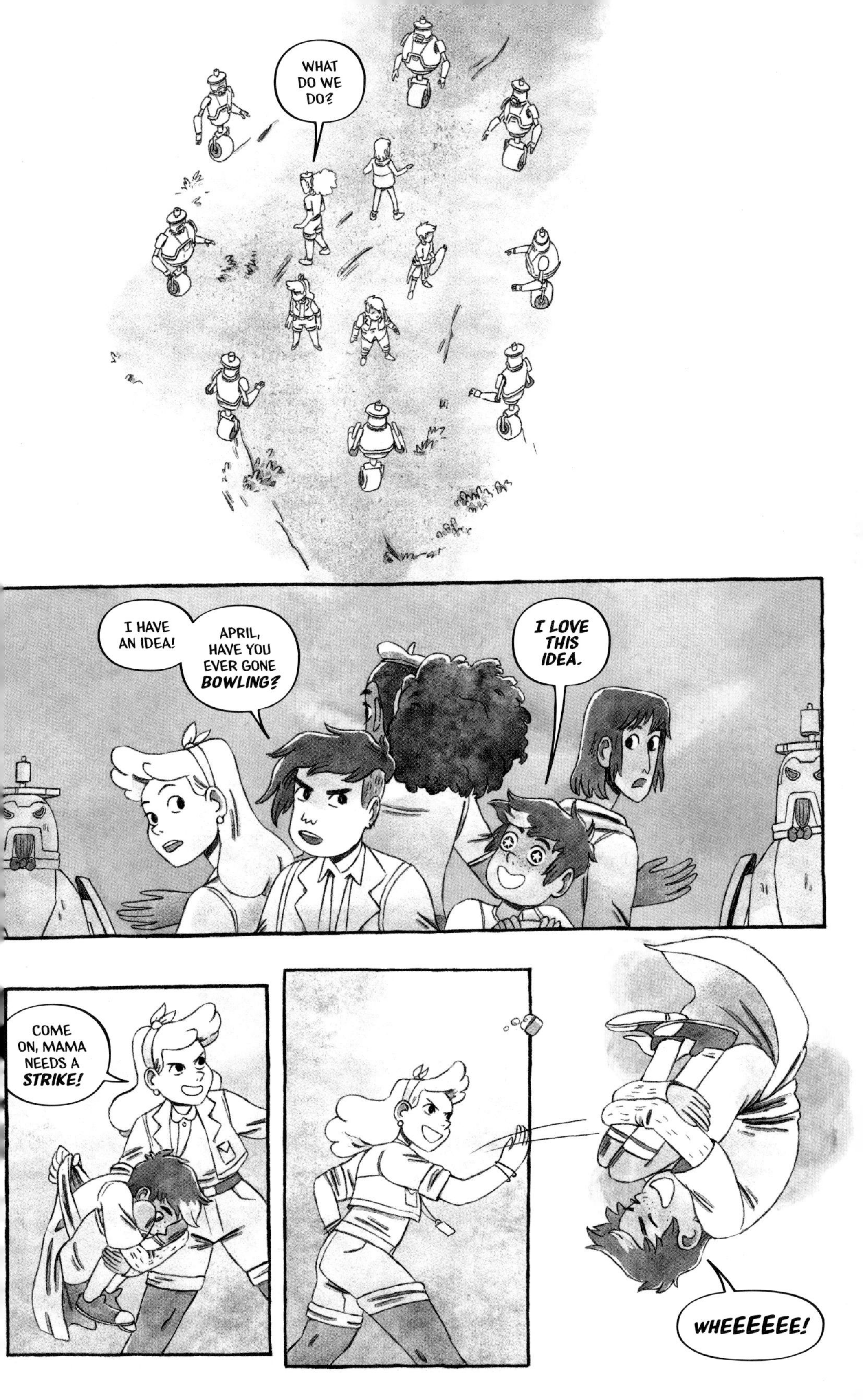
WHAT DO WE DO?
I HAVE AN IDEA!
APRIL, HAVE YOU EVER GONE BOWLING?
I LOVE THIS IDEA.
COME ON, MAMA NEEDS A STRIKE!
WHEEEEEE!

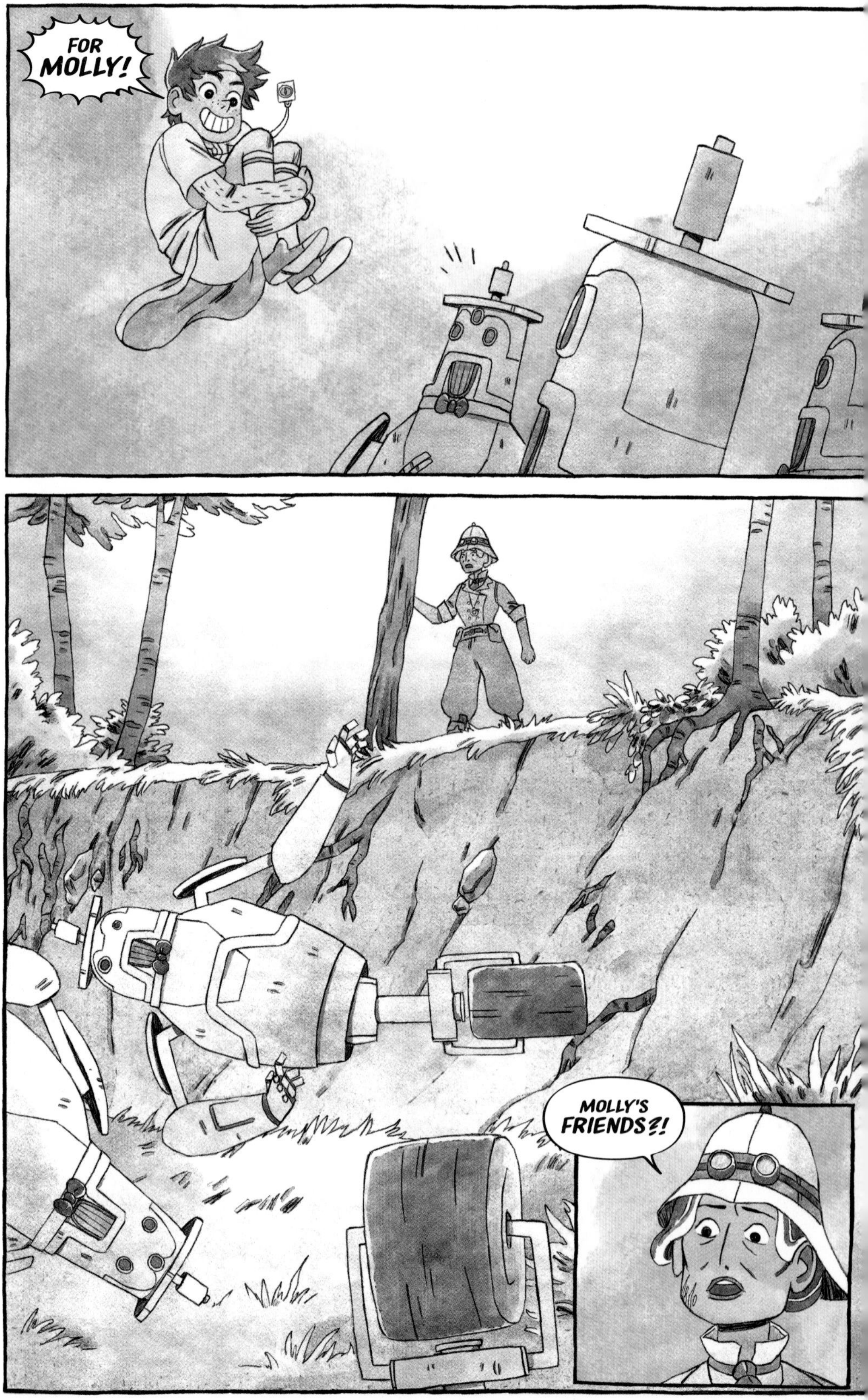
FOR MOLLY!
MOLLY'S FRIENDS?!

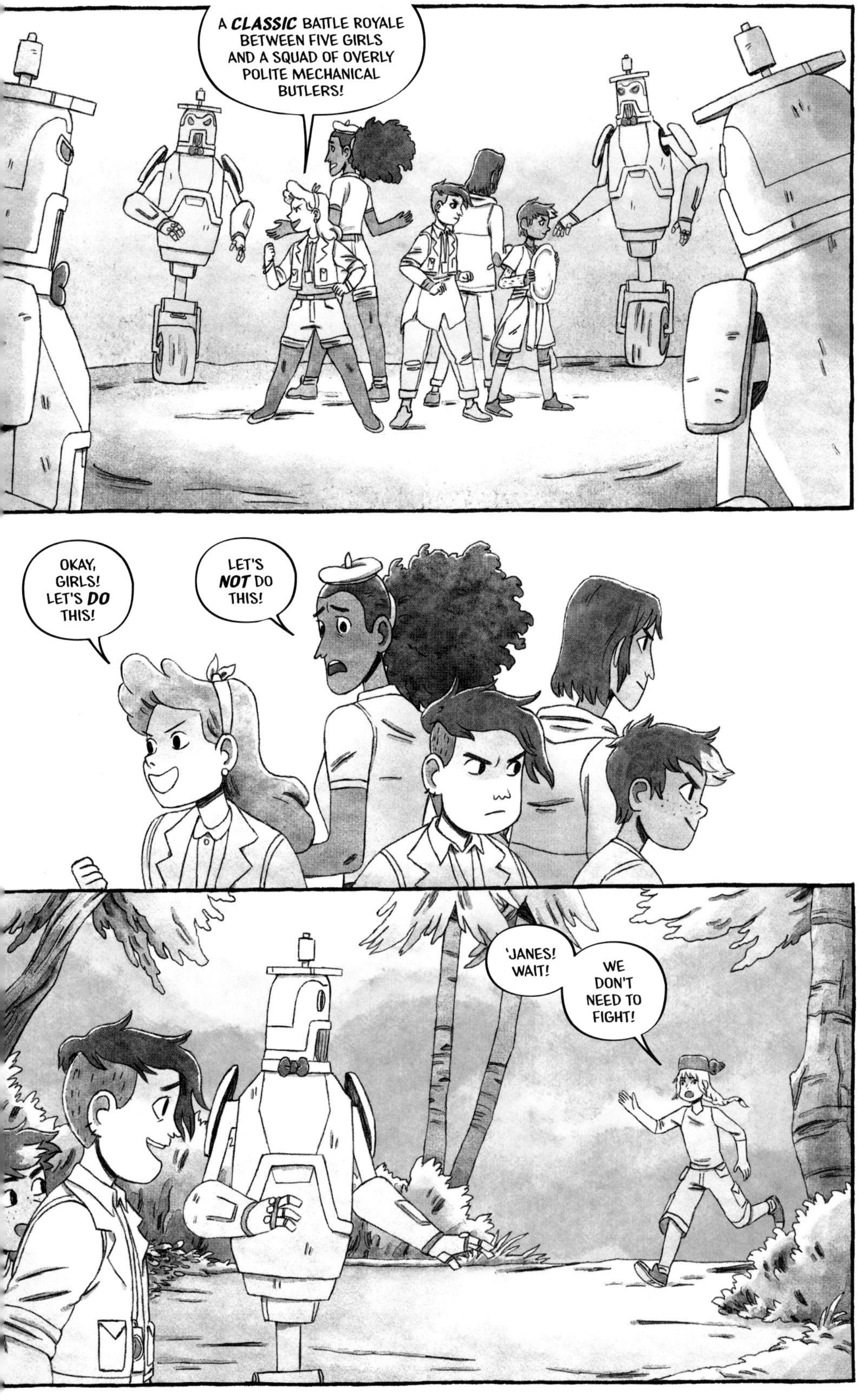
A CLASSIC BATTLE ROYALE BETWEEN FIVE GIRLS AND A SQUAD OF OVERLY POLITE MECHANICAL BUTLERS!
OKAY, GIRLS! LET'S DO THIS!
LET'S NOT DO THIS!
'JANES! WAIT!
WE DON'T NEED TO FIGHT!

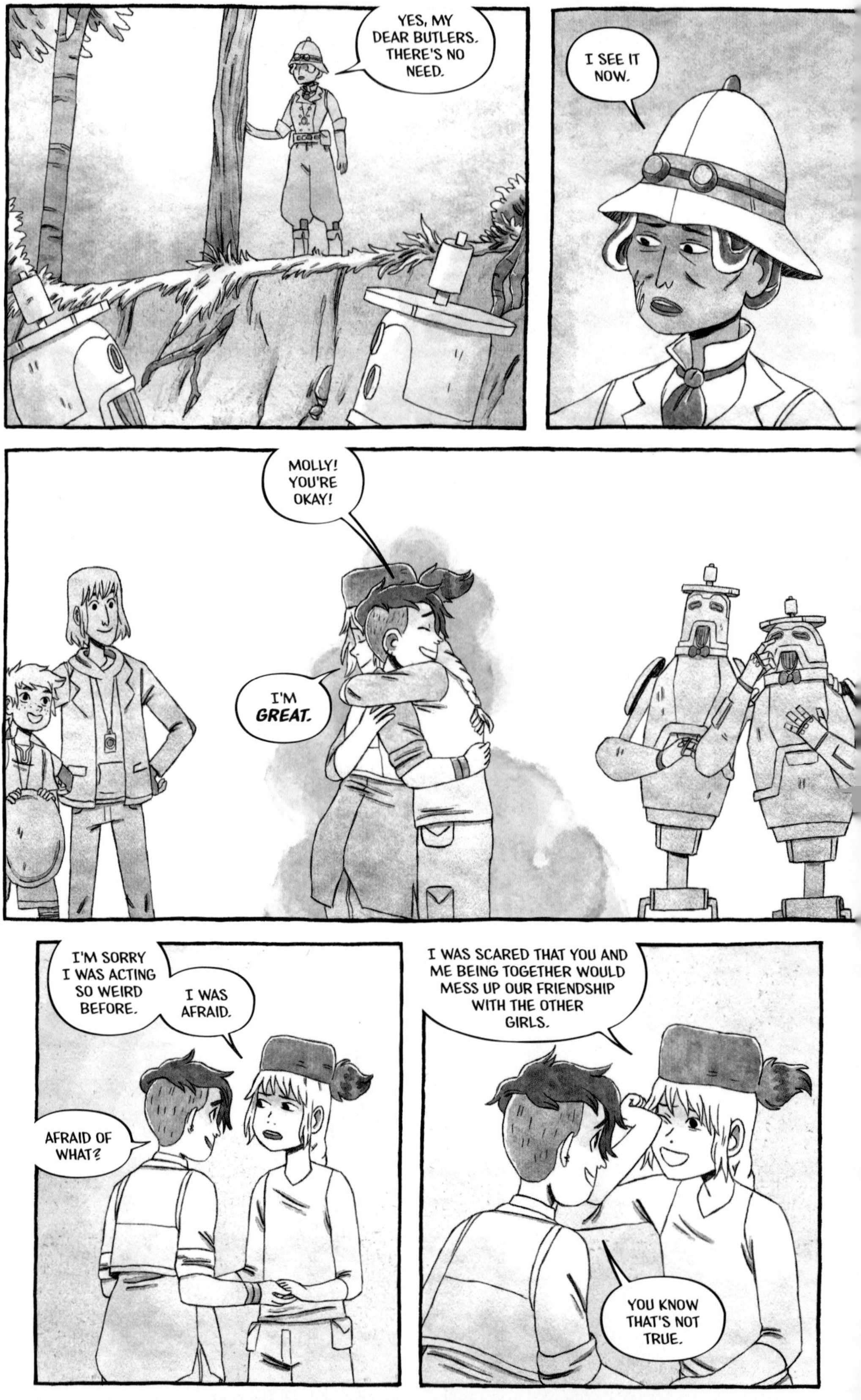
YES, MY DEAR BUTLERS. THERE'S NO NEED.
I SEE IT NOW.
MOLLY! YOU'RE OKAY!
I'M **GREAT.**
I'M SORRY I WAS ACTING SO WEIRD BEFORE.
I WAS AFRAID.
AFRAID OF WHAT?
I WAS SCARED THAT YOU AND ME BEING TOGETHER WOULD MESS UP OUR FRIENDSHIP WITH THE OTHER GIRLS.
YOU KNOW THAT'S NOT TRUE.

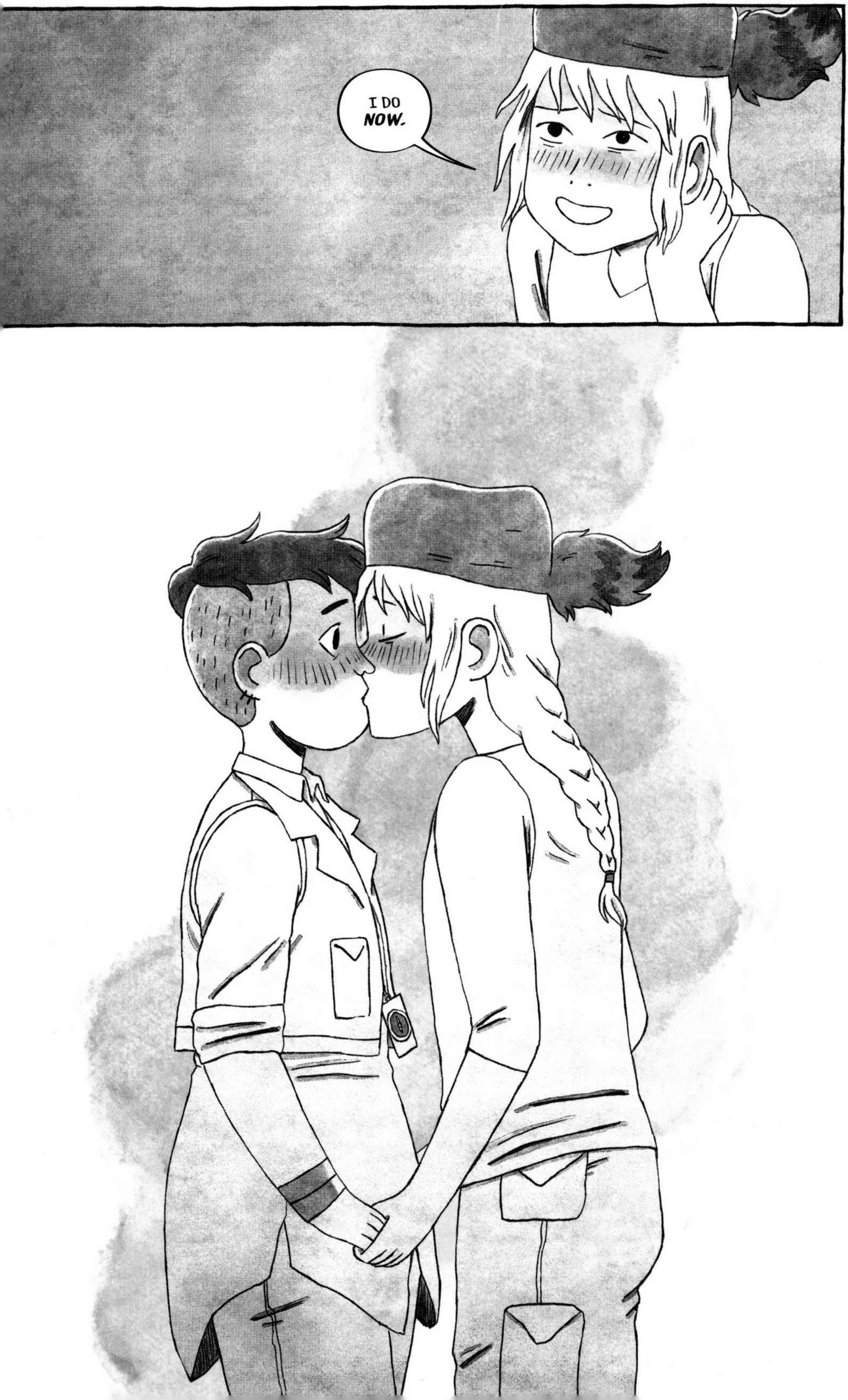
I DO
NOW.

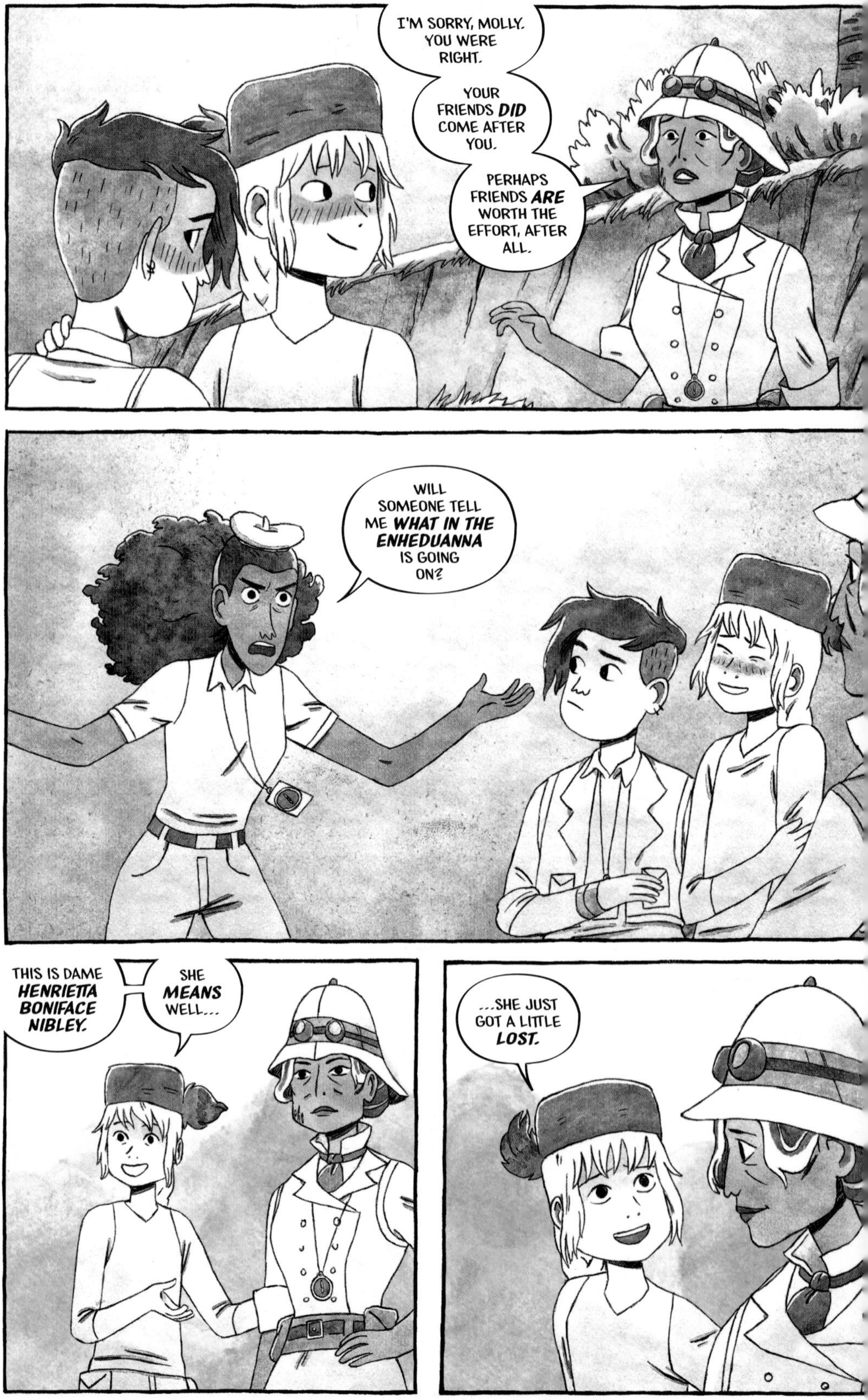

I'M SORRY, MOLLY. YOU WERE RIGHT.
YOUR FRIENDS **DID** COME AFTER YOU.
PERHAPS FRIENDS **ARE** WORTH THE EFFORT, AFTER ALL.
WILL SOMEONE TELL ME ***WHAT IN THE ENHEDUANNA*** IS GOING ON?
THIS IS DAME ***HENRIETTA BONIFACE NIBLEY.***
SHE ***MEANS*** WELL...
...SHE JUST GOT A LITTLE ***LOST.***

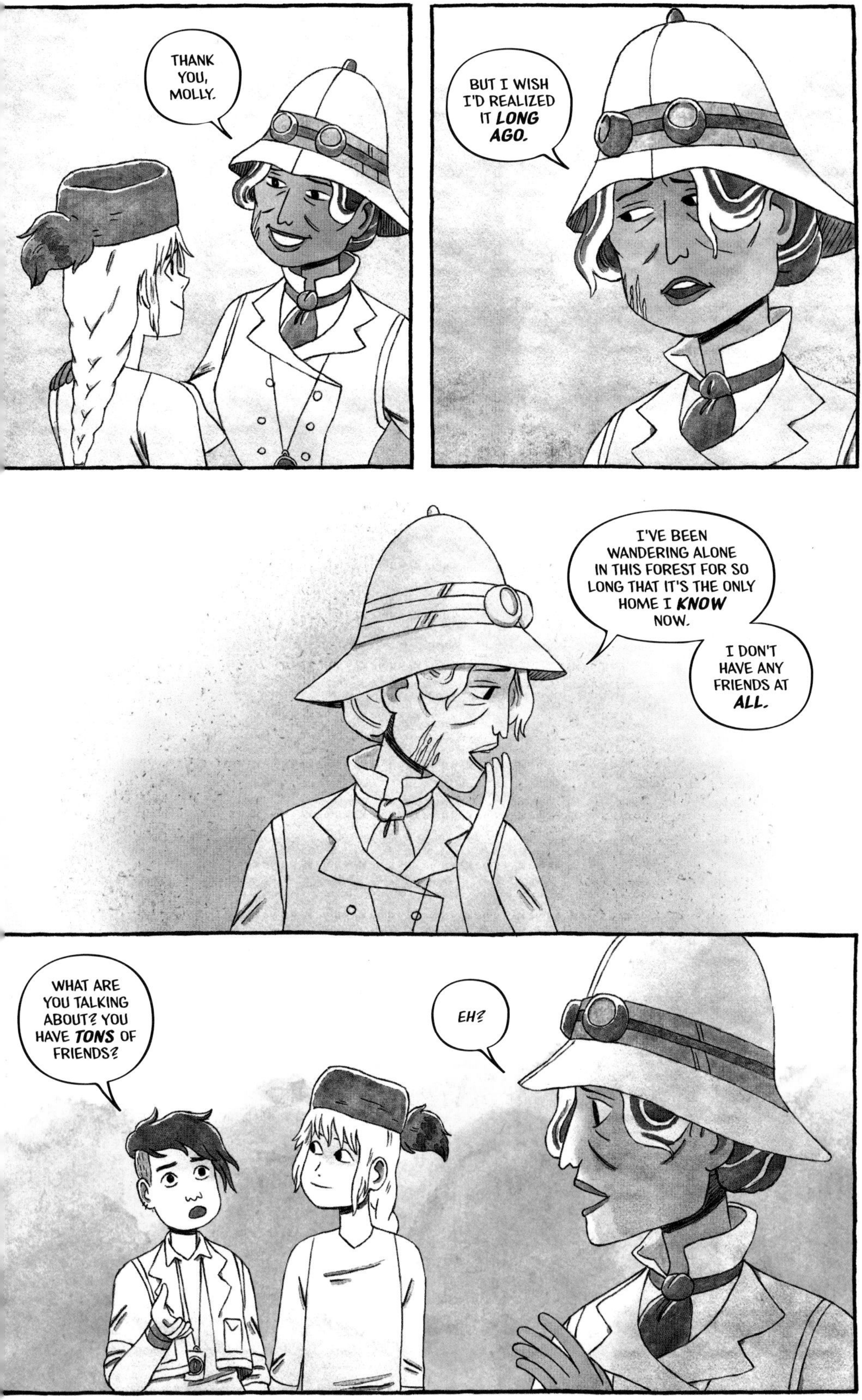
THANK YOU, MOLLY.
BUT I WISH I'D REALIZED IT LONG AGO.
I'VE BEEN WANDERING ALONE IN THIS FOREST FOR SO LONG THAT IT'S THE ONLY HOME I KNOW NOW.
I DON'T HAVE ANY FRIENDS AT ALL.
WHAT ARE YOU TALKING ABOUT? YOU HAVE TONS OF FRIENDS?
EH?

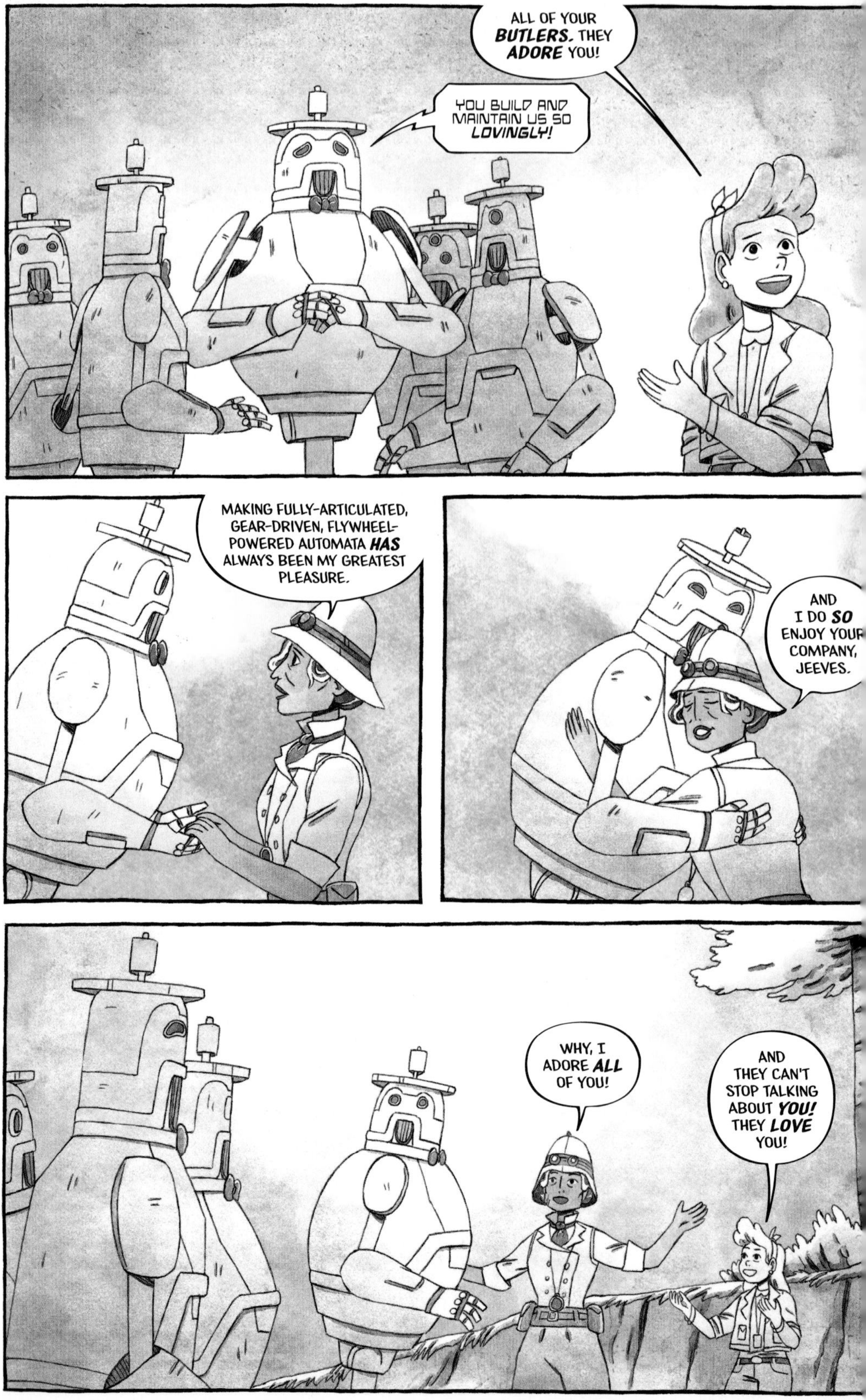
ALL OF YOUR BUTLERS. THEY ADORE YOU!
YOU BUILD AND MAINTAIN US SO LOVINGLY!
MAKING FULLY-ARTICULATED, GEAR-DRIVEN, FLYWHEEL-POWERED AUTOMATA HAS ALWAYS BEEN MY GREATEST PLEASURE.
AND I DO SO ENJOY YOUR COMPANY, JEEVES.
WHY, I ADORE ALL OF YOU!
AND THEY CAN'T STOP TALKING ABOUT YOU! THEY LOVE YOU!

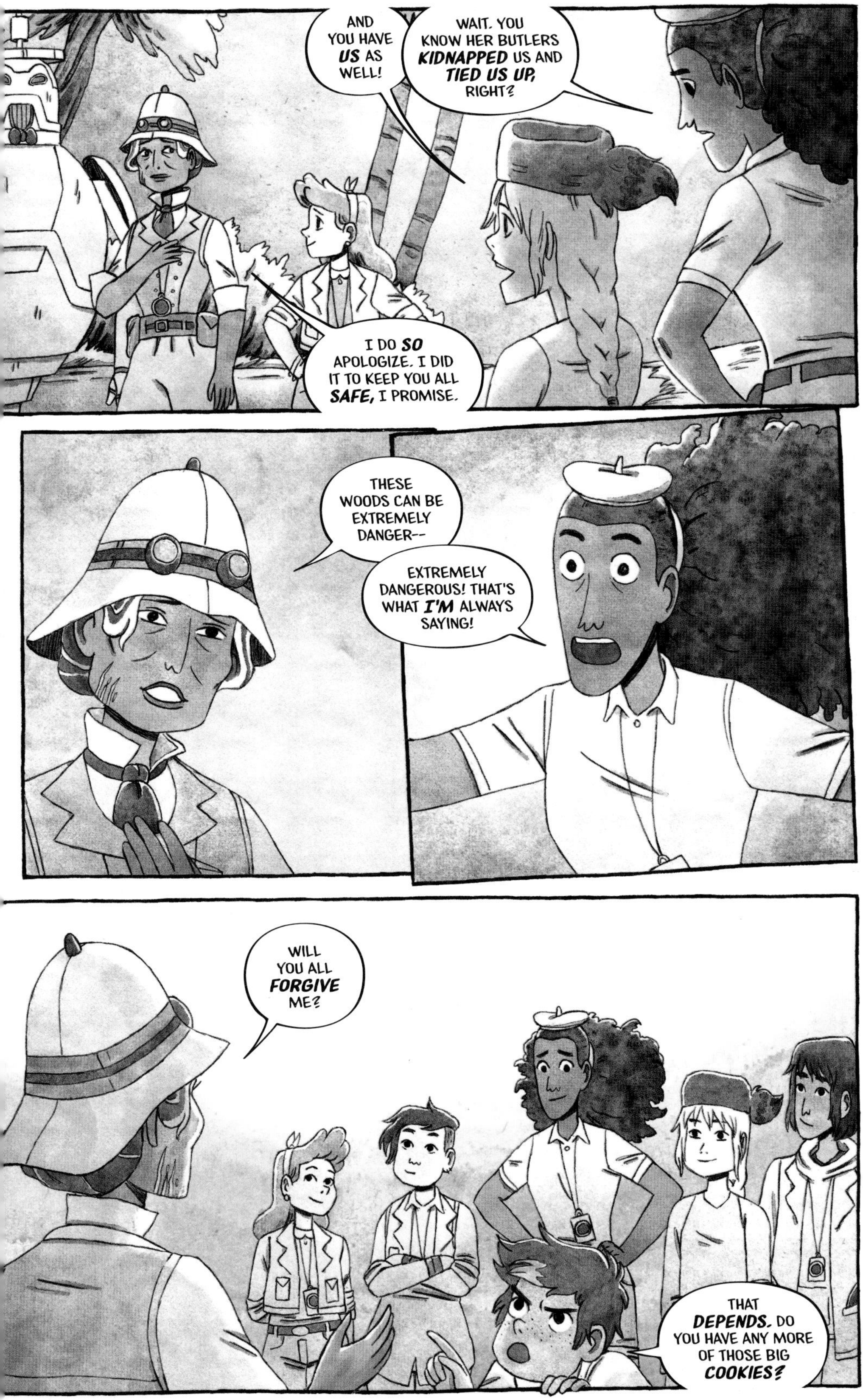
AND YOU HAVE **US** AS WELL!
WAIT. YOU KNOW HER BUTLERS **KIDNAPPED** US AND **TIED US UP,** RIGHT?
I DO **SO** APOLOGIZE. I DID IT TO KEEP YOU ALL **SAFE,** I PROMISE.
THESE WOODS CAN BE EXTREMELY DANGER--
EXTREMELY DANGEROUS! THAT'S WHAT **I'M** ALWAYS SAYING!
WILL YOU ALL **FORGIVE** ME?
THAT **DEPENDS.** DO YOU HAVE ANY MORE OF THOSE BIG **COOKIES?**

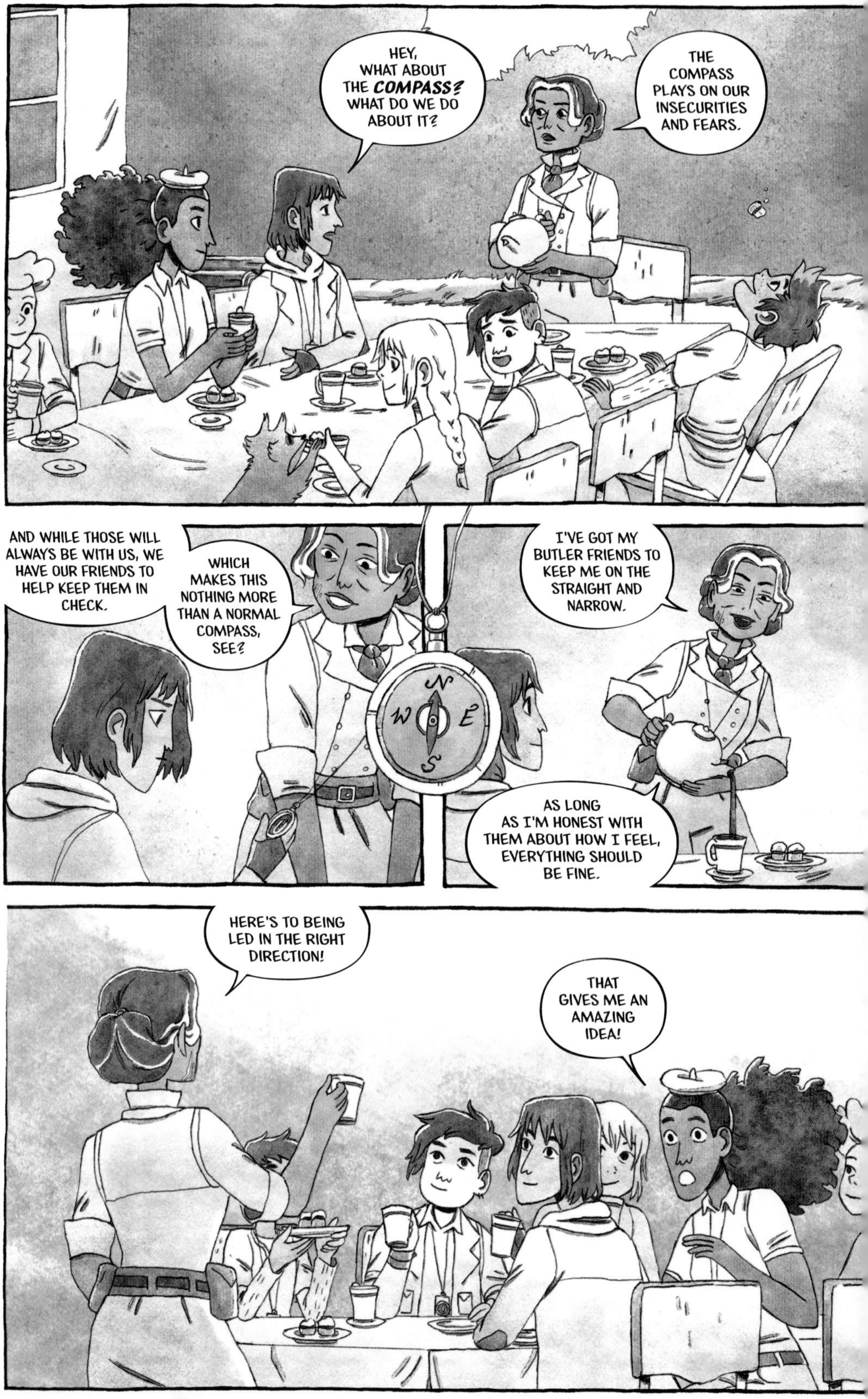
HEY, WHAT ABOUT THE COMPASS? WHAT DO WE DO ABOUT IT?
THE COMPASS PLAYS ON OUR INSECURITIES AND FEARS.
AND WHILE THOSE WILL ALWAYS BE WITH US, WE HAVE OUR FRIENDS TO HELP KEEP THEM IN CHECK.
WHICH MAKES THIS NOTHING MORE THAN A NORMAL COMPASS, SEE?
N
W
E
S
I'VE GOT MY BUTLER FRIENDS TO KEEP ME ON THE STRAIGHT AND NARROW.
AS LONG AS I'M HONEST WITH THEM ABOUT HOW I FEEL, EVERYTHING SHOULD BE FINE.
HERE'S TO BEING LED IN THE RIGHT DIRECTION!
THAT GIVES ME AN AMAZING IDEA!

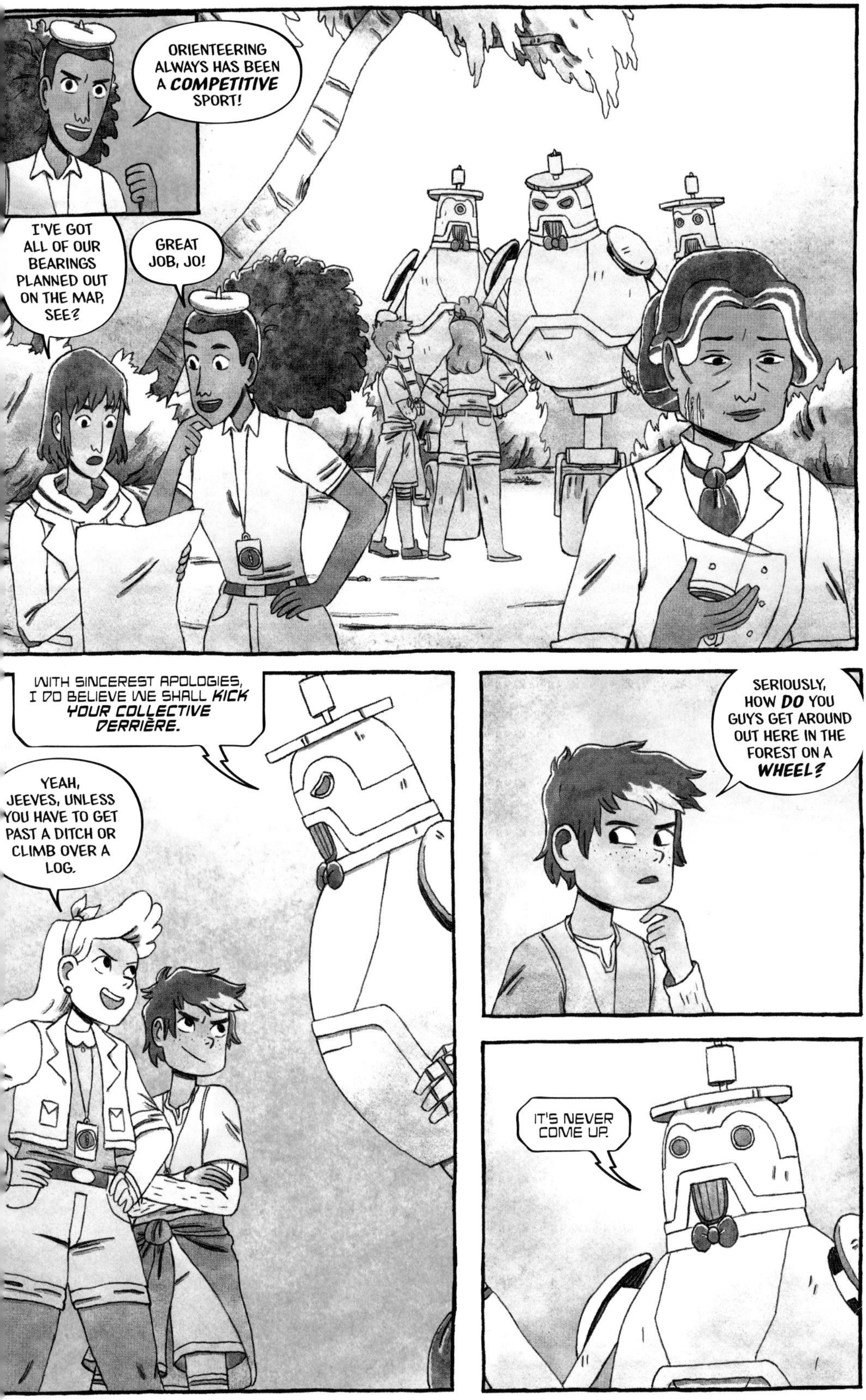
ORIENTEERING ALWAYS HAS BEEN A COMPETITIVE SPORT!
I'VE GOT ALL OF OUR BEARINGS PLANNED OUT ON THE MAP, SEE?
GREAT JOB, JO!
WITH SINCEREST APOLOGIES, I DO BELIEVE WE SHALL KICK YOUR COLLECTIVE DERRIÈRE.
YEAH, JEEVES, UNLESS YOU HAVE TO GET PAST A DITCH OR CLIMB OVER A LOG.
SERIOUSLY, HOW DO YOU GUYS GET AROUND OUT HERE IN THE FOREST ON A WHEEL?
IT'S NEVER COME UP.

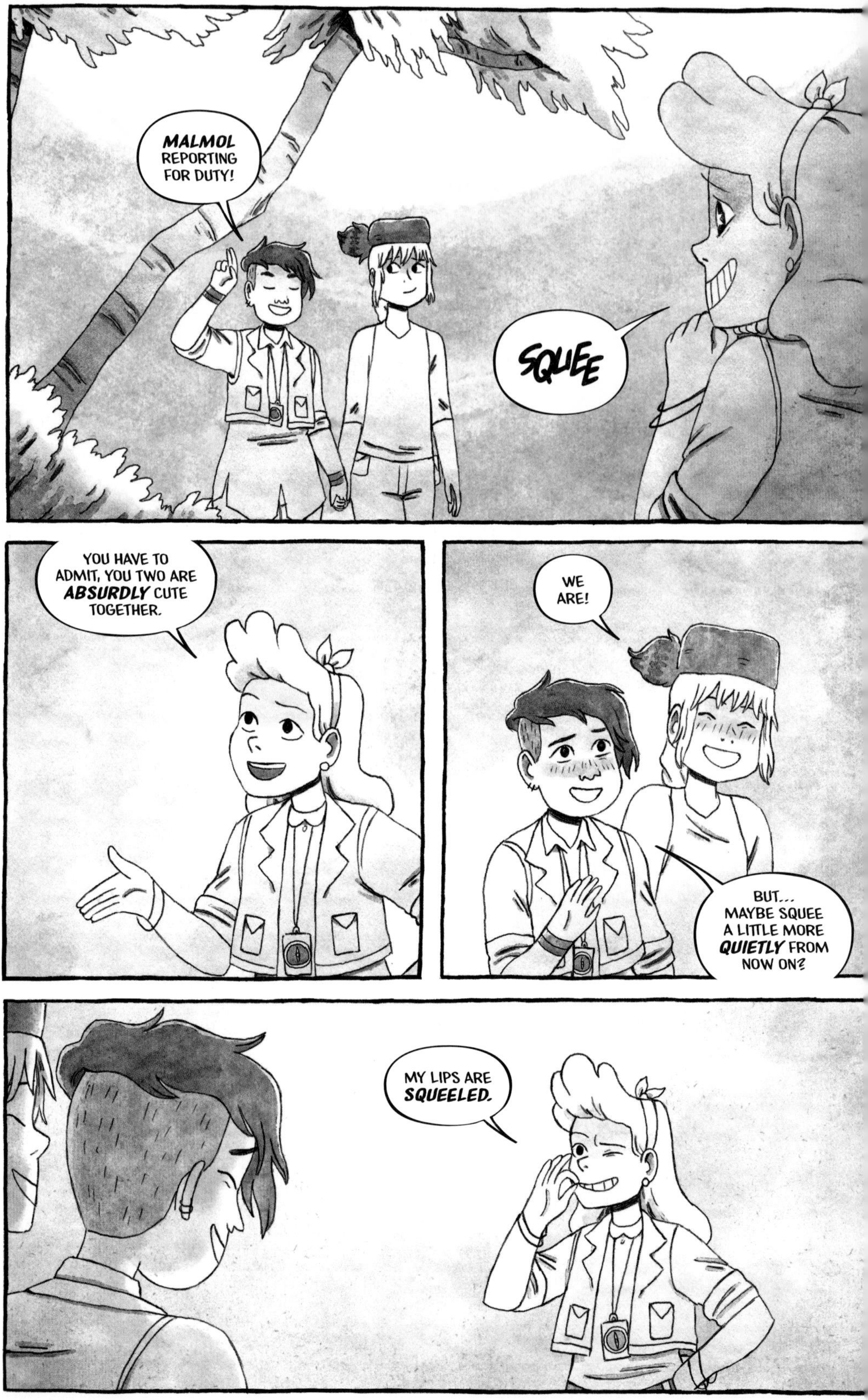
MALMOL REPORTING FOR DUTY!
SQUEE
YOU HAVE TO ADMIT, YOU TWO ARE ABSURDLY CUTE TOGETHER.
WE ARE!
BUT... MAYBE SQUEE A LITTLE MORE QUIETLY FROM NOW ON?
MY LIPS ARE SQUEELED.

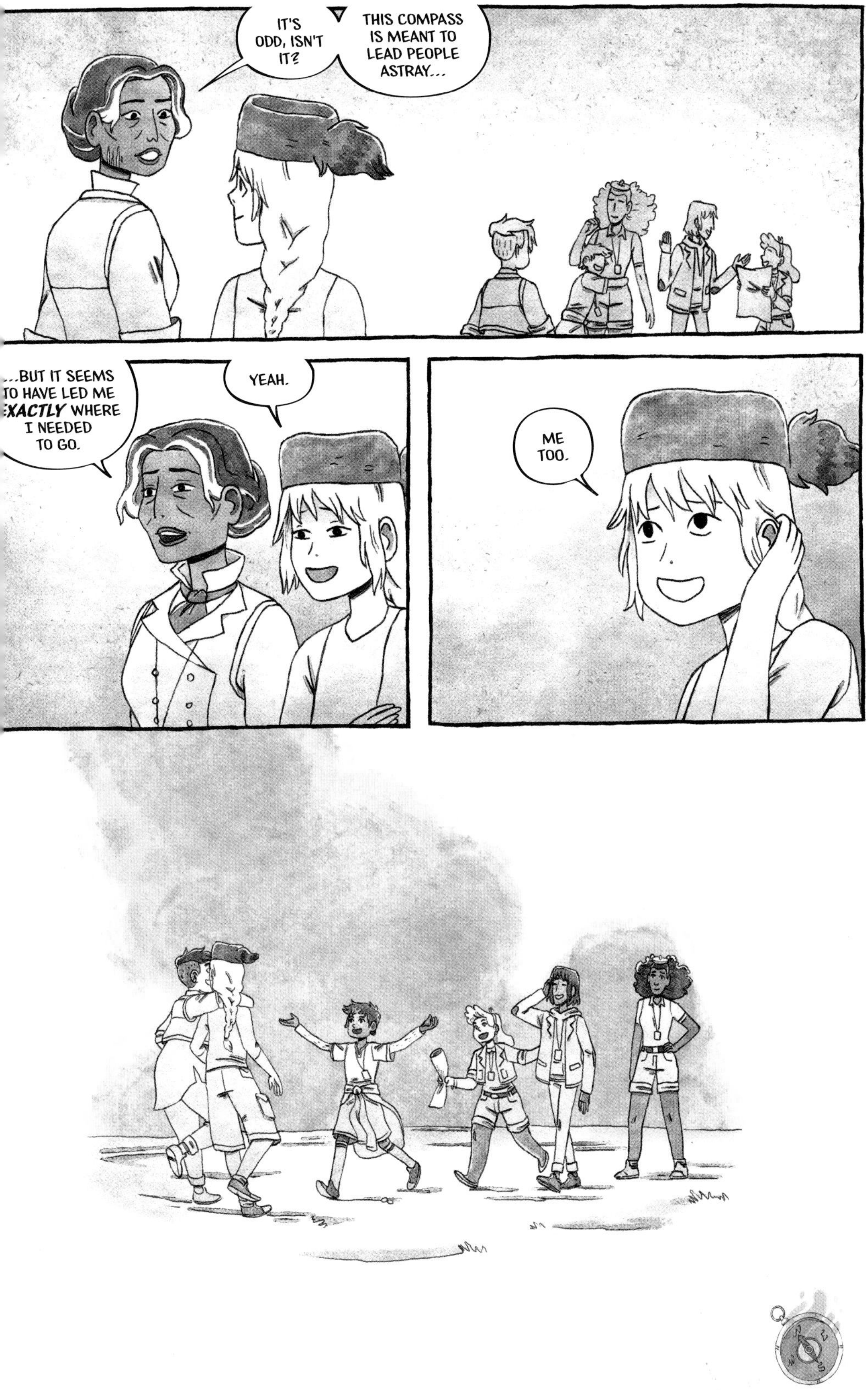
IT'S ODD, ISN'T IT?
THIS COMPASS IS MEANT TO LEAD PEOPLE ASTRAY...
...BUT IT SEEMS TO HAVE LED ME EXACTLY WHERE I NEEDED TO GO.
YEAH.
ME TOO.

Don't miss a single day at

Miss Qiunzella Thiskwin Penniquiqul Thistle Crumpet's

CAMP FOR HARDCORE LADY-TYPES!

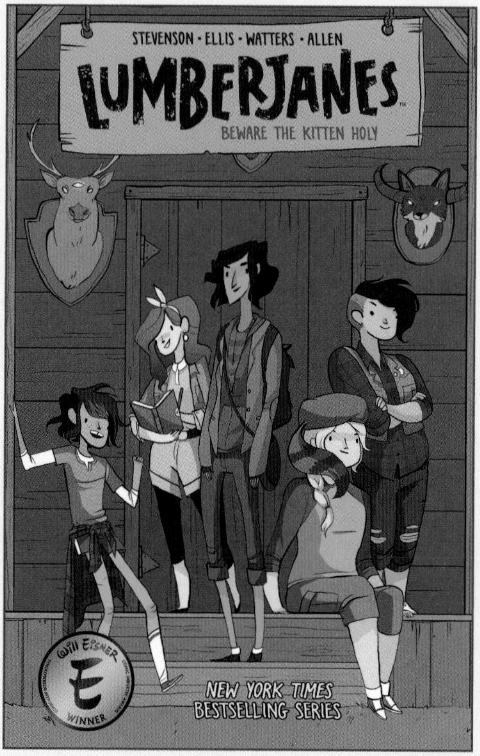
STEVENSON • ELLIS • WATTERS • ALLEN
LUMBERJANES
BEWARE THE KITTEN HOLY
Will Eisner WINNER
NEW YORK TIMES BESTSELLING SERIES

Follow the on-going adventures of the Lumberjanes in their monthly series!

LUMBERJANES Issue One

Written by

NOELLE STEVENSON & GRACE ELLIS

Illustrated by

BROOKLYN ALLEN

Colored by

MAARTA LAIHO

Lettered by

AUBREY AIESE

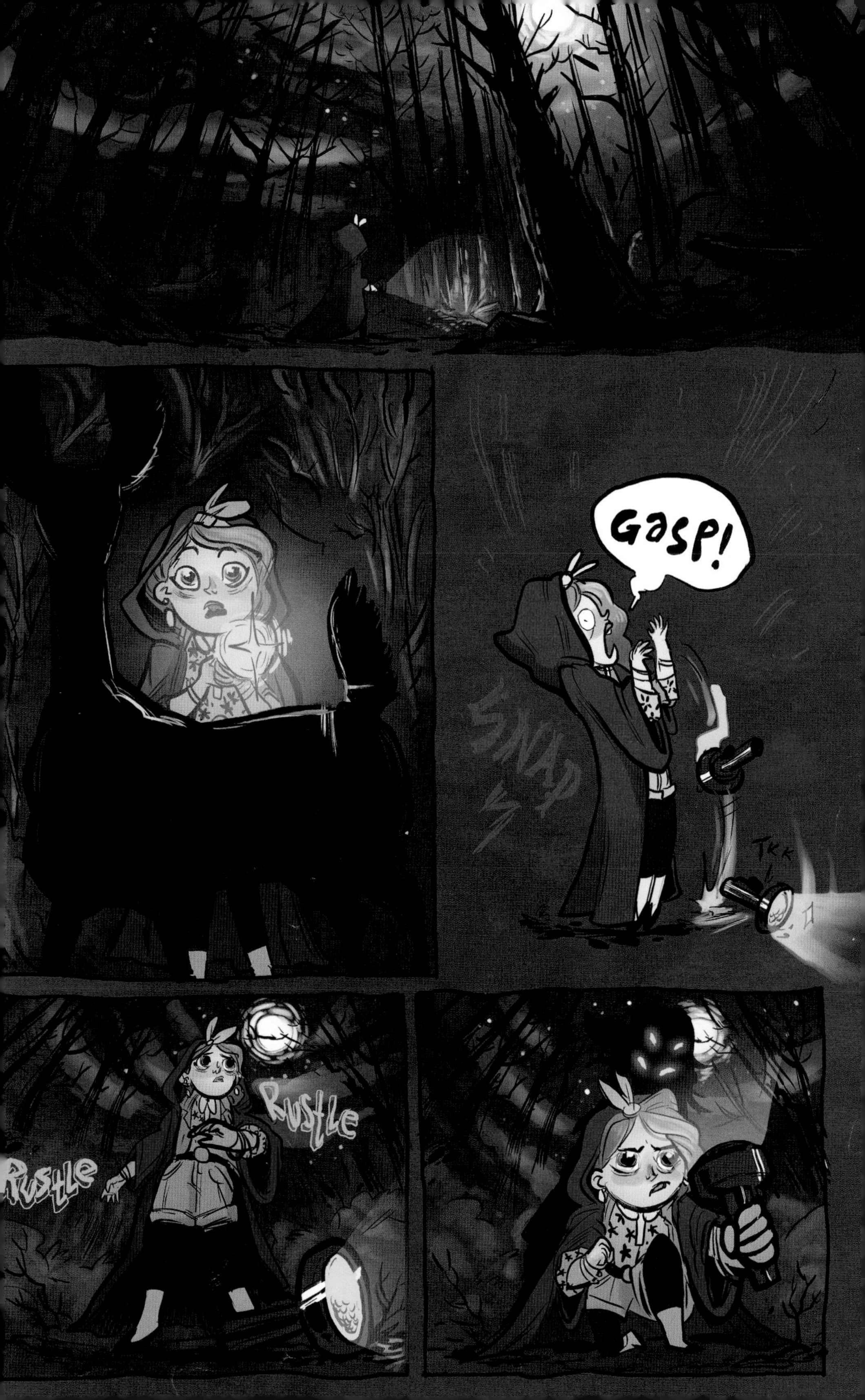
GASP!
SNAP
TKK
RUSTLE
RUSTLE

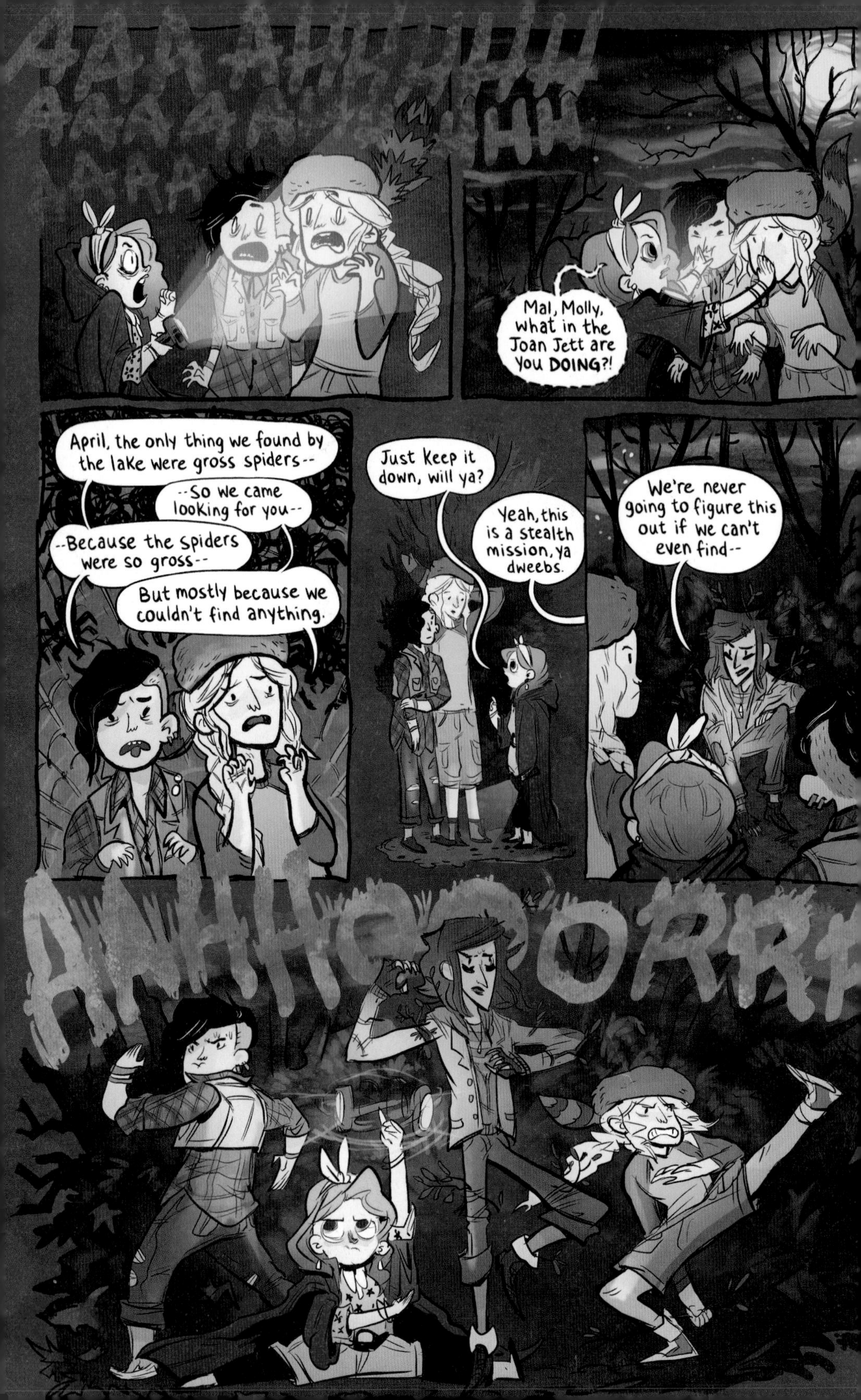
Mal, Molly, what in the Joan Jett are you DOING?!
April, the only thing we found by the lake were gross spiders--
--So we came looking for you--
--Because the spiders were so gross--
But mostly because we couldn't find anything.
Just keep it down, will ya?
Yeah, this is a stealth mission, ya dweebs.
We're never going to figure this out if we can't even find--

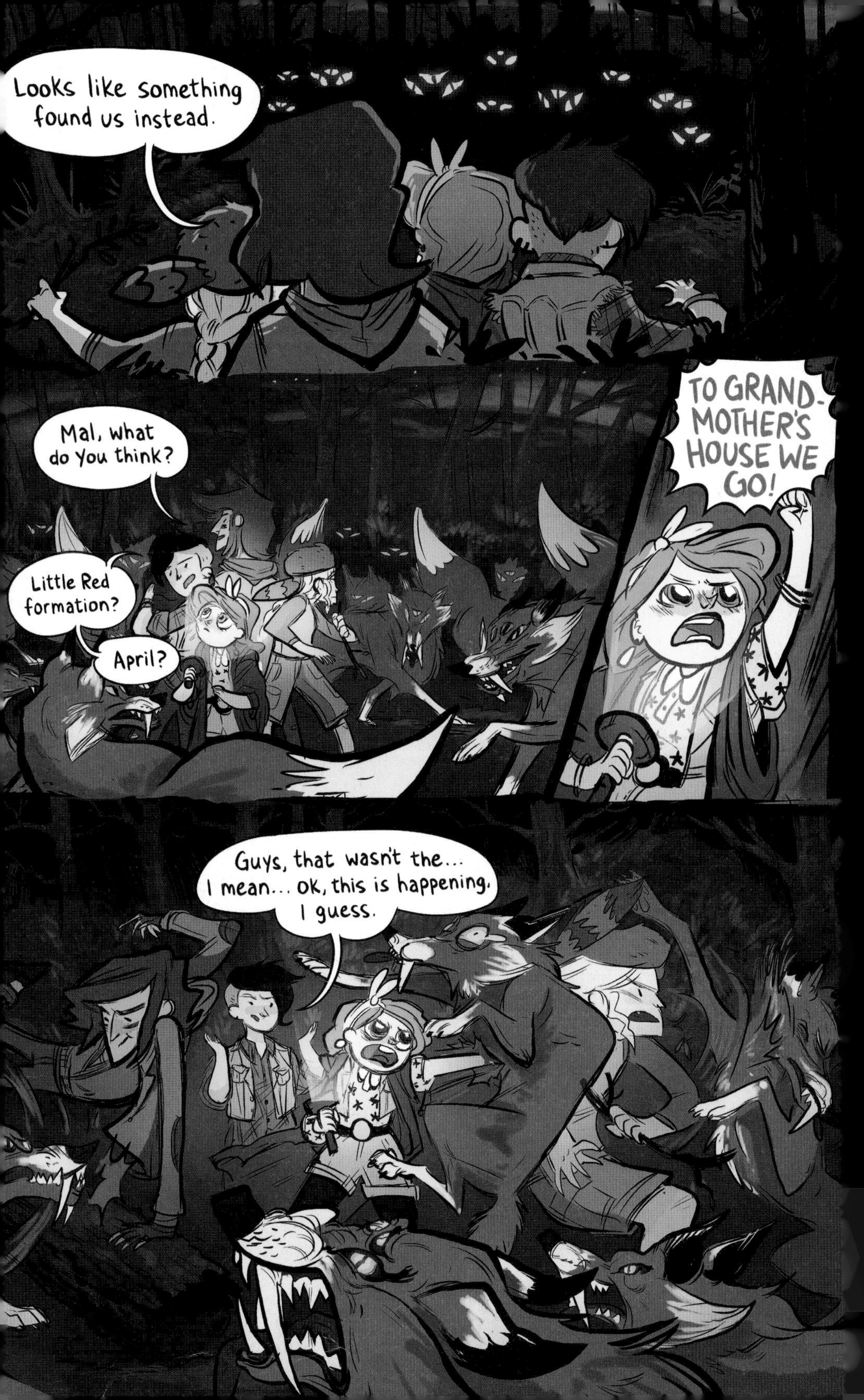
Looks like something found us instead.
Mal, what do you think?
Little Red formation?
April?
TO GRAND-MOTHER'S HOUSE WE GO!
Guys, that wasn't the... I mean... ok, this is happening, I guess.

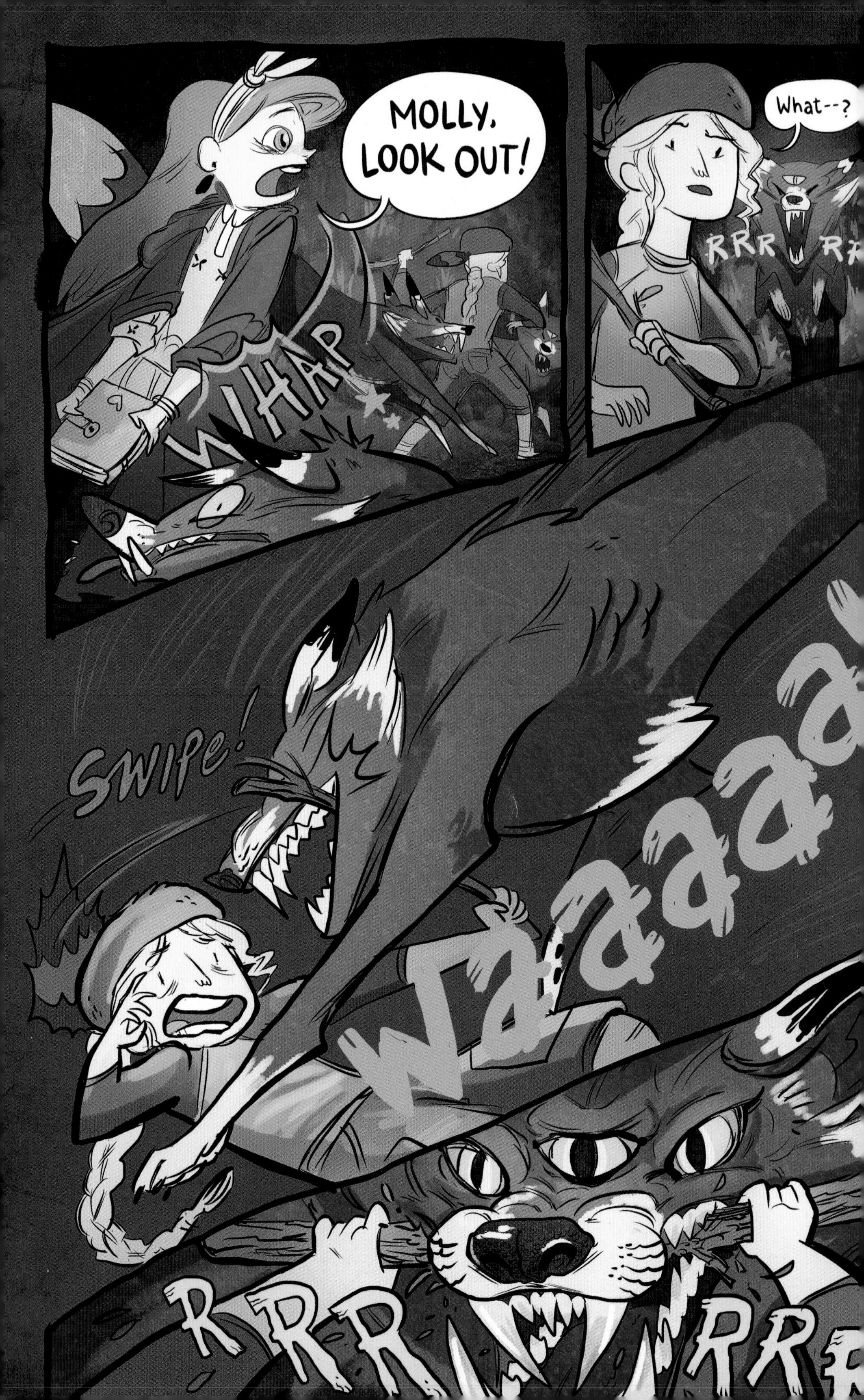
MOLLY, LOOK OUT!
WHAP
What--?
RRR RR
SWIPE!
Waaaaa
RRR RRR

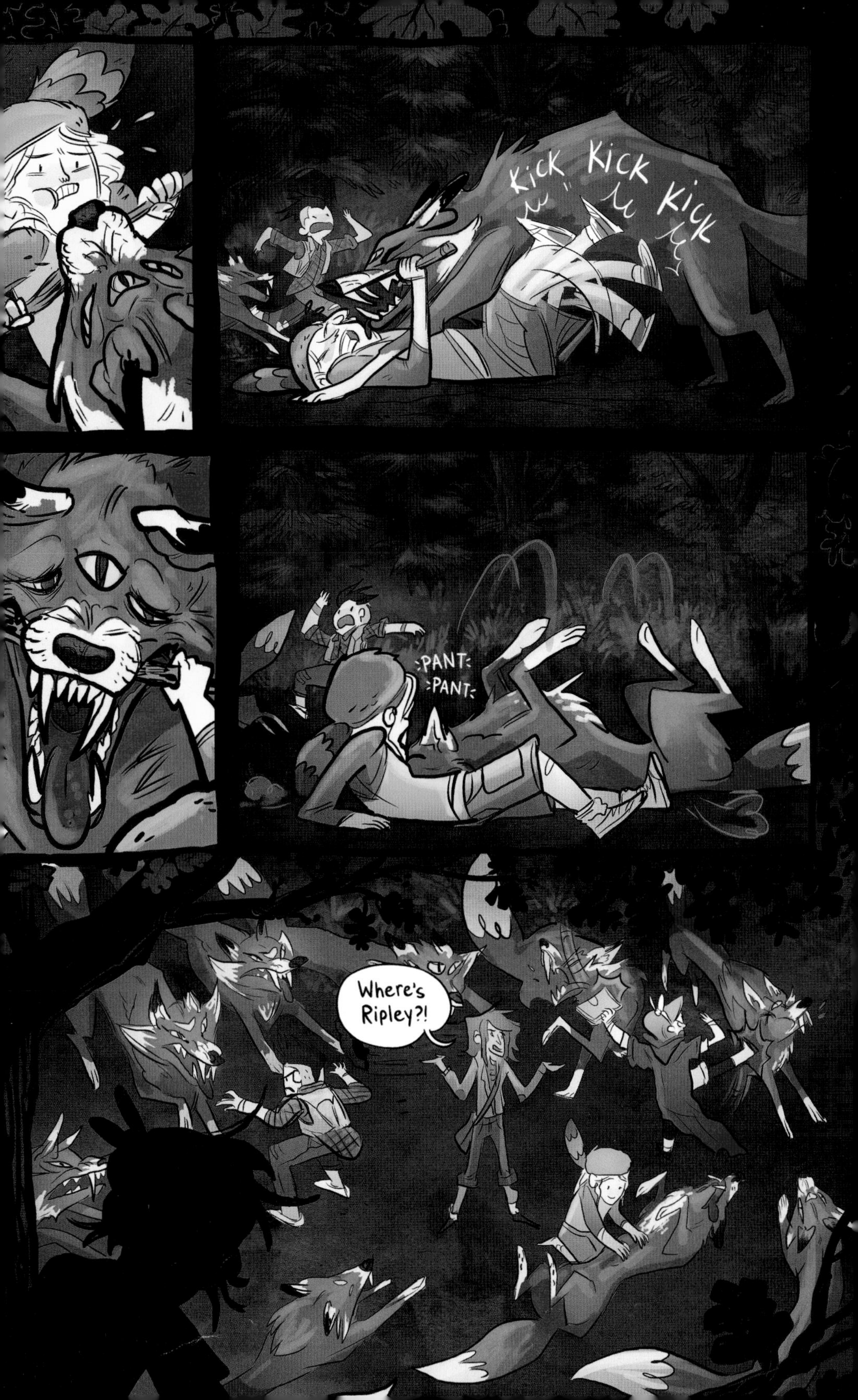
Kick Kick Kick
PANT
PANT
Where's Ripley?!

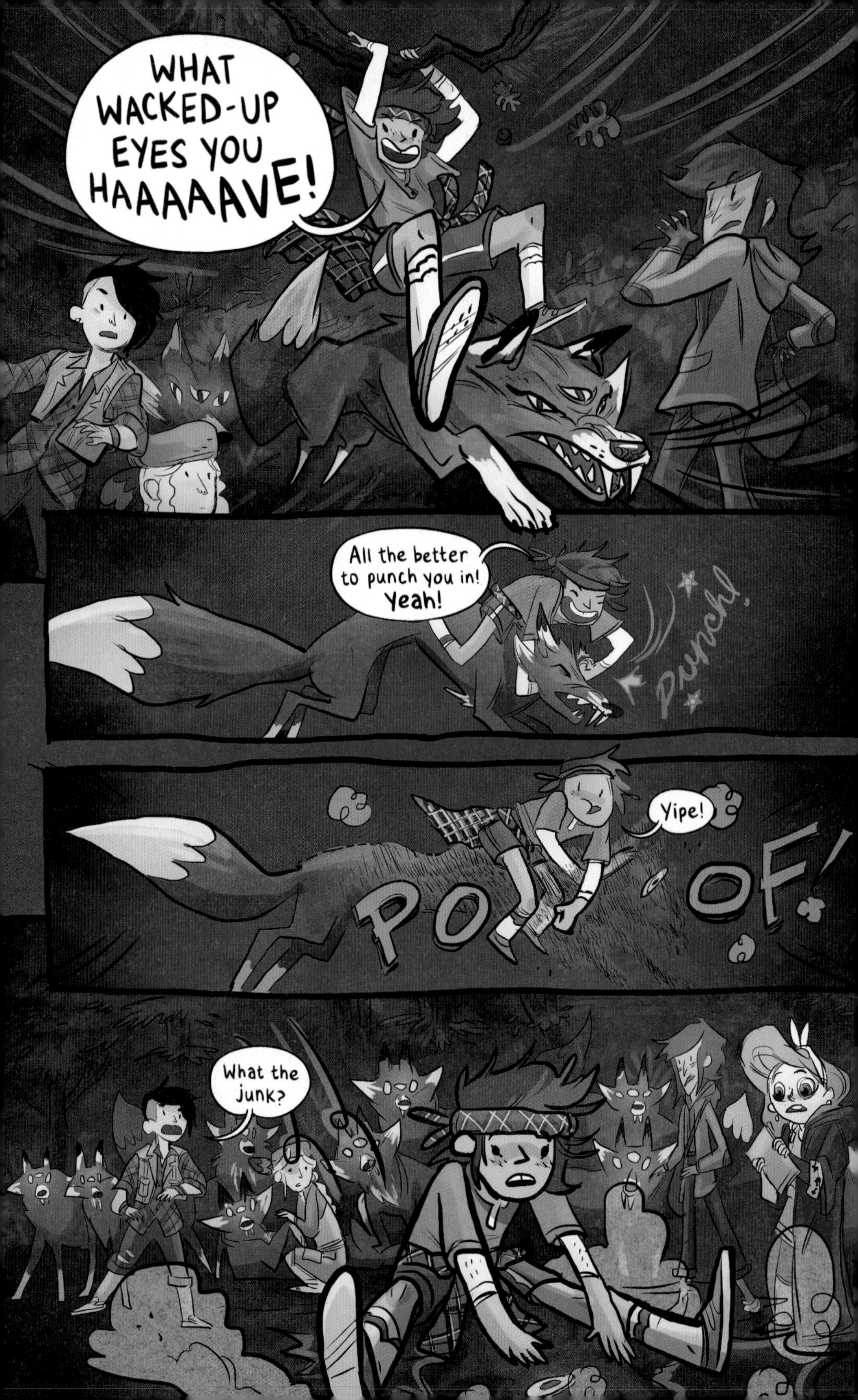
WHAT WACKED-UP EYES YOU HAAAAAVE!
All the better to punch you in! Yeah!
Punch!
Yipe!
POOF!
What the junk?

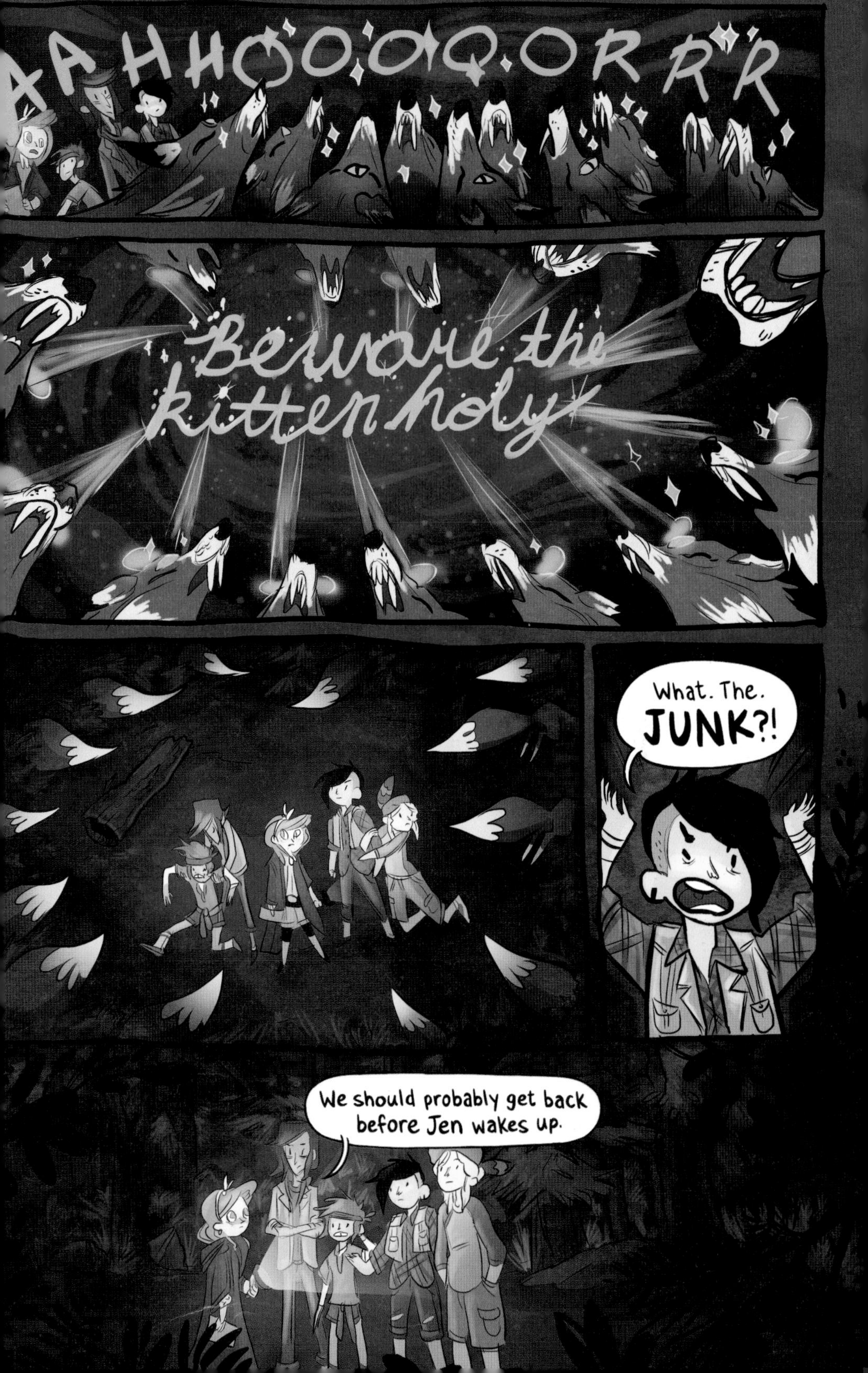
AAHHOOOOORRR
Beware the kitten holy
What. The. JUNK?!
We should probably get back before Jen wakes up.

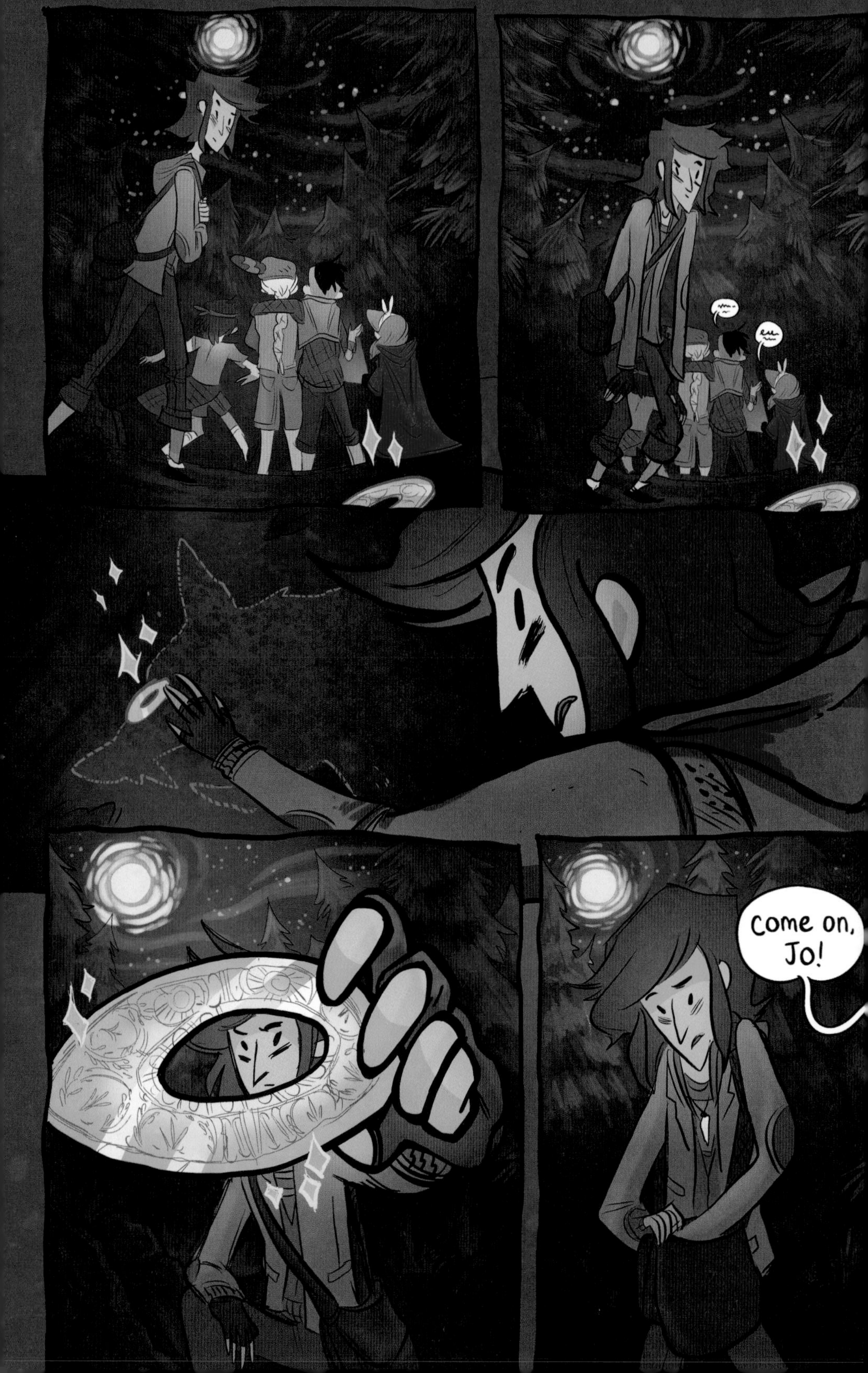
Come on, Jo!

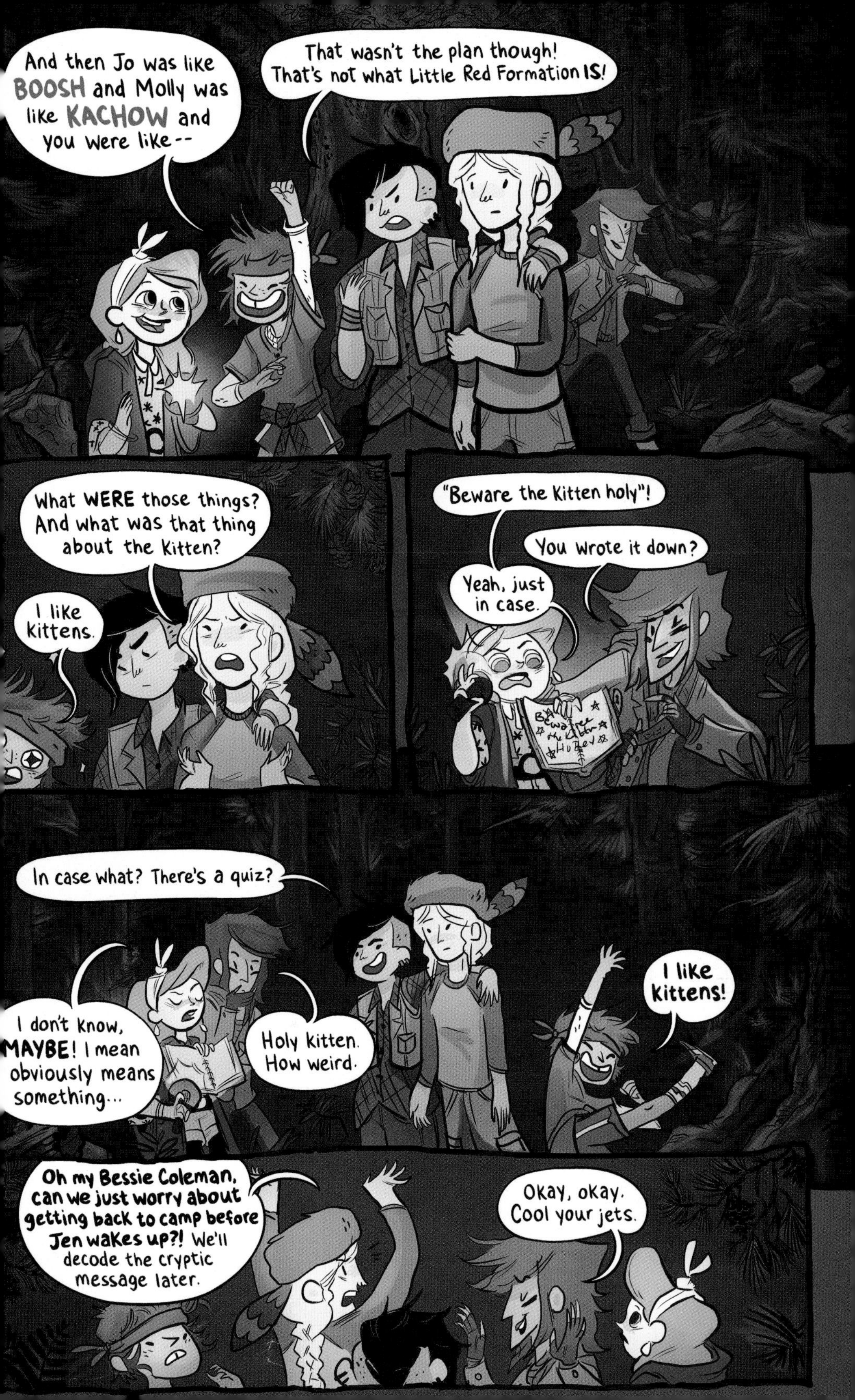
And then Jo was like BOOSH and Molly was like KACHOW and you were like--
That wasn't the plan though! That's not what Little Red Formation IS!
What WERE those things? And what was that thing about the Kitten?
I like kittens.
"Beware the Kitten holy"!
Yeah, just in case.
You wrote it down?
In case what? There's a quiz?
I don't know, MAYBE! I mean obviously means something...
Holy kitten. How weird.
I like kittens!
Oh my Bessie Coleman, can we just worry about getting back to camp before Jen wakes up?! We'll decode the cryptic message later.
Okay, okay. Cool your jets.

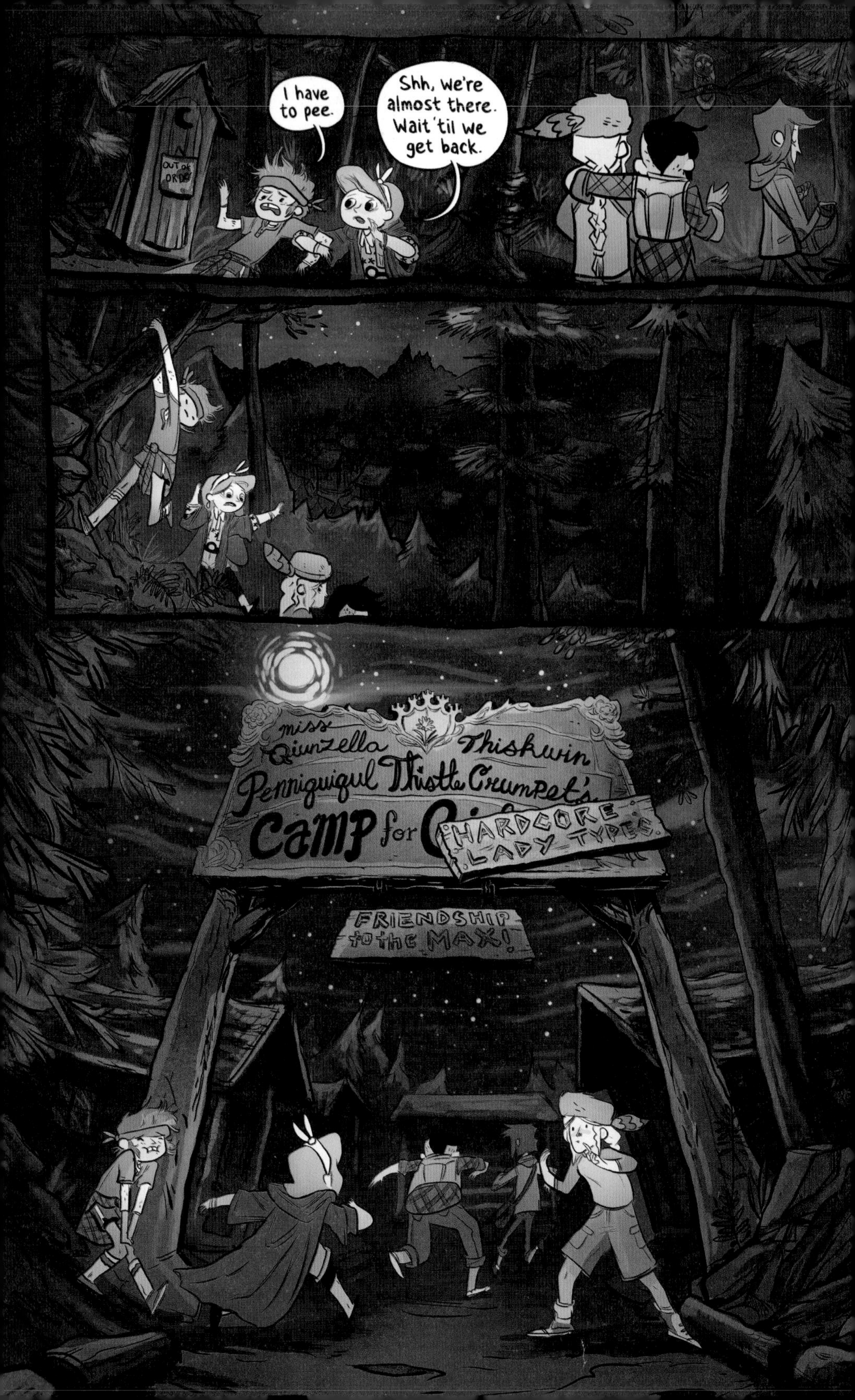
OUT OF ORDER
I have to pee.
Shh, we're almost there. Wait 'til we get back.
miss Quinzella Thiskwin Penniquiqul Thistle Crumpet's
Camp for
HARDCORE LADY TYPES
FRIENDSHIP to the MAX!

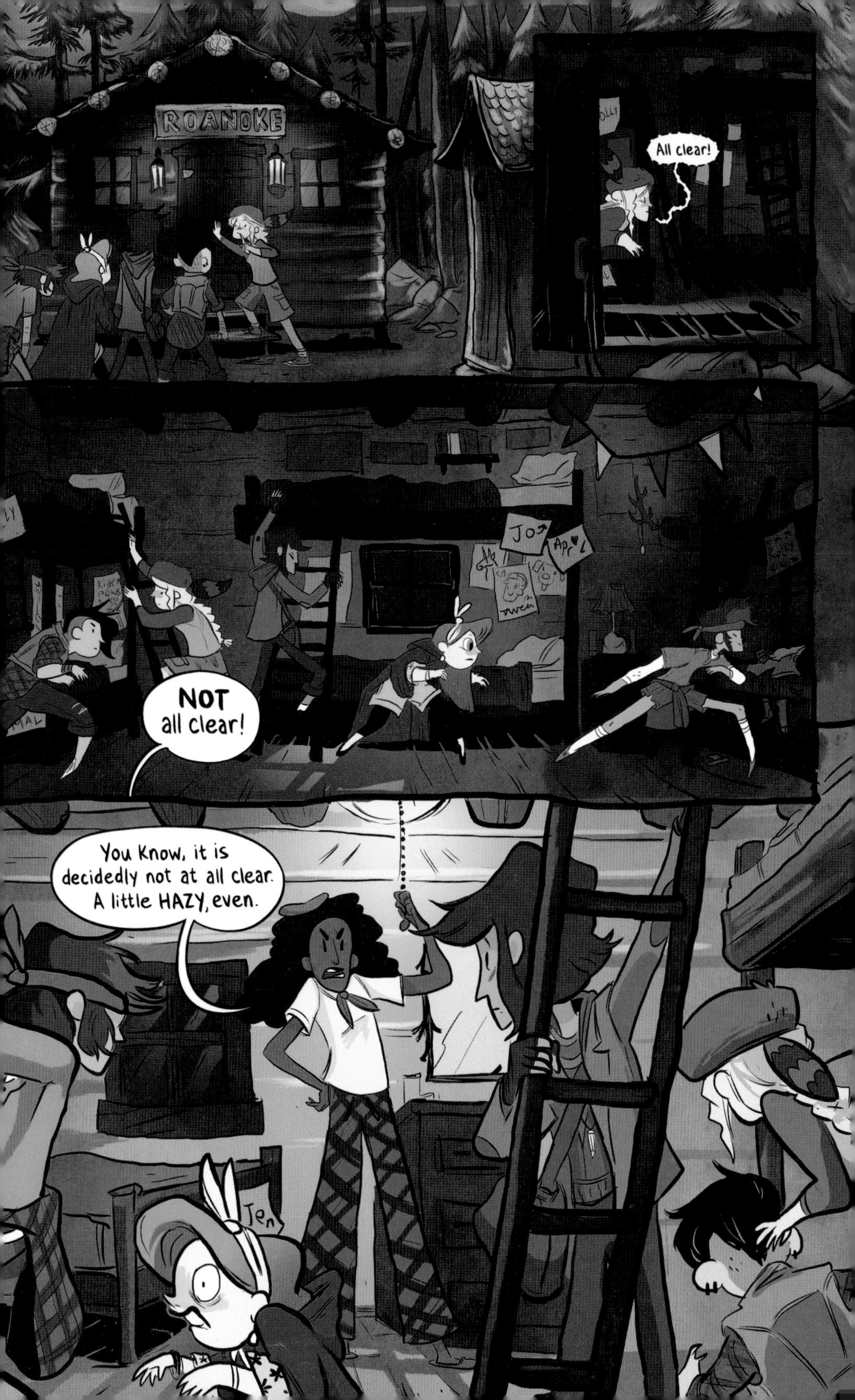
ROANOKE
All clear!
NOT all clear!
You know, it is decidedly not at all clear. A little HAZY, even.

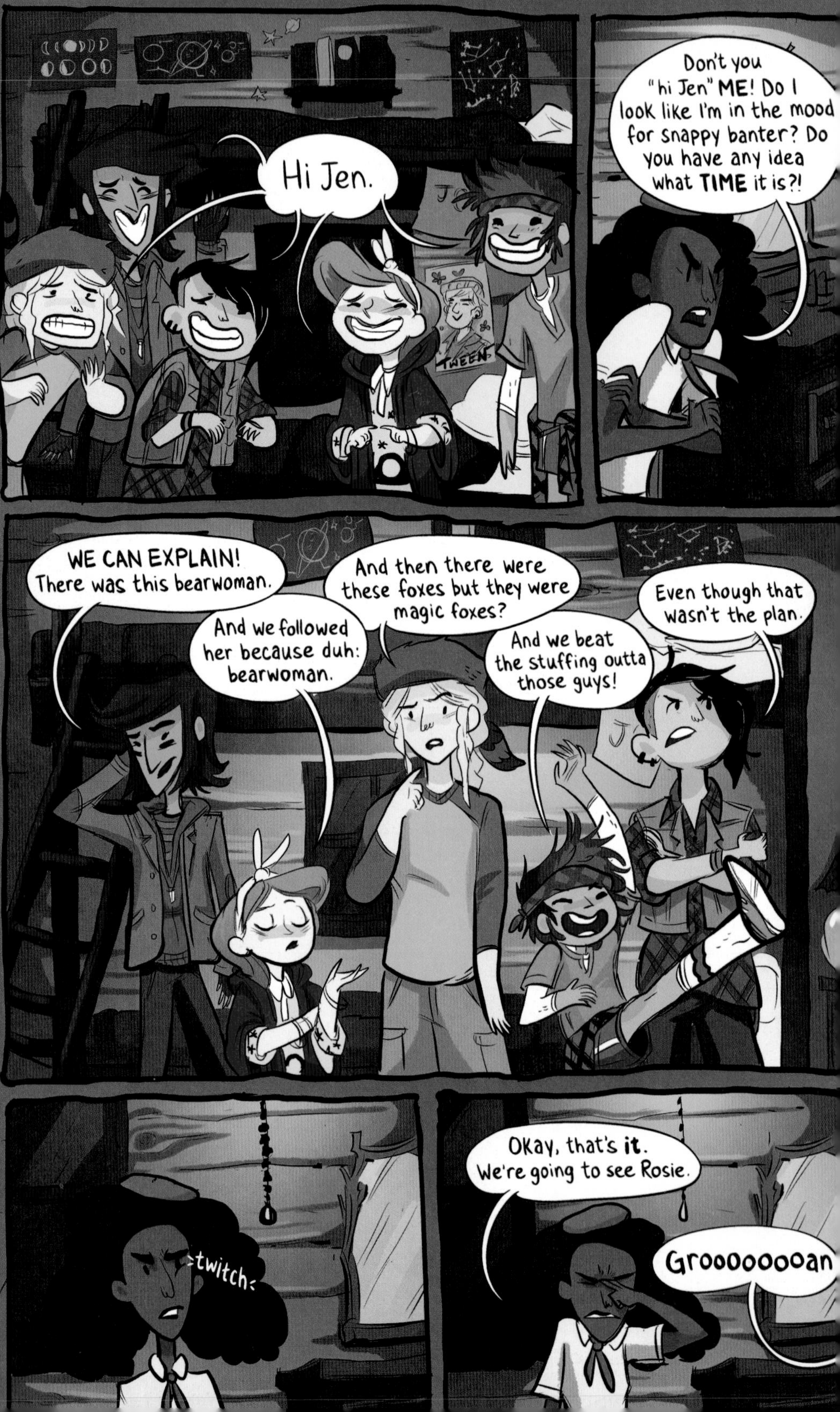
Hi Jen.
Don't you "hi Jen" ME! Do I look like I'm in the mood for snappy banter? Do you have any idea what TIME it is?!
WE CAN EXPLAIN! There was this bearwoman.
And we followed her because duh: bearwoman.
And then there were these foxes but they were magic foxes?
And we beat the stuffing outta those guys!
Even though that wasn't the plan.
twitch
Okay, that's it. We're going to see Rosie.
Groooooooan

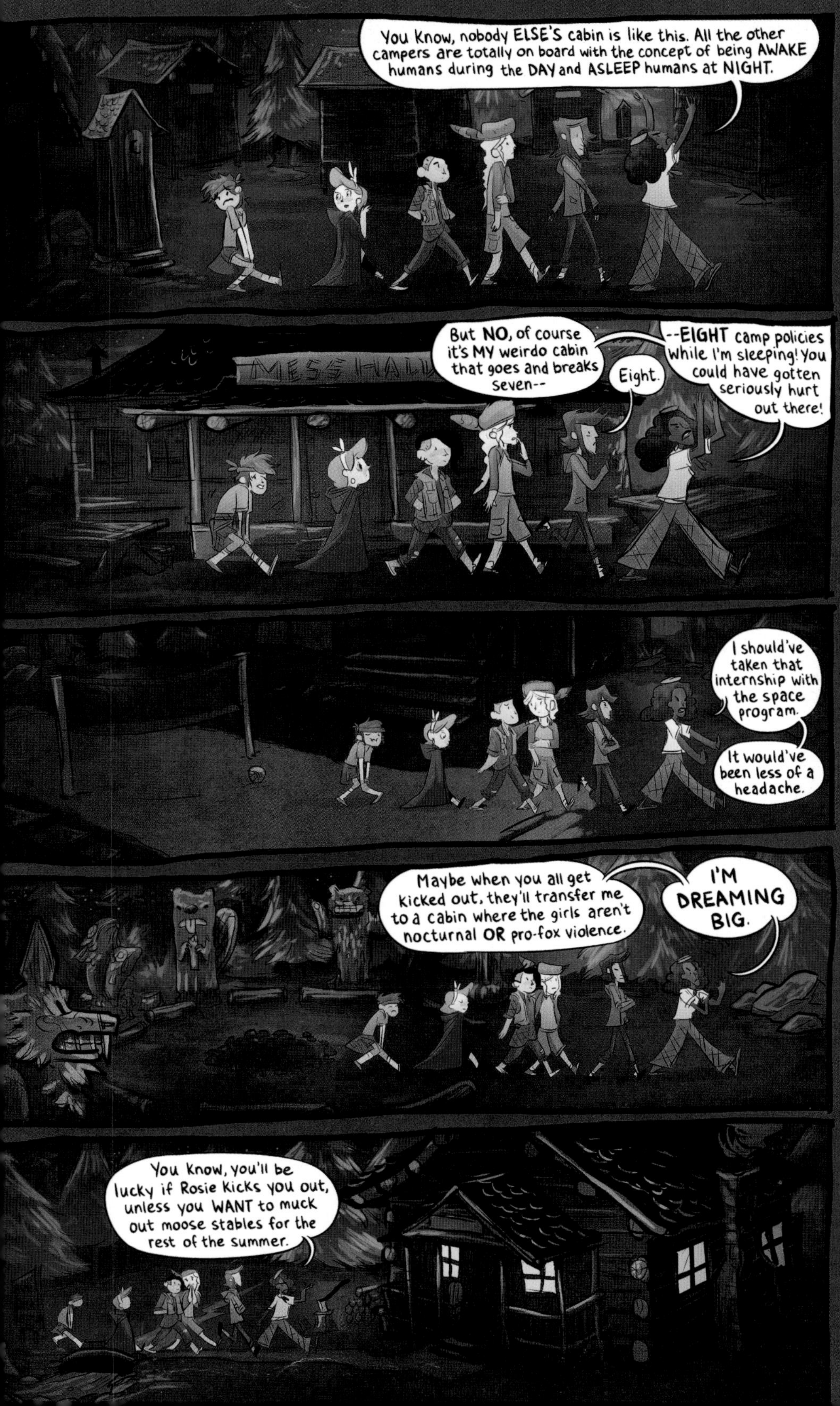
You know, nobody ELSE'S cabin is like this. All the other campers are totally on board with the concept of being AWAKE humans during the DAY and ASLEEP humans at NIGHT.
MESS HALL
But NO, of course it's MY weirdo cabin that goes and breaks seven--
Eight.
--EIGHT camp policies while I'm sleeping! You could have gotten seriously hurt out there!
I should've taken that internship with the space program.
It would've been less of a headache.
Maybe when you all get kicked out, they'll transfer me to a cabin where the girls aren't nocturnal OR pro-fox violence.
I'M DREAMING BIG.
You know, you'll be lucky if Rosie kicks you out, unless you WANT to muck out moose stables for the rest of the summer.

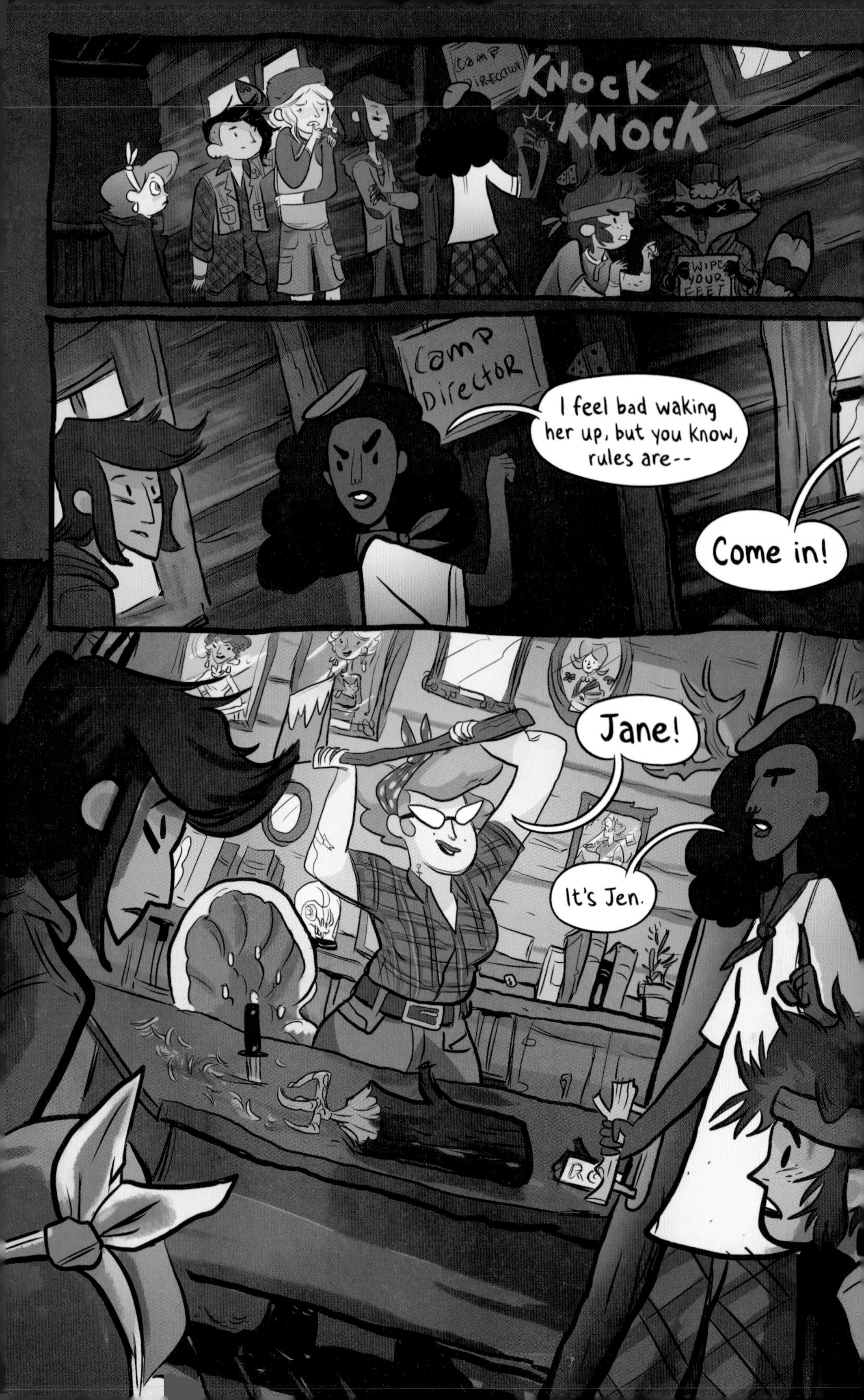
CAMP DIRECTOR
KNOCK KNOCK
WIPE YOUR FEET
CAMP DIRECTOR
I feel bad waking her up, but you know, rules are--
Come in!
Jane!
It's Jen.

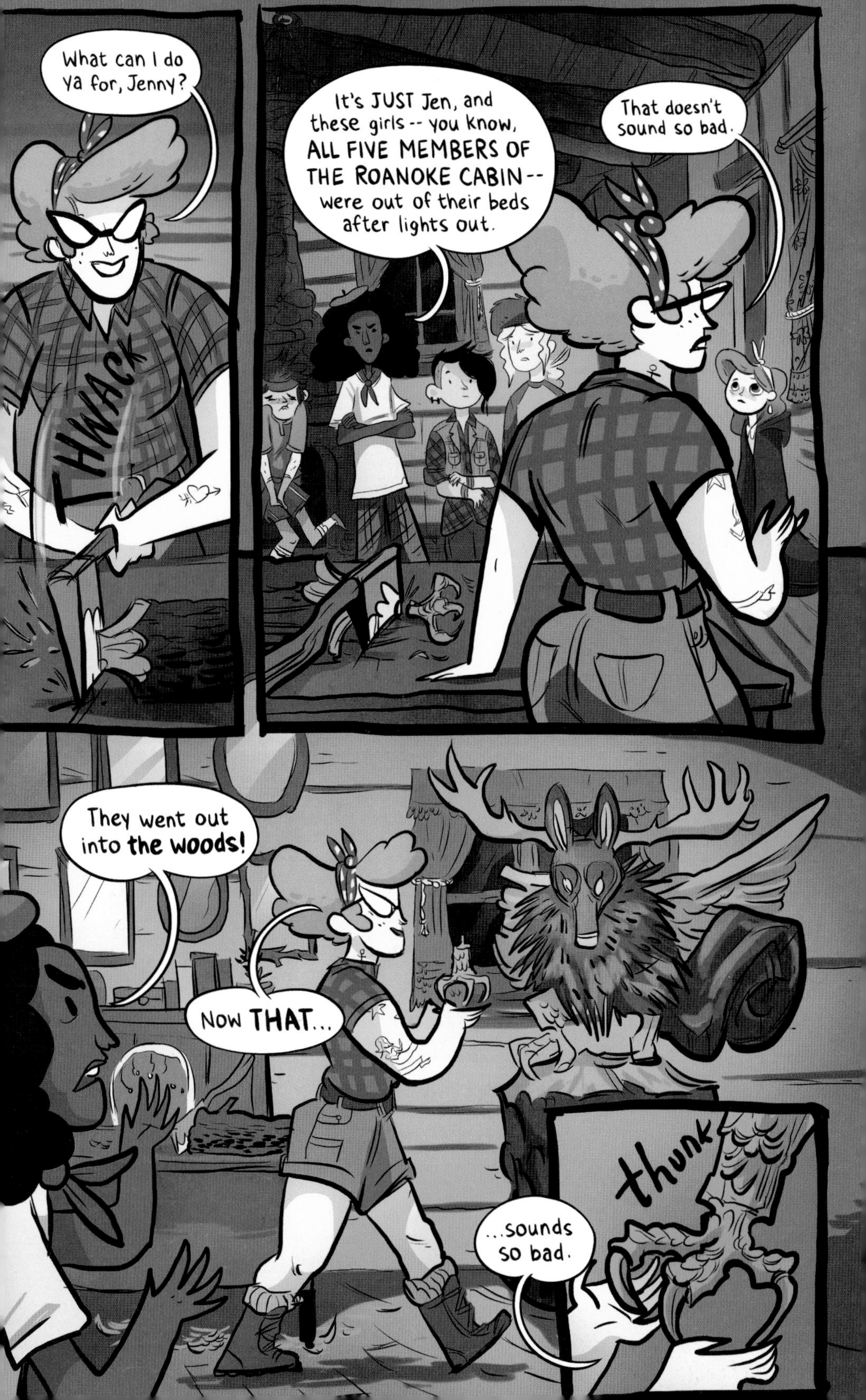
What can I do ya for, Jenny?
THWACK
It's JUST Jen, and these girls -- you know, ALL FIVE MEMBERS OF THE ROANOKE CABIN -- were out of their beds after lights out.
That doesn't sound so bad.
They went out into the woods!
Now THAT...
thunk
...sounds so bad.

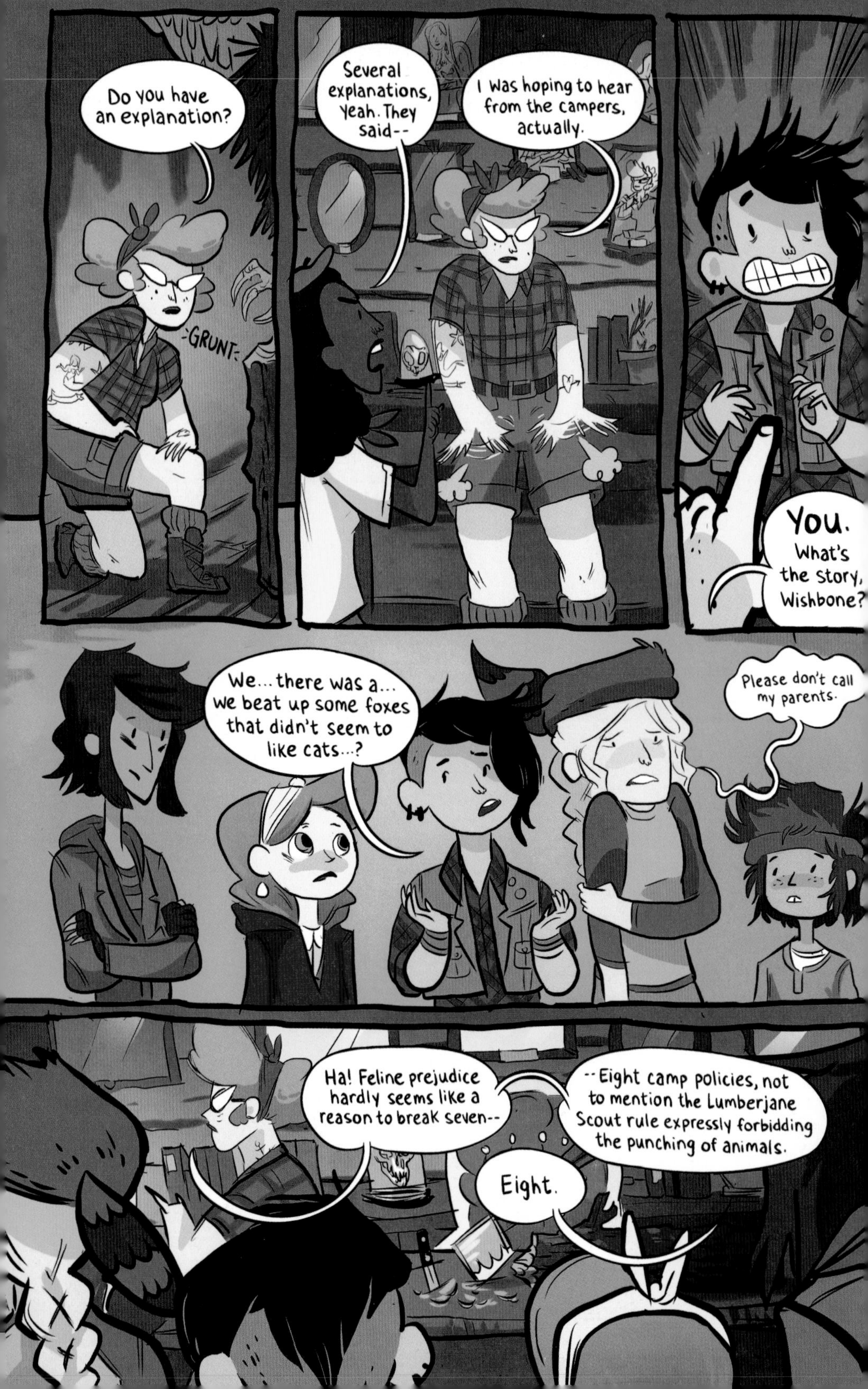
Do you have an explanation?
-GRUNT-
Several explanations, Yeah. They said--
I was hoping to hear from the campers, actually.
YOU. What's the story, Wishbone?
We... there was a... we beat up some foxes that didn't seem to like cats...?
Please don't call my parents.
Ha! Feline prejudice hardly seems like a reason to break seven--
Eight.
--Eight camp policies, not to mention the Lumberjane Scout rule expressly forbidding the punching of animals.

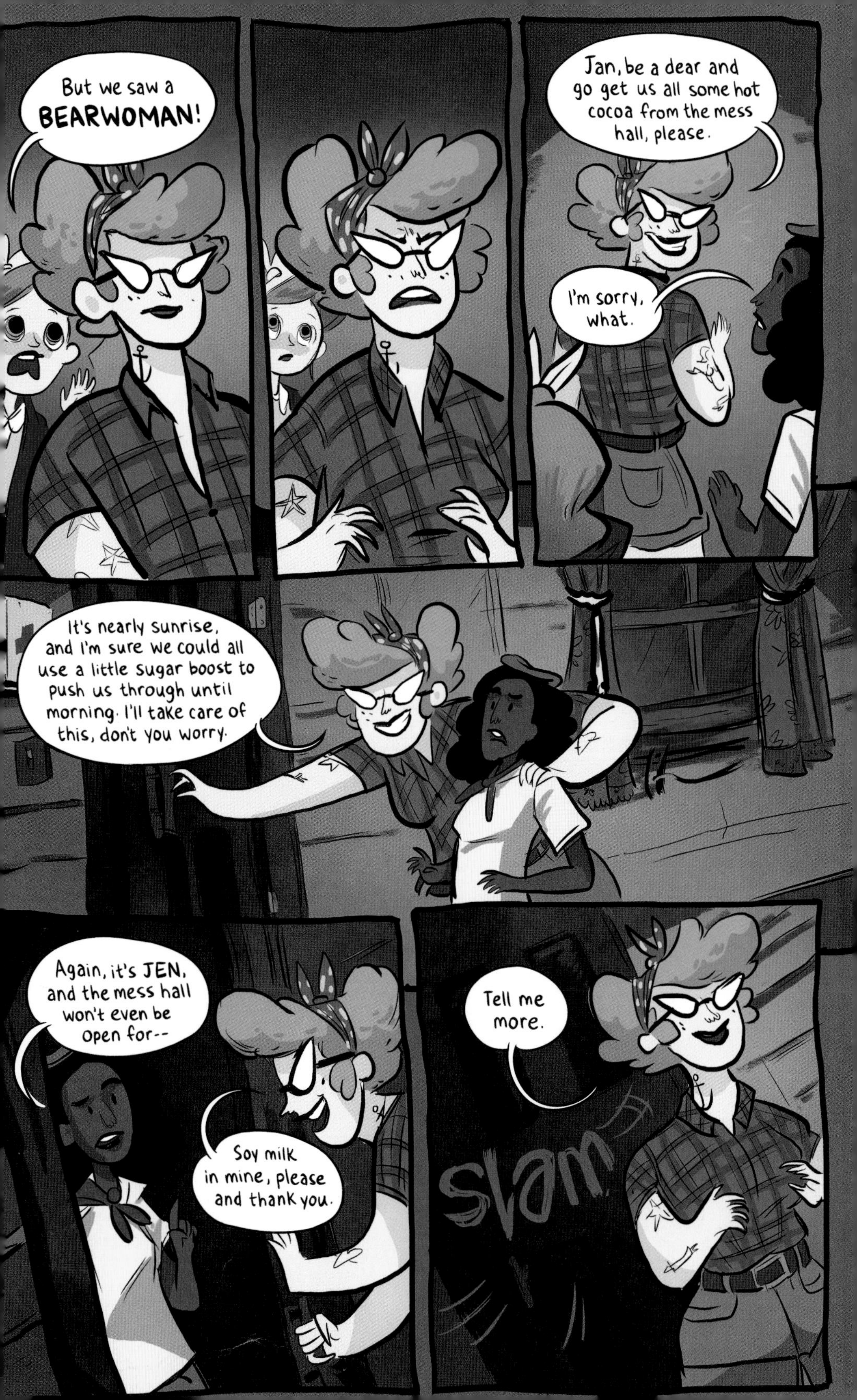

But we saw a BEARWOMAN!
Jan, be a dear and go get us all some hot cocoa from the mess hall, please.
I'm sorry, what.
It's nearly sunrise, and I'm sure we could all use a little sugar boost to push us through until morning. I'll take care of this, don't you worry.
Again, it's JEN, and the mess hall won't even be open for--
Soy milk in mine, please and thank you.
SLAM
Tell me more.

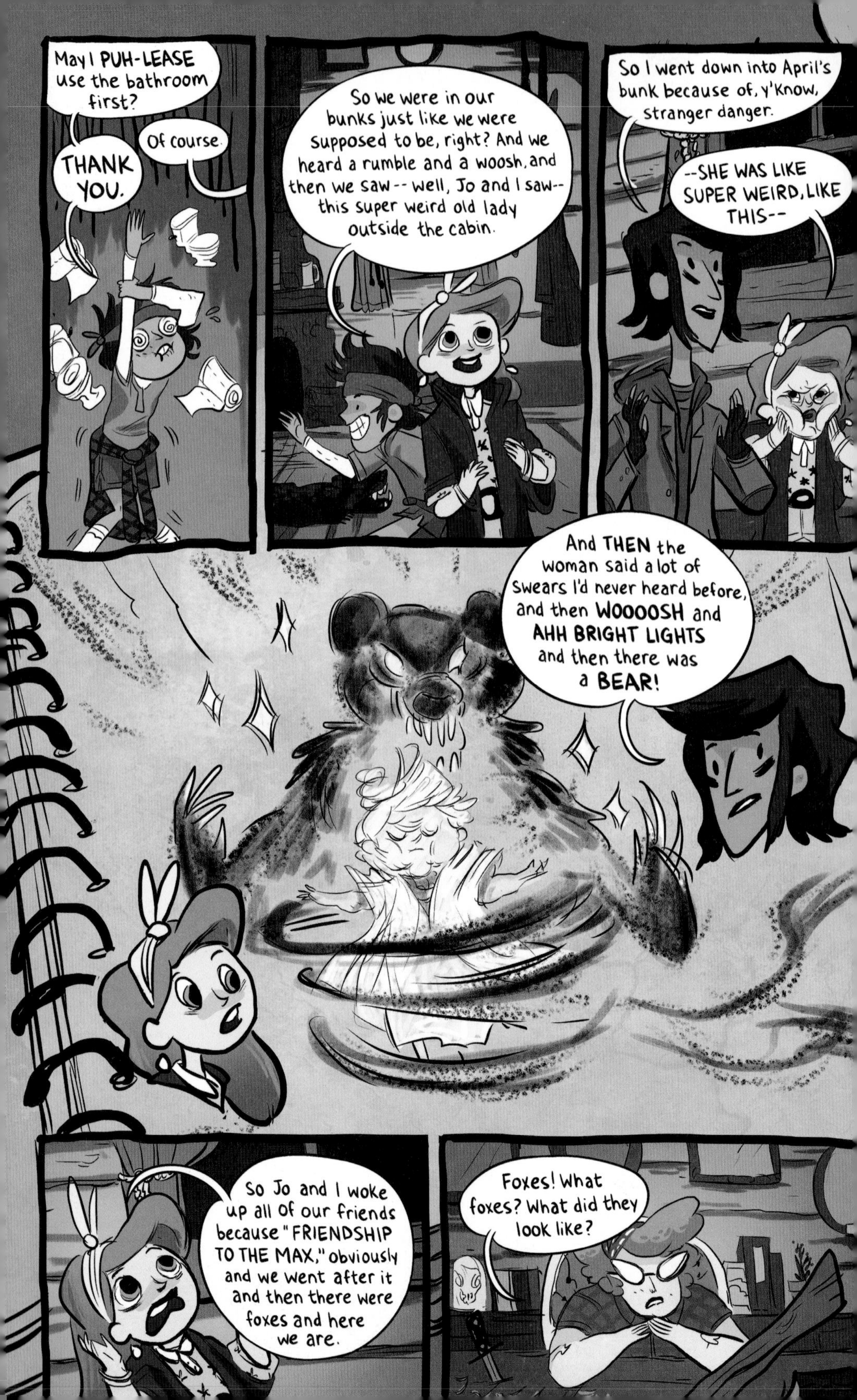
May I PUH-LEASE use the bathroom first?
Of course.
THANK YOU.
So we were in our bunks just like we were supposed to be, right? And we heard a rumble and a woosh, and then we saw -- well, Jo and I saw -- this super weird old lady outside the cabin.
So I went down into April's bunk because of, y'know, stranger danger.
--SHE WAS LIKE SUPER WEIRD, LIKE THIS--
And THEN the woman said a lot of swears I'd never heard before, and then WOOOOSH and AHH BRIGHT LIGHTS and then there was a BEAR!
So Jo and I woke up all of our friends because "FRIENDSHIP TO THE MAX," obviously and we went after it and then there were foxes and here we are.
Foxes! What foxes? What did they look like?

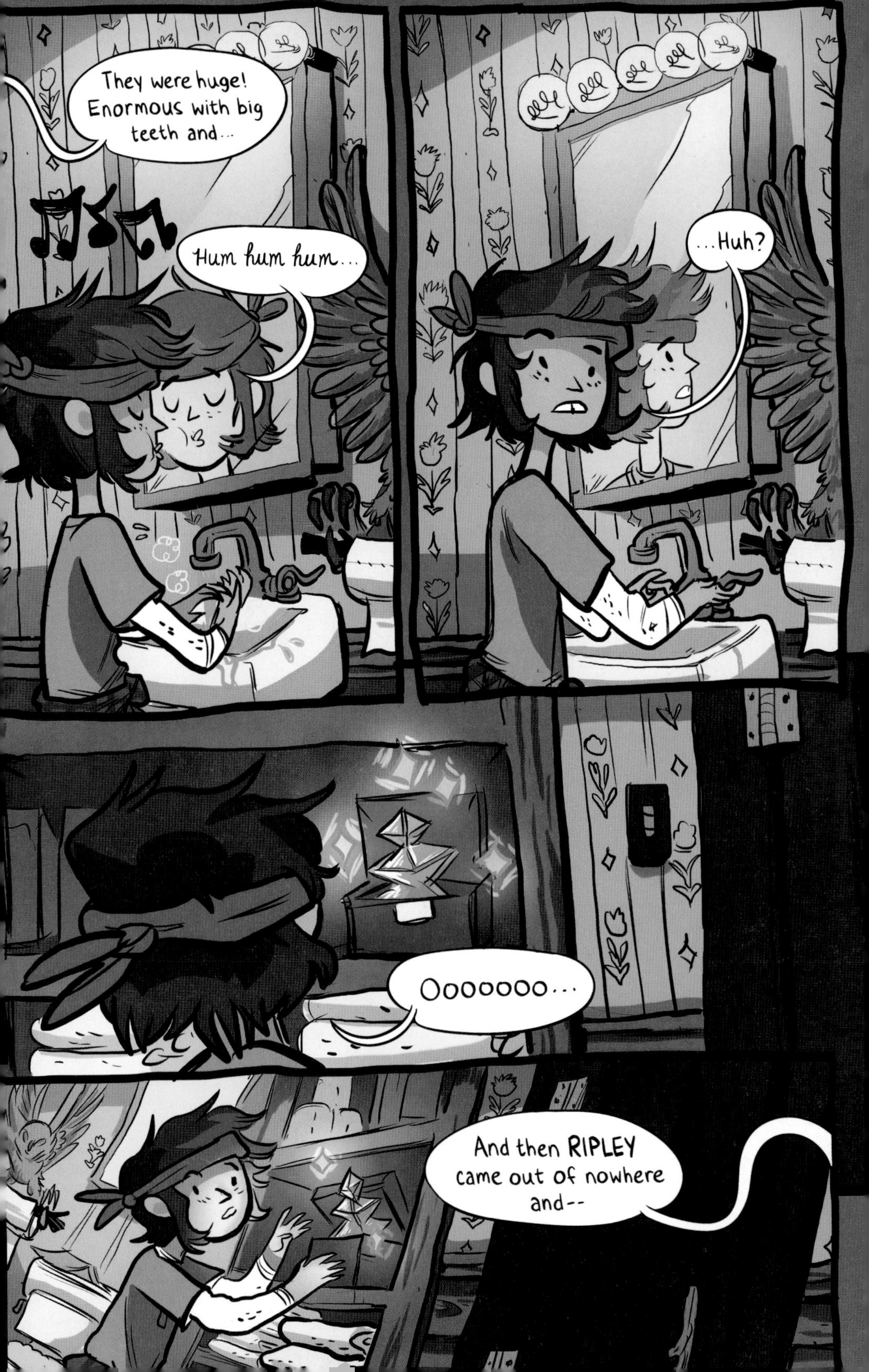
They were huge! Enormous with big teeth and...
Hum hum hum...
...Huh?
Ooooooo...
And then RIPLEY came out of nowhere and--

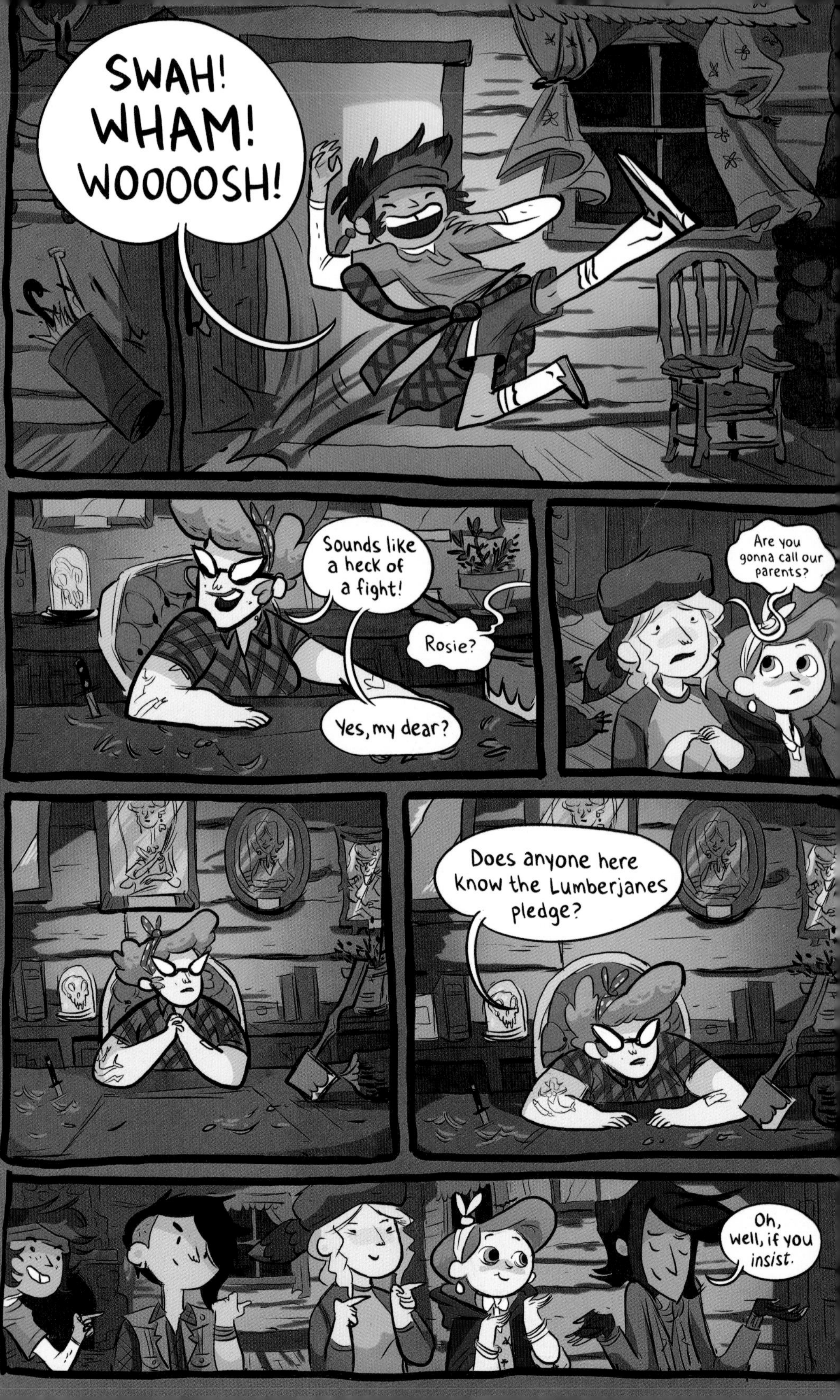
SWAH! WHAM! WOOOOSH!
Sounds like a heck of a fight!
Rosie?
Yes, my dear?
Are you gonna call our parents?
Does anyone here know the Lumberjanes pledge?
Oh, well, if you insist.

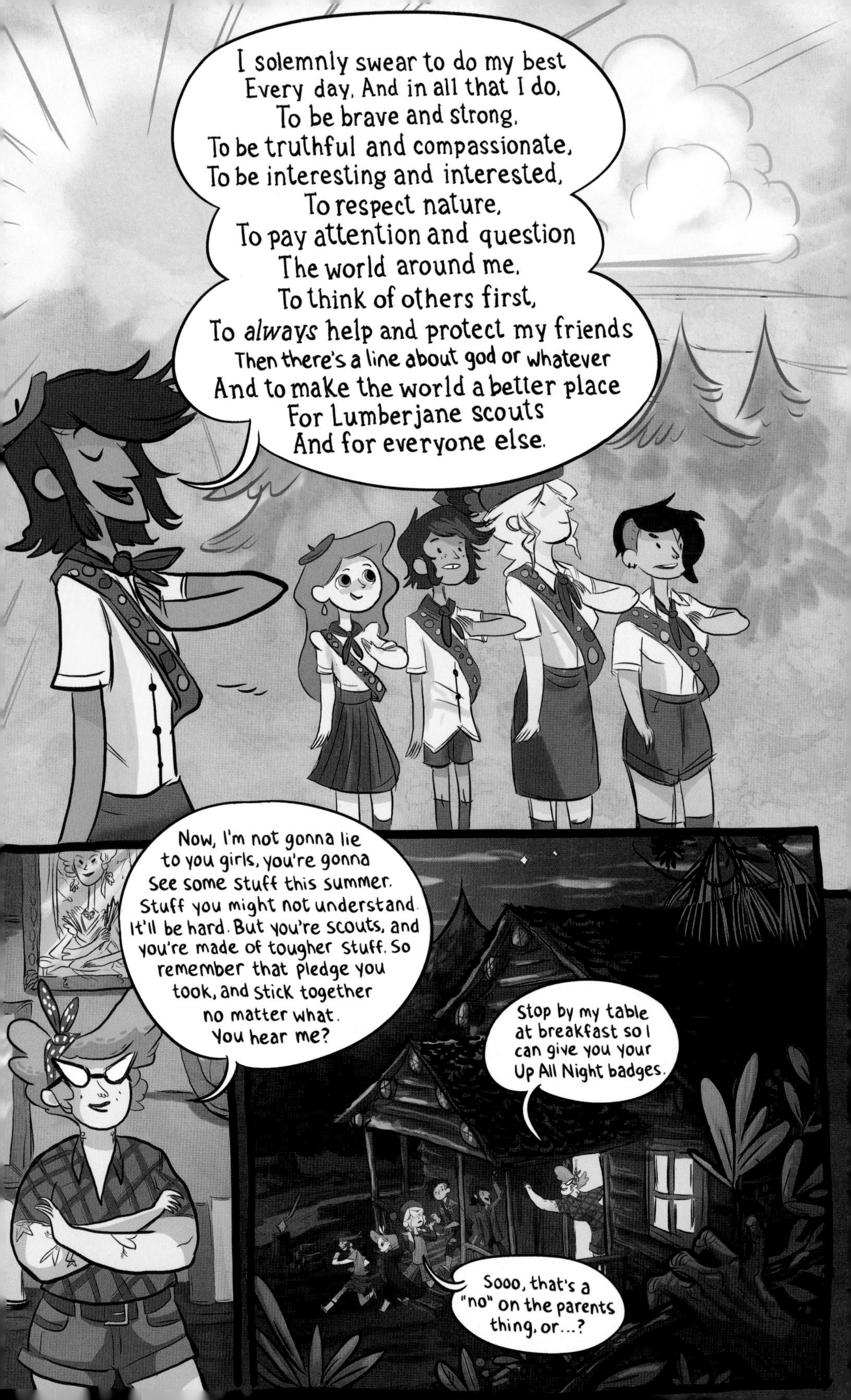
I solemnly swear to do my best Every day. And in all that I do, To be brave and strong, To be truthful and compassionate, To be interesting and interested, To respect nature, To pay attention and question The world around me, To think of others first, To *always* help and protect my friends Then there's a line about god or whatever And to make the world a better place For Lumberjane scouts And for everyone else.
Now, I'm not gonna lie to you girls, you're gonna see some stuff this summer. Stuff you might not understand. It'll be hard. But you're scouts, and you're made of tougher stuff. So remember that pledge you took, and stick together no matter what. You hear me?
Stop by my table at breakfast so I can give you your Up All Night badges.
Sooo, that's a "no" on the parents thing, or...?

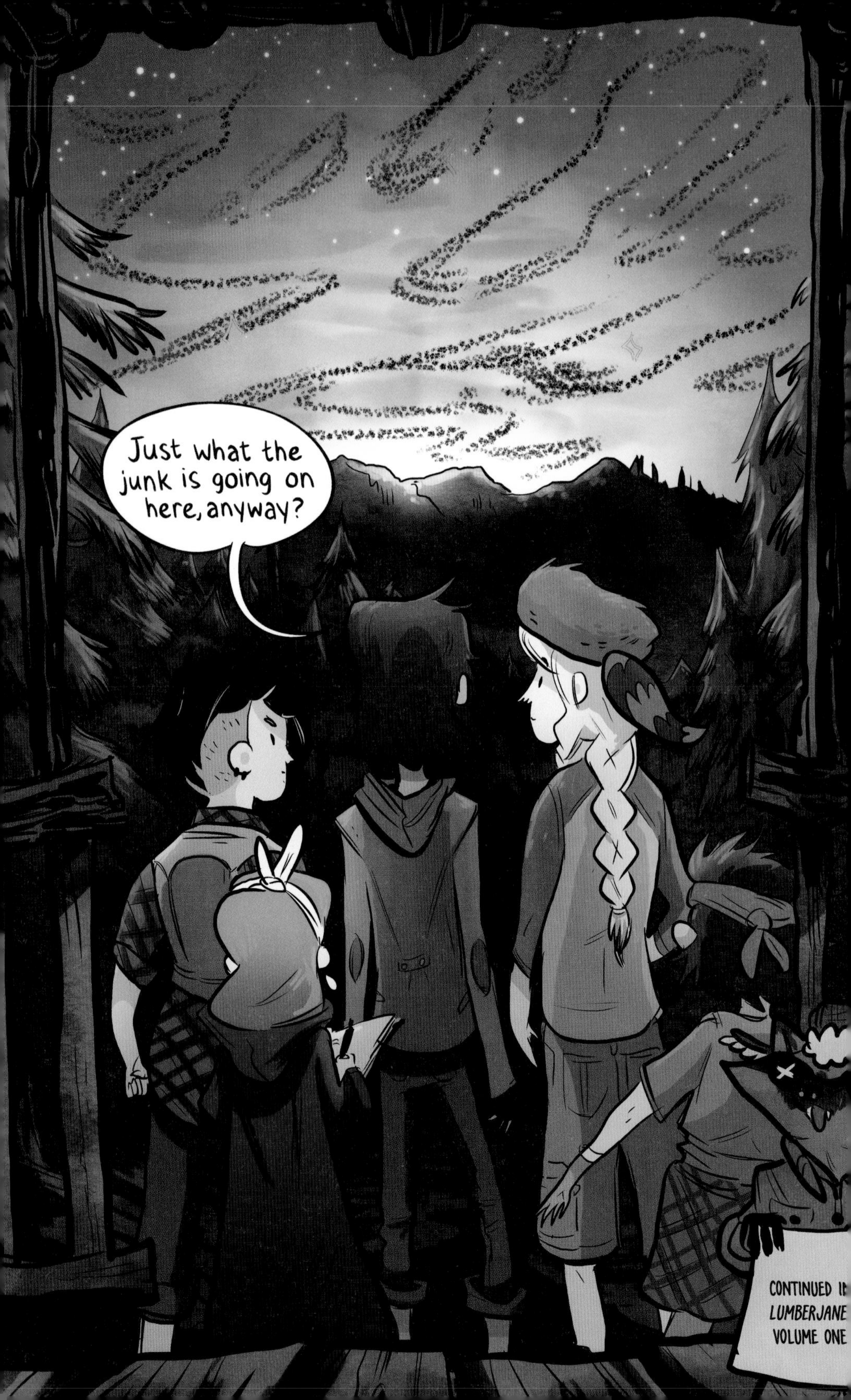
Just what the junk is going on here, anyway?
CONTINUED I
LUMBERJANE
VOLUME ONE

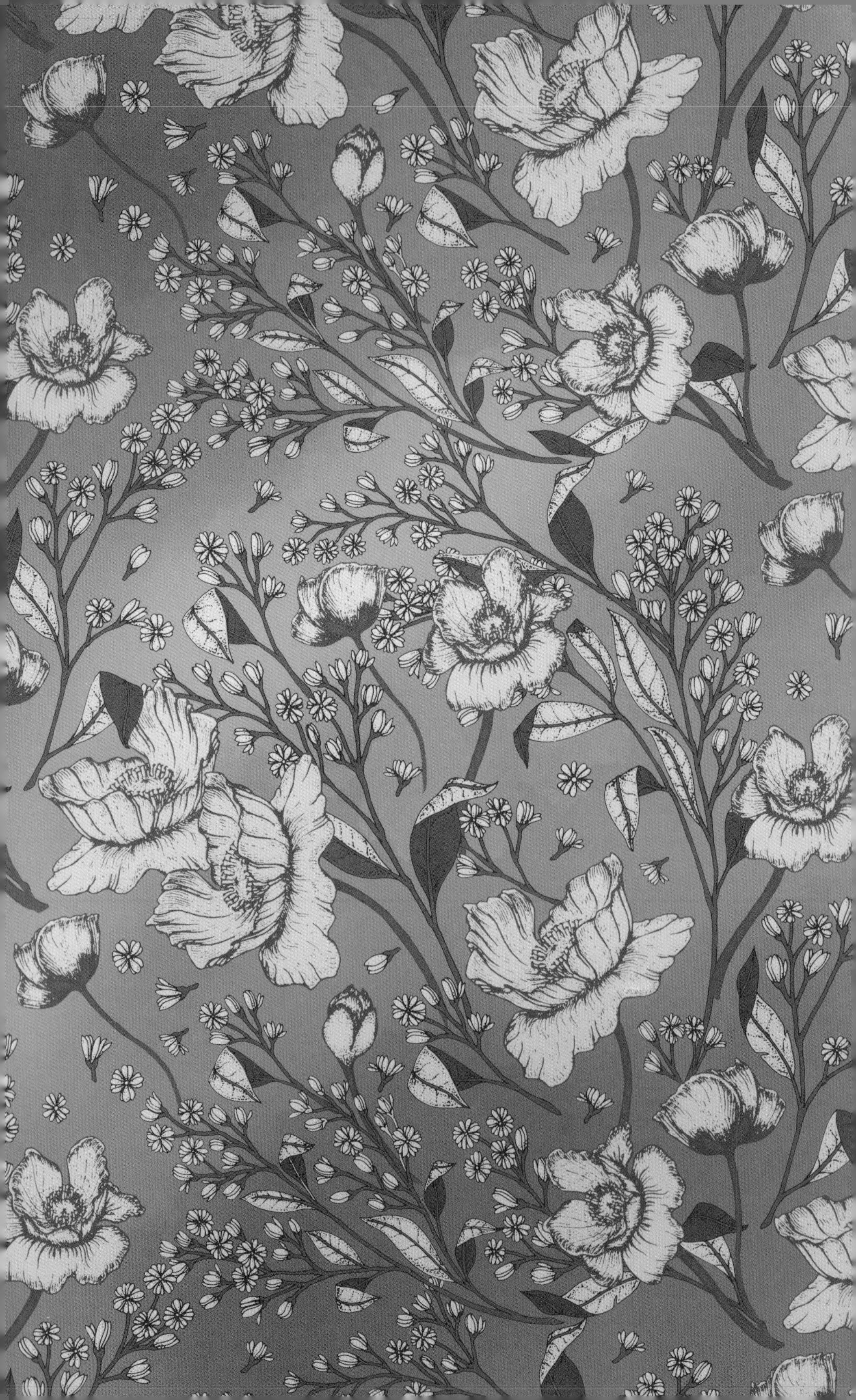

Behind the Scenes of

LUMBERJANES™

THE INFERNAL COMPASS

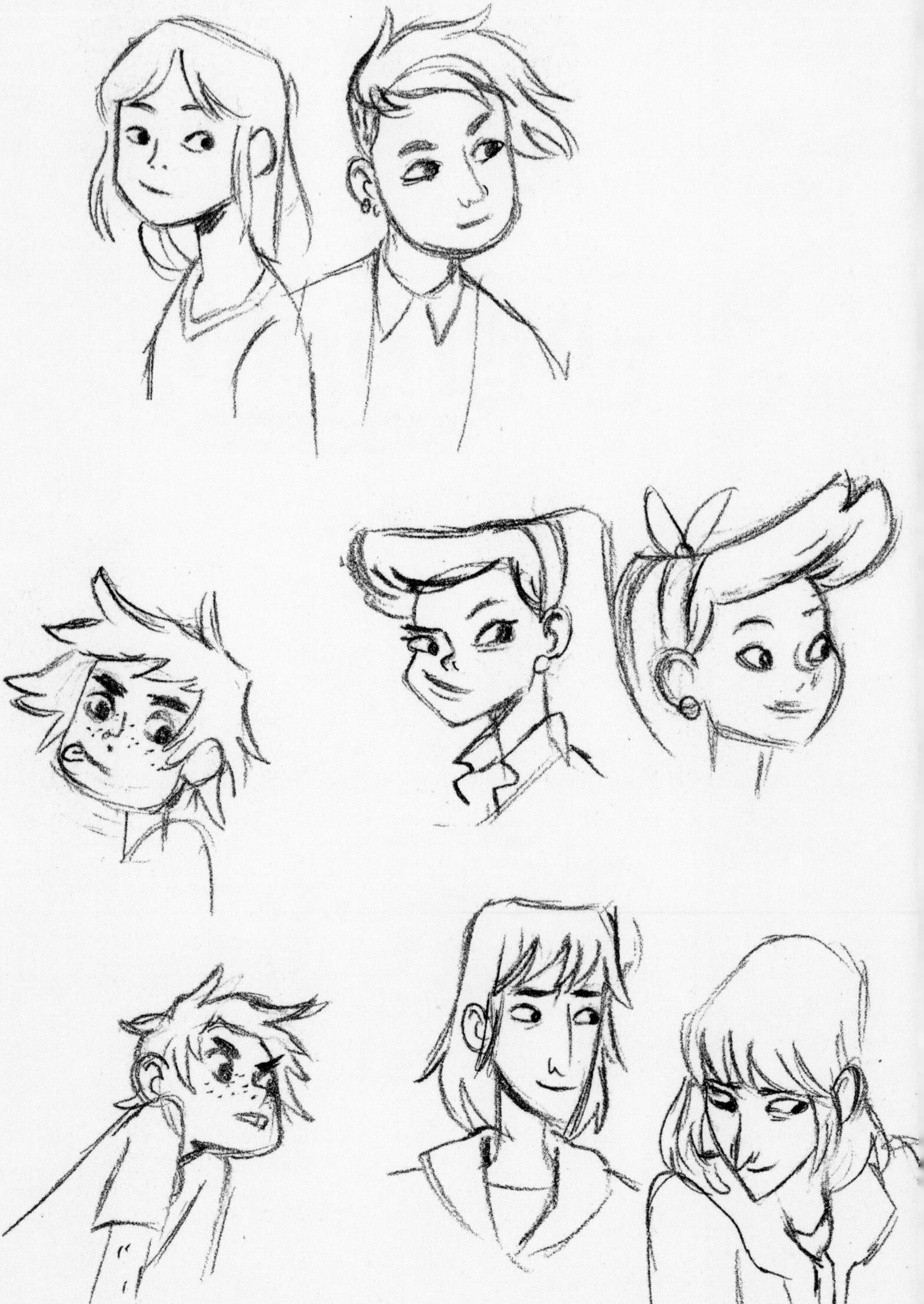

Character Designs & Concept Art by **POLTERINK**

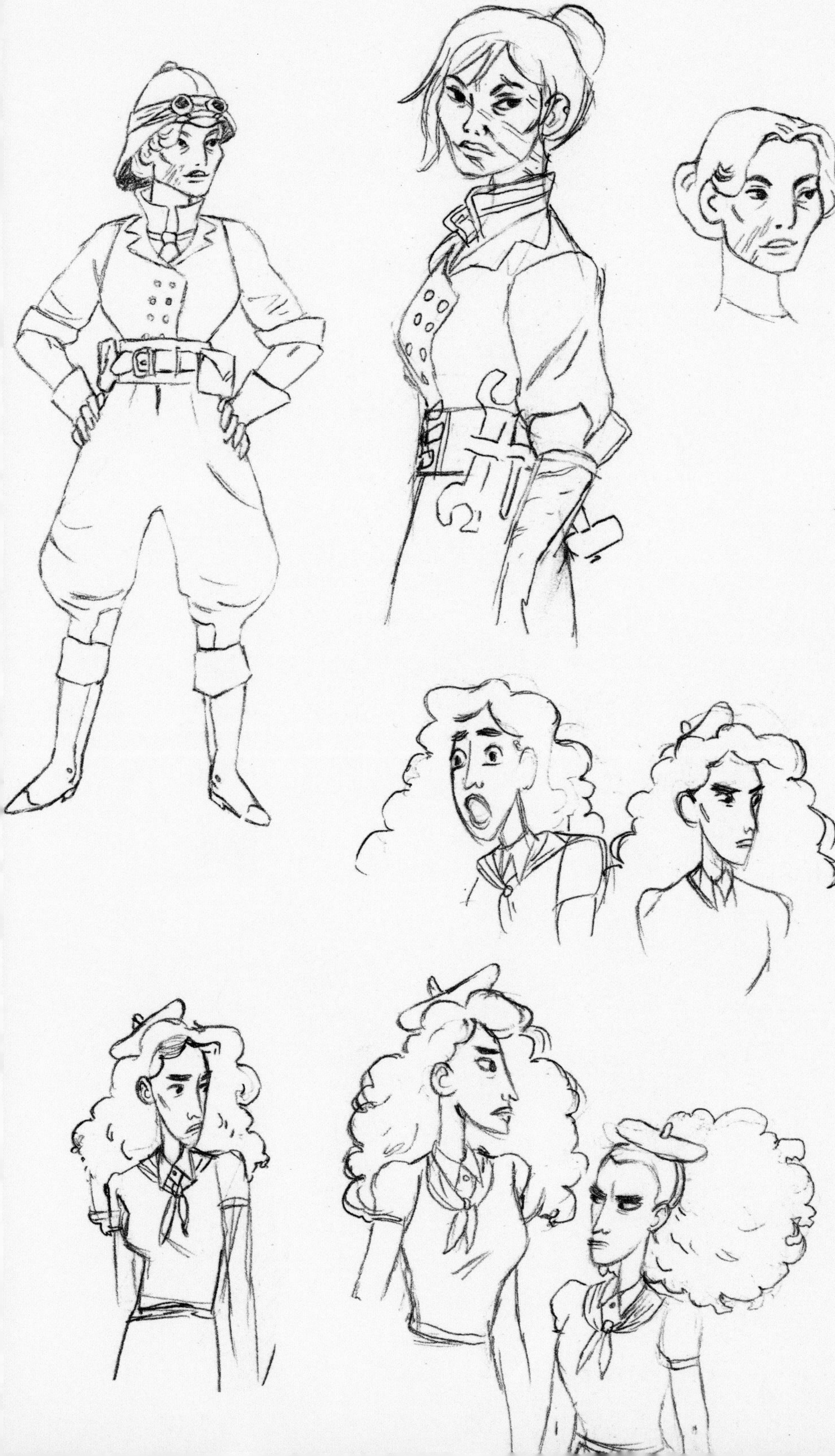

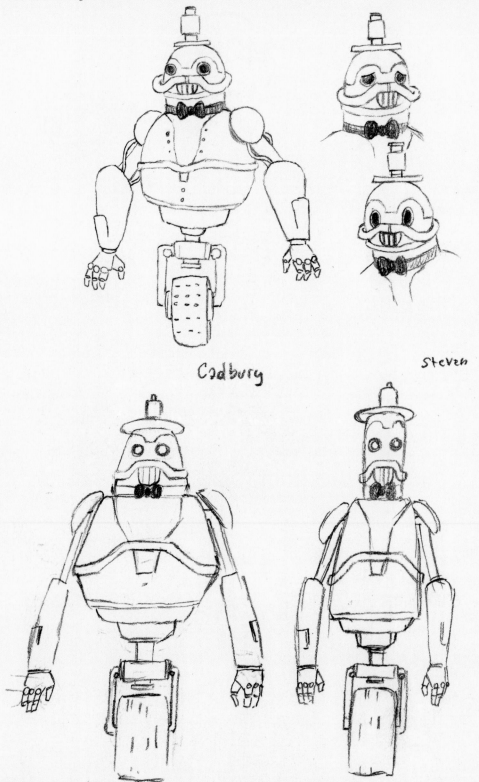

Cadbury

Steven

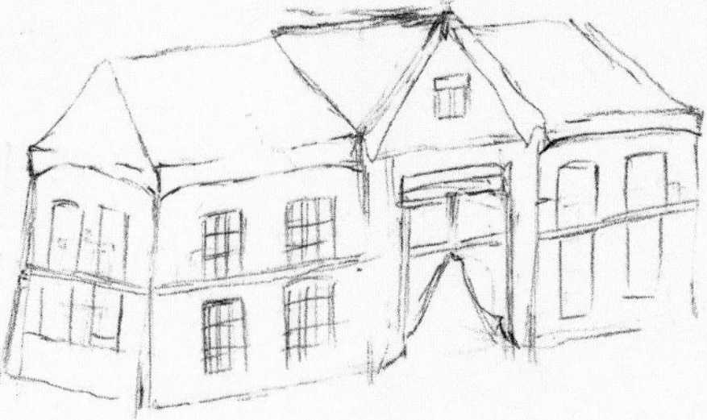

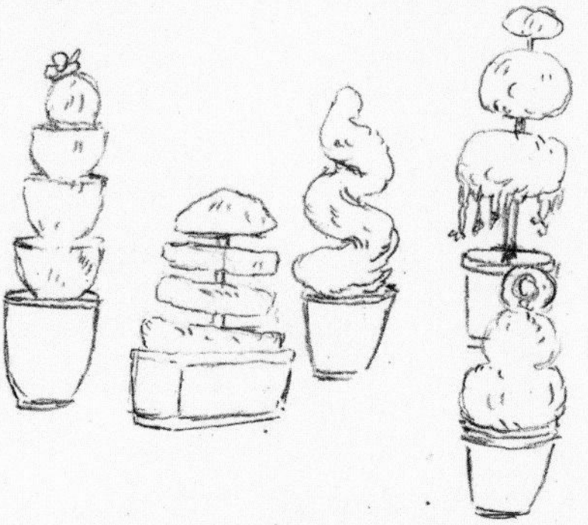

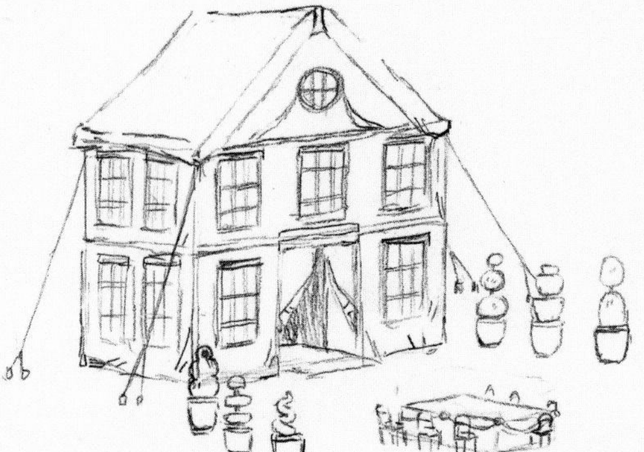

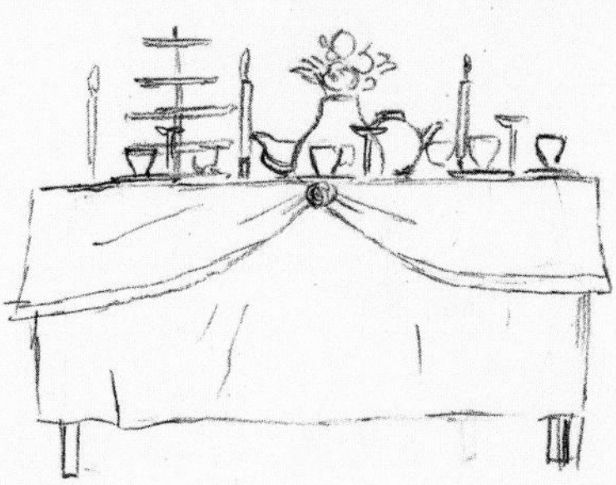

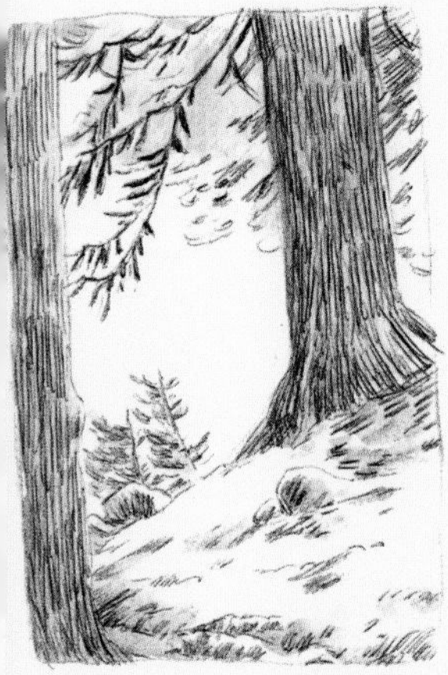

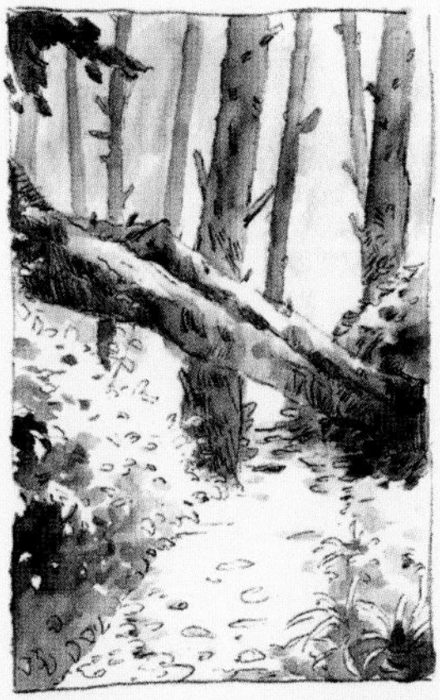

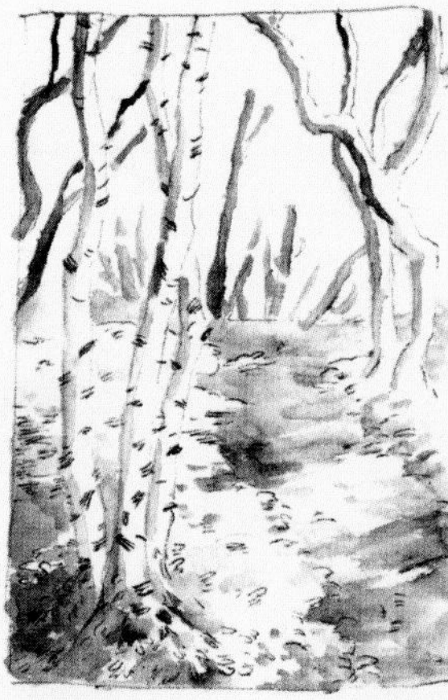

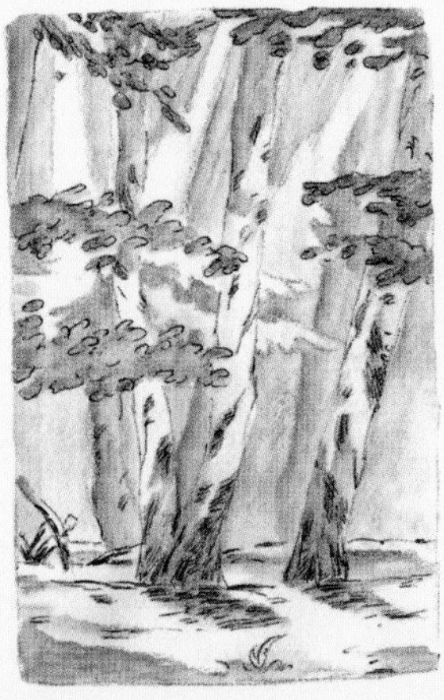

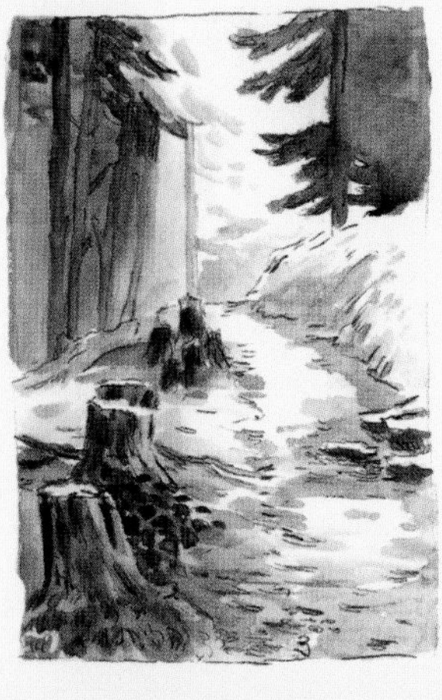

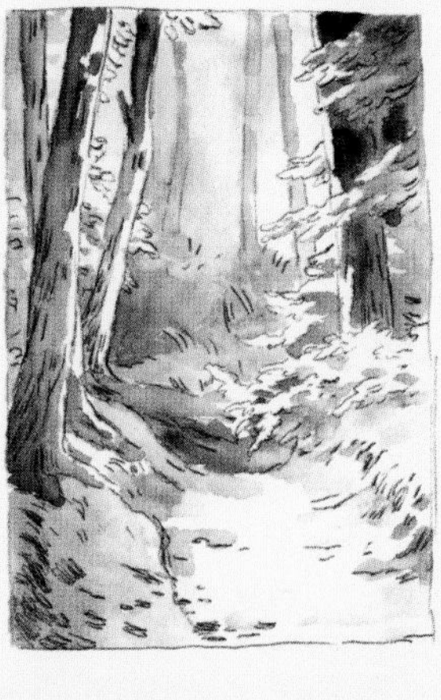

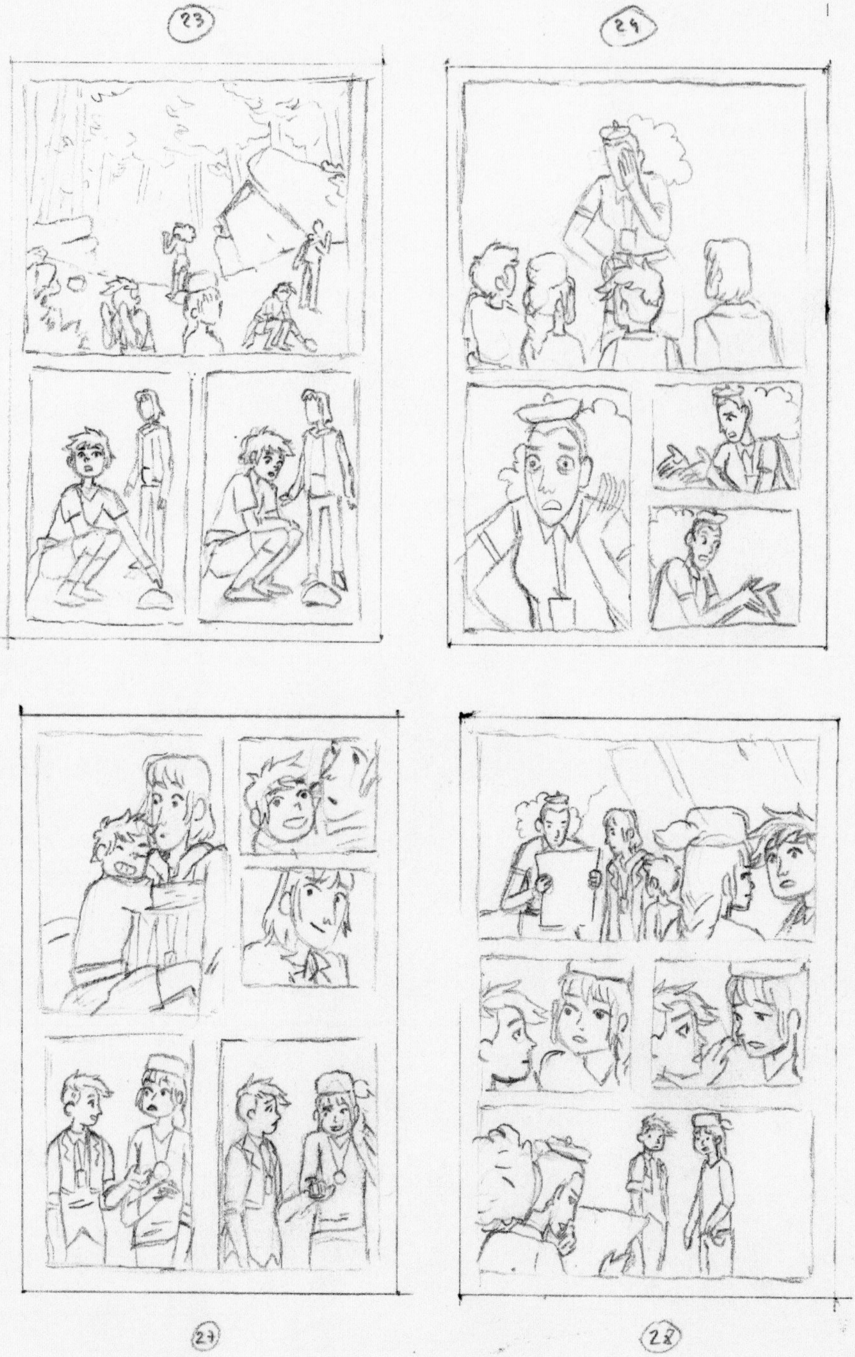

Pencils by **POLTERINK**

25

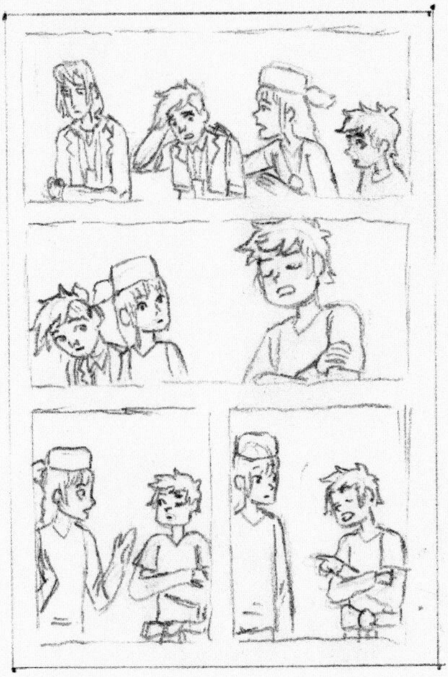

26

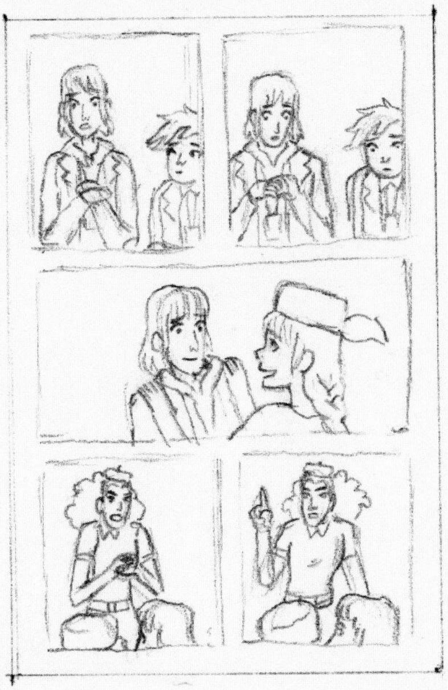

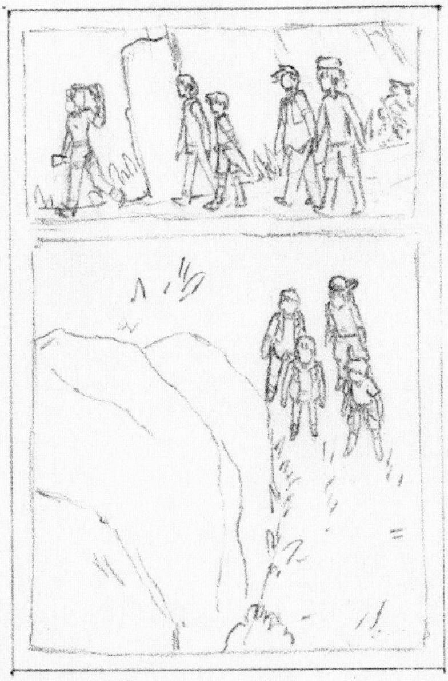

29

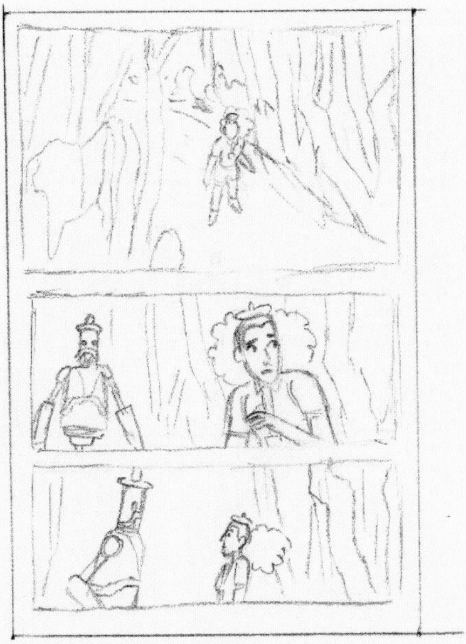

30

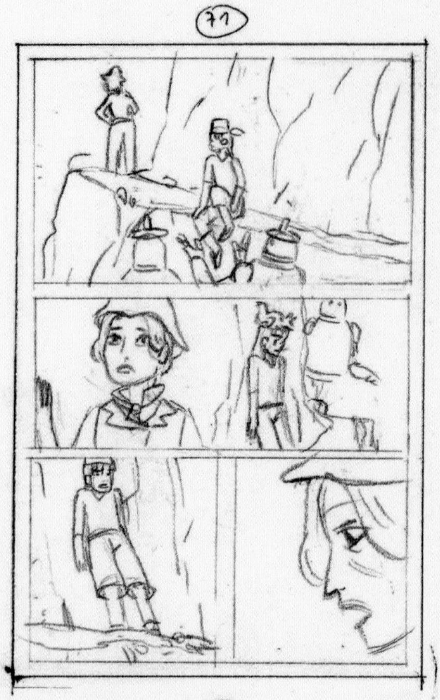
71

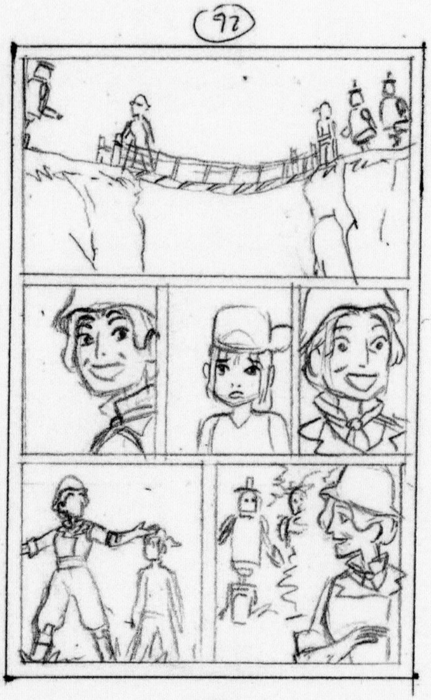
72

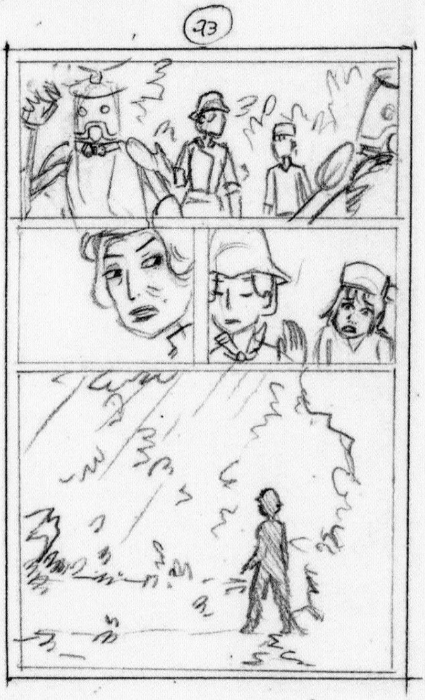
73

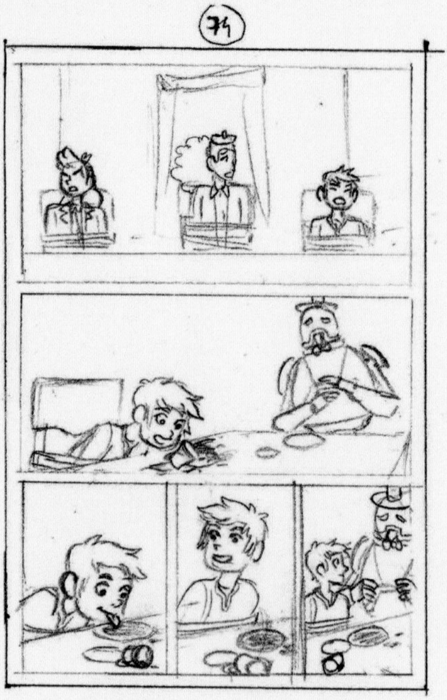
74

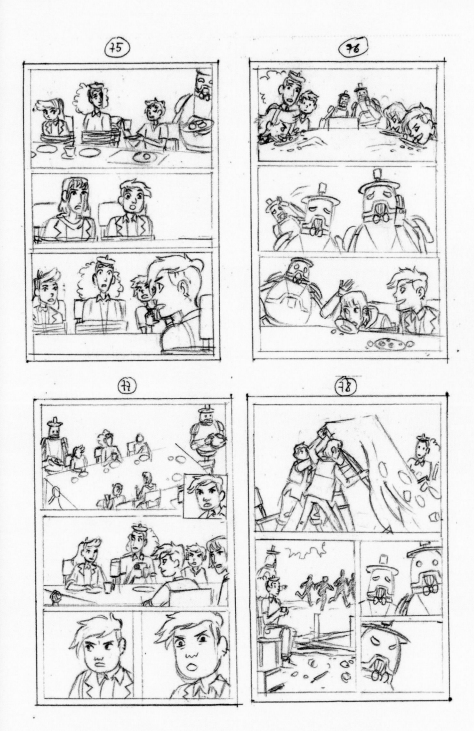

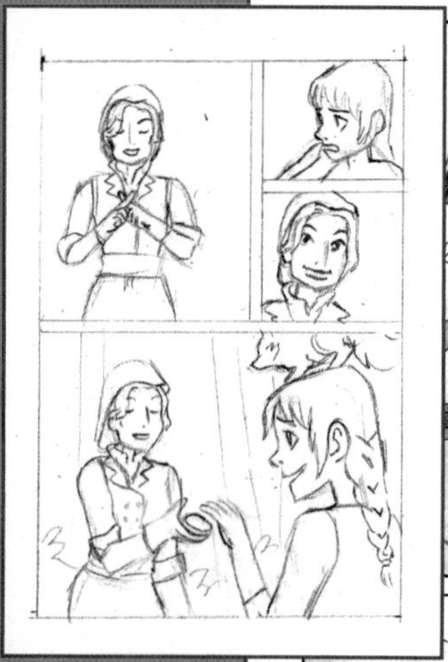

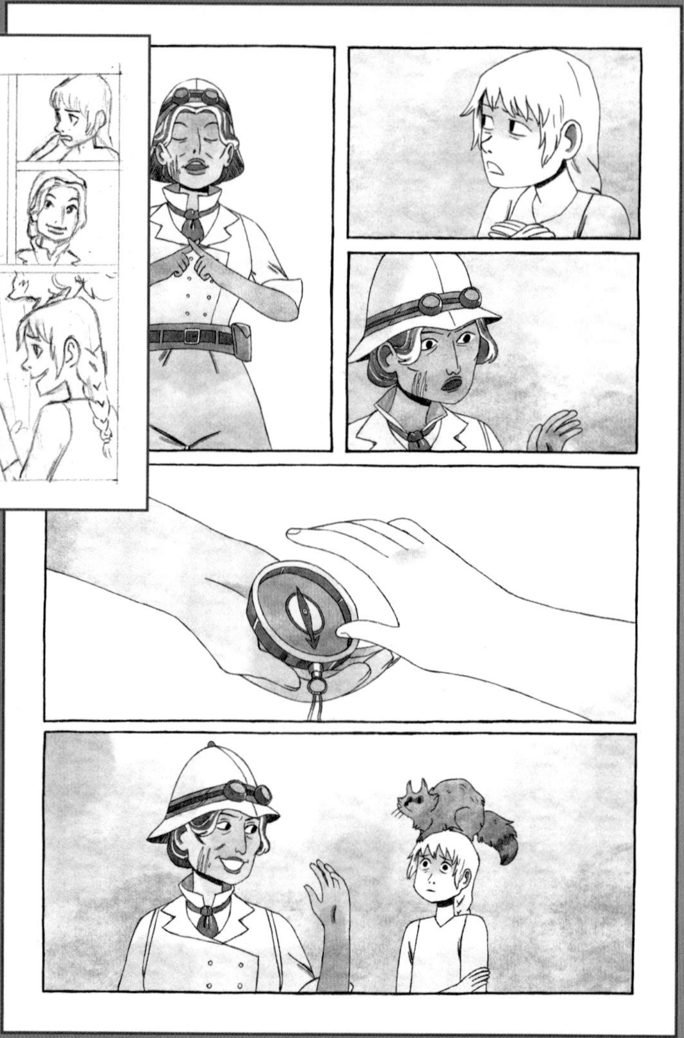

Page Sixty-Four

PANEL 1: Nibley stands up straight and gives the Lady Explorers' Club salute, which is the forefingers crossed in an X over the heart.

NIBLEY: You have my word as a Lady Explorer.

PANEL 2: Molly isn't entirely sure. Nibley wheedles her a bit.

MOLLY: I don't know...

PANEL 3:

NIBLEY: Oh, please let's not quibble over this!

NIBLEY: I do so hate a quibble!

PANEL 4: Molly gives in, still not entirely okay with all this but scared and wanting it over. She hands over the compass. Nibley trots away, waving Molly to follow, a big smile on her face.

     MOLLY: Okay. I guess so.
     NIBLEY: Brilliant! Right this way!

Page Sixty-Five

PANEL 1: Back at Nibley's camp, all the missing girls are tied up, seated at the table: April, Jen, Ripley, Jo, and Mal. Butlers and maids roll around doing their thing. A butler is pouring tea into a cup next to Mal that she can't reach because her hands are tied. Each girl has a plate with scones on it in front of her. It's very important that every girl have tea and scones.

Ripley has just leaned forward and is eating the scones like a puppy. Crumbs fly out of her mouth as she speaks. Jeeves is right behind her, looking horrified.

Make sure Mal and April are next to each other, and that April and Jen are next to each other, and that Ripley is next to Mal.

> RIPLEY: These giant cookies are delicious!
> JEEVES: Those are scones, young person.

PANEL 2:
      JEEVES: Might I interest you in a napkin?

PANEL 3:
      JEEVES: Please?

PANEL 4: Mal is struggling against her bonds, angry and scared for Molly.
      MAL: We need to get out of here! Molly's out there by herself!
      APRIL: Save your strength, Mal. These ropes are tied so well even I can't get out of them.

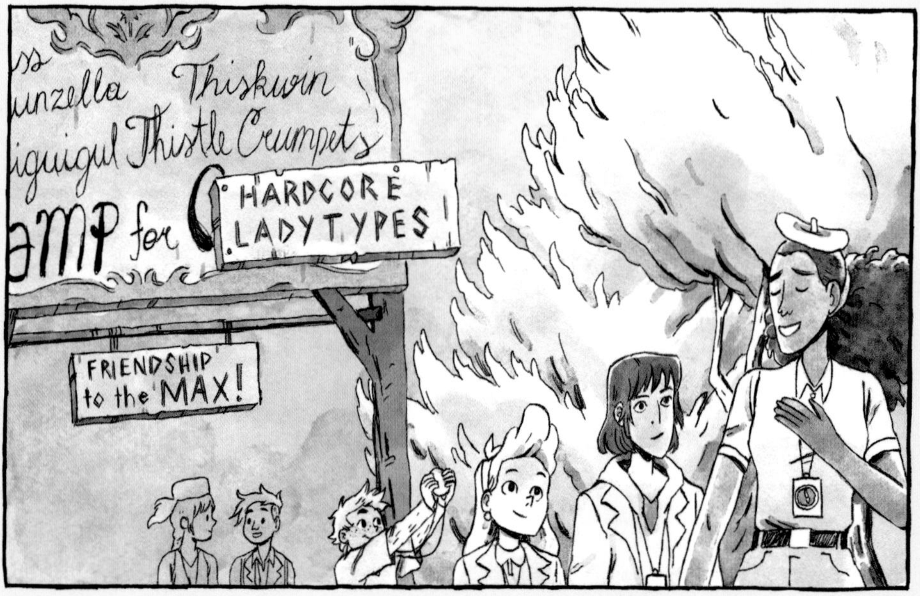
HARDCORE LADYTYPES
FRIENDSHIP to the MAX!

LILAH STURGES

Lilah Sturges has been writing comics for over a decade and believes she is finally getting the hang of it. She lives in Austin, Texas with her two daughters and a cat named Greg.

POLTERINK

polterink (also sometimes referred to as Claudia Rinofner) is a freelance artist and professional tea-drinker from Austria. As a kid she really liked spending time in the woods, feeding squirrels and building little homes for fairies out of twigs and moss.

SHANNON WATTERS

Shannon Watters is an editor lady by day and the co-creator of *Lumberjanes*...also by day. She helped guide KaBOOM!—BOOM! Studios' all-ages imprint—to commercial and critical success, and oversees BOOM! Box, an experimental imprint created "for the love of it." She has a great love for all things indie and comics, which is something she's been passionate about since growing up in the wilds of Arizona. When she's not working on comics she can be found watching classic films and enjoying the local cuisine.

NOELLE STEVENSON

Noelle Stevenson is the *New York Times* bestselling author of *Nimona*. She's been nominated for Harvey Awards, and was awarded the Slate Cartoonist Studio Prize for Best Web Comic in 2012 for *Nimona*. A graduate of the Maryland Institute College of Art, Noelle has worked on Disney's *Wander Over Yonder* and *She-Ra*, she has written for Marvel and DC Comics. She lives in Los Angeles. In her spare time she can be found drawing superheroes and talking about bad TV.
www.gingerhaze.com

GRACE ELLIS

Grace Ellis is a writer and co-creator of *Lumberjanes*. She is currently writing *Moonstruck*, a comic about lesbian werewolf baristas, as well as scripts for the animated show *Bravest Warriors*. Grace lives in Columbus, Ohio, where she co-parents a preternaturally smart cat, even though she's usually more of a dog person.

BROOKLYN ALLEN

Brooklyn Allen is a co-creator and original artist for *Lumberjanes* and when he is not drawing, then he will most likely be found with a saw in his hand making something rad. Currently residing in the "for lovers" state of Virginia, he spends most of his time working on comics with his not-so-helpful assistant Linus...his dog.

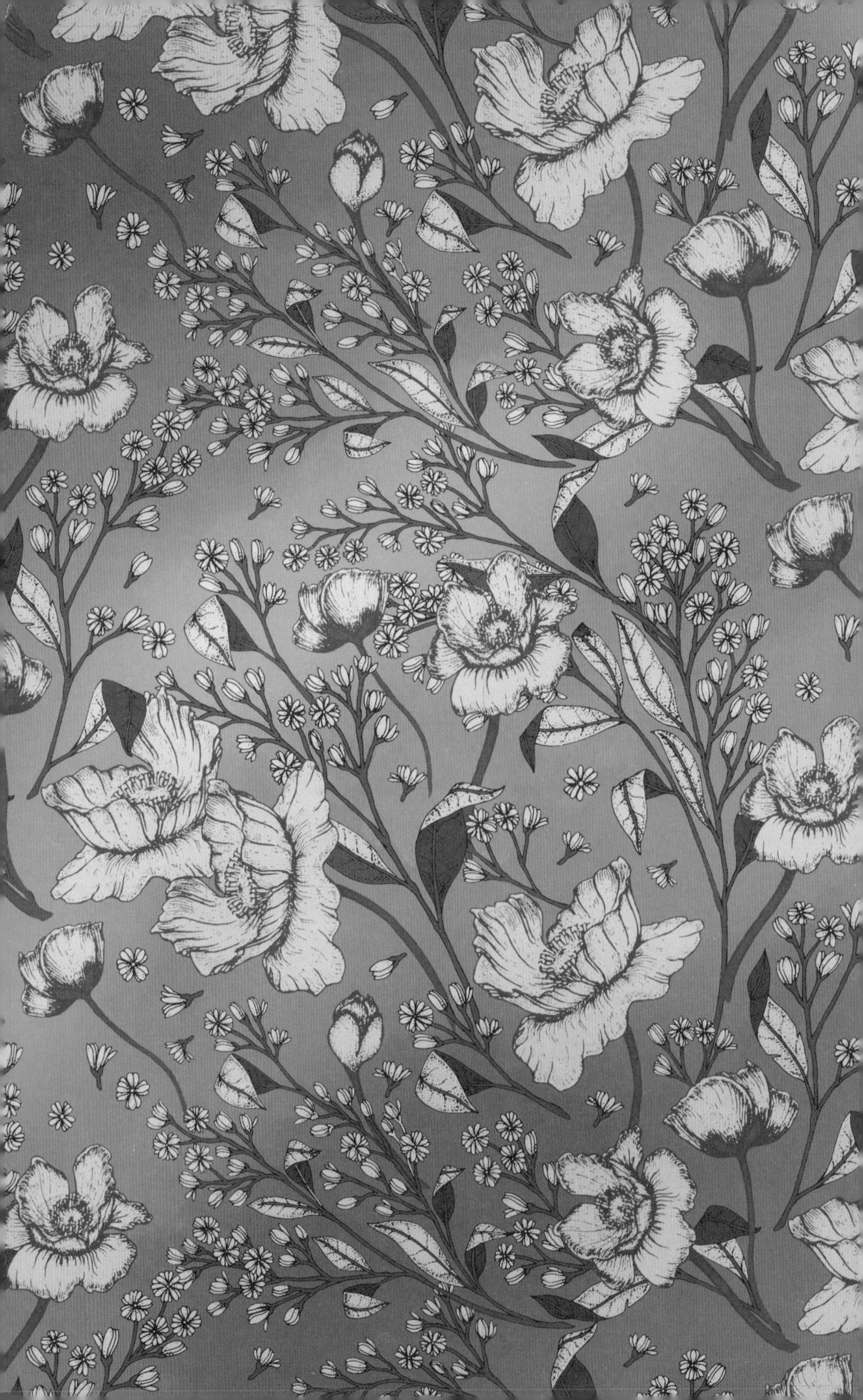

ACKNOWLEDGEMENTS

Lilah would like to thank her kids, Emerson and Camille, for being loving and kind, for having amazing senses of humor, and for explaining all the memes. You would both be excellent Lumberjanes!

Claudia would like to thank her family, who's always there to support her in any way they can and who made it possible for her to even have the opportunity to work on this graphic novel. (I love you guys!)

DISCOVER
ALL THE HITS

STEVENSON • ELLIS • WATTERS • ALLEN
LUMBERJANES
BEWARE THE KITTEN HOLY
NEW YORK TIMES BESTSELLING SERIES

Allison + Treiman + Cogan
GIANT DAYS
VOLUME ONE

RIBON • FISH • PEER
SLAM!
VOLUME ONE

Hope Larson • Brittney Williams • Sarah Stern
GOLDIE VANCE
Volume One

THE BACKSTAGERS

TYSON HESSE'S
DIESEL
IGNITION

BOOM! BOX™

AVAILABLE AT YOUR LOCAL COMICS SHOP AND BOOKSTORE

To find a comics shop in your area, call 1-888-266-4226

WWW.**BOOM-STUDIOS**.COM

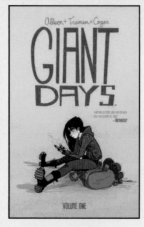

Lumberjanes
Noelle Stevenson, Shannon Watters, Grace Ellis, Brooklyn Allen, and Others
Volume 1: Beware the Kitten Holy
ISBN: 978-1-60886-687-8 | $14.99 US
Volume 2: Friendship to the Max
ISBN: 978-1-60886-737-0 | $14.99 US
Volume 3: A Terrible Plan
ISBN: 978-1-60886-803-2 | $14.99 US
Volume 4: Out of Time
ISBN: 978-1-60886-860-5 | $14.99 US
Volume 5: Band Together
ISBN: 978-1-60886-919-0 | $14.99 US

Giant Days
John Allison, Lissa Treiman, Max Sarin
Volume 1
ISBN: 978-1-60886-789-9 | $9.99 US
Volume 2
ISBN: 978-1-60886-804-9 | $14.99 US
Volume 3
ISBN: 978-1-60886-851-3 | $14.99 US

Jonesy
Sam Humphries, Caitlin Rose Boyle
Volume 1
ISBN: 978-1-60886-883-4 | $9.99 US
Volume 2
ISBN: 978-1-60886-999-2 | $14.99 US

Slam!
Pamela Ribon, Veronica Fish, Brittany Peer
Volume 1
ISBN: 978-1-68415-004-5 | $14.99 US

Goldie Vance
Hope Larson, Brittney Williams
Volume 1
ISBN: 978-1-60886-898-8 | $9.99 US
Volume 2
ISBN: 978-1-60886-974-9 | $14.99 US

The Backstagers
James Tynion IV, Rian Sygh
Volume 1
ISBN: 978-1-60886-993-0 | $14.99 US

Tyson Hesse's Diesel: Ignition
Tyson Hesse
ISBN: 978-1-60886-907-7 | $14.99 US

Coady & The Creepies
Liz Prince, Amanda Kirk, Hannah Fisher
ISBN: 978-1-68415-029-8 | $14.99 US